The Flawed Inheritance

The Flawed Inheritance

Norma Washbrook

First published in 2004 by:
Blackie & Co

ISBN: 1-904986-06-4

Printed and bound in Great Britain by:
ProPrint, Riverside Cottages, Old Great North Road,
Stibbington, Cambridgeshire PE8 6LR

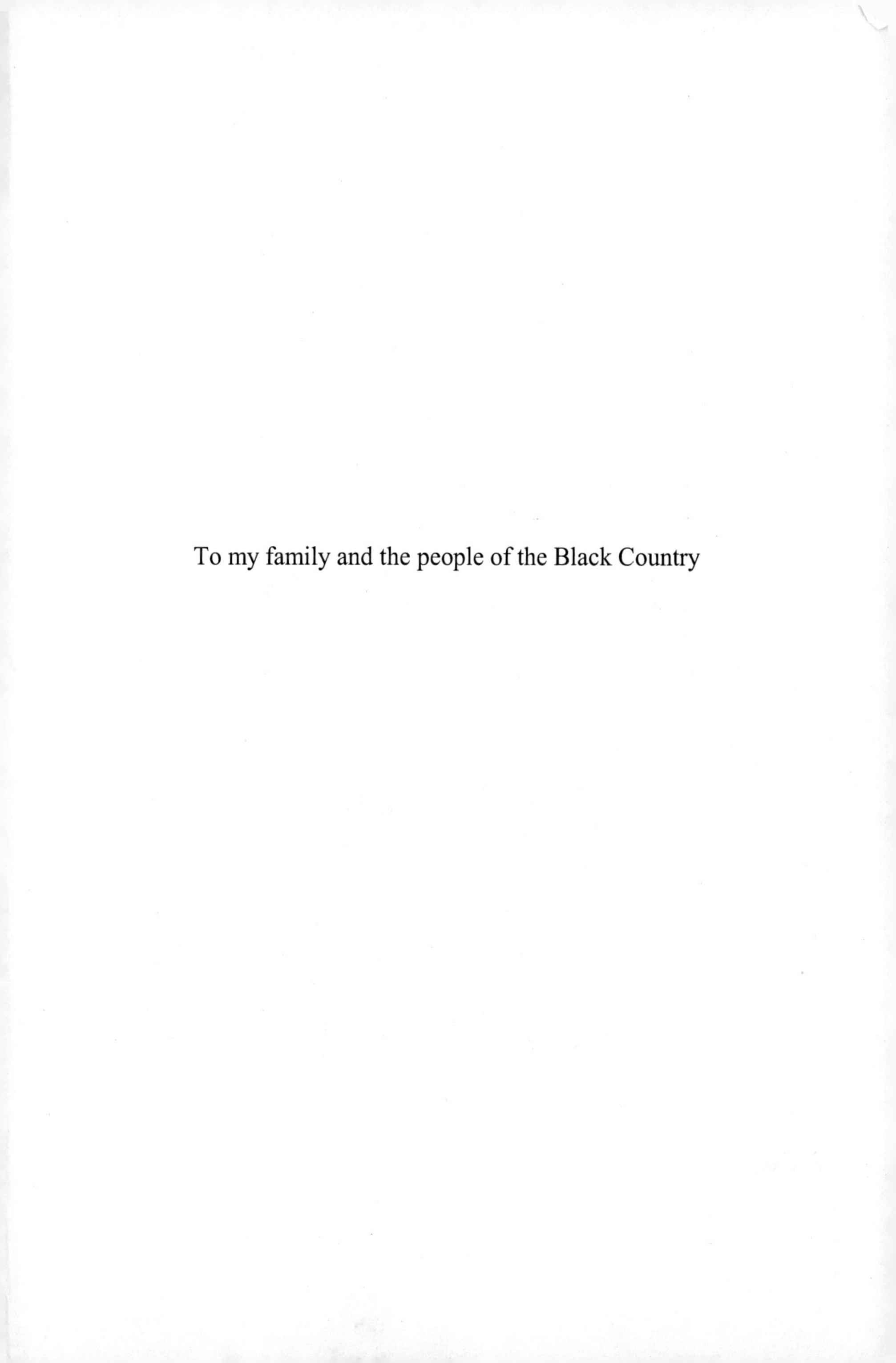

To my family and the people of the Black Country

Introduction

All was quiet in Pipers Row, except for Valerie playing with her top and whip. Ronnie stopped to watch her.

Wiping his nose on his sleeve, and inclining his head forward, he thrust his hands into his pockets.

"Gis a goo," he said. "Goo on, gis a goo."

Valerie ignored him, although she was no expert. Ronnie placed his hands on his hips and frowned.

A gust of wind blew down the entry, blowing Valerie's hair over her glasses. She missed the top yet again with the whip.

She had spent time making patterns on the top with coloured chalks. When it spun the colours blended and it looked pretty. It wobbled towards Ronnie and fell at his feet.

"Goo on, gis a goo. Doe be skinny."

Valerie glared at him. "No," she said. "My mom says not to play with you, you smell."

At that Ronnie picked up the top and threw it with all his might into the open side of a passing dustcart.

Valerie stood frozen to the spot. She paled and then she flushed. Gasping in disbelief she gave out a howl of pain and indignation.

Ronnie fled.

From that day forward Valerie Potts was Ronnie Edwards's mortal enemy.

Chapter One

Aggie Potts slapped the pastry she was making onto the scrubbed top table. Wiping her nose on the back of her hand, she pushed her hair back from her forehead and glowered at her friend Sally Holmes.

"Idle bugger?" she said. "I'll give 'em idle bugger, the cheeky bleeders. None on 'em 'as ever done a day's werk in their lives ter speak on, cheeky bleeders. Cor they see as our Herbert aye well. They only look at their selves, the selfish sods."

Sally commiserated with her friend. "Doe tek on, Agg. I ain't positive it was said, burrile find out fer sure. I only know what our Ida told me."

"Oh, it was said alright. Them lot am pison, the whole family on 'em."

Aggie sank onto a kitchen chair and wiped her floury hands on the dish cloth.

Sally smiled at her. "I tell yer what, Agg, I've a bottle of stout round 'ome. I'll fetch it an' we'll share it. Mek you feel a bit better."

Aggie grasped her arm. "Can't they see our Herbert's bad. Can't they, Sal? The doctor's bloody useless, 'e keeps on tellin' 'im it'll pass an' 'e'll get better. I think that old bugger thinks as our Herbert's idle an' just after sick notes."

Sally pushed against the table and rose to her feet. "I'll get that stout, Aggie. You get us a sandwich, we'll 'ave a bite to eat. Come down that market this afternoon, it'll do yer good ter gerrout."

She shuffled to the back door, a thin, little woman with, surprisingly, a round face and soft, brown eyes.

Aggie sighed. "Alright, Sal. What'd I do without you? As long as we'me back fer Bert's tea I'm alright ter go, so we'll get our skates on." She sighed resignedly, brushed another dewdrop from her nose and busied herself finishing the pie ready for the evening meal.

Her home was clean and, though not salubrious, was comfortable. All her married life she had put Bert, her husband, and Stan and Herbert, their sons, first. She rued the day that Herbert had married Grace Shaw. She could never see any good coming from the match. They had one daughter, Valerie, who was being reared to think that she was a cut above everybody. Despite this Aggie was fond of the child and could see no wrong in her.

She wiped the table over, deep in thought. She was approaching sixty, had worked hard all her life and could do without the worry which constantly nagged at her about Herbert's failing health. A motherly woman, who was once pretty, she kept herself and her husband neat and clean, and always put good home-cooked meals on the table. She had no great aspiration to fashion but dressed as well as she could on the money Bert gave her. She saved a little each week towards the day when Bert retired. All in all she had a reasonable life. She did not often get riled but the gossip which had reached her ears via Sally had made her wicked.

Sally's sister, Ida, had overheard Herbert's mother-in-law, Renee Shaw, talking in the market about the fact that their Grace had taken a part-time job in the local cake shop to make ends meet because Herbert was often off work sick. She had been heard to say that in her opinion he was just "boon idle". If Renee had been in her reach at that moment Aggie would have surely throttled her. Scrubbing away at the table she vented her rage until she started to feel a little calmer.

*　　　　*　　　　*

Herbert sat by the small fire in the kitchen. He felt so tired these days. His job at the local factory was not heavy, he was a storekeeper. Just walking to work was becoming an effort for him. Climbing the stairs to go to bed left him panting and breathless.

Doctor Ferguson was an acerbic Irishman who, it was rumoured, enjoyed more than just a drop of whisky.

He would say, “It’s the fags, moi lad, that’s your trouble. Give up the fags and you’ll be just foine.”

Herbert had given up the cigarettes two years ago and he was feeling worse than ever. Poking the fire he contemplated what to do to make Grace’s mood a little better when she returned from her stint in the cake shop.

Breathing heavily he managed to dust the furniture, water her plants on the windowsill, then he sat to peel potatoes for the evening meal. Valerie loved sausages and mash. She was the apple of her father’s eye, not a particularly pleasant child, however, she did love her dad. She resembled her mother, pale with glasses and straight, mousy hair, which stood the torture of being wound into rags to curl it for special occasions.

Herbert looked forward to her arrival from school. He put the kettle on a low light in anticipation of the tea that they would share before Grace arrived.

A tap on the door heralded the arrival of Aggie and Sally.

“We cor stop our Herbert, just brought yer a couple o’ oranges. We bin down the market an’ we ’ave ter get back fer yer dad’s tea.”

Herbert was pleased to see his mother, she brought a light into his life. Apart from Valerie she was the only one who understood that he was genuinely ill.

“’Allo, Mom. Sure you can’t stop for a cuppa?”

“No, really, our Herbert. Anyroad, am yer any better, son?”

“Yes, a bit, Mom. I’m hopin’ to go back to werk next Monday. I just seemed ter need a rest.”

Aggie looked closely at him. “What did the doctor say this time, son? Is ’e sendin’ yer to see anybody at th’ospital?”

Herbert sighed. “’E doe say, Mom. ’E still keeps on it’s because I smoked and it’s affected me chest.”

Aggie snorted. “’E’s too sozzled ter know what ’e’s doin’ by all accounts. Can’t yer change to Doctor Spears? ’E seems ter ’ave more oil in ’is lamp, doe ’e, Sal?”

“I’ve tried, Mom, but ’e’s not tekkin any more on so I’m stuck with old Ferguson.”

Aggie sniffed derisively. “Let’s ’ope as ’e does isself a damage when ’e’s drunk an’ then we’ll get a new doctor what knows what ’e’s doin’ fer a change.”

Sally nodded sympathetically.

Herbert said, “Grace thinks ’e’s good, says ’e was good to ’er when our Valerie was born.”

Aggie was not convinced. “I still think as ’e should send yer to the ’ospital. If yer like, next time you goo, I’ll come with yer. Anyroad, we’ve got ter goo now. See yer, son.”

She turned and waved from the door and, arm in arm with Sally, walked up the street.

Clutching her friend’s arm, she said, “’E doe ’alf look bad, Sal. I could cry when I think what ’e used ter be like.”

Sally tried to calm her friend. “Doe tek on, Aggie. ’E’s gooin through a bad patch. ’E’ll soon pick up after a rest, you’ll see.”

“I just wish as ’e was bein’ looked after better, Sal. That Grace doe see past the end on her nose, selfish little cow, ’er is. I wish as we could get ’im ’ome for a bit, build ’im up. No chance o’ that.”

Aggie sighed. Switching her mind to the meal she had to finish preparing when she got home, she managed to blot out for a while her concern for her son.

Grace opened the back door. She was cold and tired. The first sight which greeted her as she entered the kitchen was Valerie sitting on her dad's lap in front of a crackling fire, heads together over a book. She felt a stab of resentment at the cosy scene.

"Hello, Mom," said Valerie.

"'Allo, love," said Herbert.

Grace grunted and shrugged off her coat. "I'm perished I am but you two look nice and warm."

Herbert smiled at her. "Tea's nearly ready, love."

Valerie slipped off his lap and he rose to his feet. He hoped that they weren't going to have a morose evening. He had tried to make the house welcoming for his wife.

"Sausages and mash, love. Onion gravy," he said.

Grace pushed her feet into her well-worn slippers and sank onto the vacated chair.

"Me feet are givin' me some jip, I can tell yer. How they werk full time in that shop I don't know. Four hours is plenty."

Rubbing a foot, she nodded as Herbert placed a cup of tea close to hand for her.

"Do you know, there were pies left and that mingy Thelma wouldn't even offer 'em to us half price. Said as they 'ad to go back to the bakery in the mornin'. I wouldn't put it past 'er to tek some 'ome 'erself or even sell 'em on. Mean bitch."

Grace held her hands out to the fire. "You alright, our Valerie? School bin alright?"

"Yes, Mom." Not for the world would Valerie tell her mother if she had had a bad day and she couldn't tell her dad, he was too ill. So any worries Valerie had were kept to herself. As long as she had her dad to come home to she would cope with whatever life threw at her.

Chapter Two

Ivy Richards lived at number 32 Ingram Terrace. She was seventy-five and getting tired and confused. Some days she forgot to eat and, despite the kindness of neighbours, she obviously needed care.

Ivy had two daughters, Rose, who lived in Birmingham and Nellie, who lived a three-penny bus ride away. Nellie endeavoured to call on her mother every day. She had six children and did a cleaning job in the evenings between 5 and 6.30pm. Her husband, Wilf, worked at the steelworks. This was a five-minute walk away from Ingram Terrace, therefore it was with great excitement that Nellie discovered that the house next door to her mother was to become vacant.

On alighting from the bus one Monday morning, who should Nellie bump into but Maudie Rogers, an old school pal.

"Aye up, Nellie. 'Ow are yer these days?"

"Tired out, Maudie. I 'ave ter come an' see me Mom, as yer know. I doe want ter gi' me cleanin' job up but it looks as if I'll 'ave to the way things am gooin."

Maudie nodded. "Ar, it's a trek fer yer every day, my wench, but why doe you ask about Lily 'Ackett's 'ouse?"

Nellie pricked up her ears. "What do yer mean, Maudie? It aye empty, is it?"

"Not yet but 'er's goin' to 'er daughter's in Brum an' it doe look as if 'er's comin' back. If I was you I'd goo an' see old Shaw, the rent mon, an' gerra werd in afore anybody else cottons on about it."

Nellie brightened. "I'll do that. Thanks a bunch, Maudie. It could be the answer to me problems."

Nellie went down the entry to the back of number 34 Ingram Terrace. It was one of a row of ten houses. They all had a front room, a back kitchen and a scullery. Upstairs were two bedrooms and a tiny box room. Outside was a yard with a coalhouse and an outside lavatory. A gate led to the party yard and then another gate to a small patch of garden. Backing on to the party yard, attached to the coalhouses, were binneries built to accommodate two dustbins. Number 34 was an ‘entry house’ but Nellie didn’t mind that. Indeed the most noise from the entry would be caused by her own family. She couldn’t wait to talk to Wilf when she got home and prayed that he would agree to try for number 34.

The first opportunity she had to broach the subject was at nine o’clock the same evening. Wilf had been to work, finished at six, had his tea at seven, then gone to see to his pigeons. When he returned at nine he seemed in a reasonable mood so, without more ado, Nellie told him about number 34.

“Well, wench, if yer want ter move it’s alright wi’ me. It’ll be nearer to the werk, I’ll save on me bus fares and I’ll get to our Reggie’s easier ter see ter me pigeons and the allotment. The gardin aye a bad size. I might ’ave me loft theer or some fowl.”

Nellie was pleased to hear this. She got tired of Wilf being away from the house with his hobbies. Perhaps he would spend more time around home.

She said, “I’m glad you agree, Wilf. I’ll goo an’ see the rent mon termorrer. I can’t wait ter shift, I can tell yer.”

Next morning Nellie went to see old Shaw. She always made sure that her mother’s rent was left for him on a Friday. He knew she was a regular payer, however, he had to inspect her own rent book before he could recommend her to the owner of number 34.

“Come an’ see me Thursday an’ I’ll be able to tell yer if you can have it, Mrs Edwards,” he said.

Nellie couldn’t sleep for thinking and worrying in case they were turned down. However, her worries were unfounded and they were told that they could move in two weeks.

The first to know were Ronnie and Patty when they came in from school.

"When am we movin' then, Mom?" asked Patty. "Will we be able ter tek Pongo?"

"Yes, o' course we will. 'E'll 'ave a back yard same as 'ere and' a nice bit o' gardin an' all, like Granny Edwards's."

"Will we 'ave ter change school?" Ronnie asked. He hoped so. He didn't like his teacher and wouldn't be sorry to see the back of her.

Nellie nodded. "Yes, you'll 'ave ter go to the Church of England mixed, same one as I went to when I was a little gel."

"Was it nice, Mom?" Patty asked.

"It was alright. I don't expect it'll be the same teachers now. It was a long time agoo when I went."

The children were quite excited and when the others came in they could hardly wait to tell them the news.

For seventeen-year-old John it made little difference. He worked with his father at the steelworks. It would save on bus fares, however.

Mary, aged fifteen, had just started work at the Co-op. She would be able to walk to work in the High Street. Maureen, aged thirteen and a half and Barry, twelve and a half, would go to the Girls' and Boys' schools respectively. Christine, eleven and a half, would go with Patty, eight, and Ronnie, nine, to the Junior mixed. They all looked forward to the change and began immediately to prepare for the move.

Nellie had it all sorted in her mind. Mary, Maureen and Christine would all sleep round at Ivy's. John, Barry and Ronnie would share a room at number 34 and Patty would have the little box room. She hugged herself. At last she would have a front parlour.

The following Monday was half-term holiday. Nellie, accompanied by Ronnie and Patty, was on the bus going to Ivy's. Nellie was loathe to take the children with her but was sure if she left them Ronnie would get up to mischief. Barry and Christine would not be responsible for him so he had to go along.

Nellie warned them, "Now then, Patty, and you, our Ronnie, don't get spouting about us moving. I don't want all and sundry ter know our business."

"Okay, Mom," they chorused and sat as quiet as mice for the duration of the journey.

Granny Richards was dressed when they arrived but it didn't look as if she had eaten. Nellie set to to clear the ashes from the grate, then put the kettle on the gas stove and prepared to get some breakfast for her mother.

Ivy never had much to say these days but always looked pleased to see them. The children chattered away to her and got a "Yes" or "No" in reply. When Ronnie said, "Gran, would yer like us ter come an' live next door?" she smiled and nodded. Patty gave her a hug and stirred her cup of tea. Nellie was frying an egg and fathoming what to leave for her mother's lunch.

She said, "Ronnie, goo ter the shop for a quarter o' cheese an' a loaf. Doe 'ang about, look sharp."

"Okay, Mom." He took the money from his mother and ran out of the back door past number 34 and down the entry. His segged boots made a satisfying noise. He quite looked forward to his own entry. The other side of the entry was his gran's friend, Annie Pearce, at number 36. She was a bit deaf so wouldn't mind a bit of rumpus.

Ronnie chose to go to the nearest corner shop owned by Mr and Mrs Withers. Mr Withers was a quiet, genial-looking man, always wearing a brown cow gown. He rarely spoke but smiled a lot. Mrs Withers was a thin-faced, dour woman of around fifty. She looked as if she had never smiled in her life. Unbidden into Ronnie's mind came the words 'Witchy Withers'.

The shop was spotless as was her wraparound pinafore. She served the customers efficiently, rarely looking at them, speaking economically, concentrating fully on the task in hand. Nellie hated going to the shop and Annie always called the shopkeeper 'that miserable bleeder wi' a faerce fit ter stop a clock'.

If 'tick' was required, the locals would have to go to Turdy Tunley's, which was a rather dirty establishment further up the street.

Mainly the shopping was done in the High Street of the small town where there was a Home and Colonial, a Co-op, a cake and bread shop, a butcher's, greengrocer's, a cobbler's and a gents' outfitters. Most clothes shopping was done at the neighbouring, larger town. Therefore it was for quickness or 'tick' that the corner shops were used.

Returning with the loaf and cheese, Ronnie was hungry.

"Mom, can I have a piece?"

"I s'pose so," Nellie said.

She cut two thick slices of bread, spread them with margarine and put two thin slices of cheese on them. Ronnie picked up his doorstep sandwich.

"Can I goo out an' play a bit?"

"Only if you don't goo off. Stop where I can call yer. We'll be gooin 'ome as soon as I've put yer Gran's dinner ready."

"Okay, Mom."

Ronnie decided to sit on the front step of number 34. He felt quite proprietorial knowing that soon he would live here.

"Aye up, Ronnie," said a voice. "What you got theer? Looks like a bad 'and ter me. It's nearly as big as you am."

Annie's son, Jack, smiled down at him. He was a policeman so Ronnie didn't think it mattered about telling him about the move.

"'Allo," he said. "Did you know we was comin' ter live 'ere? Did yer?"

"Well, I did 'ear summat about it. Am yer glad, son?"

“Yeah, I think I am. Me mom’s gonna ’ave a front room. ’Er’s savin’ up ferra three-piece suite. We’me gonna be dead posh.”

Jack laughed. “We’ll ’ave ter pay ter come in your ’ouse then, woe we?”

Ronnie smiled. “I ’spect so.”

At that the high voice of Nellie calling her son rang out. Jack walked up the entry smiling. He felt that it soon wouldn’t be the same again in Ingram Terrace.

Chapter Three

The wind whistled round the house. It howled up the entry and rattled the window panes. Valerie snuggled under the blankets dreading the moment when she had to put her feet out of the warm bed and on to the cold linoleum.

It was Friday. After school she would come home, have her tea, then she and Grace would walk to her Granny Shaw's. This was a regular Friday visit. Granny Shaw lived in the next small town. It was a two-mile walk. Valerie couldn't remember the last time her dad had accompanied them. He could not walk that far any longer and there was no love lost between the Shaws and the Potts. Friday visits were not a hardship to Valerie, she took them for granted. Her visits to Granny Potts were not so frequent now that her dad got so tired and her Gran tried to call in when she knew that Grace was at the cake shop.

Lying in bed Valerie fantasised about what it would be like to be rich and not have to struggle all the time to make ends meet as her mother did. As she lay there, listening to the wind, she determined that one day she would have money. She would be able to make ends more than meet.

Suddenly she jumped up in bed. Her mother had cried out. She sounded hysterical. Valerie ran to her parents' room, so scared she didn't notice the icy lino.

"Mom, Mom. What's up, Mom?"

Grace stammered, "Oh my God, Valerie, yer dad's having a bad turn. I don't know what ter do. Run an' fetch Mrs Jinks. Oh no, don't do that, knock the wall, will yer?"

Shielding Valerie from the sight of her dad on the bed, Grace pushed the door to. Herbert was grey. He could hardly draw a breath. Grace had never seen him so ill and she was terrified.

Valerie ran downstairs for the poker and rattled the bars of the grate to summon Mrs Jinks. She ran to unbolt the back door. Within minutes the neighbour arrived, clad in lace-up shoes, her nightie and a tweed coat.

"What's up, Valerie?" she asked.

"Oh, Mrs Jinks, it's me dad. 'E's very bad."

"Right, I'll send our Ben for the doctor. It won't tek 'im long on 'is bike. Tell yer mom he shouldn't be long. Pop the kettle on, chick."

On her return she took a cup of tea up for Grace. She was shocked to see the state Herbert was in. He was grey and his lips had a blue tinge. His breathing was laboured and sweat beaded his top lip.

"Grace, the doctor won't be long. Ben has gone for 'im."

"Thanks, Mrs J," said Grace, her eyes never leaving Herbert's face. Her hands shook as she sipped the tea, her mind a turmoil as she silently reproached herself for doubting that her husband had been gravely ill for a long time.

The back door closed and Ben Jinks called up the stairs, "I'm back. The doctor'll be 'ere soon."

He looked at Valerie sitting hunched miserably in the fireside chair.

"Aye up, love, don't fret. The doctor'll see ter yer dad. Come on, drink yer tea."

Doctor Ferguson came through the door. He did not knock, he made straight for the stairs and into the bedroom.

"So, what's all this then?" he said, then, as Grace moved to one side and he saw Herbert lying there, looking like death, he pulled up sharp.

"He needs the hospital, my girl. I'll get him in there sharpish. Why didn't you call me earlier? He's in a bad way by the looks of things."

"He didn't seem any worse than usual, Doctor," Grace said timidly.

"Never mind about that," Ferguson cut in. "I'll arrange an ambulance. Get his stuff together."

Grace gathered Herbert's one pair of pyjamas and a towel. She told Valerie to cut the tablet of soap into two so that he could have one half to take with him and proceeded to get herself dressed.

"Valerie, Mrs Jinks will see to you. I am going to the hospital with your dad. On yer way ter school call in the shop an' tell Thelma, will yer?"

"Yes, Mom," said the child. "Can I say bye to dad before he goes?"

"Yes but only a quick one, 'e's very poorly."

Valerie went into the bedroom to give her dad a quick kiss. His skin felt clammy and damp.

"Bye, Dad. See you soon."

She tried to keep back the tears until she reached the landing. She ran into her room and, throwing herself onto her bed, she sobbed, stifling the sound in her pillow so that he wouldn't hear her.

Mrs Jinks called up the stairs, "Valerie, come round for some breakfast when you are ready. I'm going round to get Frank off to work now."

As she was told, Valerie called at the cake shop to give her mother's message to Thelma.

"I hope yer dad's soon better, chick. Give yer mom my best an' tell her we'll manage." She pushed a threepence into the child's hand. "Here, duck, treat yerself."

"So," thought Valerie, "Thelma ain't so mean after all."

The day at school was interminable. Valerie couldn't concentrate on her lessons, her tables became a mixed-up jumble in her head and several times she felt close to crying. At last came the bell for home time. Valerie ran all the way home. She went to the back door. It was locked. Mrs Jinks would know why. She knocked on her back door. It was opened by a very subdued Mrs Jinks who began to cry when she saw Valerie.

"Come in, love. Tek your coat off an' I'll mek us a nice cuppa tea."

Valerie was alarmed. "What's wrong, Mrs Jinks?"

"Well, love, yer dad's very poorly. Yer mom an' yer nan are with 'im at the 'ospital."

"Nanny Potts?" asked Valerie.

"Yes, love, and your Grandad Potts is going straight from werk."

"He must be bad then, Mrs Jinks." And Valerie began to cry.

"Come 'ere, love."

Mrs Jinks hugged her to her bosom. It smelled of mothballs but was comforting to the child who needed to be soothed at that moment. The sobbing subsided and Valerie was able to drink some tea and nibble at a broken biscuit.

"Would you like to 'ave yer tea with me and Ben, Valerie?"

"Yes, please."

Valerie took off her pixie hood and her coat and Mrs Jinks hung them on the door. Valerie sat by the fire. The Jinks' cat rolled on to her back and, purring loudly, invited Valerie to rub her tummy.

The clock ticked and the coals settled in the grate. Suddenly Valerie heard footsteps in the yard, and voices, and crying. A knock came on the back door. Mrs Jinks opened it and there stood Aggie.

"Oh, Mrs Potts." Mrs Jinks was full of concern. "Whatever is the matter?"

"Matter? Matter?" cried Aggie. "I've lost me son, that's what's the matter."

"Oh, my God!" Mrs Jinks covered her mouth with her hand. "Valerie's here."

At that a scream from Valerie and a sharp cry from Aggie rent the air.

"I day realise 'er was 'ere. Oh, my God, the poor kid," and she sank onto a chair, put her head on the table and sobbed.

Valerie stood there, white as chalk. She trembled like a leaf and would have fallen to the floor had Mrs Jinks not caught her. Her husband came through the door.

"What's up, love?" he asked

"Oh, Frank. It's Herbert, he's passed away." Mrs Jinks started to cry.

He gasped. "The poor kid. Poor Aggie. Where's Grace?"

"Still at the 'ospital," sobbed Aggie, "with 'is dad. I come ter collect our Valerie."

"Don't worry about Valerie," said Frank, "she can stop 'ere. We'll look after her. Sit you down and have a cupper tea."

Without more ado he mashed the tea and fetched a bottle of whisky from the sideboard. He laced each cup with it including a drop for Valerie. Mrs Jinks stopped crying and got down to the practicalities of the situation.

"Now then, Mrs Potts, Frank'll have his tea, then he'll go round to fetch your Stan. You need your famly round yer and Grace needs 'em an' all. I'll goo round next door an' light the fire while you stop here wi' Valerie, then Grace can come home to a warm 'ouse."

Getting things in motion, Mrs Jinks, being the good neighbour that she was, proved she was worth her weight in gold. Valerie sat as if in a trance. She felt numb. She wanted her mother and how she wanted her dad but this was not to be, ever again.

* * *

The day of the funeral was a grey, cold, winter's day. The wind had dropped but snow was threatening. Valerie got out of bed and dressed mechanically. She could hear her mother poking the fire in the kitchen and breaking up the raker which had been placed on top of the slack to keep the fire in overnight. She looked up as Valerie entered the kitchen.

"'Allo, love. Would you like some porridge for a change?"

Valerie shook her head. "No thanks, Mom. I ain't very hungry, just a piece o' toast, please."

Grace took the comb from the mantelpiece to comb her hair, then she brushed Valerie's and tied it back with a black ribbon.

"Valerie."

"Yes, Mom?"

"You won't ever leave me, will yer?"

"No, Mom," said the child.

Grace persisted. "You mean it, don't yer, Valerie? We only 'ave each other now. You promise you won't ever goo away from yer mom?"

"No, Mom. I won't ever go away from you."

Grace gave her a hug, satisfied that she would have her daughter for ever.

* * *

The funeral was so sad. Aggie cried so hard and almost fainted at the graveside. Grace and Valerie sobbed bitterly. Many tears were shed by all the family members. Mrs Jinks had stayed at the house to prepare refreshments for the mourners. She had a good fire going in the front room and had put out sandwiches and cakes. Grace had bought two bottles of sherry.

The men sat in the front room talking among themselves, the women joined them and Mrs Jinks handed round the sandwiches.

Aggie Potts stood a little apart from the rest of them. Holding her glass of sherry aloft, she said, "I propose a toast ter our son, Herbert, a nicer man yo couldn't wish ter meet." She turned to look Renee Shaw straight in the face and, leaning towards her, she said, "Now tell us what a lazy bugger 'e was, Renee Shaw. Tell us how work shy 'e was. Yo was keen enough ter tell 'in the market the other wik, warn't yer? Talking like that about a mon dyin' on 'is feet. I 'ope yo'me ashamed o' yerself. I'll never fergive yer as long as I live."

Grace stood transfixed. Bert took his wife's arm. "Come on now, Aggie, this ain't the time or the place ter carry on like that."

Aggie shrugged him away. "Don't you tell me when I can stick up fer me famly, Bert. It's about time somebody tode that poisonous old cow ter watch what 'er says about folks."

At that Aggie turned to go into the kitchen for another good cry. Mrs Jinks followed to comfort her and make another cup of tea. Valerie looked at her Granny Shaw, who was protesting to everyone that she hadn't said any such things about Herbert, and from that day, any feeling Valerie had for her, died.

The week following the funeral Grace did not go to work. Valerie did not attend school. The insurance man called and settled up with Grace. There was little money left after paying the undertaker. Grace had some savings but not a great deal. She looked up from her accounts and sighed.

"Well, Valerie, I can't see how four hours in the cake shop an' me bit o' widder's pension is gonna keep us. I shall 'ave ter get meself a factry job with more hours an' more money. Yo'me eight now, nearly nine, an' Mrs Jinks is next door to keep an eye on yer so you'll 'ave ter 'elp me an' we'll manage."

Valerie was shocked to think that her mother would be bringing the smell of slurry into the house.

She said, "Oh, Mom, I don't want you to go in the factry. Aunt Flo smells bad when 'er comes 'ome and her hands are awful."

Grace sighed. "No 'elp for it, Valerie. I shall have ter or we won't be able ter afford the rent fer this 'ouse. We'll 'ave ter move into the back ter backs. You doe remember what they was like but I do. No, I'll goo down the werks termorrer an' see what's gooin."

Next morning Valerie dressed quickly, each garment adding to the comfort of her chilled body. Snow looked likely, the sky was overcast. She was to make her way to Nan Potts while Grace was job seeking. Grace did not want to keep Valerie away from Aggie's but had no wish to go there visiting herself.

She called up the stairs, "Come on, our Valerie, the sooner we get our skates on, the sooner we will be 'ome. If I'm not back by twelve Mrs Jinks will let you in. You're big enough to walk from Aggie's on yer own now. Tell yer nan I've gone shoppin'. Don't tell 'er about job huntin'. The less 'er knows the better."

"Okay, Mom."

Grace frowned. "What 'ave I told you about sayin' okay? That's slang, that is."

"Sorry, Mom."

Aggie opened the door. "Oh, Bert, it's our Valerie." She hugged the child. "Come on in, cock, you look perished. Get thee coot off an' sit yerself by the fire. I'll mek you a nice cuppa tay."

Aggie bustled round the kitchen. She hung Valerie's coat on the back of the door.

"Yer Grandad ain't at werk today, too upset 'e is. We loved yer dad, we did, an' no matter what anybody says 'e wore werk shy an' 'e allus thought the werld of you. Let's 'ope as you tek after 'im an' not that lot over the bonk." Aggie wiped her eyes on her apron. "'Ow long yer come for, pet? Can yer stop for a bitta dinner?"

Valerie held her hands out to the fire. "Mom says to be back by twelve, Nan, but I can have a bit of toast or somethin'."

Aggie smiled. "You'll 'ave better than that, cocka. There's a stewjar in th'oven. Be just right about half eleven so you can have some o' that afore you goo."

Aggie kept her home shining but these days she did not look so smart herself. Her hair needed a perm and she looked pale and tired. Like most women in the area she had had a tough life, working in a factory and then struggling to rear two lads while looking after aged parents, the loss of whom had hit her hard, but not as hard as the loss of her son. She doubted that she would ever recover from that but here was our Valerie, not a pretty child, but she had Herbert's eyes. She just hoped that the child had not inherited the miserable outlook on life of her mother's family, especially the detested Renee Shaw, who had called her son an idler.

Too soon the clock on the mantelpiece chimed 11.30. Valerie, full of stew and warm, realised that she had to make tracks. It was only fifteen minutes' walk to home but she did not want to stay in case her Uncle Stan and Aunty Janice called in. There was always an atmosphere when her Uncle Stan was around, had been since Grace and Herbert had moved to Pipers Row and Stan was still in the back to backs in Pitts End.

He thought Valerie was a stuck-up little bugger, plain as a pikestaff but led to believe that she was something special. He couldn't be doing with Grace or her family and had made it quite clear that he considered that Herbert had been trapped into marrying Grace Shaw. As it happened, he had no intention of calling to see his parents on that day so Valerie need not have rushed.

As Valerie put on her coat, Aggie reached her purse from the cupboard.

"Ee yar, cocka, a threepenny joey for yer. Now, don't leave it too long afore yer come ter see yer old nan and grandad again, love." Aggie wiped her eyes and gave Valerie a hug. "We aye got much fambly left now, cocka, so we 'ave ter stick tergether."

Valerie kissed her cheek. "Okay, Nan," she said.

She waved from the top of the yard. As she ran down the entry she almost bumped into a lad of about her own age.

"Watch where yo'me gooin, four eyes," he retorted. "Yo coulda knocked me flyin' then."

This was her first encounter with Ronnie Edwards but it certainly would not be her last.

Chapter Four

Round the corner from Pipers Row was Platt Street. Halfway down was Salt's Fish and Chip shop. It was a thriving little business. The next chip shop was twenty minutes' walk away. Freda Salt ran the shop with the help of her parents, Eva and George, who lived next door, and that of her husband, Steve, who worked as a postman. Josie was their only daughter. She had arrived after seven years of marriage to the delight of all the family. Nothing was too good for Josie. She was Valerie's best friend. She envied her having nice things and her holidays, Josie envied Valerie having her mother's undivided attention. The business took up a lot of time. The shop opened every evening and Monday, Wednesday, Friday and Saturday lunchtimes.

The girls always walked home from school together. Valerie became grateful for the company to help shield her from Ronnie Edwards's unwelcome attentions. These happened infrequently but were always hanging like a dark cloud threateningly over Valerie. The girls didn't see each other often after parting at Josie's entry. They met each morning and played together in the playground. Freda didn't mind Josie being friends with Valerie. The child was quiet and well behaved and neatly dressed. She had misgivings about Grace being so possessive with the child but, there again, her family was somewhat protective of Josie so she felt that she shouldn't criticise.

One Friday, as they reached her entry, Josie asked, "Are yer going to yer nan's after tea, Valerie?"

"Yes, we usually do, Jose. Mom has to see Peggy to pay her club and Nan to pay her diddleum. I don't mind going and Nan would miss us if we couldn't make it." She suddenly gasped and put her hand to her mouth. "Oh, I nearly forgot. Mom asked me ter take some chips for our tea. I'd have had to come back."

She entered the shop. "'Allo, Valerie," said Freda. "'Ow's yer mom?"

"Alright, thank you, Mrs Salt."

"What can I get yer then?"

"Two bags of chips, please."

Freda put a liberal amount of batter bits into the bag with Valerie's chips. "Fourpence, please, Valerie."

"Thanks, Mrs Salt. Tarrar."

Valerie turned to leave the shop, almost bumping into Ronnie Edwards as he came bounding up the steps. He was on the verge of making some retort then, just in time, he saw Freda watching him. He knew that if he blotted his copybook he could say goodbye to generous portions of batter bits with his chips, so, giving Valerie a disdainful stare, he kept his mouth shut.

On her way home Valerie also had to call in to the butcher's shop. She had to buy two slices of belly pork for Saturday dinner. There was one lady waiting to be served. She was well dressed and smelled of perfume. Valerie liked the smell. She had an idea that it was Evening in Paris. Aunty Janice had worn some once. The woman smiled deprecatingly at the butcher.

"Two nice pieces of fillet steak, Bob," she said, "and one of your lovely pork pies. Oh, and for the weekend, do me a leg of lamb, please."

Valerie shuffled her feet in the sawdust on the floor of the shop.

"One day," she thought, "one day I shall be able to buy those things. One day I shan't be poor."

Carrying her packages home she thought of her dad and how he had suffered, how proud he had been to have her for his daughter.

"Dad, oh Dad," she thought. "How I wish he was waiting for me at home right now."

He had always made her feel special, although she was plain with straight hair and wore glasses. Now he was gone and, at the tender age of nine, she felt as responsible as her mother for keeping things together.

Valerie reached the key from its hook in the coalhouse. It was still light so she was not afraid. Lucky, the cat, wound himself around her legs, purring. She hung her coat on the back door and lit the oven. Putting it on a low light, she placed the packet of chips in to keep warm. Grace was to do fried eggs with them for a quick meal. Then she put the kettle on ready to mash the tea.

Grace finished early on a Friday. She was always relieved when another working week was over. She came in looking as tired as she must feel, bone weary, in fact. She sank onto a chair and passed a hand over her eyes. Valerie hated the smell of slurry which hung around her mother. She placed a cup of tea in front of her.

"I've got the chips, Mom, and the belly pork for tomorrow."

Grace sighed. "I don't know what I'd do without you, our Valerie. Satday termorrer, thank the Lord."

Valerie put the kettle on for her mother to have a wash. Lathe operating was hard work. Most of the girls had a kind of camaraderie, but Grace was inclined to keep to herself. She only needed the friendship of her daughter and, apart from her family, Peggy, an old school friend, who lived down the road from Renee and, of course, Thelma from the cake shop.

A plump, plain woman, she had no desire to follow fashion. She resented the fact that she had been widowed and had to go to work, resentment a stronger emotion than grief. Like her mother and her sister, she enjoyed a grumble.

Valerie was the apple of her eye. She kept the child spotless, always with freshly-ironed hair ribbons and spotless white socks and underwear.

Often she would say, "You'll never leave me, will yer, our Valerie? You'll stop with yer mom? Friends am all fickle, thay'me no good to yer."

"Yes, Mom," Valerie would agree. It was not hard to promise not to leave her mother at this stage in her young life. Apart from Josie she had few friends and her life centred around her mother, which was all she needed.

Refreshed by the wash and the cup of tea, Grace fried the eggs. With the chips and bread and butter they were greatly enjoyed. Leaving the crocks to soak in a bowl of suds they got ready for the walk to Granny Shaw's.

It was a half-hour walk to the Shaws. Valerie didn't mind walking and Grace seemed to find the energy from somewhere to make the journey.

By walking they saved money. There was a bus which would take them about two thirds of the way, which meant that they had to complete the rest of the journey on foot anyway.

Valerie didn't mind going to Granny Shaw's. she looked forward to reading the cartoon strips in the newspapers which were stacked up on a stool next to the fireplace. Gran's home was very old-fashioned, still having a Triplex grate in the back kitchen, where all household activity went on around the table.

Renee was used to the grate and, although she had a gas stove, preferred to use the ovens for most of her baking.

Grace had one old friend, her name was Peggy. She lived in the same street as Renee. She had started school the same day as Grace and they had lived near to each other all of their lives. Peggy was married to a bus driver, Keith and had two daughters, Janine, aged ten and Roma, eleven. Renee always thought that Peggy's choice of names for her daughters was rather fanciful and said so, often.

As Peggy was making Aunt Flo's wedding dress, Grace would pop to Peggy's often. Grace paid her club money and

Flo would try on the dress. They would spend a good half hour 'talking weddings'.

Keith, Peggy's long-suffering husband, was used to this palaver. His wife was good at sewing and popular because she never overcharged her clients.

On arrival Grace called out to her mother, "Just popping to Peg's, Mom. I'll sort me diddleum out with you when I get back." She called up the stairs, "Am yer comin', Flo?"

Flo answered, "Just a tick. I'm avin' me strip wash."

A few minutes later Flo emerged through the stairs door. "Glad ter get that pong o' slurry off me," she said. She looked at Valerie. "Don't you get werkin' in a factry, our Valerie. You get yerself a nice office job."

"Yes, Aunt," said Valerie, who, at nine years of age, certainly knew what she wanted from life. Being poor was not one of them and definitely not a job on any factory floor. She looked up at Flo. She had had a new perm and her hair was tightly curled. She was thirty-three and had been engaged for five years. At last the wedding was approaching. Like Grace she worked in a local factory, cycling to and fro each day, her stick-like legs pushing the pedals vigorously.

Flo's philosophy of life, like that of her sister and mother, was that it always favoured others better than it did herself. She was engaged to Fred. He worked in a local factory and was a labourer. He did not earn a big wage, his father was often ill and his mother was rather inadequate. Fred liked a smoke and a pint and also, secretly, a bet at weekends. This did not leave much over for saving. Flo was patient and, having scraped and saved hard, was relieved that the wedding was in sight at last.

The three women would enjoy a session sitting round the kitchen table bemoaning their lot. Valerie would let it all go over her head while she read the cartoon strips. One day she would be away from the environment which had her mother and aunt trapped. She didn't much care how she did it but do it she would.

Uncle Arthur didn't say much about anything. He was a loner. He worked, came home, went to the bookies and the pub and let each day drift by. As long as he had his routine and his twenty Woodbines each day he was, if not content, resigned to his lot.

He had once loved a girl deeply. When he was called up and posted abroad she had promised to wait for him. After she failed to do so he never considered another woman. She was now a plump, matronly person with three children and a husband who was a bread delivery man.

Arthur was designated to give Flo away on her wedding day. A thin, little man, who liked to keep a low profile, he did not relish the idea one bit.

Each week he gave Valerie threepence pocket money. If he had a good week on the horses or dogs he would fork out sixpence. This was treasured by her and saved. One day she wanted to open a Post Office account.

Flo was proud of her niece. Working in a factory, she would see the office girls arriving in clean blouses and skirts, neat and tidy. Setting great store on Valerie becoming one of them she would say, "Learn yore lessons an' that typewritin' an' you'll be alright."

"I will, Aunty," Valerie would say.

Valerie certainly intended to come home from work free from the slurry smell which hung around Grace and Flo and to have clean hands and nails without having to scour them with a hard brush under the kitchen tap.

Flo was trying to make her hands nice for her wedding, rubbing in hand cream and applying Snowfire to any cracks on her knuckles.

Valerie wondered if her aunt would be successful or end up hiding her work-worn hands under her bouquet.

She was looking forward to being the only bridesmaid and wearing her dress of pink taffeta with rosebuds on the bodice.

For a while, after Grace and Flo had departed for Peggy's, all was quiet. Arthur was in the scullery having a wash and shave and Renee was ironing a shirt for him. He was going to the dog track.

Valerie never had much to say to her Granny Shaw. She always remembered her Nan Potts' words at her dad's funeral.

A knock at the front door caused Renee to tut and put down the iron.

"Aye up, our Valerie, I expect that's the milk mon."

She bustled to the door, her purse clutched in her gnarled fingers, already calculating in her head the number of pints delivered that week.

The draught from the open door caught the edge of a piece of paper on the mantelshelf and lifted it slightly. Valerie half rose from her chair. She could see that it was a ten shilling note anchored by an ornamental brass cat.

The child could hear her Gran debating with the milkman how many pints he had delivered. She was transfixed by the paper rising and falling. It was beckoning to her, asking to be rescued. As if controlled by another being, quick as a flash, she was across the hearth, standing on tiptoe in front of the range. She whisked the note up and tucked it into her gymslip pocket.

Quickly sitting down she was innocently reading the paper and beginning to breathe normally as she heard Renee at the front door.

"Cheerio, Mike. Don't ferget me eggs Monday." She shut the door and came through to the kitchen. "You 'ave ter watch 'em. Soon overcharge yer, them buggers will. I'll mek another cup o' tea when I've finished this shert an' there's some broken biscuits in the tin."

She bustled to the range where the ever-boiling kettle sang over the fire.

"Just me an' you till yer mom an' Flo get back. 'Ow's school? Am yer werkin' 'ard?"

Valerie answered, "Yes, Nan."

She was not lying, she did work hard and her glasses had given her a whole new exciting world of books. She loved to read stories of rags to riches. She intended to get on and would do it one day, she knew.

"That's a good gel," said Renee. "Glad you've got some werk in yer."

*   *   *

The bombshell didn't drop until the following Monday. The clubman had flu so didn't call as usual on the Saturday, therefore the money wasn't missed over the weekend.

As Valerie came out of the school gates at four o'clock, Renee was waiting for her. Her stomach gave a flip.

"Hello, Nan. What are you doing here?" she asked, feigning surprise.

Renee leaned towards her. "Our Valerie, did you see a ten bob note on the mantelshelf on Friday?"

Valerie slid her eyes away from her nan's. "No, Nan," she said.

"Am you sure, our Valerie? I put it theer meself. It warn't theer this mornin' when the club mon called."

"No, Nan, honest," said the child.

Renee sighed. "It's worryin' me ter death," she said. "I'm gooin ter be right short this wik. The Lord only knows where it went. Yer Aunt Flo's real upset. When 'er come dinner time 'er was in a tidy state. We 'ad the kitchen upside down. I've been all of a sweat." Renee was near to tears.

For a moment Valerie felt a twinge of conscience but not for long. Surely Uncle Arthur could give her Gran some extra to help out.

As if reading her mind, Renee said, “I can’t ask Arthur fer any, ’e’s short this week. ’Ad a bad night at the dogs a Friday an’ Flo’s already gid me all ’er can. I doe know worrile do.”

“Come home with me an’ have a cuppa, Nan. Mom’ll be home by six. I’ve only got to pick a loaf up from the shop.”

“No,” said Renee. “I’ll carry on ’ome. Ask yer mom if ’er’s any idea where we can look next. P’raps ’er’ll pop over. Tarra, our Valerie.”

Renee hurried off down the street, a thin, dejected figure in her shabby, grey coat, her meagre hair scraped into a bun, shoes slipping up and down as she walked.

Valerie went into the corner shop. She didn’t often shop at Turdy Tunley’s but decided not to walk to the bread and cake shop. She felt somewhat drained today.

The shop smelled of tea, coffee, bacon, cheese and other non-specific aromas, not very pleasant. Grace would not be very pleased that the bread had been fetched from there but wouldn’t know. The proprietor had long, dirty fingernails. His wife, who presided over the Post Office counter, had been a singer of sorts. Her past life experience had not included even the basics of domesticity, thus the state of the shop premises. Very few people ever licked a stamp which had been purchased from there.

Mrs Arrowsmith, an old lady of around eighty, sat on the shop chair waiting for her tea, sugar and snuff. Her coat was once black but was now green with age and brown with streaks of snuff down the front.

Across the counter strutted the shop cat, tail in the air, pausing to pee up a muslin-wrapped slab of cheese. He added to the mingled aromas but certainly did not enhance them.

Arriving home Valerie let herself in the back door. The cat rubbed against her legs and she stooped to stroke him. Poking up the fire she then set to work to peel the potatoes, then set the table. All ready, she went to her room. Removing the top drawer of her dressing table she took out the ten shilling note. Holding it in her hand, she thought, “This is the start, this is the start.”

She jumped as she heard the back door close and hurriedly replaced the money and the drawer. Grace was back, tired as usual.

Valerie put a cup of tea on the table.

“Gran was here, Mom,” she said.

“Why’s that?” asked Grace.

“She was worried, she lost a ten bob note.”

Grace’s eyes opened wide. “’Ow’s ’er done that?”

“I don’t know, Mom, but she says it was on the mantelshelf on Friday and it’s disappeared. She wants you to pop over to see if you can think where it is.”

Grace held out her hands. “What am I supposed to do about it?” she asked. “If they can’t find it, how do they expect me to? I’m whacked, too whacked ter goo gallivantin’ over there. I’ve got me ironin’ ter do. They shouldn’t be so half-soaked. Our Flo’s got ’er ’ead full o’ that weddin’, that’s ’er trouble. I tell yer what, Valerie, we’ll ’ave a quick tea, toast an’ drippin’ then you pop an’ tell yer nan as I’ve got one o’ me ’eadaches and tell ’er as I don’t know nuthin’ about it. I’ll see her Friday as usual. Why don’t yer ask Josie ter go with yer? ’Er’ll likely be on ’er own, the shop’s open. And bring back some chips with yer.”

“Alright, Mom. Josie’s been to have her eyes tested this afternoon. I want to see how she got on. We’ll go there and straight back. We won’t be long.”

Valerie didn’t want to go but felt that she should let her mother off the hook. Also it would be a nice change to go for a walk in the evening. She seldom went out after school.

Josie was practising her scales on the piano. She spent a lot of time on her own in the living room at the back of the shop. When Valerie came to the back door she was surprised.

“What’s this, Val? You don’t usually come out?”

Valerie asked, "Can you come to Granny Shaw's with me, Jose? I have to tek a message for me mom. And I wanted to see how you got on about your eyes."

Josie put the lid down on the piano. Valerie envied her. She would have liked to play an instrument but she knew that money was tight so she never pestered Grace about things that she knew her mother could not afford.

Josie said, "My eyes are alright, just have to use a better light when I read. A bit of eye strain he said." She popped her head round the shop door. "Mom, can I go with Valerie to her nan's? We'll only be about an hour."

Freda turned from the range. "Which nan's?" she asked.

"Nan Shaw," Valerie replied.

Freda went to the till and gave Josie some coppers. "Get the buz as far as it goes, that'll mek it quicker for yer."

"Thanks, Mrs Salt," said Valerie politely.

Josie was glad to be going out. She got tired of being on her own when her parents were busy in the shop. Off the girls went in high spirits.

As the bus pulled away from the stop, Valerie looked out of the window. There was Ronnie Edwards sitting on a wall with his mates. He saw her and pulled a disgusting face. She just turned up her nose at him and looked away.

"What's up, Val?" asked Josie.

Valerie grimaced. "Oh, it's just that Ronnie Edwards. I hate him, I do."

"He's alright," said Josie, who secretly thought him very attractive.

"Well, I don't think so. I really hate him," Valerie retorted.

Renee sat reading the paper at the kitchen table. She looked up as the girls came through the back door.

"'Allo, Gran," said Valerie, feeling a bit uneasy. "Mom says to tell you she can't come over, she's got one of her bad heads. I only came to tell you. We've got to get the bus straight back."

As Valerie drew breath, Flo came through the stairs door.

"Our Valerie," she said, "can you throw any light on what could've 'appened to the ten bob note that was on the mantelshelf on Friday?"

Valerie looked her aunt straight in the eye. "No, Aunty," she said innocently.

"Well," said Flo, "It's a bloody mystery ter me. A bloody mystery." She sat at the table. "Do you want a drink or anythin'?" she asked.

"No, thanks, Aunty. Have to get the bus straight back. Thanks anyway and I 'ope you soon find the money." She turned to the door. "Come on, Jose. See yer Friday, Nan, Aunty."

As they walked across the yard she was surprised at the ease with which she had lied to Flo. She felt that she had achieved something that day, had set a precedent of some kind, which boded well for her future.

Holding Josie's hand, she cheerfully set off up the street.

Chapter Five

Ronnie danced round the front room. He sang, "Adam an' Eve an' Pinch Me went down to the river to bathe, Adam an' Eve got drownded, who do yer think was saved?"

"Pinch Me," cried Patty excitedly – so Ronnie did.

Nellie, in the scullery, heard the screams. Rolling her eyes, she let the potato she was peeling drop into the bowl.

"What's gooin on now?" she shouted. "I'll lamp yer backsides if I 'ave ter come in theer to yer."

"It's nothin', Mom," called Ronnie.

"'E's pinched me, 'e 'as." Patty's tear-streaked face appeared in the doorway.

"Right," said Nellie. "Just you come 'ere, our Ronnie." He stood defiantly in front of her. "Now then, Patty, stop yer skrikin' an' gee 'im a good pinch."

Patty brightened up immediately. She gave her brother a good pinch, using her nails.

"Ow, yo," cried Ronnie. "I day pinch you as 'ard as that, our Patty."

"Right," said Nellie. "Enuff, goo an' get some firewood, Ronnie, an' Patty, put some clean paper on the table."

Quiet reigned for a few minutes while the children did as they were asked. The back gate slammed and Pongo barked excitedly. Barry was back. He was as black as the ace of spades and hungry.

"What's for tea, Mom?"

"Klondykes," said Nellie. "It won't be many minutes, yer dad's due in from the 'lotment. I aye sid 'im all day. Pigeons, 'lotment and, I 'spect, the pub tonight," she sighed.

Often Wilf would ask her to go to the pub on a Saturday night but she hated the thought of sitting there, listening to the clap trap and noise, so she would rather stay in her own home. Wilf was obliged to go as it was the pigeon club.

Barry took the kettle of hot water into the scullery. He did a Saturday job for Gerry Taylor at the local coal wharf, filling bags. He kept his ears cocked for sounds of his dad approaching so that he could vacate the scullery and leave it for Wilf's use. He knew he wouldn't take kindly to waiting for his wash.

Ronnie came in, whistling, firewood in his hands.

"Hiya, Baz. Gorra date ternight, 'ave yer?"

Barry flicked soap at his brother. "Cheeky sod. Mind yer own poke."

"Keep yer wig on." Ronnie pulled a face behind Barry's back.

The smell of klondykes frying made Ronnie's mouth water. Nellie cut doorsteps of bread and butter to accompany them. For a while peace reigned while the three youngsters munched contentedly.

Nellie said, "As soon as your dad gets in, you an' Patty run a' play. I want yer in at half past seven sharp. I doe want ter 'ave ter run the streets lookin' for yer. Do you 'ear me, Ronnie?"

"Yes, Mom."

Ronnie would be in his mate's house. He and Terry Spooner would swop comics and play Ludo while Terry's mom and dad were at the pictures. Their Gwen would be in to keep an eye on them.

Whistling cheerily, Ronnie was stopped in his tracks by his dad in the entry. From Wilf's belt hung two pigeons, eyes glazed in death, heads lolling pitifully, disposed of, being surplus to requirements, their racing days over. Ronnie knew that he would have little appetite for the pigeon pie which would appear on the table for Sunday dinner.

Wilf said, "Mind what you'me doin'. Don't be late back and keep outa th'oss road."

"Okay, Dad. See yer."

Ronnie beat a hasty retreat down the entry. With any luck his dad would be gone to the pub when he got back.

*   *   *

Wilf's brother, Reg, and his sister, Betty, had never married. They lived together in James Street in the house where they had been born. It was three doors up from Aggie and Bert Potts. It was close enough to the school to enable Ronnie to call each lunchtime to take Reg's dinner to the foundry. For this he earned sixpence a week and Aunty Betty gave him something to eat. This helped Betty, who had a club foot, and Nellie, by feeding Ronnie.

Most of the foundry men had dinner brought in, usually a bowl of broth or stew, sometimes faggots and peas or groaty pudding, all with thick slices of bread. A bottle of tea, well sugared and milked, accompanied the food. Sometimes a sweet or savoury pasty or pie was provided. The work was dirty and hard and the men needed plenty of nourishment.

The noise from the factory was incessant and deafening. The houses vibrated with the thumps from the machinery. Ronnie and his family were accustomed to it, the women waging war on the dirt and grime or, in a few instances, 'giving neck'.

Ronnie didn't mind taking his uncle's dinner. His half hour spent with Aunty Betty was a quiet oasis in his day. She seemed to appreciate his company and he loved the old dog, Patch, who sat to share his meal.

Despite her infirmity, Betty was a cheery soul and well loved by all the family. She had a soft spot for Ronnie. One of her closest friends was Aggie Potts who had a good heart and was always available to do a good turn for a neighbour.

Ronnie sat munching his pasty.

"My tern ter collect the bread today, Aunty," he said.

"How many terday, Ron?"

"Three. We 'ad some left this morning so I can pop after school. No 'angin' about me mom says."

"Well, see that you don't, Ronnie. We don't want yer ter get inter yer mom and dad's bad books."

Ronnie cheerfully agreed and took his leave.

"See yer termorrer, Aunty. Tarrar."

True to his word, Ronnie raced out of the school gates after the bell rang and ran straight to the bread shop. Thelma had his loaves saved for him.

She said, "Now then, young Ronnie, no bitin' the corners off on the way 'ome."

Ronnie glared at her indignantly. He said, "Not me, missis. I doe do that."

"Okay, okay, son. Anyroad, 'ow many are there in your 'ouse these days?"

"I doe know, do I? I aye never in when we'me all in, am I?"

He went to the shop door, turning, he said, "Nosy bleeder," and ran off down the street.

Thelma had to laugh. He was a right 'un but she resolved to tell Nellie when she called in on Saturday.

The next Saturday morning Nellie went to the town to do her shopping. She called into the bread and cake shop to place her order for the week. Sometimes she managed to buy a sponge cake or some doughnuts. Thelma looked up from the till.

"Hello, Nell. How are yer? You'me loaded up terday, aren't yer?"

"Arr, I am that. Our Christine's s'posed ter meet me but I reckon 'er's gone an' forgot. I shall 'ave ter pop inter town this afternoon. Me mother needs some new stays an' I can't gerrit all at once. I'll have ten doughnuts an' me bread order's the same as last wik."

Righto, Nell. Anyroad, I'm glad you've popped in." Thelma paused while the customer being served by Stella went out of the shop. "I wanted ter see you about your Ronnie."

"Oh, ar, what's 'e done now?"

"Not much really, just a bit o' cheek."

"What sort o' cheek? Spit it out, wench."

"Well," Thelma paused. "'E called me a nosy bleeder. I don't suppose that's very bad but I did think I should mention it."

Nellie sighed. "An' so yer should. 'E's gerrin out of 'and. I shall 'ave ter sort 'im out. Sorry, Thelma."

Thelma grinned. "Don't be too 'ard on 'im, Nell. I reckon 'e could've bit 'is tongue out as soon as 'e said it."

"Doe you start mekking excuses fer 'im, Thelma. Anyroad, I'm off. See yer. Tarrar."

"Tarrar, Nell."

Nellie walked home, weighed down with the shopping. The first person she saw was Christine, chatting to Annie, at the top of the entry.

"Christine," she called. "Wheer 'ave you bin? I'm buggered up carryin' this lot."

"Sorry, Mom. I day realise the time. I've been round Gran's all mornin'."

Annie smiled her toothless grin. "That's right, Nellie. 'Er 'as an' you know 'ow soon time flies."

Nellie frowned at Christine. "Tek some o' this shoppin' off me an' as soon as we gerrin I want yer to goo an' fetch our Ronnie in."

Christine perked up. "What's he done now, Mom?"

"Never you mind," Nellie replied.

Christine put the shopping bag inside the kitchen door and ran down the entry. She could see Ronnie at the top of the street playing Jacks with Terry Spooner and Mickey Johns.

"Ronnie," she called, impatiently. "Ronnie."

Ronnie frowned. It was spoiling his game, his sister calling him like that.

"What yer want?"

"Our mom wants yer, NOW."

Ronnie scowled. "See yer later, Tel, Mick. Gorra goo." He scuffed the toes of his shoes along the pavement. "What does mom want me for?"

Christine shrugged. "I don't know but 'er looks proper mad so yer'd better 'urry up."

Ronnie turned and waved to his friends. "Call fer me fer the flicks, Tel."

He ran up the entry and into the back door where Nellie, lying in wait, collared him like a ton of bricks.

Grabbing him by the collar, she snarled, "Right, me laddo, no flicks for you. You'me gunna goo an' apologise ter Mrs Spears in the cake shop."

Ronnie reddened. "What for? I aye done nuthin'."

"I doe call swearin' nothin'. Fer that you can ferget the flicks this afternoon, my lad."

Ronnie looked near to tears. "I day mean it, Mom!"

"Never you mind about that. Just gerrof an' say you'me sorry. Either that or I'll tell yer dad an' 'e'll leather yer."

Ronnie thought this was the most difficult thing he had ever had to do in his life. He made his way to the shop and hung around until there was a lull between customers, then went in. He stood in front of the counter, hung his head and mumbled, "Me mom sent me, missis. I've gorra say sorry for swearin'."

Thelma tried to keep a straight face. She dismissed him with a wave of her hand.

"Okay, Ronnie. Don't let it happen again. See you next week."

There was no point in rushing home. He wasn't going to the pictures. He dawdled along the street and found himself going the long way round, via Pipers Row.

All was quiet in Pipers Row, except for Valerie playing with her top and whip. Ronnie stopped to watch her.

Wiping his nose on his sleeve, and inclining his head forward, he thrust his hands into his pockets.

"Gis a goo," he said. "Goo on, gis a goo."

Valerie ignored him, although she was no expert. Ronnie placed his hands on his hips and frowned.

A gust of wind blew down the entry, blowing Valerie's hair over her glasses. She missed the top yet again with the whip.

She had spent time making patterns on the top with coloured chalks. When it spun the colours blended and it looked pretty. It wobbled towards Ronnie and fell at his feet.

"Goo on, gis a goo. Doe be skinny."

Valerie glared at him. "No," she said. "My mom says not to play with you, you smell."

At that Ronnie picked up the top and threw it with all his might into the open side of a passing dustcart.

Valerie stood frozen to the spot. She paled and then she flushed. Gasping in disbelief she gave out a howl of pain and indignation.

Ronnie fled.

From that day forward Valerie Potts was Ronnie Edwards's mortal enemy.

Grace looked up as Valerie ran into the kitchen. She was distraught.

"Whatever's the matter, Valerie?"

Valerie could not answer.

"Come and sit down and tell me what's the matter."

After a while the child was able to tell her, between sobs, what Ronnie had done.

"Right," said Grace. "Wait till I see that Nellie Edwards. That little sod needs a good beltin'. I 'eard as 'e swore at Thelma the other day. 'E's a right little toe rag, 'e is. Don't cry now, Valerie." Grace wiped her hands on her apron. "'Ere you are, run ter the shop an' get us some broken biscuits an' a new top for yerself. Don't worry. I'll sort out Master Ronnie."

Chapter Six

"Rag bo-ans, any old rag bo-ans." The cry of Herbie Forrester, the local totter, echoed down the street. He did have a bugle once but he had made the mistake of putting it on the cart one day and some light-fingered kid had pinched it.

Herbie told everyone that he met that there was a reward out for the instrument but, so far, no one had found it.

Lily, his old nag, patiently waited, her head hanging resignedly. She liked the children to come out to pat her and sometimes, perhaps, give her an apple core or a carrot, which she would munch with her old, yellowed teeth.

She knew that Ingram Terrace was one of the streets on the home run. Her stall and hay were just round the corner.

Ronnie loved Lily. He loved the smell of her and her soft, brown eyes. One of his ambitions in life was to have a horse of his own one day.

Often he would accompany Herbie and Lily home to 'help' put the horse in. He would like to brush and pet her. Often he would call on his way to school in a morning. Ronnie, therefore, often smelled of horse. One morning he even got caught in a stream of urine. It went all over his shoes and socks. Not having the time, or courage, to face Nellie for clean socks, he had to go to school as he was. The day was warm so they dried but the smell was rather pungent. He resolved to keep his wits about him in future when visiting Lily.

* * *

Miss Hughes stood in front of her class. She was not over fond of teaching nine-year-olds. In fact, she was not over fond of teaching at all.

Tall and thin, with hair in unfashionable plaits coiled over her ears, she was rather plain. Lines of discontent ran from her nose to her mouth. When she spoke, her Adam's apple slid up and down. This fascinated her charges and prevented full concentration on her words.

She would often lose patience with some miscreant and would speak waspishly to the culprit. Boys who upset her would be sent to the headmaster for the strap. Boys and girls alike would be kept behind after school to write lines as recompense.

It would happen on the day that Ronnie had visited Lily before school and got his socks wet that Miss Hughes did her weekly hygiene inspection.

Standing in front of the class she waited for complete silence.

"Good morning, children," she said.

"Good morning, Miss Shoes," the children chorused.

"This morning I want you to file out quietly. I said, quietly! I will inspect your hands to see if they are clean."

The girls filed out first, one or two getting a frown as palms were displayed and then nails. She admonished the ones with bitten nails or grubby mitts.

Miss Hughes said, "I will see you again tomorrow morning. I expect a big improvement. If not, those of you who still have dirty hands will stay in after school and write a hundred times 'I must wash my hands and scrub my nails'. Now I will see the boys."

The boys shuffled out. Most of them had tried to keep their hands a little better but some had played on the way to school and had quite grimy paws.

As Ronnie approached the teacher, the smell from his wet socks preceded him. His hands were quite dirty from stroking Lily and he smelled generally of horse but those socks reeked.

"See me after school, Ronnie," the teacher said.

At three forty-five the bell went and, reluctantly, Ronnie went to Miss Hughes.

She frowned at him. "Now then, Ronnie, I have written a note to your mother. I am warning you about it because I have given it to your sister, Patty. This is to ensure that your mother gets it. I don't trust you to take it home."

"Oh, Miss," said Ronnie, "what've I done? I know me 'ands am dirty but I'll wash 'em. 'Onest injun."

Miss Hughes shook her head. "I think your mother should know the state in which you arrive at school. I know she does her best, my lad, and I feel that you let her down. Off you go. I have to do the detention now."

Ronnie sloped off down the corridor. Now he was for it. He'd have to make up a tale for when he saw Nellie. He didn't want her to tell his dad.

Nellie tried to keep most things from Wilf to save the children from his wrath, and his belt, but she always had him to threaten them with if things got out of hand.

Miss Hughes watched him go. He was a trial, that one. She prepared to do the detention. She was in no hurry to go home to her carping mother, so staying after school was no hardship.

As Ronnie left the school gate his friend, Terry Spooner, was waiting for him.

"'Ow did yer gerron with Old Shoesy then?"

"Okay, I s'pose," said Ronnie. "'Er's sent a note ter me mom with our Patty tellin' 'er I come ter school in a state. I doe know what 'er's worryin' about, there's plenty kids scruffier than what I am."

"Tek no notice," commiserated Terry. "Yer mom wor 'urt yer will 'er?"

"No, I doe s'pose 'er will but 'er'll goo on about summat rotten. I s'pose I'd better got off whum, it'll be werse if I 'ang about. 'Er's got ter be at werk for five tonight."

"See yer then, Ron."

"See yer, Tez."

True to form, Nellie was waiting when he got home.

"Right then, our Ronnie. What's all this about then?"

"Well, Mom, I got a bit dirty on the way ter school an' old Stuck-up Shoesy day like it."

Nellie placed her hands on her hips. "It's Miss Hughes ter you. Well, I must say, you am dirty an' what's that pong?"

"What pong? I cor smell anythin'."

Nellie screwed up her nose. "Well, I can. What you bin up ter ter smell like that?"

Ronnie decided that the best thing to do was to come clean.

"Well, Mom, it's like this. I went ter see Lily this mornin' an' 'er 'appened ter do a wee and it went all over me shoes and socks. If I'd come 'ome ter change 'em I'd a bin late fer school so I 'ad ter leave 'em."

Nellie rolled her eyes up to the ceiling. "I might a knowed it. What 'ave I told you about messin' with that 'oss? It aye our 'oss. It's a wonder Herbie doe gi' you a cloutin' fer messin' about in 'is yard."

"'E doe mind. I aye a nuisance. I only popped in fer a minute."

Nellie stood, hands on hips, glaring at her son. "Well, my lad, it's the last time. If I see or hear o' you goin' down that yard again I'll have ter tell yer dad, so be said. I'll do a note back to Miss Hughes and tell 'er it won't 'appen again."

Ronnie was devastated. How was he ever going to see Lily? He resolved that he would do it somehow on the sly.

"Sod Shoesy," he muttered under his breath. "'Er and 'er toffee-nosed ways. I bet 'er's never even stroked a 'oss in 'er life."

Nellie said, "Well, I'm off ter werk now. Doe you ferget what I've said. Get a bowl o' water and wash yer feet and put them socks ter soak in the scullery. Yer can goo an' sit with yer Gran till I get back."

Ronnie didn't mind sitting with Ivy. He could tune the wireless in to whatever he fancied. She never minded.

Sitting in front of Ivy's fire, comfortably, he reflected on his problem. He decided that by hook or by crook he would see Lily but he would have to be careful about it.

A knock came on the back door. Opening it, Ronnie was pleased to see his friend, Terry.

"Alright, Tel?"

"Alright, Ron. How did yer get on with yer mom?"

"Oh, alright, I s'pose. Just 'ave ter be careful if I want ter see Lily." Ronnie brightened up. "'Ave yer 'ad yer tea, Tel?"

"Not yet. Me mom's gettin' fish an' chips later."

Ronnie looked in Ivy's bread bin. "Would yer like a piece?"

"Oh ar, Ron, just the job. What yer got ter put on it?"

Ronnie looked in the cupboard and in a pan on the stove.

"Cold gravy alright fer yer, Tel?"

"Oh yeah. I ain't 'ad that fer ages."

Ronnie cut two hefty slices from the loaf and spread them with the dark brown, jellified gravy. The lads sat munching contentedly. Granny Ivy sat in the corner chewing on her toothless gums.

Terry turned to Ronnie. "Is 'er mutton?" he asked.

"What?" asked Ronnie.

"Is 'er mutton, mutton jeff – deaf?" Terry sighed with exasperation and bit into his doorstep.

"I doe know. I doe think so. 'Er just cocks a deaf 'un if 'er's in one o' them moods."

Terry grimaced. "We'd better watch what we'me sayin' then or 'er might tell yer mom about our plans," he warned.

"Doe be saft. 'Er doe give a monkey's what we gerrup to. We could be planning ter rob a bank an' 'er wouldn't tek no notice. All I want yer ter say is that I've bin with you any time I goo down to the yard. Herbie woe say anythin'. Okay, mate?"

"Okay, Ron. Better be gooin. Me mom'll be back soon."

Nellie finished the top office and was emptying the waste paper basket. Irene, one of the cleaners, saw that she looked worried about something.

"What's up, Nell? Yo look as if you've lost a paernd an' found a shillin'."

Nellie sighed. "It's our Ronnie, Irene. I 'ad a letter from 'is teacher today about 'im smellin'. I sends 'im ter school clean an' tidy. Can't do any more than that. I can't be behind 'im all the time."

"What yer gunna do then, Nell?"

"Well, I s'pose I'll 'ave ter write an' tell 'er that I do me best. I doe think them teachers realise how 'ard it is ter keep kids spotless."

Irene said, "Do yer want me ter 'elp yer write it?"

"Will yer, Irene? I aye very good with spellin'."

Irene found a piece of writing paper on one of the desks.

"Right then, let us think."

So, between them, they composed the following missive:

> Dear Miss Hughes,
>
> Thank you for your letter about Ronnie smellin'. You being not married you doe know what is the smell of a man. Our Ronnie is sent out clean every morning and I can't do any better than that. He has promised to be more careful an' not see the 'oss.
>
> Yours respectful,
>
> Nellie Edwards Mrs.

“I think that sounds alright, Nell. ’Ave yer gorran envelope?”

“Yes, ta. I got one at ’ome. Thanks ever so, Irene. I’ll sleep tonight now.”

Deciding that she would give the letter to Patty in the morning, Nellie went about her cleaning in a more cheerful frame of mind.

Chapter Seven

It was Saturday. Grace and Valerie went to the High Street to do the weekend shopping. Valerie loved the smells in the Home and Colonial, a mixture of coffee, tea and smoked bacon, all mingled together to make a tantalising combination.

From there they made their way to the bakery to buy bread and to see Thelma. As they approached the shop Ronnie Edwards emerged, just ahead of his mother. Nellie had decided that he should accompany her to help with the carrying and to keep him out of mischief.

Valerie looked at him from under her eyelids. “You’me for it, Ronnie Edwards,” she whispered harshly. “Wait till me mom sees your mom.”

Ronnie poked his tongue out at her. Nellie followed him out of the shop, her mind on her next purchases.

Absentmindedly nodding to Grace, she was quite taken unawares when Grace spoke to her.

“Just the one I wanted to see, Nellie Edwards.”

Nellie stopped short and gathered her wits.

“What’s up wi’ you then? What can I do fer yer?”

Grace pulled herself up to her full height of five feet two and glared at Nellie.

“Sort out your Ronnie, that’s what. ’E’s a naughty little sod, ’e ’is. Our Valerie broke her little ’eart last Saturday. It comes ter summat when ’er can’t play in ’er own street wi’out other folks’ kids comin’ an’ upsettin’ ’er.”

Nellie reddened. “Wot’s ’e done then?” she asked defensively.

“’E throwed ’er top in the dustcart, spiteful little beggar.”

Nellie had difficulty not to smile. “Am yo sure ’e did it? ’Er coulda lost it down the drain.”

Grace snorted. “’E done it alright. ’Er was broken-’earted.”

"Right, I'll see about it," said Nellie and she stalked off up the street after Ronnie, who had hurried off in front.

As soon as Nellie got home she sent Patty next door. Ronnie had put his bag of shopping on the kitchen table and she was certain that he would be round at Ivy's.

She was right. Patty came back, Ronnie in tow.

She glared at him. "Right now, Ronnie. I doe want no lies. Is it right what Grace Potts 'as tode me about your throwin' Valerie's top on the rubbish cart?"

Ronnie shuffled his feet and stared at the floor. "'Er said I smelled, Mom. 'Er's a nasty little cow."

Nellie bristled visibly. "'Er shouldn't a said that but you shouldn't a done what you done an' don't call folks cows either. I think it's about time I 'ad a werd wi' your dad. You'me gerrin out of 'and. I'm gerrin sick o' folks complainin' about you an' that swearin's gorra stop an' all."

Ronnie hung his head. He realised he may have gone too far this time. He hated Valerie Potts and her stuck-up mother.

He appealed to Nellie. "Can I still goo an' play after me dinner, Mom? Can I?"

Nellie sighed. "I doe know if I can trust yer outa me sight. Oh, goo on."

Nellie was still smarting about Valerie saying that Ronnie smelled and this tempered her annoyance with her son to some degree.

"I'll tek me sandwiches with me, Mom an' me an' Tel ull goo over the fields. Can we, Mom?"

Nellie was putting away the shopping, her mind on her mother's dinner.

"Okay then, but remember, me laddo, behave yerself an' tek that blasted dog wi' yer. 'E aye 'ad a proper run fer two days."

She put four doorsteps of bread and margarine with some thinly sliced corned beef into some newspaper and

Ronnie filled a pop bottle with water. He reached a khaki knapsack from the peg on the back door, put Pongo on a string and set off to call for Terry.

*　　　　*　　　　*

Christine had had a lovely morning with her Aunty Betty. Like Ronnie, she loved to spend time at James Street. She felt rather special when she was there.

Betty liked to iron Christine's dresses. She bought different ribbons and slides to put into her long, blonde hair, which she loved to brush and try in different styles.

Betty had a sewing machine. She could not manage a treadle with her bad foot so a little hand machine had been purchased. She would enjoy making dresses for her nieces for special occasions. She was quite a talented seamstress. Also, for a modest fee, she would turn sheets side to middle or make curtains for her neighbours.

She and Reg lived contentedly together. Neither had met anyone special with whom to spend their lives.

Betty had inherited her mother's button tin. Over the years in it had been collected odd buttons, bits of lace, hooks and eyes, press studs and odd beads from broken necklaces. Christine loved to sort out the tin.

Taking the tin from the cupboard, she asked, "Aunty, do you want these beads for anything special?"

Betty smiled. "I don't think so, chick. Why? Were you thinkin' o' doin' summat wi' 'em?"

"Well, if I can have a needle an' cotton I wouldn't mind mekkin meself a necklace."

Betty nodded. "O' course yer can. I'll sort one out for yer."

For an hour or so Christine sat happily threading her beads.

Betty was ironing. Looking over her shoulder, she said, "Some o' them beads was yer nan's, God bless 'er soul. 'Er would've liked you to 'ave 'em, our Christine. I'll find you out a fastener."

She tied the fastener onto the ends of the cotton and placed the necklace around her niece's neck.

Looking in the mirror the child thought that it was the prettiest thing she had ever owned.

"Well, love," said Betty, "I think that you'd better mek tracks. Yer mom'll be back from shoppin' an' wonderin' where you've got to."

"Okay, Aunty." Christine hugged her aunt and gave her a kiss on her lovely, soft cheek. "See you Tuesday after school an' I'll bring Patty."

Betty waved from the doorstep. "Tarra, chick."

She loved that child as much as she loved Ronnie and the rest of her nephews and nieces. Although she occasionally wondered what it would have been like to have a family of her own, she was happy to share her brother's offspring.

Christine made her way home, singing happily, fingering her necklace. In the distance she saw Ronnie with his knapsack over his shoulder, and Pongo trotting at his side, coming towards her.

"Off ter call fer Terry, I bet," she thought.

"Hiya, Chrissie. Where yo bin?" he called.

"Aunty Betty's. Look what she helped me to make."

She held the beads away from her neck for him to admire. She must have pulled harder than she intended. The cotton snapped.

"Oh no," she cried. "Me beads, me beads."

In a colourful cascade they fell to the pavement.

"Doe cry," Ronnie said. "Thay'me only a few beads. Nothin' ter cry about, our wench." He started to help her to pick them up.

"'Ere, I'll give yer a bit o' paper off me sandwiches ter put 'em in."

Christine calmed down a little and she set to to collect them.

"Orlright now, are yer?" he asked.

She nodded.

"I've gorra goo now. Tel'll think I aye comin'. Tarra, see yer later."

Christine walked home disconsolately. She would have to rethread the beads, making sure she used stronger thread, if her mother had any.

Ronnie knocked on the door to Terry's house. Mrs Spooner answered it.

"Is Terry comin' out, Mrs Spooner?"

She nodded. "When 'e's ate 'is dinner. I s'pose you'd better come in an' wait ferrim."

Terry was sitting at the kitchen table. It took a moment for Ronnie to fathom out exactly what his repast was, then the smell gave him a clue. It was Oxo and bread that his mate was eating with relish.

Looking up from his meal, Terry asked, "Gorrany spug, Ron?"

"No, Tel. Me mom wouldn't let me gerrany. 'Er says if I keep on swallerin' it, it'll wrap itself round me 'eart an' I stuck some on the 'eadboard an' it got all tangled up in our Barry's 'air. 'E 'ad ter 'ave it all cut out. 'Ave you gorrany, Tel?"

"Nah, I've spent me pocket money on caps fer me gun."

Mrs Spooner came into the kitchen.

"Mom, can I 'ave some pieces ter tek wi' me?" he asked.

"I s'pose so. Now doe you get comin' in late, our Terry. Me an' yer dad'll be gooin down the club. I want yer in by six o'clock, well before we goo out. Our Gwen'll be 'ere an' you can't 'ave any pals in while we'me out either." She glanced at Ronnie as she spoke. "'Er says you woe do as yo'me tode when yer mates am around."

Terry packed his newspaper-wrapped pieces into Ronnie's knapsack. As he did so the front door closed with a bang.

"Is that yer dad, Tel?"

"Ar, I think so."

At that Ronnie headed for the back door. The arrival of the head of the household had that effect on visitors to families in the area, be it pals of the children or a neighbour popping in for some reason.

Untying Pongo's string from the drainpipe in Terry's backyard, Ronnie and Terry made their way to the wasteland, which all the locals called 'The Fields', bent on an afternoon of adventure.

The lads were soon joined by Mickey Johns and Freddie Perks. They decided to relive the cowboy and Indian films which they attended regularly at the Saturday crush. They all wore their snake belts. For the ones who did not have a toy gun, a piece of wood, pushed into their belt, sufficed.

To the delight of Pongo, Mickey had brought along his terrier, Judy. He became very enamoured with her. The lads were so engrossed in the game that they failed to witness the extent of Pongo's passion which took place behind a clump of gorse.

The afternoon soon passed. The sandwiches were shared, leaving just one in the knapsack. The lads drank from the bottle of water, impervious to the crumbs which inevitably went into it and certainly not wiping the bottle neck as it was passed round. That would have been sissy. The dogs drank from the brook and enjoyed the bits of sandwich given to them.

The afternoon wore on. Mickey and Freddie made their way home. Half an hour later, after enquiring the time from a man walking his dog, Ronnie and Terry decided to follow them.

Terry said, "I'll 'ave ter goo now, Ron. Me mom'll kill me if I aye 'ome before 'er and me dad goo ter the club."

"Okay, see yer, Tel."

"See yer, Ron."

Ronnie made his way down Foundry Street. Coming towards him was Herbie Forrester, the rag and bone man. Before Ronnie could call out to him, he disappeared into the entry at the side of the Haymaker's Arms, where he would get a cooked meal from the landlady.

Ronnie wondered how Lily was faring. He looked around but there was no one in sight. He ran, Pongo in tow, down to the opening which led to Herbie's yard. He approached the stable. The padlock was hooked through the hasp on the door but had not yet been closed to lock it. Quick as a flash, he pulled the door open, slipped inside and pulled it to.

There was his beloved Lily. She snickered in welcome, then edged away from Pongo.

"Doe worry, gel. Pongo woe 'urt yer."

Ronnie tied the dog up, threading the string through a ring in the wall away from the horse. He stroked her neck and blew into her nostrils, revelling in the smell of her. It was semi dark in the stable and, to Ronnie, homely. He picked up her brush and began to brush her, taking care not to go to the back end of her, as Herbie had taught him, in case she kicked.

He sat on the straw in the corner and shared the last sandwich with Pongo. He filled his water bottle from the bucket and then let the dog take a drink. Slaking his thirst he sat, contemplating the horse.

The sun came weakly through the small window high in the wall. Flies buzzed round the glass. It all had a soporific effect and Ronnie, sitting with his back to the wall, nodded off to sleep.

*   *   *

Ivy sat in the corner watching Nellie sewing a patch on to Wilf's overalls. The radio played cheerfully in the background. Young John was upstairs getting ready to go out. Mary was washing her hair in the scullery. Wilf was reading the paper and having a smoke. He was ready to take himself off to the pub. He was in a good mood and was confident that he and Reg had done well with the pigeons that day.

Nellie relished the peace which reigned over her household. She had had a strict upbringing. Although Ivy was a docile old soul, that hadn't always been the case. Many were the smackings Nellie and her sister had suffered, as children, for the slightest misdemeanour. Trouble, it seemed, had followed Nellie as much as it did Ronnie, most of it unintentional.

She did her utmost to shield her kids from harm. On the very rare occasion that Wilf had corrected one of the lads she had been upset for days afterwards. She was finding it more difficult these days to prevent Ronnie being walloped. It only needed someone to confront Wilf with one of his pranks, instead of herself, and 'all would be up'.

Christine and Patty came through the back door.

"We'me starving, Mom."

Nellie looked up from her sewing. "What, again? Well, you'd better have a piece."

Putting the overalls down, she reached a loaf from the bread bin, cut two doorsteps and spread them with beef dripping.

"Thanks, Mom," said the girls.

Wilf glanced at the clock. It was half past seven.

"Wheers our Ronnie then? Time 'e was in."

Nellie shifted uneasily on her chair. "'E woe be long now. I expect 'is stomach'll be rumblin'."

Wilf frowned. "Rumblin'? I'll rumble 'im if 'e doe gerrin soon, runnin' the streets this time o' day at 'is age."

Nellie said, "Some kids am out all hours."

Wilf shook his paper aggressively. "I doe care what other kids do. I want mine in th'ouse at a proper time."

Christine wiped her mouth on the back of her hand. "Shall I goo an' see if I can find 'im, Mom?"

Nellie smiled gratefully. "Yes, luv, if you've finished yer piece, would yer?"

Christine nodded.

Patty asked, "Shall I goo with her, Mom?"

"No," said Wilf. "I doe want all me kids on the streets. You can stop an' shape up fer bed."

Patty's face fell. She liked to listen to the wireless with her mom on a Saturday night and stay up a bit later, no school next day.

Nellie winked at her. "Get ready, then you can sit wi' me an' shell some peas fer termorror's dinner."

Patty brightened and when Maureen came in from the scullery, her head wrapped in a towel, she went through to have a wash.

Twenty minutes later Christine returned alone.

"No signs of our Ronnie, Mom."

Nellie asked, "When did any on yer last see 'im?"

Christine replied, "I sid 'im this afternoon on me way back from Aunty Betty's. 'E 'elped me pick me beads up."

Wilf suddenly lost interest in his newspaper. "Did yer goo round the Spooners?"

"Yes, Dad. Terry's bin back since six o'clock."

Nellie had a sick feeling in the pit of her stomach. She went to the foot of the stairs.

"John, JOHN," she called.

"Yes, Mom." John appeared at the bedroom door.

"Our Ronnie aye in. I don't want the girls runnin' the streets after 'im, I want you an' Barry ter goo an' look fer 'im. It's gone eight. 'E knows 'e aye gorra stop out after eight."

John frowned. He was going to his mate's house to play cards and they were sneaking a jug of beer from the outdoor of the Haymaker's.

"Aw, Mom, cor we give 'im another half hour? If he aye back then, we'll goo an' look ferrim." Under his breath, he muttered, "I'll clip 'is earole when I see 'im, bloody little pest."

Nellie knew that Mary wasn't going out so she asked her to take Ivy round home. Maureen decided to go with her. She wanted to listen to the wireless and, at Ivy's, they could please themselves.

"Right," Wilf said. "you lads goo an' find yer brother an' tell 'im I'm waiting ter 'ear wheer 'e's bin till now."

Nellie made a pot of tea. "Want one, Wilf?

"Tea doe mix wi' beer, if I ever get out ternight," he grumbled.

Wilf was getting madder by the minute. It was a quarter to nine and no sign of the lads.

"If they doe come back wi' 'im I'm gooin ter the bobbies."

Nellie wrung her hands. "Do you think that'll be necessary, Wilf? 'E might've only forgot ter ask the time an' be playin' somewhere."

"I doe think so, Nell. 'Is mate aye sid 'im since six o'clock. Wheered 'e goo when 'e knowed 'e'd gorra be in?"

When John and Barry came back at nine-thirty without Ronnie, Nellie was starting to feel a bit hysterical.

"Well, that's it," said Wilf. "I'm gooin meself. You two goo over the fields an' tek a torch an' I'll goo round ter Reg's an' see if 'e's bin round theer."

John was fed up to the teeth. He had been looking forward to his card game and now he wouldn't be able to go.

Between them, Wilf, Reg, John and Barry scoured the area, all to no avail. Wilf decided to go to the police station. The desk sergeant was Jack Pearce, Annie's son.

"Aye up, Wilf. What can I do fer yer?" he asked.

"It's our Ronnie, Jack. 'E's gone missin'. 'E aye bin sin since six o'clock. We've looked everywhere ferrim. 'Is mother's gooin mad wi' worry."

"Don't worry, Wilf. We'll ask the beat bobbies ter look out fer 'im. 'E'll tern up, you'll see, large as life."

"I 'ope so, Jack. We'me worried ter jeth."

Wilf left the police station and made his way home. He had never felt so bad or so helpless in all his life. Although he had started out being angry with his son, this had now dissipated and he felt nothing but concern.

Herbie came out of the Haymaker's. He had drunk more than usual and was tired. He made his way along to his house. As he shuffled through his entry, something in his fuddled brain told him that he had forgotten to do something. For a minute or two he couldn't register what it was, then a flash of inspiration told him that he had left the padlock off the stable door.

He went across the yard, unhooked the padlock and fastened it through the staple. Inside the stable, Pongo stirred and growled softly, then he settled himself down into the straw and snuggled up against Ronnie. Ronnie slumbered on. In his subconscious mind he dreamed someone was calling to him. He just turned over and sank into a deeper sleep.

At number 34 Ingram Terrace, Jack Pearce was talking to the family. He was now off duty but concerned about the whereabouts of young Ronnie. He was trying to piece together his movements and to jog their memories, hoping for a clue, however slight, which could help to find him.

"What does he like to do best?" he asked.

Nellie wiped her eyes. "Just the things any kid does," she answered.

"Anything special?"

"Football," said John.

"All the games the kids play," said Nellie.

Wilf put his arm round her. "'E'll be alright, love. Don't ferget 'e's got Pongo wi' 'im. 'E loves our Ronnie."

Nellie gave a watery smile. "Ar, 'e loves animals, 'e does. 'E's allus 'angin' round that 'oss of Herbie Forrester's."

She gasped, her hand to her mouth.

"What's up, Nell?" said Jack.

Nellie looked at him. "We never thought o' that 'oss. 'E's allus goin' ter that stable. 'E gorrin ter trouble the other wik fer messin' round theer an' gooin ter school smellin'. I tode 'im never ter goo theer again. Do you think as 'e could 'ave sneaked into that stable again?"

"We'll soon find out," said Jack.

Ronnie stirred in his sleep. He wanted to wee. He sat up and rubbed his eyes. For a moment he couldn't think where he was. It was very dark, very little light came through the panes of the dusty stable window. Lily shuffled and stirred, catching her hoof on the cobbled floor. Pongo stretched and yawned. Slowly, it dawned on the child where he was. He was desperate to wee so he stood and did it against the wall.

"Pongo, are you theer?" he asked.

The dog leaned against his leg. "Wharram we gunna do now, mate? I can 'ardly see."

Ronnie felt his way along the wall to the stable door. He pushed but it wouldn't budge.

"Oh blimey," he said. "Oh blimey. I'm for it now, Pong. Me dad'll kill me."

He sank down on to the straw and began to cry.

"I want me mom," he wailed and, burying his head in the dog's side, he sobbed.

Jack and Wilf made their way to Herbie's. They hammered on his front door. An upstairs light came on in the house next door and the window slid up.

A voice called out, “What’s all the racket? Doe yer know what time it is? Some folks’ve gorra goo ter werk in the mornin’.”

Jack called back, “Sorry, mate.” Turning to Wilf, he said, “That’s Monty Chapman. ’E’s never werked in ’is life, never mind on a Sunday.”

Again he hammered on the door to no avail.

“We’ll goo round the back an’ ’ave a look at the stable.”

Jack led the way through the opening.

“Ronnie,” called Wilf. “Ronnie.”

They heard a voice calling faintly, “Dad? Is that you, Dad?”

“Yes, son, it’s me an’ Jack. Doe worry. We’ll get you out. We’me tryin’ ter wake Herbie.”

Wilf was weak with relief. He had had visions of his youngest son drowned in the canal or murdered. Now he knew where he was, he silently thanked the Lord.

Jack tried hammering on Herbie’s back door. After a few minutes it opened and Herbie, not a pretty sight, emerged.

“What the ’ell’s gooin on raerned ’ere?” he asked.

“Our Ronnie’s locked in the stable, ’Erb,” said Wilf. “Sorry we ’ad ter wake yer. ’E sounds frit ter jeth. Can you lerrim out?”

“Yes, o’ course I can. I day realise ’e was in theer. I day put the lock on till late. ’E musta bin asleep or summat.”

Without more ado he took the key from its hook behind the back door, shuffled across the yard and unlocked the padlock.

Ronnie stood there. Pongo growled at the men. Ronnie held tightly on to his string. Wilf held his hand and led him away.

“Goodnight, Herbie, and thanks,” he called to the rag and bone man.

Ronnie turned and, through his tears, managed, “Goodnight, Lily.”

Wilf had to smile. He turned to the policeman.

"Comin' fer a cuppa cocoa, Jack?"

"No thanks, Wilf. I'm late off me shift. The missis will be worried so I'd better get back. See yer termorrer when I pop in to me mom's."

"Goodnight then, mate. I really appreciate what you've done." He held out his hand for Jack to shake.

Looking down at Ronnie, Wilf thought, "The poor kid, 'e's wore out."

He said, "Come on, son, let's get yer back. Yer mom's worried stiff about yer."

The child could only nod as he walked along, Pongo trotting beside him.

When they walked in Nellie was overcome with emotion and relief. She hugged Ronnie and shed a tear, then she held him by the shoulders and looked into his tear-stained face.

"Doe you ever do anythin' like that again," she said.

Ronnie managed to say, between sobs, "Sorry, Mom. I fell asleep. I day mean ter frighten yer."

"Well, stop blartin' now. Thank God you'me safe. I'll mek yer a cuppa cocoa. I expect Pongo's 'ungry an' all."

Barry stood up. "I'll feed 'im, Mom."

John ruffled Ronnie's hair and said, "Well, ar kid, you've cost me a gaerm o' cards, little perisher."

Wiping his nose on his sleeve, Ronnie looked round at his family and smiled.

"Glad I'm 'ome," he said.

Next morning Ronnie went round to Annie's to say 'thank you' to Jack. He was just about to depart to referee a football match.

"'Allo, Ronnie," he said. "You look better this mornin'. Did yer get ter sleep?"

"Yes, Mr Pearce. Ta for 'elpin' me dad ter find me."

Jack patted him on the head. "All in a day's werk, son, all in a day's werk. Cheerio, lad. Cheerio, Mom."

With a cheery wave, Jack went across the yard and down the entry.

Annie sniffed. She looked at the child closely.

"You'me just like yer Granny Ivy when 'er was your age. We've allus bin pals, yer know. Me an' 'er used ter knock around tergether right from infants class at school. Us an' that Peggy Burns, Peggy Venables as was. 'Er aye very partic, 'er aye. You should see 'er dishcloths. Thay'me black as the ace o' spades. They look as if 'er's blacked the graert wi' 'em. I wouldn't gee yo a thank you for anythin' as 'er cooked. Yer Granny Ivy was allus spotless."

Annie wiped her nose on the corner of her apron. She put her hand on Ronnie's shoulder and bent her head to his.

"Should yer like a bit o' me cake, cock? I med it yesterdi."

Looking at the dewdrop which had reformed on Annie's nose, quick-thinking Ronnie said, "Well, Aunty Annie, I aye got room fer one yet but I'd like ter tek one with me fer later, if yer doe mind."

Annie smiled. "In that case, I'll put one fer yer mom an' all."

She dug out a brown paper bag from the table drawer, putting into it two generous slices of fruit cake.

She said, "I used up all me cracked eggs on this. I gerrum cheap from the market. Do you gerrit, Ronnie? Cheap, cheap."

Ronnie laughed. "Thanks, Aunty Annie. See yer."

He waved from the doorway. Annie gave him a toothless grin and waved, then, scratching her head between her dinky curlers, she turned back to the stove.

Much as Ronnie had come to love Annie, he couldn't bring himself to eat that cake. He went along the party yard and chucked it over the wall to Mr Rogers's chickens.

Chapter Eight

It was a nice day for Aunt Flo's wedding. Grace had washed Valerie's hair the night before and wound it into rags. She had new shoes and socks and Betty had completed her pink, taffeta dress.

She was the only bridesmaid and felt her responsibilities deeply.

Grace wore her navy blue suit. She had used one of her clothing cheques for a new blouse. She always took her club money to Peggy's so that the neighbours wouldn't see the club man calling at Pipers Row. Not that it mattered. Most of the folk in the area depended on cheques for their clothes and bedding.

Valerie was excited. She had felt special in her dress when she tried it on. She wished that her dad could be here to see her. She had called in to Granny Potts on the Tuesday.

"Gran, can you get to the church to see me on Saturday?"

Aggie frowned. "I doe know yet, Valerie. I'll see what yer Grandad says. I aye still right wi' that lot but it aye your fault. I'm not promising anythin' but I'll try."

Valerie gave her Gran a hug. "Thanks, Gran. I'll look out for yer."

Aggie was touched. She was not used to being hugged.

"I miss yer dad, Valerie. I think about 'im every day of me life."

"And me, Gran, and me."

Valerie knew exactly how she felt. She had a bond with Aggie that she would never have with Renee.

Grace brushed out her hair. Without her National Health glasses and flushed with excitement, the child almost looked pretty.

Brushing away a tear, Grace said, "Come on, love, we'll miss the bus and we 'ave ter get yer frock and headdress on at

Gran's. I bet Aunty Flo is all of a two an' eight this mornin'. I can just imagine it."

On arriving at Renee's they were welcomed by Peggy waiting to assist Valerie with her dress.

"Ooh, yer look lovely, pet," she said, "and wait till yer see yer Aunty Flo."

At that Flo came through the stairs door. Grace and Valerie gave a little gasp. She was transformed. Her dress fitted like second skin, her headdress and veil, borrowed from a workmate, suited her perfectly.

She exclaimed when she saw her niece, "You look lovely, our Valerie, an' the weather's 'oldin' out fer us. I'm dead nervous."

Grace said, "Doe be nervous, our Flo. The vicar's lovely an' you look a picture."

"Do you think Fred'll like me frock?" asked Flo.

"Course he will, anybody would," Grace answered.

A knock on the door heralded the arrival of the Cortina car which had arrived to take Renee, Grace and Peggy to the church. It was to return for Arthur and Flo.

Flo trembled as she waved them off.

"I'll be glad when it's all over, our Valerie."

"You'll be alright, Aunty," the child said. "Uncle Arthur looks smart an' you look lovely."

Happily the trio set off for the church.

It was rather daunting, walking down the aisle behind her aunt and Uncle Arthur. Fred was waiting for them. He was beaming, looking very smart in his suit, hair well Brylcreemed and shoes highly polished.

Valerie had never seen him looking so smart. His family all sat on their side of the church, his two brothers and their wives, with his parents and their two grandsons.

On Flo's side sat Renee, Grace, Betty and some of Flo's workmates from the factory.

There was an audible sigh as she walked in. She was hardly recognisable in her wedding finery and had a distinct glow about her.

The service was soon over. Emerging from the church Valerie spotted Aggie and Sally standing by the gate. They waved and Aggie put her thumbs up to let Valerie know that she looked very nice.

The photographs were taken, then confetti was thrown over the couple, mainly by Flo's workmates.

The reception was being held round the corner from the church in the upstairs room of The Acorn pub. There was a lovely cake, made by the mother of Fred's sister-in-law, and a spread of sandwiches, salad, sausage rolls, trifles and something Valerie had never seen before – cheese and pineapple on cocktail sticks.

Aunt Flo had allowed Josie to come as company for Valerie and the girls waited in anticipation for the speeches to end so that they could tuck in.

Uncle Arthur managed to make a brief speech, wishing the happy couple all the best and thanking Valerie for looking so nice.

Fred, who had had a couple of drinks to fortify him, was quite funny and the relieved laughter which followed his speech preceded a happy couple of hours.

Valerie and Josie played with Fred's little nephews and they all tucked in to enjoy the food.

They all went back to Renee's to get changed out of their finery and for the adults to have yet another glass of sherry.

Flo and Fred were going to Blackpool for a few days and then taking up residence in a small, terraced house, round the corner from Renee, in Bragg Street.

The bus ride home was, for Valerie, somewhat an anti-climax to her day. Grace was nodding tiredly, Josie chattered on about the lovely dresses and the flowers, and Valerie wondered what she had to look forward to now that the wedding had come and gone.

It was Monday. Josie was away from school with a cold. Valerie walked along the pavement methodically fitting her feet into the pavers, trying to keep to a pattern.

She felt that by doing this she would reach home unscathed. No taunts of 'Four eyes' would follow her along the street. No cat-calls of 'Stuck up', 'Snotty cat' or 'Lady Muck' would reach her ears.

Valerie knew that whenever she walked with Josie she would escape any taunts. Children who offended her would be deprived of batter bits from the shop or even barred totally. It was as well to keep on the right side of Josie Salt.

Valerie sighed. It was only ten weeks until Ronnie Edwards would be at the boys' senior school. She and Josie would be at the girls' school. She would rarely see her tormentor after then.

Now that she was eleven she did even more to help her mother. Indeed, her mother was as dependent on her emotionally as ever. Sometimes the child felt the burden without quite realising what it was.

Reaching her own entry she broke into a run, glad to see the light at the end, knowing it was clear. Turning into her yard, she opened the coalhouse door and retrieved the back door key. She bent to stroke the head of the cat.

"You are my friend, Lucky. You and Jose. Blow the rest on 'em. I don't care if I am stuck up. Thay'me all rough they am."

Lucky gazed at the door hopefully and Valerie let her into the kitchen. A note on the table listed the things to prepare for the evening meal. Valerie peeled the potatoes and cut them into chips, putting them into cold water to stand. She then cut slices from the loaf and spread them with margarine. The fire was damped down with slack and ready for someone to poke it into life. Valerie did so and added a few nuggets of coal.

A knock came to the back door. It was Mrs Jinks.

"Alright, Valerie?" she called.

"Yes, Mrs J, thanks."

"Okay, chick. Call me if you need anythin'."

"I shall. Tarrar," said the child.

She knew that Connie was always at hand. It gave her a sense of security.

Mrs Jinks's son, Ben, always had a kind word for her. He was twenty-eight and, as far as they knew, he had never had a girlfriend. "Too shy," his mother would say. "Too reserved, our Ben." Secretly she mourned the grandchildren she may never have if Ben never met 'the right one'.

Ben had had a miserable time at the shoe factory. He could not stand the ribald jokes and comments of the women on the production lines. Fortune had smiled on him when he won the football pools. It was a closely-kept family secret. He had bought his parents' house and purchased a shoe repair business in the town where he was content to work alone. He was contented with his lot and not looking for a wife at this stage in his life.

Left alone, Valerie gave Lucky some milk and went upstairs to her room. Often it was at this time that she missed her dad. She found solace in reading. Her latest book was *Anne of Green Gables*. She had an hour to spend whilst waiting for her mother to return from work. Settling down, she opened her book.

Tomorrow she would go to the library to see if they had *Anne's House of Dreams*.

Patty was round at Ivy's house. Like her sisters she appreciated the peace. They were listening to the wireless together. The child had been making dolls from pegs and had now decided to do some of her corking. Aunty Betty had given her some oddments of wool. It was growing nicely, all the colours of the rainbow. She would ask her aunt to coil it into mats for her chest of drawers when it was long enough.

Ivy sat dozing. The peace and the warmth made Patty drowsy. She had a sore throat and a nasty headache coming on. She felt very tired. Putting her arms on the table and resting her head on them, she immediately fell asleep.

This was the scene which met Nellie's eyes when she walked in. Ivy stirred and smiled sleepily at her daughter. Nellie placed her finger on her lips and indicated that they should let Patty slumber on.

Returning to her own home, she called to Christine, who was in her room reading.

"Yes, Mom?" She appeared in the stairs doorway.

"I'm going to werk now, Chrissie. Ronnie's at the swimming baths, the others'll be in soon. All the dinners are in the oven. Yer dad's is on the bottom shelf. Mary'll be back shortly. Pop round in a few minutes an' see if thay'me alright next door, will yer?"

"Okay, Mom."

Christine rolled up her magazine and decided that she might as well read it round at Ivy's. Peace would be shattered in her own house when the family all arrived.

Nellie set out to do her cleaning job. She enjoyed the break from the daily grind at home and the company of Irene and Vera, the two bright sparks she worked with. The money was not a lot but it was paying the weekly instalments on her beloved three-piece suite and Nellie had her heart set on a carpet for the front room to replace the lino and mats. Betty was making new curtains, things were slowly taking shape. She felt contented.

Christine sat in Ivy's, listening to the wireless. She was almost dropping off to sleep herself when the back door opened and closed with a thud. It was Wilf. Since the escapade with Ronnie, when he was missing, Wilf was even more concerned about the whereabouts of his offspring and less likely to chastise them, except for the worst misdemeanour.

"Aye up, our Christine. Nobody in round 'ome. I wondered where you all was. I'm starving. I could eat a scabby 'oss."

Christine stretched. "'Allo, Dad. Me mom's left all the dinners on a low light in the oven. I'll come round with yer. Our Mary'll be in in a jif."

Wilf looked at Patty, still fast asleep. He was inclined to leave her where she was. He brushed her hair back from her face. She was very flushed, perspiration stood out on her forehead.

He shook her shoulder gently. She did not react. He panicked and picked her up. She was floppy like a rag doll. He looked at Christine.

"'Ow long's 'er bin like this?"

"Not long, Dad. I think 'er's bin asleep about an hour. Me mom sin her before 'er went ter werk an' come an' asked me ter pop an' check on 'er, then I nearly dropped off an' all. Do you think 'er's real bad, Dad?"

Wilf stroked Patty's hair and spoke to her urgently.

"Patty, come on. Wake up, love. Come on." He turned to Christine. "Get a wet rag, Chris. We'll wipe 'er face."

The child did as she was bid. Wilf tenderly wiped his daughter's face. She stirred and tried to open her eyes. She grunted and was promptly sick all down Wilf's trousers. She began to cry hoarsely. Wilf felt out of his depth and somewhat panicky.

"Chrissie, goo an' fetch yer mom from the werk. Tell 'er our Patty's real bad."

He carried the child to the front room where it was cooler and wiped her face and hands with the wet cloth.

Patty whimpered pathetically. She ached all over, her head was splitting and the light hurt her eyes. She wanted her mother.

Nellie, Mary and Christine arrived together. Nellie had come post-haste at Christine's request. She always felt panicky when one of her children was ill. The doctor thought she was a rather fussy mother, although she did not bother him unnecessarily.

She was surprised at how well Wilf had coped with the situation but when she saw Patty, her heart sank. The child was becoming delirious. She was muttering and moaning.

Turning to her husband, she said, "Goo an' get the doctor, quick, Wilf. 'Er's real bad."

She held Patty and rocked her back and forth.

Mary made her mother and nan a drink and stood in the doorway, feeling helpless. Suddenly the doctor was there. Holding Mary by the upper arms, he moved her out of his way before the girl had chance to realise that he had arrived.

Briskly, he said, "Well, Nellie. What's up now?"

Nellie looked up at him. "'Er's real bad, Doctor, or I wouldn't 'ave sent for yer."

Doctor Ferguson looked at the sick child. He felt her neck for enlarged glands and lifted an eyelid.

"Keep her cool and give her some aspirin. Get her home to her bed and I'll pop by in the mornin'."

Nellie was not happy. She could see that her child was very ill.

"Do you think as 'er ought ter goo ter 'ospital, Doctor?" she asked.

"No, no. I'll see her tomorrow. Sponge her down and keep her cool."

He snapped his bag shut and, nodding to Wilf, he made his exit.

Nellie looked at her husband. "I aye 'appy about it, Wilf. You know 'ow I 'ate 'ospitals ever since me dad was in but I feel 'er'd be better theer. I s'pose we'd better do what 'e says an' tek 'er 'ome ter bed. 'Ow I'm gunna get an aspirin inter 'er, I doe know. 'Ave ter try, I s'pose."

In her own bed and sponged down, in a cool nightdress, Patty did look a little more comfortable. Nellie tried to get her to take water from a spoon but had very little success. She sat with her and, eventually, lay her head on the bed an dozed off.

At two o'clock in the morning, Nellie awoke with a start. The bed was shaking. Patty was having a kind of fit. Nellie shouted to Wilf, who stumbled across the landing, hair on end, half asleep and panicky, into the room.

"Oh, my God!" he exclaimed. "What's up wi' 'er, Nell?"

"'Er's 'avin' a tern. Oh, Wilf, what shall we do?"

"I'll goo fer that old bugger. 'E'd better do summat. 'E shoulda sent 'er into 'ospital like you said. 'E's bleedin' useless."

Wilf was getting into his trousers and shoes while he was berating the doctor. He ran down the stairs. Fifteen minutes later he was back.

"'E's sendin' the ambulance, Nell."

Nellie had not undressed, so was ready.

"I'm gooin with 'er. Wake the kids an' tell 'em. I doe know 'ow they can sleep through all this."

Without delay the ambulance arrived and Patty was carried by two compassionate, encouraging men out to the vehicle.

Wilf and Nellie went with her, leaving a dazed, unhappy John, Barry and Ronnie to worry about their sister.

*   *   *

That morning, Thelma and Stella were putting out the bread and cakes in the shop. They worked steadily, knowing that the first customer would arrive at nine o'clock.

Stella had a sister, Paula, who lived in Ingram Terrace. At ten minutes to nine, she knocked on the door of the shop.

"Trust our Paula to be on the front row afore we'me ready," grumbled Stella. She turned to the door and mouthed, "Gi' us a minute."

Opening the door, she said, "You'me early this mornin', our Paula."

Paula grimaced. "I've bin ter the doctor's, aye I. Me back's killing me again. Anyroad, I've heard as one o' Nellie Edwards's babbies 'ad ter goo ter th'ospital in the night."

"Which one?" asked Stella.

"One o' the gels, I'm tode. 'Er's pretty bad. They 'ad ter call the ambulance."

Thelma turned from the window where she was displaying éclairs.

"What's that, Paula? One o' Nellie's, you say? 'Er'll be devastated, and Wilf. Let's 'ope it ain't too serious."

The three women stood, looking concerned, all cheer gone from the day.

* * *

Patty had been taken to the isolation hospital. Fortunately it was only three miles away and accessible by bus.

She was placed in a room on her own. Nellie and Wilf could only look at their daughter through a glass window.

The ward sister was kind but firm and listed the rules to the couple: No children to visit. Visiting times to be strictly adhered to. Not more than two visitors and parents only for the time being.

They looked at their daughter lying so still and pale in the pristine bed. There was an electric fan to cool her and a drip, giving her fluids. They felt bereft.

Nellie, always used to caring for her children, wanted to run into the room and take over from the nurses.

When Patty had been settled, the sister came to tell them that the doctor was ready to talk to them. They sat in the ward office, on the edge of their seats, Nellie nervously twisting her handkerchief.

Doctor Page was tired and he looked it. He had been up most of the night and needed a wash and shave. Now, he had to tell these parents that their daughter had meningitis and was gravely ill.

Nellie sat as if she had been struck and Wilf, who had never cried in front of her in all of their married life, broke down.

"We are giving Patty the best care," the doctor said. "We have new antibiotics now and they are more effective."

"Could she die, Doctor?" asked Nellie.

"Now, now, you must be optimistic, mother. We will do our best for her."

Sister opened the door and brought in three cups of tea.

"Thank you, Sister," said Doctor Page. "I think that mom and dad understand the position now. I'll leave them to your care and I shall see them later today."

He walked wearily to the door, silently praying that he would be able to save their child.

On their return from the hospital they were greeted by all the family, desperate to know how Patty was. They explained to them that she was very ill.

Nellie said, "I ain't bin ter church fer years, Wilf. I think I'll pop in an' say a prayer fer our Patty. Will yer come wi' me?"

Wilf nodded. All their children decided that they would come along.

Annie Pearce was awaiting their return. She had cooked some faggots and peas and had them waiting, hoping that the appetising smell would tempt them to eat.

“I ’ope yer doe mind, Nellie. I gid Ivy ’er dinner and ’er’s alright, so doe worry about ’er. Sit yer down an’ try ter eat a bit before yer goo back ter th’ospital.”

Nellie thought she would never eat again but she did manage a little and felt somewhat better and more able to cope.

Ronnie grieved inwardly for his sister. Being the two youngest they had been close. Although they fought, and had the normal sibling rivalry, their loyalty to each other had been absolute. He sat on the back doorstep, stroking Pongo.

“Please, God,” he prayed, “please, God, let our Patty get better.”

Patty was in hospital for ten weeks. She recovered slowly and the hard work of the staff paid off. One thing they could not avoid was that Patty lost her hearing.

Nellie sobbed when the news was broken to them then, lifting her chin resolutely, she looked at Wilf.

“At least ’er’s alive. We still ’ave our Patty. There’s ’elp for ’er an’ we’me a famly. We’ll look after ’er. All I want now is to get ’er ’ome.”

The family, including Pongo, were overjoyed to have Patty back home. They were philosophical about her hearing loss and were eager to help her all they could. She was to attend residential school as soon as there was a place for her. Eleven-year-old Ronnie was optimistic.

He said, “P’raps it’ll come back. P’raps our Patty’ll ’ear a little bit.”

He knew he would miss his sparring partner but had the school holidays to look forward to.

Chapter Nine

1961

Grace had gone to Renee's. Valerie didn't want to accompany her. She had pleaded to be allowed to go to Josie's instead. Eventually Grace relented.

"I s'pose you do get fed up wi' 'earin' the moans and groans. I must admit, I do, meself. Go on then, just for this once. I'll be goin' round ter Peggy's. I doe know if our Flo'll be there. 'E doe like 'er comin' ter me mother's too often. Miserable devil, 'e is. I thought once 'er was married 'er'd 'ave a game with 'im. 'Is brother's the same. 'Is wife can't look for 'im, by all accounts." Grace put her coat on. "I'll be back about nine, so see you're here when I get in, our Valerie."

Valerie mentally hugged herself with glee.

"Yes, Mom, course I will."

Half an hour later, Valerie and Josie sat eye-holing potatoes at the back of the chip shop. Josie looked at her friend closely.

"Valerie, do you ever want to get married?" she asked.

"I don't know. I haven't really thought about it. I expect Mom would have to live with me, though. I couldn't ever leave me mom on her own."

Josie tossed a potato into the bucket of water.

"Would you like lots of children, Val?"

"Oh, yes, I think so. Two girls and two boys. Would you, Jose?"

"Not before I had me own business and made lots of money, then I'd just run it, have somebody else do the hard work for me."

Valerie contemplated this last statement. It appealed to her. Someone with a business could become rich and have a lovely home. Yes, that's what she would like. Why hadn't she thought of it before?

"Are you going to the flicks tomorrow night, Val?"

"Yes, I think so. Me mom wants to see the new Doris Day film."

Josie sighed. "My mom's in the shop, as usual. I expect I shall just listen to the wireless or watch TV. Maybe I'll do me piano practice."

Valerie thought about asking Josie to accompany them to the pictures but realised that to do so was asking for trouble. She had better ask Grace first. She looked forward to their outings together.

Josie dug another eye from a potato.

"Do you like that Bobby Powell, Val?"

"Not really. Why? Do you?"

"'E's alright but I like somebody better." Josie looked coy.

Valerie gave a short laugh. "Come on, who is it?"

Josie blushed. "Well, I only like him a bit. It's Ronnie Edwards."

Valerie glared at her friend. "'E's horrible. Fancy liking him!" she exclaimed.

Josie was indignant. "Well, he's always been alright with me. I know he used ter torment you but he's grown out of that now."

"I still can't stand him, Jose. He makes me flesh crawl, he does."

Valerie viciously stabbed at the potato she was holding. If Josie really liked Ronnie she would have to do something about it.

Valerie left Josie's in good time to reach home before her mother. She prepared some sandwiches for supper and put the kettle on a low light ready for the cocoa. She felt that Grace was less likely to sulk if she came home to a welcome and perhaps she wouldn't mind her going to Josie's another time.

It was nine-thirty and Valerie was getting concerned. Grace was always home for nine o'clock. She waited in the front room, looking through the window. She was about to put on her coat to go out to meet her mother when she saw her cross the street.

Opening the front door, she greeted her with, "Mom, I was worried about you, you are late."

Grace, puffed from walking, went into the room and sat on the settee.

"I didn't want you ter worry. I came as quick as I could get away."

"Is anything the matter?" asked Valerie.

"No, not really," answered Grace, sliding her eyes away from her daughter's face.

"Come and have your supper then. Would you like tea or a cup of cocoa?"

Grace shrugged off her coat. "Oh, cocoa will be fine, thanks."

She put on her slippers and sat in the easy chair. Valerie brought in the cocoa.

"Is Gran alright, Mom?"

"Oh yes, she's alright."

"And Uncle Arthur?"

"Yes, yes, 'im an' all." Grace bit into her sandwich.

Valerie wasn't satisfied. She felt that her mother had something on her mind.

"Peggy okay, Mom?"

Grace turned to look at her. "You won't leave it till I tell yer so I s'pose I'd better. You'll know soon enough anyway."

"What, Mom?"

"Well, I doe know 'ow ter tell yer really." Grace was getting flushed. She sipped her cocoa. "Anyway," she said, "What it is, well, what it is, yer Aunty Flo's gunna 'ave a babby."

There, it was out. Valerie sat deep in thought.

"Well, she's married, Mom. You have to be married to have a baby, even I know that."

"Yes, six years." Grace was keen to change the subject.

Valerie took Grace's empty cup. "I bet me nan's pleased."

Grace bridled. "Pleased? Pleased? I doe think so. Our Flo's no spring chicken, yer know."

Valerie didn't know what that implied. Although she was fifteen, Grace had not told her anything about the facts of life. What her monthlies had to do with reproduction, the girl still did not know so she was nonplussed about it all.

* * *

An urgent knocking on the front door awoke Grace. She sleepily looked at the alarm clock on her bedside table. Half past six. Soon be time to get up anyway but who could be calling at this time on a Monday morning? She pulled her coat on over her nightdress and pushed her feet into her old slippers. Valerie, also awake, met her mother on the landing.

"Who's that knocking, Mom?" she asked.

"I doe know, do I, Valerie? Get some clothes on, in case."

Opening the front door, she was taken aback to see Janice, her sister-in-law, standing there.

"Oh, Grace, whatever shall we do?" she asked.

"Come on in. We doe want ter wake the street," said Grace, looking round to see who was about.

Janice moved into the house, then Grace saw that she had Paul with her. He had not been to Grace's since he was small and she had quite a shock to see him.

Showing them into the front room, Grace was about to apologise for her attire when Janice burst into tears.

"It's Bert, Grace. He had a funny turn this morning when he got into the depot. He must have gone into the gents and when ’e was late tekkin ’is bus out they went ter look ferrim and, Grace, he was collapsed on the floor. Stan an’ ’is mom are at th’ospital. We doe know what’s ’appenin’.” She wiped her eyes. “If anythin’ ’appens to ’im it’ll finish Aggie. It’s bin seven years since ’Erbert died an’ ’er aye got over that yet.”

Grace frowned. “I know ’ow long it’s been since Herbert died, Janice, an’ we ’aven’t got over it yet either.”

Janice looked up with a start. She felt rather hurt by Grace’s tone.

“Well, I was going to ask if Valerie could stop with Paul but I see we are causing a problem so I’ll go.”

Grace then realised how curt she had been and, although she was loathe to let Valerie stay off school, she felt that it was the least she could do.

“Valerie can come back with you. I’ll pop in dinner time to see how things are or you can leave him here. I’m sure Mrs Jinks would have him for you. ’Er’s as good as gold.”

Janice thought for a moment. “I’ll tek ’im back to Aggie’s, then we’ll know what’s gooin on. See yer dinner time then, Grace.”

Paul was not impressed. He was eight and thought himself old enough to stay in the house on his own. He didn’t particularly like Valerie. When he saw her at Aggie’s they virtually ignored one another.

Grace saw the supervisor of the assembly line.

“I’m ’avin’ ter pop out dinner time, George. Me father-in-law’s took bad. ’E’s in th’ospital. I’ll try ter be back on time.”

George was firm but fair. He knew Grace was a good timekeeper, very rarely even quartered, so he felt a little leeway could be given.

“You goo, me wench. I ’ope ’e’s alright. ’E’s a good sort is Bert. I was playin’ dominoes wi’ ’im last Friday. I day think ’e looked so well. What’s the trouble wi’ ’im?”

“’E collapsed at werk. He’s on earlies this week. ’E always goes on ’is bike, as yer know. They found ’im in the gents.”

George frowned. “Poor Aggie. ’Er’s ’ad it rough. Anyroad, see ’ow things are an’ thanks fer lettin’ me know.”

At lunchtime Grace made her way to Aggie’s with dread. She knew that she had neglected her in-laws but felt that she was tired all the time. Going to see Renee on a Friday was enough to fit in and the weekend was taken up with shopping and housework. Valerie had tried to call weekly but Grace had not been very helpful to the child, who had been made to feel guilty and had tailed the visits off.

On reaching James Street she saw Sally Holmes disappear into the entry with a covered tray in her hands. Grace thought, “I hope she isn’t feeding our Valerie. She’s fifteen and quite capable of getting herself and young Paul some food, surely.”

Always on the defensive, Grace walked down the yard. She always knocked at the back door before she entered. Sally stood at the stove. Hearing the door open, she turned.

“Oh, Grace, it’s you. Valerie and Paul are in the front room. I’m just doin’ a bite to eat. I said ter Valerie that Janice could’ve left Paul wi’ me but ’er was in a panic and never thought. It’s understandable. I’ve put Aggie up ter bed. Janice’s with ’er.”

Grace looked at the older woman. “Why? What’s gone on?” she asked.

Sally put her hand to her mouth. “Oh, my God. Yer doe know, do yer? Well, wench, sorry I ’ave ter be the one as tells yer but Bert’s passed away. Talk about lightnin’ striking twice. ’Ow that poor wench’ll stand up to it, I doe know.”

Grace was nonplussed. “Do you think I should go up, Sally?”

Sally turned, teapot in hand. “If yer like. You can tek the tray up. I’ll gi’ the kiddies a bite ter eat. I doe s’pose

Aggie an' Janice'll feel like anythin'. Stan's devastated. 'E loved 'is dad, 'e did."

Climbing the stairs carefully, Grace gently pushed the door of Aggie's room open. Janice turned from the bed where her mother-in-law lay, unmoving.

"Cup of tea," Grace whispered.

"Thanks," whispered Janice. "Stan's gone for the doctor. I think Aggie's in shock."

"Oh," said Grace. "I'll go down. Call me if you need anythin'."

Janice nodded

Going into the front room she found Valerie and Paul playing a quiet game of cards. Valerie looked up at her mother questioningly.

"How's Grandad, Mom? Is he very bad?"

"No, Valerie." Grace wondered how to tell them, then realised there was no course of action except to be truthful.

"Would you like a cup of tea, Valerie, and a drink of pop, Paul?"

"Yes, please," they answered.

In the kitchen, Sally was wiping away a tear. "Have yer told them, Grace?"

"In a minute, when I've given 'em their drinks. I'm dreadin' it, I can tell yer."

Sally nodded sympathetically.

Handing the tea to Valerie and putting Paul's pop on the table, she didn't look at them as she said, "Grandad was very poorly when they found him, you know."

Valerie's eyes widened. "He's not dead, is he, Mom?"

Grace put her arm round her. Paul blanched.

"He is, he is," he shouted and burst into tears.

He shrugged Grace's arm from his shoulders. Throwing himself onto the settee, he sobbed for his Grandad.

Sally came into the room.

"Do yer want ter come round ter Sally's, cocker?" she said to him, stroking his head. "I reckon our Smokey'd like ter see you. Did yer know 'er's got three little kittens ter show yer?"

The child sat up, wiping his eyes on his sleeve. He silently went to Sally and, holding her hand, accompanied her to the door.

Valerie was numb. Her Grandad had always been nice to her. She felt as if all the people she loved were going away. She only had Grace and resolved to always look after her.

Ten days later, Valerie attended Bert's funeral. She felt so very sad. It seemed so final. Again she missed her dad. She had only women close to her. She intended to see Aggie more often, realising that she had, unintentionally, with the thoughtlessness of youth, neglected her gran.

Janice was so kind to her, different from Flo, who only seemed to have her own world of dissatisfaction to dwell in. Yes, she felt closer to the Potts at this stage of her life. In fact, without realising it, she needed them.

* * *

It was Josie's birthday. She was a month younger than Valerie. They would both be fifteen years old. It was June and at the end of July they would be leaving school.

Valerie called in on her way to school to deliver the card and the scented soap that she had bought for her friend.

"Thanks, Val," said Josie. "Just the kind that I like. I have had mainly money from mom and dad and me gran and grandad, so will you come with me on Saturday to choose something?"

Valerie frowned. "I'd like to, Jose, but I'll have to ask mom first. It depends on what she's got planned."

Valerie did not hold much hope of Grace letting her go but decided she would give it a try.

That evening, Valerie prepared the evening meal, setting the table with a clean cloth, then she dusted through the house. She had the appetising faggots and peas ready as Grace came through the door.

Her mother sank onto the chair. She was flushed and looked tired.

"Mom, why don't you give up the factory job? I'll be at work soon and we'll be able to manage."

Grace looked at her with a sceptical expression on her face.

"Manage? Manage? I'm just about sick o' managing. When I see some folk an' the way they can afford things it meks me blood boil."

"Don't get upset, Mom. I just don't like to see you so tired all the time. Think about it. P'raps you can go back to the cake shop with Thelma and do less hours. Only a few weeks now 'til I leave school. Miss Banks says she will help me to get an office job and I can go to night school for shorthand and typing to improve me speeds."

Grace relaxed her expression. She could see that her daughter was trying her best and she certainly couldn't carry on much longer doing the job she had held down for the past seven years. Her hands were getting stiffer and her eyesight was deteriorating.

"Alright, I'll think about it. I don't know if Thelma's got any hours at the shop. I'll ask her on Saturday when I pop in but don't get yer 'opes up."

After tea, when the washing up was done, they sat podging the new rug. Valerie could see that her mother's mood had changed for the better, so broached the subject of Josie's invitation to go shopping on Saturday.

"By the way, Mom, Josie liked her soaps."

"That's good. I always think you can't go wrong wi' a nice tablet o' soap. We 'ad enough in the war usin' plain soap fer everythin'. Yer nan allus used Fairy. Mind you, we can't grumble, we've all got reasonable complexions. Yer Grandad used ter say, 'Yo doe need none o' that mekkup on yer faerces'. 'E was dead against even a bit o' face powder, was yer Grandad."

Valerie continued. "Josie says she's had money for her birthday."

"Oh, ar?"

"She would like me to go to town with her on Saturday to pick something. I told her I didn't know what I was doing on Saturday."

Valerie slid a sideways look at her mother. Grace's expression didn't give anything away. Inside she was a bit annoyed that her daughter would want to spend time on a Saturday with anyone but herself.

"I thought we was goin' shoppin' together, Valerie. We doe 'ave that much time tergether, what wi' me werkin' an' you at school. Then you see yer Nan Potts every Thursday."

"I call to see Nan Potts straight from school, Mom, and I'm always here with the chips when you get in."

Valerie was near to tears. Grace was always rubbing it in about her going to Aggie's. She gave up hope of going out with Josie and, giving a resigned sigh, applied herself to the pegged mat.

After a long silence, Grace spoke. "I s'pose yer'd better go off wi' yer friend. I don't want it said that I stop you doin' things wi' yer mates. I'll manage the shoppin' on me own. We doe need too much this wik." And, with a martyred air, Grace went into the kitchen to put the kettle on.

*   *   *

The milk bar was crowded with young folk. It was a popular meeting place and on Saturday afternoons it was difficult to find a seat.

Josie and Valerie had been lucky to find stools at the end of the counter, facing the door. They sat happily discussing their purchases and the music they had listened to in the cubicles of the record shop. Josie took out the gold chain she had bought with her birthday money.

"Do you think me mom and dad will like it, Valerie?"

"Yes, it's just lovely. Try it on."

Josie was trying to undo the catch. Through the corner of her eye, Valerie spotted Ronnie Edwards coming through the door with Terry Spooner and Mickey Johns. They were laughing at some joke or other. She ignored them and concentrated on Josie's struggles with the catch on her chain.

Josie looked up and Ronnie smiled at her. He gave Valerie the briefest nod.

Josie flushed, then said, "Blast it, I can't get this dratted thing to open."

Valerie tried to help but had to agree it was not going to budge.

"Well," said Josie, resignedly, "when we've finished our coffee and sandwiches, back it will have to go to the shop."

Valerie sympathised. "P'raps they'll have another one the same, Jose."

Josie put the chain back in its little box. "I hope so. I wanted me mom and dad to see what I'd spent me money on."

She placed the box on top of her bag then, placing the bag on her stool, she said, "I'm just popping to the loo. Won't be a sec."

Ronnie had obtained a seat just behind them. Moving his chair so that Josie could pass, he smiled at her. Josie blushed but did not speak to him. Valerie sat, sipping her coffee.

Ronnie got up and went further along the counter to buy a drink. He had placed his jacket on the back of his seat to reserve it.

Valerie had to think quickly. She glanced round. No one was looking at her, everyone was talking and laughing. Quick as a flash, she took the little box from the top of Josie's bag and dropped a spoon on the floor. Bending to pick it up, she popped the box into Ronnie's jacket pocket.

Her heart beating rapidly, she casually sipped at her drink, trying to breathe normally. As Josie returned, Ronnie glanced at her, then glanced away. Valerie noticed him do it and her friend's slight flush. She was disgusted to think that her best friend could like her worst enemy.

The necklace was not missed until the girls reached the jeweller's. Josie was near to tears.

"I must have dropped it. What am I goin' to do, Valerie?"

"We'll go back the way we came," she answered. "We'll find it, don't worry. It must have fallen out of your bag."

The girls retraced their steps, looking at every inch of the pavement as they went. Back in the coffee bar there was no sign of Ronnie and his mates. Valerie asked the man behind the counter if anyone had handed it in.

"No, cock," he said, shaking his head. "Sorry."

By now Josie was beside herself with worry.

"Do you think somebody could've pinched it out of your bag, Jose?"

Josie widened her eyes. "Never! Do you really think somebody could've done that?"

"Who knows?" said Valerie. "Stranger things have happened."

Josie wept all the way home on the bus. She dreaded facing her parents and grandparents, who had given her the money. They would think she couldn't be allowed to go shopping on her own again.

Mrs Salt was sympathetic with her daughter. Her father rebuked her for being 'so half-soaked'.

"Right, Josie," he said, "I reckon I'll take a walk later on down to the police station. See what they suggest."

Freda brightened. "P'raps somebody'll hand it in."

Steve pulled a wry face. He said, "You'me 'opin', aye yer? I'd say that's gone fer good but I'll goo an' see anyroad."

Valerie turned to Josie. "I'd better get home, me mom'll be wondering where I am. I hope you get your necklace back, Jose."

She walked home, deep in thought. She was a little nervous about what she had done in case it backlashed at all.

Grace was pleased to see Valerie come home in time to have a bite to eat and then get ready to go to the cinema.

On being told about the missing necklace she tut-tutted. "I bet it's bin pinched," she said. "It comes ter somethin' when you can't tern yer back fer five minutes without some light-fingered so and so pinching things out o' yer bag."

Valerie assessed her mother's mood. "Mom," she said. "What do you think about Josie coming to the pictures with us? Do you think it would help to take her mind off that necklace?"

Grace grudgingly agreed. She would have rather gone with just Valerie but supposed it wouldn't hurt for once.

They set out to call for Josie. As they were shown into the living room at the back of the shop, Steve arrived. In his hand he held the small box containing the gold chain.

"Oh, Dad, you've got it. Where was it?" Josie cried.

Steve smiled. "Jack Pearce was on the desk at the nick. He said it had been handed in."

Valerie looked perplexed. "Who by?" she asked.

"Ronnie Edwards. He said he found it in his coat pocket, in the coffee bar."

They all fell silent, then Grace said, "A likely tale. It wouldn't just walk in theer by itself."

Mrs Salt agreed. "Yes, he's allus bin a bit of a lad, 'as Ronnie."

Steve turned to his wife. "Yo cor goo sayin' the lad took it. If 'e did, why did 'e 'and it in to Jack? P'raps somebody put it in ’is pocket ferra joke. ’E an’ ’is mates am allus foolin’ round. We ’as ter tell ’em off in the shop often enough.”

Valerie said, “He could’ve been frightened of being found out. Borstal isn’t very nice.”

Josie shrugged. “Anyway,” she said, “I’ll never be sure about him again.”

Chapter Ten

Vera Salt was wiping the counter over. She was a stickler for cleanliness. Nobody could say that her chip shop wasn't spotless.

Steve was mopping the floor. He had finished his round early and always helped when he came in.

Vera said, "Our Josie's decided what 'er wants to do when 'er leaves school, Steve."

He finished wringing the mop. "Oh, yes? At last? 'Er's bin a vet, a nerse, a typist. What's 'er decided on now?"

"'Airdressin'."

"Well, that's a chaernge. Do yer think 'er means it this time?"

"Yes, I do. 'Er's asked me to see if Freda's got anythin' when I go termorrer to 'ave me perm."

Steve thought for a moment. "Well, 'er won't 'ave far ter goo. It's only down the road. Doe you think er'll like it?"

Vera shrugged her shoulders. "You guess is as good as mine, Steve. All I know is 'er won't want to ter sit at a desk all day like Valerie's gonna do. 'Er wouldn't 'ave the patience."

"You'me right, me wench," he said. "Let's 'ope as 'er settles. I s'pose one day 'er could 'ave 'er own shop, like we 'ave."

"One step at a time, Steve, one step at a time."

"Well, as long as 'er realises that 'er starts at the bottom an' 'er won't be permin' 'air for a long time."

Vera nodded. "I've already told 'er that. 'Er still wants ter do it."

Steve took a couple of swipes with the mop. Laughing, he said, "I s'pose 'er'll be able to do all our 'air in a year or two. Save us a fortune, that will."

*　　　　*　　　　*

Valerie sat in the head teacher's room, waiting for the deputy headmistress, Mrs Jameson. She was to be advised on her career.

Mrs Jameson was tired. She felt a headache coming on. She swallowed two Aspros and prepared to face her pupils for the afternoon.

She entered the room and was relieved to see Valerie sitting there, an easy child to deal with.

"Right then, Valerie, what do you plan to do with yourself?"

"Office work, Mrs Jameson. I want to improve me shorthand and typing."

Mrs Jameson smiled at her. "Well, that is quite possible. There is a vacancy for an office junior at the shoe factory. I can arrange an interview for you, if you wish."

Valerie was pleased. "Thank you, Mrs Jameson."

She couldn't wait to get home to tell her mother.

Josie was waiting outside the school gate.

"How did you get on with Mrs Jameson, Val?"

"Okay. I'm going for an interview at the shoe factory for office junior."

Josie laughed. "Well, you'll never go barefoot, Val. I hear the workers can buy the seconds. That'll be great."

"What about you, Jose?"

"Well, I'm going to work at the hairdressers in the High Street, you know, the one that Maureen Edwards works at."

Valerie froze. She didn't want her friend to become pals with one of the Edwards family.

Josie went on, "Just what I wanted. So handy for home and I'll be able to do your hair for you, won't I?"

The two girls walked on, chatting about their future. Mrs Jameson watched them go. She passed her hand over her eyes wearily. Another year over, more pupils ready for the big, wide world, to spread their wings. She was beginning to feel old.

Valerie was interviewed by Mr Rolf, the office manager. He was in his fifties, smartly dressed, a typical ex-army man. After questioning her, he seemed satisfied and pleased that she would be attending night classes at the commercial college to further her shorthand and typing. He doubted if there would be any problems with flirtations or distractions in Valerie's working day. He was a pretty good judge of character and felt that here was a young lady who would give years of service to the company.

On her return from work, Grace questioned her deeply about the job.

"What time will you have to be there for, Valerie?"

"Half-past eight, Mom."

"That's good. You'll be able to get the eight o'clock bus and be in plenty o' time. What time do yer finish?"

"Quarter past five."

"Ooh, that's not bad. You'll still get 'ome before me."

Valerie looked intently at Grace. "Mom," she said, "do you think you'll be able to get a lighter job? We'll manage."

Grace was touched by her daughter's concern. "I'll 'ave ter see, Valerie. P'raps I'll be able to goo on the assembly line. At least I'll be sittin' down. I'll ask termorrer. I doe want ter goo back in the cake shop. Me feet ain't up to it."

"Ask tomorrow then, Mom. You can't carry on forever like you are."

Grace sat in reflection, drinking her tea. She didn't relish the thought of Valerie attending night classes twice a week. She would miss her company but then they would have the weekends together.

* * *

"Ronnie, come in 'ere a minute. I've got summat ter tell yer."

Wilf went into the front room, leaving the door ajar. Ronnie's heart sank. He searched his memory to try to think what he had done lately. Maybe something had caused his father's displeasure. He could not think of anything. He had spent his leisure time playing football, visiting Lily and Herbie and generally knocking around with his mates.

He entered the front room. Nellie had lit a small fire to prevent the furniture getting damp. It had been a rainy month. Wilf stood, warming his backside. He looked at his son, not unkindly. The lad felt a little better.

"I've sorted a job out for yer."

Ronnie brightened. He wanted to work with his father and John at the steelworks.

"What's that then, Dad?" he asked.

Wilf lit a cigarette. He was only going to have a couple of puffs. Nellie didn't like smoking in her parlour.

"Well, yo know I goo ferra pint in Th'Aymekker's?"

"Yes, Dad." Ronnie didn't want to work in a pub. What was Wilf getting at?

"Well, I got you a job. I was talkin' ter Bobby 'Aynes an' 'e needs a new lad."

Ronnie felt sick. "Bobby Haynes, the butcher? But, Dad, you know I can't stand cruelty ter animals."

"Doe be saft. Thay'me all gunna be jed when yo see 'em an' yo'll get used ter it. Anyroad, yo woe be messin' wi' the mate ferra long time. Yo'll 'ave ter learn 'ow ter do it fust."

Ronnie felt defeated.

Wilf went on, "It beats the factry an' the coal yard an' the 'ours aye bad. Half day on a Thursday an' three o'clock on a Satdy."

Feeling trapped, Ronnie knew it was no use arguing. It appeared that his future, for the present anyway, was cut and dried.

"Okay, Dad. I s'pose I'll gee it a goo but I never thought I'd mess wi' raw meat."

Wilf grinned. "Yo've allus bin glad ter eat it, like the rest on us."

Ronnie had to agree. "Ar, you'me right there, Dad."

He turned and went into the kitchen. Nellie stood at the stove, stirring the custard.

"Alright, our Ronnie? Dad tell yer about the job?"

"Yes, Mom. Not what I thought I'd do when I left school. I s'pose I'll get used to it. Anyway, old Pongo'll 'ave plenty o' mate."

"Ar," said Nellie, "and we, I 'ope."

*　　　　　*　　　　　*

With some trepidation Valerie opened the door to the office block of the shoe factory. She was to report to Mrs Shelley, the office supervisor. There was a counter in the outer office behind which was situated a switchboard and a receptionist. Jenny Dawes was a plump, pretty, happy-go-lucky girl. She looked up as Valerie came in.

"Hello," she said. "Are you the new junior?"

"Yes," said Valerie. She suddenly felt self-conscious about her rather old-fashioned coat and pleated skirt. Jenny looked very smart. "I have to report to Mrs Shelley."

"Yes, of course," said Jenny. "Old Shelley's bark is worse than her bite. She'll look after you, don't you fret. I've been here two years. Started as junior meself and I've been okay."

Valerie felt a little better. She just nodded and smiled weakly. The door to the inner office opened and Mrs Shelley emerged. She was stylishly dressed in a navy suit and sparkling white blouse. Her hair was permed and her make-up understated and perfect.

"Come along, Miss Potts. I will show you your duties."

She led the way to the post room.

"I will expect you to be on time every day. You will have an hour for lunch and ten minutes for each tea break. You will be responsible for the post and for making tea for the sales office. Each person will give you tea money every Monday for the week. As you come in each morning you will bring up the milk. Each morning you will sort out the mail and take it to the appropriate departments. Messages from the sales office will be taken to other departments. You will see to all outgoing mail and take it to the local Post Office at five o'clock, in plenty of time to catch the last post. Vernon will show you how we buy the stamps and how to balance the post book. He will spend a week with you before he goes to the accounts department."

Valerie's head was spinning. She wished she was back at school and had never seen the shoe factory. She felt that she would never remember all that she was told and would never find her way around the factory.

Vernon, a spotty youth of sixteen, was obviously unimpressed with her. He would show her the ropes reluctantly and couldn't wait for the week to end so that he could start his new job.

* * *

Saturday morning was always busy at Tresses. Josie, now the new junior, got there early in anticipation of the rush. Freda was already there looking through the appointment book. Josie unpacked the clean towels and filled the kettle ready for the tea, mainly drunk on the hoof by the busy staff. The washbasins and mirrors had all been left sparkling clean at closing time the day before. She liked working at the shop. It had been strange at first. The layout had not been complicated.

Freda, the proprietor, shared the premises with her husband, Joe, who ran the barber's section. The shop was double fronted, with the staff room in the middle, and rules were set down to prevent equipment straying from one section to the other. Each section had its own towels in different colours, although customers often brought in their own and equipment was jealously guarded. Occasionally shampoo was loaned in an emergency.

On the occasions when the staff were able to take refreshment in the staff room, laughter was often heard as Joe, or his son, Roger, would tease the stylists. Of course the junior would come in for some good-natured ragging. It was too much for the men to resist.

Josie longed for the day when she would be qualified to do perming and cutting. She was learning fast. Already her mother and nan had let her set their hair and felt quite confident in her. One day she would have her own shop but, at this stage in her life, that seemed very far away.

At eight-thirty sharp the first customer arrived, from then on it was non-stop. The time fled and at ten o'clock they were all panting for a cup of tea. Josie went into the staff room to brew up. Next to the tea caddy was a brown paper parcel. Joe had noticed her go in and popped his head round the door.

"Aye up, Jose, you must 'ave an admirer. That parcel come fer you this mornin'. Delivered by 'and, it was."

Josie was surprised to say the least. She didn't know who could have left her a present.

"Thanks, Joe," she said.

He grinned. "Am yer brewin' up, Jose? I'm gaggin'."

"Won't be long," she said.

Freda popped her head round the door. "Tea, Jose?" she asked. "Me feet am killin' me today. I'll be glad when it's two o'clock. What's that you've got there?"

Josie put the parcel back on the cupboard. "I don't know yet," she said. "I'll open it in a minute when I've mashed the tea."

"Okay," said Freda. "Don't forget to show me."

Waiting for the tea to stand Josie began to unwrap the parcel. She took off the first layer, then the second, the third, fourth and fifth, then she saw that it was one of the capes belonging to the barber shop. She unfolded it and shook it, preparatory to hanging it up in the shop, then – *plop* – something fell out and landed on her foot.

Her screams brought staff and customers crowding to the doorway.

"For God's sake, Josie, whatever's the matter?" Freda stood, scissors in hand, afraid of what she was going to find. "Have you scalded yourself or somethin'? Yer nearly had me cut Mrs Davis's earole off."

"Sorry, Freda." Josie could only point to the offending object on the floor.

"A bleedin' sheep's eye." Freda forgot her shop voice. "It's them bleedin' butchers again. I'll bloody kill 'em. Wait till I see 'em. Upsettin' my shop."

Joe turned away, covering his mouth with his hand, stifling his chuckles. He had a good idea who had packed that parcel.

Chapter Eleven

Valerie settled in at the shoe factory better than she had thought. She soon got into the routine and found the rest of the workforce helpful.

Jenny Dawes, the telephonist/receptionist, was particularly friendly. One day she suggested to Valerie that, when she had been there for a while, she would teach her how to operate the switchboard. Valerie looked forward to that. The evening classes tired her but she was determined to stick it out to get her shorthand and typing speeds up, then she would qualify for a job in the typing pool.

Grace missed her when she attended the college but realised that the girl had to do it to get on.

While at work, the time flew. Valerie appreciated being able to give her mother money to help out and she saved up for items of reasonably priced clothing for herself.

She was not envious of the other girls but did want to always look neat and clean. This she achieved by Grace getting a clothing cheque for her, and taking the money to Peggy each week. Good-natured Peggy had made her a couple of dirndle skirts, which looked as good as shop bought, so she managed to look quite smart.

One day she was taking post to the accounts department when she realised that a young man was looking at her. She blushed and turned away but not before she had registered a little about him.

Norman Proudfoot was eighteen. He was studying to be an accountant and also attended the college. He was a quiet, bespectacled, shy lad. The girls who worked at the factory frightened him to death. He much preferred someone who was quietly dressed, reserved and not pushy. Someone like Valerie but how would he ever get to talk to her? She was as shy as he was.

*   *   *

Valerie had a week's holiday. She didn't know what she was going to do with it but, what with washing all the net curtains and generally spring-cleaning the house, she found the time was flying.

On the Friday she sat on the bus going into town. She wanted to buy fabric for a summer dress. She sat reflecting on her life. Her ambition, at the moment, was to be a private secretary. She was doing well with her shorthand and typing speeds now and felt that she was getting nearer to attaining her ambition.

Looking up, she saw her cousin, Paul, waiting to get on the bus. She didn't really want to speak to him and hoped that he wouldn't spot her when he got on. But he did. Waving to her, he made his way down the bus and sat next to her.

"'Allo, Valerie. Long time, no see. I go to Gran's on a Saturday but I never see you there."

"No, I don't get much time now that I'm working, Paul."

"Where are you workin'?"

Valerie smiled. "At the shoe factory."

Paul widened his eyes. "Mekkin shoes? I never thought you'd do that."

Valerie laughed. "No, I'm in the office and I go to college for typing and shorthand."

"Oh, pardon me, I'm sure," said the lad, cheekily. "Anyway, me nan's not well."

Valerie was concerned. "Isn't she? What's wrong with her?"

"I doe know but 'er 'as ter keep gooin ter bed. 'Er says as her ain't goorany goo in 'er, accordin' to me mom."

Valerie felt so guilty. She hadn't been to see her Gran for ages. She knew that Aggie must be ill to keep taking to her bed. She wasn't that type at all.

"I'll be down to see her soon. I've had this week off. I've got to go in the main weeks for the stocktaking, so I'm having me time off."

Paul stood up to get off the bus. "Cheerio, Val. I'll tell me Gran I've seen yer."

She waved to her cousin and resolved to call on her nan as soon as she could.

Stan Potts sat, eating his grey peas and bacon. He wiped his mouth on the back of his hand.

"Well, Janice, I don't see why you 'ave ter do everythin' fer me mother. You ain't her only daughter-in-law. You'll never get that job you've set yer 'eart on."

Janice put the teapot down in front of him. "Grace has ter werk, Stan. We can manage. We have up ter yet and I hear as 'er ain't too well wi' the arthritis these days."

Stan grunted. "You'me too saft be 'alf, our Janice. Young Valerie only comes on 'op and a catch an' all. 'Er thinks 'er's somebody, 'er does and 'er was on the back row when looks was gid out. Dresses as old-fashioned as 'er mother. Grace doe do a lot fer 'er own mother from what I 'ear. I sid Freddie Burke th'other day and he says if Renee ever gets bad it'll be Flo what'll have ter do everythin' over that end an' all."

Janice stared at him. "Renee aye bad is 'er?"

"Not yet but, let's face it, Grace day look after our Herbert a fat lot."

Janice agreed. "I know, Stan, but think about it. 'Er aye 'ad much of a life 'erself, really."

Stan sniffed. "'Er'll see as that young Valerie doe 'ave much of a life an' all. Selfish cow."

Valerie decided to finish her shopping quickly so that she would not upset Grace by going to Aggie's the next day and spoiling her mother's Saturday. She got off the bus at the bottom of Aggie's street and met Janice.

“’Allo, Valerie. Coming ter see yer nan? ’Er’ll be pleased.”

“Sorry nan’s not so well, Aunty Janice. I saw Paul on the bus. I’ll try to come more often but I’m working, as you know, and I go to night classes.”

Janice smiled. “Yes, I know. Thelma told me. You’re at the shoe factory, ain’t yer?”

“Yes, in the offices. I have this week off.”

“Aggie’ll be pleased,” said Janice.

She was and shed a little tear when the girl came in.

“I aye got no energy, Valerie. That doctor doe gee me anythin’ wot’ll do me any good. I aye bin right ever since I lost Bert. The doctor says that’s what’s the matter wi’ me an’ I’ve got ter put me mind ter gettin’ meself right. I do try but after a few days I get wore out again. I’m older than Bert, yer know, I’m nearly sixty-eight. Me mother lived ’til ’er was eighty. It was me dad what died early. It was ’is ’eart, just like our Herbert, ’e was.”

Valerie was sympathetic. “Don’t worry, Nan. You need a good rest. I’ll come and see you next week.”

She bent and put a kiss on Aggie’s cheek. “Bye, Nan,” she said.

Aggie waved from the fireside chair and smiled at her granddaughter.

Afterwards, Stan said to Janice, “Me mom’s chuffed Valerie come. Anybody’d think as Princess Margrit ’ad called in, the fuss as ’er med. We’me theer all the time an’ all we gets is the moans and groans.”

Janice put her hand on his arm. “Course your mom appreciates what we does, Stan. ’Er knows as you’ve changed yer shifts to ’elp ’er an’ I’m always here. Our Paul’s the light of her life and don’t ferget Valerie’s all ’er’s got of Herbert.

Stan shifted uneasily in his chair. “You’me right, I reckon. Doe tek any notice o’ me. Just sour graerps.”

Janice said, "I think Valerie'll try ter come more often now 'er's sin 'ow bad yer mom is."

Stan sniffed. "I should 'ope so. Anyroad, that's if 'er mother'll let 'er."

Despite Grace's grumbles, Valerie did call to see Aggie each Thursday after work. She took care to stay for just half an hour to prevent any sulks when she got home. She had tried to explain to her mother how poorly Aggie was but it did not seem to sink in.

On the second Thursday who should she bump into, coming out of the chip shop, but Norman Proudfoot. He stopped and smiled at her.

"Hello, Valerie. What are you doing in this neck of the woods?"

She flushed slightly. "I'm going to see my Gran, she lives in James Street. She's not well," she said, in her 'office voice'.

Norman laughed. "Well, blow me, I only live around the corner. We can walk down together if you like."

Valerie nodded. "Okay," she said.

She was surprised how nice Norman was away from work. They walked along self-consciously, Norman wheeling his bicycle, both thinking of something to say.

"How long have you lived round here then?" she asked.

"Only two years. It's closer for dad to get to work. Me sister works at the Home and Colonial, our Desmond works at the steelworks, me dad works at the Town Hall. Me brother's getting married in a few months."

Valerie sighed. "I don't have any brothers and sisters, just me and mom. Well, here I am. Tarra, see yer."

Norman waved. "See yer, Valerie. Tarra." And he went on his way, whistling cheerily.

As Valerie entered Aggie's back door, Janice was standing in the kitchen. She smiled conspiratorially.

"Who was that chap you was with then, Valerie?"

Valerie blushed furiously. "Only a lad from work," she said. "He lives just round the corner. I don't know him that well."

Janice gave her an old-fashioned look. "Don't let yer mom 'ear that you'me gettin' friendly wi' lads or 'er'll 'ave an 'eart attack."

Indignantly, Valerie protested. "I don't go with lads, so don't you go tellin' her that I do, Aunty Janice."

Janice laughed again. "I shan't tell her but if you want a chap, you 'ave one an' tek no notice."

Aggie was in bed but seemed a little stronger. She held out her hand to her granddaughter.

"Come on, me wench. 'Ow's things? 'Ow's yer mom, any better?"

Valerie bent to kiss her. "She's still got the rheumatics, Gran. She's got a job sitting down, still, on the assembly line. She's doing less hours now but I can give her some so we'll manage. I'll get better money when I get into the typing pool."

Aggie was lost in thought for a minute, then she looked at Valerie.

"Screws is 'orrible," she said. "I doe s'pose the quack's give 'er anything any good fer it?"

"No, Nan," Valerie agreed.

"Me neither, cock, me neither."

Again Aggie sat lost in thought then, leaning forward toward Valerie conspiratorially, she said, "Valerie, when I die there'll be a bit of insurance, enough ter bury me. Yer Grandad left me alright so there'll be a bit fer you and Paul and Stan and Janice."

Valerie shifted uncomfortably on the chair. "Now, Gran, don't talk like that."

Aggie clutched her hand. "I want ter know things are straight. It won't be a fortune, just a bit fer you to put in the Post Office, towards when you set up home on yer own."

Valerie couldn't imagine that ever happening but thanked her Gran and gave her a kiss.

She stood up. "Better make a move, Gran. Got to get the chips on my way home. See you next week. Tarra."

As she turned to wave in the doorway, Aggie beckoned to her to come back.

"I'm only telling you, cock. There's an old brown ambag in the back of the wardrobe. If anythin' 'appens ter me, you'll know where to look. Don't ferget an' keep it to yerself."

"Oh, Gran, you'll get better."

"I 'ope so, cock, I 'ope so." Aggie waved feebly from the bed.

It became a regular thing for Valerie and Norman to walk along on a Thursday evening. It went on for six weeks before he plucked up enough courage to ask her out.

"Er," he said, "er, Valerie, what do you do on a Sunday afternoon?"

"Well, not a lot really. Just sit with me mom really."

She blushed as he bent towards her. "Er, well, er, would you like to go for a walk this Sunday? In the park or somewhere?"

Valerie thought about it for a few seconds, then decided she would mange to get out somehow and she accepted.

Sunday morning dawned bright and sunny. Valerie lay on her bed, reading her book. Grace was bustling round downstairs. Valerie lay agonising over how she could broach the subject of going out after dinner. No way could she say she was meeting a lad. Grace seemed to have a mental block about her daughter and the opposite sex. A subject never to be countenanced, even though the girl was approaching seventeen. Even going out with Josie had to be earned days in advance to soften up Grace.

Valerie lay, planning her strategy. She would act normally and not pay any extra attention to her appearance to raise her mother's suspicions. Downstairs Grace had made tea and toast.

"Valerie, breakfast," she called.

Valerie dressed quickly.

"Sorry it don't run ter bacon this week. P'raps next week, eh?"

"It don't matter, Mom. I like toast. Shall I fetch the paper?"

Grace poured the tea. "No, eat yer breakfast first, then you can fetch it."

They ate companiably, listening to the service on the wireless. Valerie was on edge all the time.

"Guess who I saw yesterday, Valerie? That Mr and Mrs Stevens. Thay'me a funny pair. I reckon as they'd spile another couple they would. His mother went berserk when 'e married 'er but, lookin' at 'em, I reckon as it was meant ter be. Their Doris 'as gone ter live in Sheffield, married a lorry driver 'er met at the werk. They doe seem too bothered about it. I'd goo mad if you done that. I couldn't manage without you, our Valerie."

Valerie nodded, methodically spreading jam on her toast. She quailed inwardly at the thought of telling Grace she was going out after dinner.

Grace took her plate to the sink. "By the way, I saw Thelma's sister yesterday. 'Er's out of th'ospital. Come out on Thursday. 'Er says Thelma'd like me ter pop round. I thought I'd pop round after dinner. Do you want ter come?"

Valerie felt like cheering. "Oh. Oh no, Mom. I could do with popping to Josie's. She offered to tidy me eyebrows for me. Give my love to Thelma."

Grace nodded. "I will. I dare say I shan't stop long. I 'ad enough o' sickness when yer dad was bad."

The morning dragged. Valerie could hardly eat her dinner. She was excited and apprehensive. It was her very first date. She wondered if Norman would want to kiss her. She hoped not, not yet anyway.

Norman hung around the park gates uncertainly. He wasn't sure whether he wanted this date or not. Valerie had been the only girl who, so far, hadn't seemed to notice his spots. They were clearing up, slowly. Valerie thought he had kind eyes and nice teeth. His hair wasn't bad either and he was always clean.

Norman liked Valerie's hair. It was always tied back tidily and she was not silly and giggly like most young girls. He spotted her hurrying along the road. She was flushed and a little breathless. He grinned when she reached him.

"You made it then."

"Hi, Norman," she said, shyly. "I like your suit."

It was his turn to flush. "I thought we would go for a walk and then, maybe, a row on the lake."

Valerie looked away from him. "A walk's okay but we'll leave the boats, if you don't mind. Somebody might see us."

Norman was surprised. "Does that matter?"

"Me mom thinks I'm at me friend's. She doesn't seem to think I should go out with lads."

Norman's eyes widened. "No harm in a walk in the park, surely, Valerie?" he said.

She shook her head. "No. No, you're right."

They walked along. Shyly, Norman caught hold of her hand. Valerie blushed again. She liked the feel of his fingers, they felt quite strong. Suddenly, she felt happier than she had for a long time.

Grace knocked on Thelma's front door. Harry answered it.

"'Allo, Mrs Potts. Long time, no see."

"'Allo, 'Arry. You're gettin' taller by the day."

Grace entered the front. She noticed that it was sparsely furnished but spotlessly clean.

"Come through, Grace," Thelma called from the kitchen. She sat on the fireside chair, feet up on a stool. She looked surprised. "No Valerie?"

Grace slipped off her jacket. "No. 'Er's gone ter Josie's. Summat about 'er eyebrows wantin' straightenin'. Doe know why, they look alright ter me."

Thelma smiled. "That's gels for yer. I s'pose I should be glad I've gorra lad."

Grace looked at her friend closely. "'Ow are yer terday, Thelma? You still look a bit peaky."

"I'm better today. I didn't come down till twelve o'clock. Jerry done some soup an' a roll. I'm a bit sore but I s'pose it'll ease as time goes on. I'll be off work another six wiks. They've put in a temporary manageress. I shall get bored stiff here. Be glad when I can get back ter normal."

Grace frowned. "Doe rush things. Let the famly look after themselves fer a bit."

Thelma laughed. "That'll be the day. It's a good job I've got me sister or the 'ouse'd be stinkin' by the time I could do it."

"Shall I mek you a cup o' tea, Thelma?"

"Yes, please. Jerry's gone down the allotment. He'll be a couple of hours at least."

Harry called, "Gooin ter play footie, Mom. Okay?"

"Yes, okay, Harry. Just be back fer yer tea. Yer dad's bringin' faggots and peas from yer Gran's."

Turning to Grace, she said, "'E's no trouble. Just lives fer 'is football. Always off over the park, 'e is."

*　　　*　　　*

Flo's baby was born in hospital on a Friday. She would have liked to have had a home confinement. Like all her family, she had a dread of hospitals. However, the doctor and midwife would not hear of it. Flo was thirty-nine and a risk.

The baby was a scrawny little mite but was perfectly formed and had a good pair of lungs. Contrary to the belief of many that he would have some defect, because of his mother's age, he was perfect.

Fred was over the moon. He never thought he would be a dad and, at forty, he realised that he had cut it a bit fine.

The Acorn pub resounded to the sounds of Fred, his brothers and his mates, wetting the baby's head. Granny Shaw was her usual philosophical self.

"They'll know thay'me married now," she said, "and I reckon I'm too ode to be a Gran again."

Grace agreed. "All I 'ope is our Flo's never left ter rear 'im on 'er own like I was wi' our Valerie."

Renee snorted. "Doe yo worry on that score, wench. Freddie Burke's as strong as an 'oss an' doe ever ferget, me wench, the devil allus looks after 'is own."

Grace and Valerie went to see Flo and the new baby, Mark, on their return from hospital. Valerie had knitted a matinee jacket and Grace had crocheted a shawl, with much grumbling about her stiff fingers.

Flo was as pleased as Punch with the gifts. She was glowing and had never looked so well in her life. Fred, for the moment, was as proud as a peacock.

"Youda thought as 'e was the only one who'd ever 'ad a babby," said Grace.

"Oh, but he's a lovely little chap," said Valerie.

"Not as nice as you was when you was a babby, though," said Grace. "And why did you offer ter babbysit for

’em, our Valerie? You don’t get much time at ’ome as it is, what wi’ yer night classes an’ poppin’ ter see Josie.”

“That’s only two evenings, Mom. I try to be at home as much as I can.”

Grace just sniffed.

*   *   *

It was six months later and Aggie was sinking rapidly. Janice and Stan, with the help of Sally, took turns to sit with her. The doctor admitted, at last, that she was very ill. He offered to get her a bed in the General Hospital but, as there was little to be done for her, they decided to leave her in her own bed. The district nurse called in twice a day to administer an injection.

One Monday morning, on his way to school, Paul, at Janice’s request, called to tell Grace and Valerie that time was running out for his Gran.

“Mom,” said Valerie, “I’d like to go to sit with Gran for a while. You won’t mind if I go after work tonight, will you? I know it’s Monday and I’ll miss a night class but I can catch up.”

Grace looked at her daughter. She could see that the girl was concerned.

“Course. You go, if it’ll make you feel better. I s’pose ’er always thought a lot of you, Valerie.”

Stan was on the late shift. Janice welcomed Valerie. She looked dead tired.

“I’m so glad you’ve come, gel. Your gran always thought a lot of you. I could do with poppin’ round ’ome for a bit, I ain’t been today. If yer need anythin’ Sally’ll come but yer Gran’s had her injection and should sleep now, so it’s just a matter of somebody sitting here.”

Valerie smiled at her aunt. “You carry on, Aunty Janice. I’ll be okay and, as you say, Sally’s next door.”

Sitting by the bed, Valerie thought she had never seen anyone look so ill since her dad had died. She would never forget him and how he had suffered.

Aggie barely seemed to be breathing, she was very peaceful.

Janice came in with a cup of tea. "I'm off now, Valerie. I shan't be too long, love. Are you sure you'll be alright? You can knock the wall for Sally. I reckon she'll be in before long, anyway."

Valerie smiled at her aunt. "Stop worrying, Aunty. I said I'll be okay. I'll read me magazine."

As she sat, leafing through the pages, she glanced over at the wardrobe. She was transfixed for a moment. Gran's bag was in there and inside it, known only to her, was the money for Stan, Paul, Janice and herself. She felt a little hurt that no mention had been made of Grace. If Gran had anything, surely it would have been split between Stan and Herbert, if he had lived. To her mind, because Herbert had gone, his share should have come to her or her mother. Valerie calculated that if it was being shared equally between the four of them, Stan's family would be getting three quarters of Aggie's money and Herbert's family only a quarter.

The house was quiet. Aggie was so peaceful. Did she dare to take a look? No, she didn't. Again, she tried to concentrate on her magazine.

She stood up and looked out of the window. There were a few girls preparing to skip in the street and a couple of housewives canting on the corner. She slipped quickly downstairs and slid the bolt on the back door. She put the catch on the front door lock. If Sally called she could make up some excuse. Returning to the bedroom, she took a deep breath and crossed over to the wardrobe. Hands shaking, she opened it. Searching towards the back, under shoes and boxes, she found the handbag.

Opening it, she found four brown paper envelopes neatly rolled and secured with a rubber band. Each had a name printed on it. They were not sealed. She unrolled the one bearing her name and gasped. It contained some five pound notes, twenty of them. She had never seen so much money. It was wrapped around a brooch which was Aggie's. Quickly she checked Paul's envelope. He had the same amount of money and a gold watch chain. In Stan's was two hundred pounds and in Janice's was a hundred.

From each envelope, including her own, Valerie took out fifty pounds. Neatly rolling them up, as before, with the names showing, and securing them with the rubber bands, she placed them as she had found them and secreted the bag in the back of the wardrobe. She bundled the money together and pushed it to the bottom of her own handbag. Aggie slumbered on.

Feeling justified in sharing the money out, to her mind in a fairer manner, she hurried to take the catch off the front door and unbolt the door to the kitchen. Hurrying back upstairs, she sat, looking unseeingly at her magazine. She gave a start as she heard a quiet tap on the bedroom door. Sally popped her head round.

"Sorry, wench," she whispered. "Did I mek yer jump?"

She looked at Aggie lying so still in the bed and wiped away a tear. "God bless 'er. 'Er does look peaceful. 'Er aye bin the same since Bert went. I reckon 'er's just broken-'earted, poor wench."

She put a hand over Valerie's and looked into her face. "'Ave you 'ad a cuppa tea, love?"

Valerie nodded. "Yes, thanks but I'd like another one if there's one going, please." She felt it would help to settle her nerves.

Sally was glad to be doing something. "I'll pop the kettle on then. 'Ow's yer mom, Valerie?"

"About the same, thanks, still battling on."

"Yes, cock, we 'as ter, doe we?" Sally nodded and turned to leave the room. "I'll put yer a bit o' me cake an' all, stop the grubs bitin' till yer gets yer tea."

"Thanks, Sally."

The old woman smiled and thought to herself what a nice young woman Valerie Potts was turning out to be.

Janice returned. She looked fresher, having managed to wash her hair. She looked at Aggie and was satisfied that nothing had changed since she had left.

"Thanks, Valerie," she said. "Sally stops a lot but I don't want to put on her all the time. I'm sure that Aggie would be glad ter know that you've bin with her. She allus thought a lot o' you."

Valerie smiled. "I know, Aunty, I know."

Aggie lasted another two days, finally drawing her last breath at two on the Wednesday morning. Stan was sitting with her. He was devastated. He blamed the doctor for his half-soakedness but was unsure what to say or do about it. Janice was a brick and took over all the arrangements.

The funeral, ten days later, on a Friday, was well attended. Aggie was well liked in James Street. She had been a good neighbour to a lot of people and they collected for a nice wreath for her.

Janice and Sally cleaned the house and arranged refreshments for after the burial. Thelma had organised sausage rolls, bread and cakes. To help Janice, Grace and Valerie had arranged to collect them on their way to James Street.

Thelma was sympathetic. "I bet you'll miss yer nan, Valerie?"

She nodded. "Yes, I shall, a lot." And she meant it.

Thelma asked Grace, "Did you 'ave any trouble gerrin the day off work?"

"No," said Grace. "We'me allowed a day off for close relations."

"Oh, that's good," said Thelma. "You can do without any worry on a day like this." To herself she thought, "I wonder what Grace would say if she knew my lad had seen Valerie in the park with a chap." She had decided to keep shtum about it. Best not to rock the boat. Valerie seemed such a nice girl.

Sally was grieved to lose her friend. Reg and Betty Edwards paid their last respects. They would miss their kindly neighbour. Nellie Edwards sent a card. All in all it went off well. Again, Valerie felt the loss of her dad and felt it deeply that she had lost the person who knew him best.

Stan and Janice had the job of sorting out the house. They had toyed with the idea of applying to rent it themselves but had been offered one of the new council houses. Pitts End was to be demolished.

They found that sorting Aggie's personal effects was a long, depressing task. They had to keep having a break when emotion overcame them. Janice came across the old brown handbag three days after the funeral and discovered the envelopes therein.

She gave it to Stan, who was nonplussed, and she suggested they open the envelopes when they were all together.

On Monday evening, when Valerie arrived home from college, Grace sat waiting for her.

"Valerie, sit down a minute," she said.

Hanging her coat on the back of the door, she looked at her mother expectantly.

"I've got summat ter tell yer."

"Oh yes, what's that, Mom?"

Grace poured her a cup of tea. "Well," she said, "Janice was here. She says she wants you to call in tomorrow after work. 'Er didn't say what for. Anyway, I'm not bothered, I'm sure it's none of my business. I know you'll tell me, anyway. Have you any idea what it's about?"

"No, Mom, I can't say that I have. Well, we'll soon see, won't we? What's for supper?"

"Welsh rarebit." Grace turned to the stove. "It's all ready and I've done the sandwiches for termorrer. It's quiet 'ere on me own when you'me out."

Valerie cringed. Same old story.

The next day dragged at work. Although Valerie knew what Janice wanted her for, she would be glad when it was all over and she knew she had got away with her deviousness.

She arrived at Aggie's house without seeing Norman, about which she felt a little disappointed deep down. Sally was in her garden, unpegging her washing.

"'Allo, wench," she said. "Nice ter see yer again. Am yer bearin' up?"

"Yes, thanks, Sally. It does seem strange coming here without me nan around though."

"I know, cocka. I can't get used ter 'er not bein' 'ere either." She sighed and wiped her eyes on her pinafore. "I think they've nearly finished the sortin' out now. I'll be gettin' new neighbours. It won't be the same without your nan."

Valerie nodded sympathetically.

Sally shuffled down her yard. "Nice wench, yes, nice wench," she muttered to herself.

Stan, Paul and Janice were all sitting at the kitchen table. The house seemed to echo. Most of the furniture had gone, the curtains were waiting to be taken down and there were a few ornaments on the table.

Janice greeted her, "Come in, Valerie. We're just going to have a cuppa tea. Sit yer down."

Stan nodded to her and Paul said hello. Janice sat down. She sighed.

"I'll be glad when it's all done, Valerie. I can't think I've ever done anything so sad in all me life. We've kept some of the furniture for the new house to remember yer Gran by. Is there anything you'd like to keep, anything from these bits on the table? You're welcome to take yer pick, you know."

Valerie pondered. She spotted the little shepherdess that had graced her nan's mantelpiece in her bedroom.

"I'd like her, if I could, Uncle Stan. If nobody else wants her."

"Tek it, by all means an' anythin' else you like."

So she chose a dish with raised flowers on it as well.

"Do you think Sally'd like something, Stan?" asked Janice.

"I 'spect 'er would. We'll find summat out when we've finished," he said.

When they all had been given a cup of tea, Janice produced the brown handbag. She handed it to Stan.

"Your Gran's left us all an envelope and we thought we should all open them together," she said.

Deep down Janice thought this the best thing to do as Grace was such a sceptical person. Stan passed each envelope to its respective owner.

"We haven't disturbed this till we was all together," he said. "We've got no idea what's in 'em. Each one's got our name written on it, it's me mom's writin'."

Paul opened his first. His eyes popped and his jaw dropped.

"Look, Mom, money."

"'Ow much, son?" asked Janice.

Paul counted. "Fifty pounds! I aye never sin that much money. Aye me Nan good ter think o' me like that?"

"Yes, 'er was," said his mother.

Stan said, "An' me grandad's old watch chain, Paul. 'Er allus said it was for 'er first grandson."

Valerie was next. She produced the fifty pounds and the brooch. She showed it to Janice, who exclaimed at its daintiness.

On opening her own envelope Janice was overcome to see that she also had fifty pounds and Stan was overwhelmed with his portion.

"Just what we need for the new house, Jan," he said. "I never knew me mom had all this money. 'Er could've spent it on herself, gone on 'olliday or summat. Just like 'er to put it away fer us." And he shed a tear.

Valerie pinned her brooch to her jacket. "I'll always treasure this and remember me nan," she said.

Paul looked up at her. "I'm saving me money in the Post Office," he said. "Any idea what you're gonna do with yours, Valerie?"

"Yes," she said, "I'm going to buy a television for me mom."

Chapter Twelve

Bobby Haynes proved to be a fair and generous employer. Despite his qualms about working in butchery, Ronnie found that he soon got used to it. At least the job was clean, inside and near to his home. He appreciated his weekly wage and found that Bob was generous, both with bits for Pongo and the odd pie or cut of meat for the family. In return, and for a small fee, Nellie washed the cloths and the white clothing worn in the shop.

The days flew by. Ronnie was always busy. He enjoyed the constant banter between Bob and Andy and himself and the rather ribald repartee between them and the customers.

Andy was getting married. He was going to move into the flat over the shop. It had been vacant since Bob and his wife, Tess, had moved into a detached house in Pipers Row, a house coveted by Valerie when she passed by. They had three children, two girls at infant school and a boy at junior school and they had a golden retriever bitch called Jessie.

Patty was progressing well. She was due to leave school in July. She had become accustomed to boarding in the week and returning home for the weekends. She would miss her non-hearing friends but looked forward to being with her family.

Aunty Betty had a sewing machine with an electric motor. She was doing outwork for a soft furnishing company and Patty was going to work with her at home. She was looking forward to earning her keep. She had done very well with lip reading and, as she had heard for twelve years of her life, her speech was good.

One Sunday, as the Edwards family were eating their midday meal, Pongo stretched out on the hearth and quietly died. The whole family mourned him but especially Ronnie and Patty. He was buried in the patch of back garden. The house seemed empty without him.

On his way down the entry, the following morning, Ronnie met Annie.

"'Allo, Ronnie, sorry ter 'ear about Pongo. Ah know what yo'me gooin through. I lost my Lassie years agoo. Do you know I still 'ear 'er sometimes? They never leave yer, yer know. 'Er was me best friend after Dennis died."

Ronnie could only nod.

"Tarra, son. Have a good day at werk. Tell that cheeky bugger, Andy, I'll see 'im later in the wik."

"Okay, Annie, see yer."

Bobby could see that Ronnie was quieter than usual. When the shop went quiet, and they were drinking a cup of tea, he asked the lad what was wrong.

"It's nothing, really, Bob, only our Pongo died yesterday and we all miss 'im, specially our Patty."

"Sorry ter 'ear that, Ron. We love our Jessie. I don't know what our house would be like without 'er. Patty leaves school next month, don't she?"

"Yes. 'Er's looking forward ter werkin' with me Aunty Betty. 'Er's already learnt ter use the machine an' 'er'll be mekking curtains and covers. 'Er can't very well werk in a factory or shop 'cause of 'er 'earin' problem, so werkin' wi' Betty's gonna be a godsend."

Bob nodded. He had a soft spot for Patty. She was a cheerful, pretty little thing.

Next morning, Bob arrived at the shop. Walking into the back room, he put a cardboard box on the table. When Ronnie arrived, he beckoned and took him through.

He said, "Don't tek yer jacket off, Ronnie. Yer'd better tek this round 'ome first."

Ronnie was curious. "What is it, Bob?"

"Tek a look."

Ronnie lifted the flaps of the box. There, on a blanket, was a golden retriever pup. Ronnie lifted him out. A little, pink tongue licked his face, then the pup nipped his nose with sharp, little teeth. Despite himself Ronnie was quite emotional.

"Thanks, Boss," he said. "Our Patty'll just love him. 'Ow much do we owe yer?"

Bob grinned all over his good-natured face. "Nothin' at all, lad. It's a gift. Your sister deserves it, all she's bin through. 'Er's bin a little Trojan. I'm glad the pup's gooin ter a good 'ome. Now, goo on, tek 'im whum."

Nellie was alone in the house when Ronnie appeared at the door.

"What's up, son? You ain't 'ad the push, 'ave yer?"

"No such luck. I've brought a present 'ome."

When Nellie saw the pup, her eyes filled with tears.

"The 'ouse is quiet when you'me all at werk these days. 'E'll be company, 'e will an' our Patty'll be over the moon when 'er gets 'ome at the wikkend."

Without more ado she set to to make the pup a bed.

"Shall we give 'im a name or wait fer our Patty?" Nellie asked.

"Wait for Patty, I think, Mom. Bob meant him specially for her. I'd better be gettin' back to the shop."

"'Ave yer asked him 'ow much we owe him, Ron?"

"'E says we doe owe 'im anythin'. 'E's glad the pup's comin' ter a good 'ome."

Nellie stroked the little head. "Oh, 'e's come to a good 'ome, alright," she said, gazing dotingly at the little fellow.

Patty christened the pup 'Prince'. He soon learned to come to his name. The family soon learned to put things out of the reach of his needle-sharp teeth and to keep doors and gates closed for his safety.

He had an adoring fan club but the one most besotted with him was Patty. She called at the shop to thank Bob, giving him a big hug and a kiss. He was quite dewy-eyed when she left.

There grew between Patty and the pup a special bond. He seemed to know that she was unable to hear. If her attention was needed he would take her hand in his soft, retriever mouth or gently tug at her skirt.

Ronnie worked extra hard for Bob. He seemed to grow up and mature, becoming more sensible by the day.

* * *

Anything that Valerie wished to keep secret she hid underneath the long, bottom drawer of her dressing table. To get at it she had to lift the whole drawer completely out. This hiding place was where she kept any money and her Post Office savings book. She managed to deposit five pounds a week from the legacy money when she took the post from the shoe factory to the local Post Office. No one knew her there, not like the counter at Turdy Tunley's, where she could be spotted paying it in. On one occasion she deposited twenty pounds. If, by any chance, Grace ever saw the entry she would say that she had won the sweep at work. As Valerie cleaned her own room every week, it was unlikely that Grace would ever find her secrets.

The television set was a great success. They had gone into town together and spent a Saturday morning choosing one, feeling very rich to be able to pay cash for it. Being able to watch the box meant less grumbling from Grace when Valerie wanted to spend the odd evening with Josie.

On Sunday afternoons she liked to go to Flo's to see Mark. She would take him for a walk in his smart, coach-built pram, going into the park over the bank, near Renee's. More often than not Norman would join her. He was getting more persistent about going out properly. He wanted to take her to meet his family. Occasionally they would go to the cinema in the town, with Josie covering for Valerie. All in all, it was becoming a strain.

Valerie had mastered her job. Jenny had, good-naturedly, shown her how to operate the switchboard. However, she was beginning to get on Valerie's nerves, always boasting about how she need not work. Her father owned the fruit and vegetable shop in the High Street. He wanted his daughter to work with him, to learn the ropes of the trade. She had demurred and decided to work in an office, thus the job at the shoe factory.

On a few occasions, Jenny had been late for work and Mrs Shelley had taken her to task for it.

She had resented the talking to and said to Valerie, "I'm sick o' this poxy job. No need for her to go so much about a few minutes. You covered for me. The board wasn't left, was it?"

Valerie sympathised with her.

Jenny was ill with the flu. Her father rang to say she would be away for a few days. Mrs Shelley asked Valerie to man the switchboard and the reception and recruited a reluctant Vernon to help with the post.

Valerie thoroughly enjoyed being in reception. She felt that it would be a step up if she could carry on with it. There was a typewriter which she could use to practice on in her lunch break and Mrs Shelley gave her some typing to do. She had developed a good telephone manner, having seen a film in which a telephonist featured.

On the fourth day that Jenny had been away, Valerie was sorting the post on the reception counter. She saw an envelope with Jenny's writing on it, addressed to the personnel department. She hoped that Jenny was giving in her notice but decided to check it. Looking around, there was no one to see, so she put it into her bag.

That evening, while Grace was watching television, she washed up the tea things and steamed open the envelope. She was disappointed to see that Jenny had not given notice, just a sick note for two weeks. Apparently Jenny had flu and tonsillitis.

Valerie screwed it up and took it out to the dustbin with the tea leaves.

*   *   *

Josie was trying to talk Valerie into having a home perm. She had done Vera's hair beautifully and felt that Valerie's severe style did nothing for her. She talked her into saving for some stylish new glasses but Valerie dithered about the perm and, mistakenly, consulted Grace.

"I don't know what you want ter mess with yer 'air for. I can't be doin' with all the prinkin' an' permin'. Can't yer be satisfied wi' what God gid yer? I s'pose if you want a perm, you'll 'ave one, no matter what I say. But doe come cryin' ter me if it terns out all frizzy and you look a freak." Of course it suited Grace for Valerie to look as plain as possible. She added, "An' there's nothin' wrong wi' them glasses, either."

Josie found Maureen Edwards was a nice girl to work with. She was helpful and, though fully qualified, did not order her about. She had a boyfriend, Chas, who worked at the local garage as a mechanic and who would often meet her from work. They were saving to get engaged.

She would tell them stories about her family, especially Ronnie, making them all laugh at his antics. Her concern for her sister, Patty, was obvious. She loved to spend time doing her sister's hair and taking her shopping.

Christine Edwards was training to be a nurse. Maureen was proud of her. She would tell her workmates how hard it was for her sister and how, at the time, she felt like giving up, then something would occur to give her the heart to carry on. One of her concerns was the health of Ivy. Often the customers would ask about the old lady who was becoming more feeble. Nellie was caring for her virtually full time now.

John was still at home. He was twenty-five and did not seem to bother about girls, he just enjoyed his motorbike and the company of his mates.

Mary was engaged and hoping to take on the tenancy of Ivy's house, which she had lived in for so long and, of course, Ivy couldn't be left to live alone.

Barry worked full-time for Gerry Taylor, the coal merchant. He was having driving lessons so that he would be able to do the coal deliveries. He could hardly wait for the day when he would be able to drive the big wagons.

*　　　　　*　　　　　*

The rent man called, as usual, on the Friday. Nellie, as always, had her own and Ivy's rent money ready.

"I have a letter for you, Mrs Edwards," he said. "I can tell you what is in it. The landlord is going to modernise the houses. He is going to put in a bathroom and update the kitchen."

Nellie was overjoyed but perplexed.

"'Ow's 'e gonna do that then?"

"Well, there will be a doorway, from the kitchen through to the coalhouse, that will be knocked through to the outside lavatory and the binnery to make one room. Then there will be a new bath, washbasin and toilet put in."

Nellie frowned. "Will all the 'ouses be done at the same time?"

He laughed. "I don't think so."

"Good," she said. "We'll 'ave ter use me mom's while it's being done."

It would mean a lot of mess but it would be worth it. Nellie hugged herself. She could hardly wait for Wilf to get home to tell him. No longer would they have the jaunt to the slipper baths to get clean. They would have hot, running water. What luxury! Instead of giving Ivy a wash down she would be able to put her into a nice, soapy bath.

As she prepared the evening meal she recalled the years when the children were small and she had to get the brick boiler going to fill the galvanised bath every Friday. She sometimes wondered how she had coped. She remembered the joy when she was able to buy a gas boiler with a hand-operated agitator. That had been a big step up from the poss tub. Now she had an electric washing machine. What bliss! And soon they would have a proper bathroom. She marvelled at the progress which seemed to be galloping towards her.

* * *

Jenny returned to work on a Monday. She was summoned to Mrs Shelley's office. She looked in on Valerie and asked her to man the switchboard for a while.

Valerie waited apprehensively. Jenny pulled a face and knocked on the supervisor's door.

"Come in."

Mrs Shelley sat at her desk, reading a letter. She did not look up, just continued to read.

Jenny was getting annoyed. She coughed for attention.

Mrs Shelley looked up.

"Oh yes, Jenny. Are you better?"

"Yes, thank you, Mrs Shelley."

"Well, long time, no see or hear from you." Mrs Shelley looked at her over her glasses.

Jenny was taken aback. "I sent a sick note in. Me mom posted it. You should have had it a week last Wednesday at the latest."

Mrs Shelley raised an eyebrow. "Well, we didn't get it. You know the rules. You always have to supply a sick note. Having two weeks off without a note is not permissible."

Jenny saw red. She leaned across the desk. "I'm telling you I sent a note in, Mrs Shelley. Are you calling me a liar?"

The supervisor bridled. "Don't speak to me like that, Jenny Dawes. All I know is that personnel have complained about one of my staff not sending in a note. It's a reflection on me if one of my girls disobeys the rules."

Jenny was tired and still weak from her illness. Her parents had wanted her to have another week at home. She didn't want this woman looking at her as if she had crawled out of a piece of cheese. Her dad could keep her at home for as long as she liked. She didn't need this poxy job. She drew up to her full height and looked Mrs Shelley in the eye.

"I think I'd rather work for me dad in the shop than stop in this God-forsaken hole. You can keep your job."

She walked out of the office. Valerie saw her hurry past without a word.

Mrs Shelley came into the outer office.

"Valerie, I would like you to carry on with the switchboard and reception indefinitely," she said.

She went into her office and closed the door. Sitting at her desk, she rubbed a hand over her eyes. "At least Valerie's reliable," she thought. "A nice girl."

*　　　　*　　　　*

Norman was anxious for Valerie to accompany him to his brother's wedding. They had managed to go to the cinema a couple of times with Josie giving an alibi. Once, Valerie had skipped an evening class so that they could go to the theatre. Her excuse to her mother for being late on that occasion had been a fire drill at the college, causing her to miss the bus.

Grace always insisted on Valerie being home by nine o'clock or, on a rare, special occasion, ten. Any later and Valerie would get the 'silent treatment' for a couple of days. It was hard work keeping Grace sweet. The new television set helped, it gave her something else to watch besides the clock.

Valerie was scheming. How could she go to the wedding? What could she wear? How late dare she stay out? Again Josie had to be her excuse.

The wedding was to be at two-thirty. Valerie would have to leave home at one o'clock to get ready and be at the church on time. She had a brainwave. She would not have to implicate Josie.

"Mom," she said. "I've been asked to work on Saturday for an extra stock take. Half of us are going in for the morning and half for the afternoon. I have to be there for one o'clock. If it takes a long time, I might be late."

Grace tutted. "I wanted to see the musical this week."

Valerie thought.

"Can't Thelma or Peggy go with you? It can be my treat with the extra money I'll earn on Saturday."

Grace nodded. "I s'pose I could ask Thelma. 'Er don't go out on a Saturday. 'Er husband's in the pigeon club so he always goes to the pub. I'll ask her."

"Right," thought Valerie, "how to dress?"

She could wear her new navy suit, put on an old blouse and shoes and change at Josie's. She would have to be very careful not to be seen but how could she avoid it? She racked her brains for an alternative, then, in a flash, it came to her. Janice. She had kept her counsel when she had seen her with Norman. Perhaps she would help.

During her lunch hour next day she got on the bus to Janice's in Pitts End. The door was answered by a dusty Janice, complete with turban and overall.

"Oh, what a surprise, our Valerie. You'll 'ave ter excuse the mess, we're packin' up ter move. We're gooin to our new 'ouse termorrer."

Valerie's heart sank. "Oh, I see. I was going to ask a favour but I don't think you can help me now."

Janice smiled. "Try me," she said.

Valerie explained her predicament.

Janice thought for a moment. "I think you should just stand up to your mom and tell her the truth."

Valerie hung her head, then looked at her aunt. "I can't, Aunty. You don't know what it would be like if me mom got wind about me going out with Norman. If things got serious with him, I would have to tell her but, as it is, we're just friends and I don't want to upset the apple cart at this stage."

Janice felt that she didn't want to condone Valerie being untruthful but then she thought, "What's the harm? She's only goin' to a weddin', not for a dirty weekend."

"Well, Valerie, it's no further for you to get to our new house. It's on the new estate, number 24 Leslie Street. You turn first left off the main road. The bus stops right by it. I'll be in on Satday sortin' meself out. If yer want ter pop an' get ready, it's alright by me an' it's unlikely anybody yer know will see yer. In any case, I'm yer aunty an' you can be visitin' me. It ain't far from yer chap's. Yer can pop after the weddin' on yer way 'ome ter change. I shan't be gooin out."

Valerie kissed her aunt. "Thanks, Aunty. I wish things were different but you know how me mom is an' it may not come to anything with Norman, although he's ever so nice."

She caught the bus back to the factory, feeling greatly relieved.

Saturday dawned bright and clear. A lovely, June day. At 34 Ingram Terrace all hell was let loose. The whole family was attempting to get ready for the marriage of Mary to Desmond Proudfoot.

Aunty Betty had worked for weeks, sewing the bridal gown and dresses for Maureen, Christine, Patty and Desmond's sister, Rose. Norman, the groom's brother, was to be best man.

Annie Pearce was coming to keep an eye on Ivy. She was next door, getting her ready. Jack was taking them in his car. If it all got too much for Ivy, he would bring them home early.

Wilf was proud of his daughter. He liked young Desmond. He was from a respectable family but wasn't averse to having a pint in the Haymaker's with his prospective father-in-law.

Nellie had a new perm and her suit was from Marks and Spencer. Her hat, chosen by Christine, took years off her.

Ronnie answered a knock at the front door.

"Flowers are 'ere," he called. He laid the box on the table in the front room. Mary took the lid off and gasped. There it was, her dream bouquet, buttonholes for all the family and sprays for the prayer books her bridesmaids were to carry. They all looked lovely. Maureen had coiled their hair up into bouffant styles and studded flowers into the coils.

Grace noticed that Valerie was wearing her new suit.

"Aren't you going to get all dusty, stocktaking?" she asked.

Valerie shook her head. "No, Mom. I only have to type the lists. My other suit needs cleaning. Anyway, I've got an overall in my bag."

"Suit yerself," said Grace. "Your 'air looks smart in that French pleat, nice and tidy."

Valerie patted at it. "Yes. Josie showed me how to do it. Well, Mom, it's nearly half past twelve. I'll have to go. Have a nice time at the pictures."

Grace sniffed. "I don't know if I'm going yet. I'll pop to the shop, see if Thelma wants ter go. 'Er still gets tired since her op."

Valerie made her escape. "Cheerio, Mom. Don't get too much for supper, one of the girls will pop out to get something."

Janice was waiting for her. "Give me your blouse an' I'll run the iron over it. Have a use of me lipstick."

Valerie looked doubtful.

"Go on, it's the same shade pink as yer blouse. You 'air looks nice. Hang on a minute."

Janice left the room. When she returned she had in her hand a lovely, silver hair slide.

"This'll match yer earrings."

Valerie was touched. "Are you sure, Aunty Janice? I hope I don't lose it."

"You won't. Here, I'll put it in for yer."

Clipping the slide along the French pleat, she stood back to admire the effect. She ironed the blouse and supervised the application of the lipstick. Valerie changed and Janice was pleased with her appearance.

"Go on, you've just got time to walk round to St Peter's before they all arrive. Have a lovely time."

Valerie rubbed her lips together. The lipstick felt unfamiliar. She felt quite glamorous.

Walking up to the church she had a feeling that some of the people hovering round the doorway were a little familiar to her. She went in and sat near the back, on the bridegroom's side. The church began to fill up. Norman arrived with his brother. He paused to speak to her.

"You look nice, Valerie. See you after." Then he moved to the front pew to sit with Desmond.

She looked round as the bride's family entered the church. She had the shock of her life. There were Nellie Edwards and Wilf, followed by Barry, John and, worst of all, Ronnie. She felt like disappearing into the floor. She hadn't realised that Desmond was engaged to one of the Edwards girls but, of course, she had never met any of Norman's family, so how was she to know?

She sat fretting. How was she going to get through the afternoon and evening? Should she just walk out? She looked at Norman. He looked so proud and happy as he joked with his brother. No, she couldn't just leave and let him down. She had to stick it out somehow.

Grace called into the shop. Thelma agreed to go to the cinema. She had had a row with Jerry and was still smarting.

"I don't go out on a Saturday night as a rule, usually too tired after a day 'ere but I'll go 'ome and have half an 'our on the bed an' I'll be as good as new." She added, "Poor Valerie, 'avin' ter werk on a Satday. Never mind, I expect 'er'll be tired termorrer but 'er can 'ave a lie in."

"Yes," said Grace, "then I s'pose 'er'll be wantin' ter go an' see our Flo's babby. 'Er dotes on 'im. 'Er ain't sid 'im for a fortnight."

The reception wasn't as arduous as Valerie had feared. Norman introduced her to his parents and relatives. Everyone was so happy and everybody mixed well.

In the cloakroom Nellie said to Christine, "Is that Valerie Potts young Norman's with then, our Christine?"

"Yes, Mom."

"Kept that quiet, day they?" said Nellie. "Our Mary never said."

"P'raps she didn't know, Mom. I don't think his mom had met her before today."

"Really," said Nellie, her eyes wide. "Well, that's a turn up for the book."

Valerie sat listening to Norman's Aunty Em telling her all about her nephew.

"'E was a lovely little kid, 'e was. Allus good at sums. Wants to be an accountant. Where do you live then?"

Valerie thought for a moment then decided that she may as well come clean.

"Pipers Row, the other end of town."

"Oh, I know, that's where Connie Jinks, Connie Smith as was, lives. I went ter school wi' 'er. Nice wench. I was glad to 'ear o' their bit o' luck, though it's s'posed to be a secret."

Valerie looked at her enquiringly.

"I shouldn't a said anythin', it's the sherry talkin'. Anyroad, I know you won't tell anybody, will yer?"

Valerie shook her head. "No, whatever it is, I'll keep it to myself. I think of lot of Mrs Jinks."

"Well, young Ben had a win on the pools. He bought his dad's house and his cobbler's shop. Quite a lot it was, by all accounts. Connie told her dad and he told me. They looked after 'im well in 'is ode age. Used to live by me mother."

Valerie was astonished. All the time Connie had been paying the rent for Grace and had never said anything. But, thinking about it, she didn't blame them for not broadcasting it around. People could be very jealous.

Ronnie ignored Valerie and she him. He was secretly annoyed about her being there and asked Mary how it had happened.

She said, "Our Ronnie, don't be so nasty. The invite was for Norman to bring a friend. I day know 'e was seein' Valerie Potts, did I? Anyway 'er 'asn't done anything ter make me dislike 'er. I don't really know 'er."

Ronnie scowled. "Well, I do. I've never got it out of my head that 'er could've put that necklace in my pocket."

Mary was shocked. "Never! I don't think so, our Ronnie. 'Er seems a nice, quiet gel ter me."

Ronnie bent his head to his sister. "Sly, more like," he said.

At eight-thirty, although the reception was going with a swing, Valerie told Norman that she would have to be going. She also explained that she had to call in at Janice's to get changed. Norman was flabbergasted.

"Are you sure you need to go so early?" he said.

"Oh, yes. I've really enjoyed myself. Your family are very nice." She said her goodbyes, shook Desmond by the hand and kissed Mary on the cheek.

"Going so soon, Valerie?" she asked.

"Yes, I have to get back, Mary. Thank you for a lovely time and all the best to you."

She made her exit. Norman walked with her down the road. They arranged to meet next afternoon, in the park, over 'the bonk'.

Janice was agog to hear about the wedding. Stan was in the bathroom, getting ready to go out and Paul was at a friend's house.

Valerie described the dresses and the reception as she got changed.

"You'll never guess who the bride was," she said.

"Who?"

Valerie grimaced. "Mary Edwards."

Janice thought for a moment, then the penny dropped. "Nellie Edwards's daughter?"

"Yes."

Janice's eyes widened. "Oh, Valerie. I think you're gonna 'ave ter come clean. Grace's sure ter find out now. You needn't tell her about the weddin' but you'll 'ave ter tell 'er about Norman. If 'er finds out from somebody else all 'ell'll be let loose."

Valerie scrubbed at her lips to remove the lipstick.

"Why don't me mom want me to have a boyfriend, Aunty? I'm seventeen now and old enough."

Janice knew only too well but she said, "P'raps when 'er sees what a nice chap Norman is, 'er'll change 'er mind."

"I don't know how to introduce them."

Janice wagged her head. "Sleep on it, wench. Summat'll turn up."

When Valerie had gone, Stan came in, buttoning his clean shirt.

"'Ow did 'er gerron at the weddin', Jan?"

"'Er enjoyed it. Now, Stan, don't you go tellin' anybody about it."

"Course I won't. Be nice ter see that wench break away from 'er mother, though."

Janice shook her head. "I can't see it happening somehow."

Stan grinned. "Miracles do 'appen sometimes," he said.

On Norman's return, Desmond had a pint waiting for him. Ronnie came across to have a word.

"How're you enjoying the wedding then, Ronnie?" Norman asked.

"Great, just great. Our Mary looks 'appy. Your Desmond's an okay bloke."

Norman smiled. "Yes, yes, he is. How are you getting on with the butcherin'?"

Ronnie said, "Oh, great. I'm surprised really, I never thought I'd tek to it but I 'ave. I'd like me own shop one day."

Norman frowned. "Would yer? That'd be a responsibility. I'd rather work with somebody else's money meself. I'm startin' a new course at college, bookkeepin' and accountancy. It's every Friday, seven till nine."

Ronnie pondered. "I could do wi' a course like that. I was alright with maths at school but it's another matter when you've got yer own business."

Norman slapped him on the shoulder. "You'me determined to get that shop then?"

"Oh, ar," said Ronnie.

"Why don't you enrol wi' me then, for the bookkeepin'? We could go together."

Ronnie felt flattered to be asked. "Righto, Norman. I think I will. By the way, 'ow long you bin going out wi' Valerie Potts?"

Norman took a swig of his beer. "Not long. Anyway, we ain't gooin out as such. We're just friends really."

Ronnie was relieved to hear it. Norman turned to watch the dancers and his gaze rested on Patty.

"What a pretty little thing," he thought.

Chapter Thirteen

Baby Mark was coming on beautifully. Valerie was quite besotted with him. Even Grace and Renee had a soft spot for the little lad.

At four months he had filled out and smiled beatifically at his admirers. Flo broached the subject of his christening with Fred.

"Who do yer want fer our Mark's godparents then, Fred?"

He scratched his head. "I 'adn't really thought about it," he said. "I s'pose me brothers'll stand fer 'im."

Flo buttered a slice of bread meticulously. "I've had a thought, Fred."

"That's a first."

"Cheeky sod. No, I had a thought about Mark's godmother."

"Goo on, spit it out. I 'spect you want that grumpy sister o' yourn."

Flo placed the piece on the plate alongside his bacon and egg. "I reckon our Valerie'd like to do it. 'Er idolises our Mark."

Fred dipped his piece in his egg yolk. "Well, ar reckon everybody as sis 'im does that. Yo know, I reckon yo'me right. 'Er doe seem a bad sort o' wench, in spite of 'avin' your Grace fer 'er mother."

Flo bridled. "Doe talk like that. I know there's no love lost atween you an' my famly, Fred, but your lot aye that special."

He held up his hands. "Okay, okay, 'ave it yer own road. Valerie it is."

He wiped his bread round his plate, pushed it into his mouth, picked up his paper and prepared to pick a winner.

*　　　　*　　　　*

Josie was going out with Freda and Joe's son, Roger. They were regular picture goers. She had taken him home to meet her parents. Steve had already made his acquaintance when he had been to the shop for a haircut. He thought him a nice enough lad. Josie had tried to talk Valerie into going out in a foursome with them. She had been doubtful.

"I don't know, Jose. We don't see each other much these days, what with me at college on a Monday and Thursday and Norman there on a Friday. As you know, me mom likes me to go to the pictures with her on a Saturday as a rule and, in the week, she likes me in by nine o'clock."

Josie secretly thought that Grace was very unfair and selfish. One evening, when setting her mother's hair, she spoke about it.

"Well," Vera said, "Grace Shaw was allus a funny wench. We used ter go to the youth club at the Methodist Church over the bonk. Grace was there. 'Er 'ad a crush on the young minister. 'Er day think as we knowed but everybody did. Everywhere 'e was, Grace was. All the services, all the fêtes. He was nice to all on us but Grace must've took it to 'eart. Anyroad, he went away fer three months, back 'ome, an' when he come back he brought his fiancée with 'im. Broke 'er 'eart it did. Never went to chapel again. Then when nobody thought 'er'd ever gerra chap, 'er met Herbert Potts. 'E day 'ave a chance. Grace 'ad med up 'er mind ter 'ave 'im and 'er did. His mom warnt very 'appy about it but I reckon as 'er mother must've clapped 'er 'ands. I doe think as Grace was very easy ter live with. Flo's a moaner but 'er never was as bad as Grace. Valerie seems a nice enough gel. 'Er sticks to her mother. I 'ope as 'er doe spoil 'er life for 'er."

Josie agreed. She was a bit young to understand how a possessive mother could manipulate, so it was hard to see Valerie's point of view at times.

Although she was quite fond of Roger, Josie still, deep down, had a niggling regard for Ronnie Edwards but the necklace incident had left her with doubts. Anyway, Roger was okay. He was a laugh and they enjoyed their outings.

* * *

Sunday was dull but dry. Flo was trying to soothe a fretful baby. Fred was grumbling about the crying.

"Why's 'e so cranky, blartin' all the while? Can't I 'ave a bit o' peace on a Sunday after bein' at werk all the wik?"

Flo glared at him. "You miserable bugger. Can't you see the poor little soul's teethin? I can't 'elp 'im cryin'. Do you think as 'e's the only babby what cries?"

She was near to tears herself. The house was a tip, her hair was a mess, her husband was a selfish pig. She felt like walking out and taking baby Mark with her. Flo knew there would be little welcome at Renee's, whose philosophy was 'you mek yer bed so yer lie on it'. So she had nowhere to go.

Just as she was contemplating pouring the dirty washing-up water over Fred's head, a knock came on the back door. It was Grace with Valerie. Flo didn't know whether to be glad or sorry to see them.

"Aye up, our Flo. Are you alright?" said Grace over Mark's screams.

"No, I aye. Our Mark's teethin' and I can't gerranythin done."

Valerie held out her arms for her cousin. He was hot, flushed and fretful.

"Shall I take him to the park for you, Aunty?"

Flo was grateful. "Oh, would yer? Fresh air'd do him good. That might settle him off. I'd be able ter get 'is lordship's dinner and get me nappies done."

Valerie put Mark in the pram. He was indignant about being put down. She rocked it vigorously and he quietened.

"See you in about an hour, Aunty."

Grace sat at the kitchen table. "Shall I peel yer taters, Flo?"

"Oh, would yer? The meat's done an' I shelled the peas last night."

Grace set to with a will. Fred came in from the lavatory, paper in hand. He grimaced behind Grace's back.

"'Allo, Grace. Don't usually see you on a Sunday. I expect young Valerie's gone to the park, 'as 'er?" He grinned at Flo. "I reckon there's a chap around somewhere."

He went into the front room to study form. Grace froze. She wouldn't encourage him by asking what he meant.

The potatoes peeled and her cup of tea finished, she said, "I think I'll tek meself off for a walk, Flo, while you and Fred 'as yer dinners."

Flo was relieved to hear it. "Okay, Grace, thanks. See yer later."

The park was ten minutes' walk away. Grace was a slow walker so it took her about fifteen. There were children on the slides and roundabouts, lads were playing football, prams were being pushed, couples were strolling, some with arms around each other. She walked round the outer path, but there was no sight of Valerie and Mark. She sat on a bench for a while.

Deciding to make a move, she suddenly spotted Valerie pushing the pram. Walking alongside her, wheeling his bicycle, was a tall, young man. She stood stock still, knowing that she could not be seen. She was unsure what to do. Valerie bent over the pram to soothe the baby. The young man took out a bag of sweets and offered it to Valerie. She smiled up at him. Grace felt a stab of panic. She was going to lose her daughter, she was going to end up on her own. How could she bear it? She sank onto a bench screened by a shrub. She sat for a while to compose herself, then walked slowly back.

Flo had a cup of tea ready when Grace returned.

"That was quick, our Grace. Did yer see Valerie on yer travels?"

Grace shook her head. “No, I didn’t go very far, just inside the park and back. I think I’ll carry on home, Flo. Tell our Valerie I’ve got one of me ’eads comin’ on.”

Flo pushed the nappies down in the bucket. “Are you sure, Grace? Valerie’ll be upset if yer goo without ’er.”

“Just tell her I’ll see her at home.”

Grace wanted to face Valerie on her own territory and she needed to think up a strategy.

On her return, Valerie was surprised, and shocked, to find that her mother had gone. She had a sense of foreboding. Could Grace have found out about Norman? No, not since they had arrived at Flo’s, surely? Flo didn’t know about him . . . did she?

“Was Mom alright, Aunty Flo? She wasn’t upset or anything?”

Flo picked Mark up from the pram.

Stroking his head, she said, “’E’s a lot cooler now. Oh, no, I don’t think so. ’Er just popped out for a walk while we was ’avin’ our dinners, then she come back an’ said ’er was gooin. One of ’er bad ’eads comin’ on an’ ’er wanted to get ’ome.”

Valerie’s heart plummeted into her shoes. She stood as if rooted to the spot. She realised that her mother could have seen her with Norman.

“I’ll carry on then, Aunty. I hope Mark soon gets over his teething. I’ll try to pop again soon.”

“What a nice gel,” thought Flo. “Our Grace don’t know ’ow lucky ’er is ter ’ave such a good daughter.”

As Valerie walked home, she plotted what she could say to Grace. She dreaded facing her. She dreaded the ‘silent treatment’ more than a row. In fact, she wished her mother would just row for once.

Grace sat with the cat on her lap. The room was silent, apart from the purring and the tick of the clock. She did not look up from the Sunday paper she was reading as Valerie came through the back door.

Valerie hung up her jacket on the door and put the kettle on. She washed the dinner things which had been left soaking in the bowl. Still no word from Grace.

Valerie decided to keep quiet and let her mother have first say. She could see the signs of a big sulk. She made sandwiches for tea and did extra for the Monday's lunch packs. She then poured two cups of tea. She decided to take her tea up to her room. Taking her jacket from the back door and, picking up her cup and saucer from the table, she crossed to the stairs door. As she reached it, Grace spoke.

"I s'pose everybody knows about your romance except me?"

Valerie turned. "What did you say, Mother?"

Grace bridled. "I said I expect every Tom, Dick and Harry knows about your romance except me. I bet I'm the laughing stock of the place."

Valerie just stood there, cup and saucer in hand.

"Well?" Grace said. "Does everybody know?"

Valerie turned. "There is no romance, Mother. Norman's just a friend from work, that's all. Just a friend."

Grace snorted. "He looked more than a friend ter me."

Valerie saw red. She plonked her cup of tea on the table. The tea splashed onto the cloth.

"Mother, I'm a grown woman. If I want a friend, I shall have a friend. I can run my life myself."

Grace reared up. "It's a good job I'm a thinkin' as your dad ain't here to hear you talkin' ter me like that. Run yer life? Run yer life? You ain't got the sense you was born with. Lads am only after one thing. Before you know where you are you'me in a load o' trouble."

Valerie glared at her mother. "I don't know what you mean but I can tell you I shan't get into any trouble. All I've done is gone for a walk and Norman happened to be in the park."

Grace sat down and turned her back on her daughter. "You'll be the talk o' the place," she said.

Valerie went upstairs to her room, sat on her bed and cried.

* * *

Ronnie had continued to visit Herbie Forrester and Lily. He called at least twice a week for a chat and fuss of the old horse. When he started at the butcher's he took over the delivery of Herbie's supplies. He was a great one for his fry-ups. When the weather was suitable, Herbie would walk Lily to the fields and tether her to graze. He rarely took the cart out now, being content to potter round the yard and the stable and to call into the Haymaker's for his lunchtime pint.

Herbie's meat order was the same each week. On a Monday, Ronnie would bring a meat pie and chitterlings. Wednesday was the bacon, black pudding and sausage order. On Friday he would take a nice piece of steak or a couple of chops.

Herbie frequented the Salt's fish and chip shop regularly. Vera always had a kind word for him.

"How's Lily, Herb?" she would ask.

"'Er's alright, a bit stiff in the joints, like me," he would say and do his phlegmy laugh.

No one had been further than the kitchen at Herbie's. As no work had been done to the house, everyone presumed it was the same as when his mother had been alive.

Nellie did his bits of washing, which Ronnie collected each Monday, hanging the bags on the handlebars of his bike. The curtains were never washed. They looked really bad. Nellie told Ronnie to ask Herbie if she should fetch him some new nets from the market.

"I doe think I want new nets at my age," he told him. "Tell yer mom thanks but they'll see me out, I reckon."

"Okay, Herbie. Do you want me ter fetch Lily for yer?"

"Ar, yo can if you like. I'll just 'ave a walk up to Turdy's fer me bit o' grocery, then I think as I'll 'ave a rest. I seem ter be dead tired lately."

"You'me gerrin old, mate, that's all." Ronnie put his hand on the old man's bony shoulder. "Doe get overdoin' it." He waved and went off down the entry, whistling.

* * *

Drainpipe trousers were all the rage. *Rock Around the Clock* was on at the pictures. Grace tutted in disgust. She would have to miss her cinema outing. Valerie had been asked to go with Josie and Roger. She had not spoken about it to Norman. She stood ironing her blouse for work next day.

"I don't s'pose you're going to *Rock Around the Clock* then, Mom?" she asked.

Grace gave a derisive laugh. "Course not. As if I'd want ter be with all them saft kids."

Valerie concentrated on her ironing. "I wouldn't mind going, just to see what all the fuss is about. Josie's going."

"I should think 'er wants summat ter do. Anyroad, 'er'll never get in. They say as they queue fer miles, saft devils."

Valerie finished her blouse. "Well, I thought I might go with her to keep her company."

Grace was flabbergasted. Valerie was, in a quiet way, standing up to her.

"Well, suit yerself. Don't come cryin' ter me if there's trouble. I don't s'pose as I can stop yer. I'll just have ter stop in on me own again."

The compressing of her mother's lips told Valerie that she was in for a hard time if she did go.

* * *

After closing time at three o'clock on Saturday, Ronnie called in at the barber's to get his hair done. Roger was a dab hand at doing the D.A. and Ronnie rather fancied himself with one. They played together for the early closing football team and a match had been arranged for the following Thursday. They chatted animatedly about the team and football in general.

The interconnecting door to the staff room was open and, through the mirror, Ronnie could see Josie washing up at the sink. She had a trim figure and her hair was stylishly arranged. He thought she was lovely. She waved to Roger through the doorway and Ronnie felt a stab of jealousy, which quite surprised him.

He hadn't contacted Josie since the sheep's eye prank. He knew that he wouldn't stand much of a chance with her since the necklace incident but he still admired her from afar. Josie must have told Maureen that he was in the shop. She came to the doorway.

"Hiya, Ronnie. Don't let that Roger loose on yer 'air, you'll end up lookin' a right freak."

Roger turned round. "I don't think so, not like your customers. You can always pick out the Maureen Edwards' disasters."

Maureen laughed. "Cheeky sod," she said. Returning to the ladies' section, she said, "Our Ronnie'll look a right Ted when Roger's finished with 'im. Our dad won't be very pleased. I reckon Prince'll nip the seat out of his pants when 'e gets 'ome."

Josie laughed and shrugged. She wasn't really interested in Ronnie Edwards . . . was she?

Valerie decided not to go to *Rock Around the Clock.* She stayed in, listening to the radio and practising her shorthand.

After an hour, she told Grace, who was watching TV, "I'm just popping round to see Mr and Mrs Jinks. I haven't seen them properly for ages, have you?"

Grace shook her head. "No, I haven't. I wonder if they're alright."

"I'll just be about half an hour then.

Valerie knocked on the Jinks' back door. Ben answered. She could hear the TV on in the front room.

"Come in, Valerie. I ain't seen yer for a bit. Are you alright, an' yer mom?"

"Yes, thanks, Ben. We must be like ships passing in the night, not to have seen each other. How are your mom and dad?"

Ben put the kettle on. "Well, mom's got a bad back. She's bin in bed for a wik. The doctor says as all 'er can do is rest. Me dad an' me 'ave bin managin'. I've bin closing the shop early to get home."

Valerie was sympathetic. "Oh, Ben, you should have said. We could have done some washing for you or something."

"Well, we wouldn't say no to the washing, Valerie. As I'm in the town I bring the shopping and me dad does the cookin' but, as you know, the washin' soon piles up."

"Parcel it up," she told him. "I'm not going out. I'll soon put it through the washer for you."

Ben beamed. He liked Valerie. He was a painfully shy man but had known her all her life, so he was at ease with her.

Connie was glad to see her and bemoaned her enforced idleness.

Valerie told her, "Can't be helped, Mrs J. You'll soon be better if you rest."

After she had gone, Connie said to Ben, "What a lovely young woman our Valerie's turned out to be."

"Yes, 'er 'as, Mom," he said.

On her return, Grace spotted the bundle of washing.

"What's that you've got there, Valerie?"

"Oh, just a bit of washing. Mrs Jinks is laid up. They're managing but for the washing."

Grace sniffed. "Well," she said, "I s'pose it won't hurt fer us to do a bit o' washin' for 'em. They've 'elped us enough when your dad was bad an' now we've got the washer. Best thing we've ever 'ad. Only twenty more weeks ter pay on it. Be glad when it's paid for."

"Payments always seem to take a long while but there's many a thing we wouldn't be able to have without them," Valerie said.

Norman was getting tired of his sporadic relationship with Valerie. He saw her at work occasionally. She did not encourage him to chat in reception, she wanted to keep on the right side of Mrs Shelley. They would sometimes see a film or go for a walk in the park, still arranged surreptitiously, so that Grace wouldn't get wind of it. All in all, things were not progressing.

Desmond and Mary were renting Aggie Potts's old house. Norman would call to see them on a Friday night now that his night class was finished and they would have a game of cards and a fish supper.

Often he would see Patty and Christine there and Maureen and Chas. They were lively evenings and, gradually, Norman felt more at ease with the sisters. His shyness began to subside and, also, his skin was becoming clearer, thus adding to his confidence.

He especially liked Patty. He admired her courage and the way she dealt with her deafness. She was always cheerful and a pretty girl.

Ronnie would sometimes turn up with a pork pie to share or some ham off the bone for sandwiches. He regaled them with stories and jokes and talked of the motorbike he would own one day. He had his leg pulled. They said his only girlfriend was Lily because she was a captive admirer. He would just laugh. He knew who he liked.

Valerie was progressing at work. She had passed her shorthand and typing exams and was now assisting Mrs Shelley to take dictation from the directors of the company. Mrs Shelley knew that she was not a distraction and was thoroughly reliable.

The night classes had now finished. Valerie missed them as a reason to get out of the house, therefore she decided that when the new term started, she would enrol on a bookkeeping course on a Wednesday evening. She had ambition to do well. She aimed to climb the ladder. She still desired to be rich.

During her lunch hour, once a week, she managed to call to see Janice. She could only stay for half an hour to natter and eat her sandwiches.

Janice asked her, "Do you still see Norman now, Valerie?"

"Only once or twice a week. You know how me mom feels about it."

"Have you taken him home yet, duck?"

"No, Aunty. She might be rude to him and I couldn't bear that. It's best left as it is."

Janice nodded. "Yes, p'raps but it seems such a shame. She'll come round one day, you'll see."

Valerie sighed. She very much doubted it.

Grace didn't manage to get to Renee's every Friday. She now had to get the bus as far as it would go as her feet were getting worse. She still enjoyed seeing Peggy and Flo would bring Mark to see her mother and Arthur. Arthur doted on the little lad. He was saving a pound a week for him in a tin upstairs.

Valerie was going to Josie's to have her hair trimmed.

Grace grumbled to Renee and Flo, "I don't see her half the time. If 'er ain't at night class 'er's at Josie's or out wi' that chap."

Flo passed the biscuits. "'Er ain't out every night, Grace an' 'er's got ter 'ave a bit o' life of her own, ain't 'er?"

Grace fumed. "I don't stop 'er, I'm sure. Many's the 'our I spend on me own. I don't grumble."

"Oh, no?" thought Flo. She said, "I bet you see more of your Valerie than I do of Fred. 'E's never in. When 'e's on mornin's 'e spends the afternoons at the 'lotment, when 'e's on afternoons 'e's in bed half the mornin' then at the 'lotment. Friday nights, when 'e can, 'e guz ter the dogs wi' Arthur. Satday and Sundy 'e's at the pub of a dinner time an' snoring all afternoon. I may as well be single. I spend nearly all me life on me own."

Renee pursed her lips. "Thay'me all the saerm, them Burkes."

Flo bridled. "Well, Mother, me dad was no saint. I remember the rows 'ere when I was a kid."

Renee sniffed. "You shouldn't speak ill of o' the dead." And she shuffled to the front door to pay the milkman.

Valerie found the bookkeeping course fascinating. She enjoyed working with figures. "One day," she thought, "I shall be keeping books for my own business."

The other girls on the course were very friendly. They were a jolly group. They would invite her to go with them for a drink after class but she would have to refuse. They thought she must be meeting a boyfriend and ragged her about it mildly. She didn't admit to them that she had to get home at a reasonable time to appease her mother.

Work was going well. She was, as usual, punctual and keen to do her work efficiently. Social life consisted of a, now weekly, outing with Norman, lunchtime visits to Janice, occasional Sunday visits to Flo and Mark and the odd evening at Josie's.

Josie talked of her relationship with Roger and their outings but insisted that it was nothing serious.

Valerie had to make sure she spent enough evenings in with Grace. She helped to clean through the house to keep her mother sweet. Shopping on a Saturday together was essential for domestic harmony, Grace stopping to chat occasionally, proud of the fact that she had her daughter with her. She felt like saying, "Look how my daughter's sticking to me." Little did she know what people were saying about her being a possessive mother and spoiling her daughter's life.

Norman's mother was becoming concerned about his relationship with Valerie. She had tentatively spoken about it to Mary, who was tactful but honest.

"Well," she said, "her mom's very possessive of her, by all accounts. Her dad died when she was about nine, you see. Josie, her friend, works with our Maureen. She's a good mate to 'er. Josie wants her to be more modern but it's her mother. 'Er likes to dictate what Valerie wears and what 'er does."

Mrs Proudfoot got the picture. She'd come across situations like this before. She realised her son was on a hiding to nothing if he got seriously involved with Valerie Potts. What could she do about it? Nothing. She would just have to sit back and wait for it to fizzle out.

John Edwards was smitten. He had never bothered much about girls. He had seen enough of his sisters. He just enjoyed life, going out on his motorbike and meeting his mates for a drink. He earned good money now and Nellie encouraged him to save. She had his board money every Friday and he gave her his savings which she took to Turdy Tunley's to deposit in his Post Office savings account.

Mary and Desmond had asked him to come to the Friday evening sessions but he hadn't bothered. He liked to play snooker.

One Friday, at a loose end, he decided to call on them for a change.

Desmond’s sister, Rose, was there. She was twenty, an attractive girl with a sharp wit. He had forgotten that he had met her at the wedding. Over a game of Ludo, and a fish supper, they fell in love.

Chapter Fourteen

Ronnie knocked on Herbie's back door. He could hear Lily shuffling around in her stable. It was half past five and he was on his way home from work. He had Herbie's fry-up ingredients. He banged harder, still no reply. He grew concerned. Going round to the Haymaker's he knocked on the window of the snug.

Bertie Rounds looked over the frosted glass and mouthed, "What do yer want?"

"A werd wiv yer," mouthed Ronnie.

Bert reluctantly came to the door. He had been having a pre-opening time nap.

"'Ave yer sin Herbie terday?"

"No. No, can't say as I 'ave."

"Thanks," said Ronnie. He went back to Herbie's and tried to look through the kitchen window. He couldn't see a thing. He wondered what to do, who to turn to. Jack Pearce came to mind. He doubted if he would be at his mother's at this time of day, so decided to go to his own house.

Jack lived in Bakers Fold in a police house. Ronnie got on his bike and rode round there. His wife answered the door, apron on, just about to dish up the evening meal. They were going out.

"Jack," she called. "Somebody here for you." She whispered to him, "Don't be long." She wasn't overjoyed about him being bothered on his day off.

Jack came to the door in his shirt sleeves. "Well, if it ain't young Ronnie. What can I do for yer?"

"Mr Pearce, it's Herbie. He ain't answering the door. He must be in, Lily's locked in the stable. Can you come?"

"Course I can. Be just a mo. I'll meet you round there."

On his way back, Ronnie called in Turdy Tunley's. He hadn't seen Herbie either. Jack reached the house just after Ronnie. He hammered on the door. Still no reply.

"'Ave they sin 'im at the Haymaker's?"

"No. I checked that, and Turdy's."

"Well," said Jack, "we'd better break in." Without more ado the door was forced. No sight of Herbie.

Jack looked in the front room. "He ain't in there. I doubt he could gerrin there, it's full o' boxes."

They went upstairs. The front bedroom was packed to the ceiling with boxes. Herbie was in bed in the back bedroom. He lay very still. Jack looked at him, then turned to Ronnie.

"Sorry, mate. I think 'e's gone."

Ronnie was stunned. "Gone?" he said. "Gone? 'E can't be gone."

Jack put his hand on the lad's shoulder. "I'm pretty sure 'e 'as, son. Can you pop round for the doctor?"

Ronnie staggered a little. "Yes, I'd better."

He sped on his bike to the doctor's house. His wife answered the door. Ronnie blurted out his message.

"Doctor will be with you shortly," she said.

On his journey back to Herbie's, Ronnie's main thoughts were of Lily. What was going to happen to her now? He could have wept.

Jack was in the kitchen. He asked, "Does Herbie have any relations, Ron?"

"Not that I know of, Mr Pearce. We never saw anybody an' 'e never mentioned anybody either."

"Right" said Jack, "we'll 'ave ter look inter things then."

At the back of the clock, on the mantelpiece, were sundry bills and envelopes. One, a long parchment type one, was sealed. It was addressed to 'Whoever it May Concern'. When the doctor had certified Herbie's death, Jack gave it to him to open.

"I don't know what this is, Doctor, but I think we should open it."

"Yes," said Doctor Briars. "It may give us a clue to the whereabouts of his relatives."

He read the missive inside. It was crudely written but made sense. Doctor Briars looked at Jack.

"Who is Ronnie Edwards?" he asked.

"That's me," said Ronnie. "Why?" He was puzzled. Why had Herbie mentioned him?

"Well, it seems that Mr Forrester wants Ronnie Edwards to go to Foster and Shaw's solicitors if anything happens to him, which, of course, it has."

Ronnie was astounded. He had never seen a solicitor in his life. He doubted if there was anything for Herbie to leave, then he thought, "Lily, he wants me to look after Lily."

Doctor Briars said, "Anyway, my lad, we will get the undertakers to come to see to Mr Forrester and tomorrow you should go to the solicitor."

Ronnie was speechless, then he thought of Lily. "I'll see to Lily, then I'll have ter pop ter me gaffer's to ask for a mornin' off termorrer."

Jack nodded. "I'll ask Ben Jinks to change the back door lock. You can settle up with him later. I'll stop till the undertaker comes."

Ronnie stammered, "Yes. Yes, thanks, Mr Pearce. I'd better see to Lily. I'll let you know how I get on."

"Cheerio, son." Jack was sorry the poor lad had had to see Herbie.

Ronnie took the stable key from the hook at the back of the door and went into see to Lily. She snickered and nuzzled him. She had kicked her water bucket over and needed some hay in her net.

Ronnie automatically fed and watered her. He patted her neck.

"Sorry, gel. Yer boss's gone but I'll look after yer." He felt like crying. "See yer termorrer."

He took his leave and set off for home, passing the undertakers' van on the way. He called at Bob's to ask for the morning off. He could see that the lad was upset and was sorry to hear about Herbie. Another old character gone.

Nellie, also, was upset to hear of Herbie's death. He was a loner but well liked. She knew Ronnie was fond of the old chap and how much he loved old Lily. She wondered what would happen now. On hearing that Ronnie had to see the solicitor, she decided to accompany him.

"Do yer want me to come with yer, Ron? Two 'eads is better than one."

"Would yer, Mom? I'll go early ter see to Lily and tek 'er to the field. 'Er's bin penned up an' needs a break."

"Okay, son, you'll feel better if you do that."

Ronnie barely slept. He would miss Herbie and the fate of Lily played on his mind. Next morning, Lily settled in the field and Ronnie smartly dressed, he and Nellie made their way to the solicitor's office in the main town.

The building was rather imposing. Apart from the local Town Hall, they had never been in such a posh place. They felt somewhat overawed.

A receptionist sat behind a large, carved desk. She looked up as they entered.

"Good morning," she said. "How can I help you?"

Ronnie answered, "We're here to see Mr Forrester's solicitor. He died yesterday and there was a note asking me to come here. I have a letter."

"You don't have an appointment then?"

Ronnie's heart sank. "No. I didn't realise I needed one. The doctor and the police told me to come. I have a letter."

The receptionist scrutinised it. "Wait here a moment. I will see if Mr Foster has time to see you. Please take a seat."

Ronnie and Nellie sat, nervously waiting. The room was panelled and impressive, smelling of beeswax polish. Nellie pitied the cleaning lady. They both wished they were somewhere else.

The girl came back. “You are in luck. Mr Foster can see you. Go on through.” And she held the door to the inner office open.

Mr Foster was quite young. An affable man, he stood and stretched his hand out to Ronnie and then Nellie.

Waving to the chairs in front of his desk, he said, “Now then, there is a note from Mr Forrester. Well, Mr Forrester did make a will, which we have here. He saw my partner some months ago. I shall get it from the safe.

Nellie looked at her son. She was feeling confused, still not comfortable that they should be here at all. He was obviously feeling the same. They sat in silence waiting for Mr Foster to return.

The solicitor opened a long envelope and produced a typewritten sheet of paper. He scrutinised it for a few seconds then passed it over for Ronnie to read.

“I can’t concentrate, Mr Foster. Can you read it for me, please?” the young man said.

“Of course. Well, it seems that Mr Forrester wanted you to be his main beneficiary. Apart from one or two small legacies to Mr and Mrs Rounds at the Haymaker’s Arms, the rest of his estate is bequeathed to you.”

Ronnie was numb, like a statue, unable to move. Nellie sat there in the same state. All that was heard was the ticking of the large clock and the typewriter in the next room.

Mr Foster picked up the phone. “Miss Perks, will you please bring in a tray of tea?” He turned to Ronnie. “This seems to be a shock to you, Mr Edwards.”

Ronnie shook himself, mentally. “It certainly is. I dain’t think Herbie thought that much of me. I only helped him a bit with Lily and did a bit o’ shoppin’ for him. I liked him. I’ll miss him a lot.” Despite himself, tears filled his eyes.

The tea appeared. Ronnie felt a little bit better after a couple of swallows and Mr Foster felt that he could continue.

"Mr Forrester has left his house to you, also Lily and her stabling, which was his property. He asks that you care for her for her lifetime."

Ronnie gasped. "I didn't know as Herbie owned his own 'ouse. I thought as it was rented an' o' course I'll look after Lily. I think the world of her, I do."

Mr Foster smiled and continued. "There will also be a sum of money to come to you when all the funeral expenses have been met and, of course, the other small legacies."

Ronnie gasped again. "I don't expect any money. Hasn't Herbie got any relations, Mr Foster?"

"No. He had a sister but she died some years ago and, of course, his mother died some fifteen years ago, as you may know." He sipped his tea. "Come to see me next Monday, by then I will have arranged the funeral. You may have the keys to the house and the yard, so that you can look after the horse. I would leave the house as it is until after the funeral."

Ronnie said, "Oh, I will. It would be disrespectful to mess with Herbie's things before he's even buried. And, Mr Foster, will you make sure that the undertaker knows that he has to have the best, and a good headstone as well?"

Mr Foster smiled. "Of course I will. By the way, there was a little note on the will. Mr Forrester did not want you to spend any of the money on a motorcycle."

Ronnie gave a short laugh. "I'm not surprised. When I used ter tell him I wanted one he used to call them death traps."

The solicitor stood up and shook their hands. They emerged, blinking, into the sunlight of the street. They still could not comprehend what had happened.

On their return home, they saw Jack's car outside Annie's. Ronnie knocked on the back door. Jack answered.

"How did yer get on then, lad?" he asked.

"Well, Mr Pearce, I still can't believe it. The solicitor says Herbie's left me his 'ouse an' I've ter look after Lily."

Jack smiled. "'E knew what 'e was doin'. 'E knew you loved that old 'oss. I'd better give you the new keys. Ben Jinks changed the lock and you've got the stable key already."

Ronnie took the keys. "Thanks, Mr Pearce. It ain't all sunk in yet. The solicitor's arrangin' the funeral. We'll all know on Monday."

Jack said, "Let me know when it is. I'd like to be there if I can."

Annie came through from the front room. "An' me. I liked old Herbie. Went ter school wi' 'im, I did."

Ronnie turned at the door. "Do you think as you could keep it to yourselves about the will? I don't want all and sundry ter know me business."

Annie smiled and agreed. "I understand, lad. We won't tell a soul. It doe do fer the nosey buggers round 'ere ter know yer business. We'll keep shtum, doe you worry."

"Thanks," said Ronnie. "I'll let yer know about the funeral."

Ronnie apologised to Bob for having to ask for more time off. He arranged to see the solicitor at four-thirty, after closing, on the Monday, then had to ask for the following Friday afternoon for the funeral.

"Doe yo worry, lad. Yo've never 'ad any time off since yer started. The missis'll come in Friday an' give us 'and. It'll mek a change for 'er. Er says as 'er misses the shop sometimes. The kids can goo ter the nan's from school."

Ronnie had explained to Bob that he would be looking after Lily but had not gone into detail about the rest of the legacy.

It was rather a quiet funeral. Ronnie, Nellie, Wilf, Jack and Annie Pearce and Mr and Mrs Rounds from the Haymaker's attended. They all went back to the pub for a drink and a sandwich. They would all miss the old chap.

Two weeks later, a letter came for Ronnie. It was a statement from the solicitor and a cheque for the balance of the estate for nineteen hundred pounds. The letter enclosed stated that the deeds to the house were being transferred to Ronnie and, when he had time, he could call in to discuss the safekeeping of them. Ronnie had opened the letter after finishing work for the day and seeing to Lily.

Again, he was in shock. He hadn't been able to face going into the house to start sorting it out. Nellie ministered to him. She understood how he must feel. He needed to gather his thoughts and to make plans.

A family meeting was held at 34 Ingram Terrace. It was decided that Herbie's house would be cleared. Maureen and Chas were to be married and would rent it from Ronnie. The rent money would pay for Lily's keep and for veterinary bills. She was getting very old now. It was also decided that the ownership of the house would be kept as a family secret, as would be the money which Ronnie had inherited.

The story which was agreed upon was that Maureen and Chas would be renting the stable as well as the house. They would assist Ronnie with Lily's care. As many other landlords were installing bathrooms into their properties, it would not appear strange that the Foundry Street house was being updated.

Four weeks after the funeral, the wedding was arranged for ten weeks' time and the family girded their loins to clean and decorate.

Ronnie gave all his siblings, and Nellie and Wilf, a hundred pounds. They all protested but he wanted to share his good fortune. After the bathroom had been installed and the decorating done, the rest of the money was put into a savings account for the day when he was to have his own shop.

On a wet Saturday, armed with cleaning and decorating materials, Nellie and Mary made a start. Maureen and Ronnie would arrive after work with John and Chas to do the heavy lifting.

The front room was full of boxes, as was the front bedroom. Nellie decided to clear out the back bedroom first. The bed was stripped. It was quite clean, due to Nellie's ministrations and they dragged the mattress outside. The pillows were put into the dustbin, together with curtains, towels and tea towels.

"We could do wi' harnessing Lily to the cart," joked Nellie.

They emptied drawers and wardrobes, parcelling up the clothes for the Sally Army. Some of the clothing was out of the Ark. They even came across some of old Mrs Forrester's things, which Herbie must have been loathe to part with.

Nellie stood, hands on hips, to survey the room.

"It all needs decoratin', top ter bottom," she said. "We'll all 'ave ter muck in, won't we?"

When the menfolk arrived they decided to work from the top to the bottom of the house. Firstly, they would have to tidy out the stable to accommodate all the boxes. These would have to be explored at a later date.

Lily had never had so much fuss for ages, or seen so much activity. She stood in the yard, watching them move boxes, an old mangle, poss tubs, old harnesses and various bits which Ronnie was loathe to throw away. It took two weekends to clear the house. Some of the old furniture was usable, so they decided to clean it up and keep it. Some was burned with other rubbish in the yard.

The following week, the builder began work on the bathroom. A doorway was knocked through to the old brewhouse and a sizeable amenity was made.

Weekends and evenings were spent decorating. All the family set to with a will, scraping ancient paper from the walls and burning off paint. A new fireplace was fitted in the front room and the old black grate was removed from the kitchen.

Maureen wanted a new electric cooker and a modern sink unit was purchased.

Nellie and Wilf bought them a Formica table and four chairs in bright yellow for a wedding present. Reg proved to be a dab hand at paperhanging and Betty made a bedspread and matching curtains as her wedding gift. It took all of the ten weeks to get the house ready. Maureen and Chas wanted a small wedding at the Chapel in the High Street. Betty made the wedding dress and Patty, the only bridesmaid, made her own.

Nellie couldn't believe how quickly her children were leaving home. Ivy was physically fit but getting more confused. She spent most of her time at Nellie's, sitting in the corner, letting life go on around her. Christine was living at the hospital, so there was only Maureen sleeping round at Ivy's and soon she would be gone to Foundry Street. Annie came up trumps, as usual.

"'Ow are yer gonna cope wi' Ivy when there's nobody ter sleep round there, Nellie?"

"I don't know, really. I've still got the lads at home. Patty can't sleep round there. 'Er wouldn't hear if her nan got up in the night. Me mom sleeps like a log but there's just the off chance that 'er might get up."

"Well, if you'me stuck, I'll tek tern about wi' yer when Maureen's married. Just till yer get summat sorted."

Nellie hugged her. "Annie, you're a brick. I daresay summat'll turn up. I've got that much on me mind at the minute, I can't see me way ter sort me mother out. I don't know what I'd a done if you adn't sat wi' 'er while we was sortin' the house out."

"Doe worry, love. You've bin a good daughter ter Ivy an' I know 'er wore allus fair wi' yer." Annie turned at the door. "The 'ouse'll be quieter fer you when Maureen's married. They all fly the nest, doe they?"

Nellie sighed. "Yes, Annie, they do."

After doing up the house, Ronnie decided to open a building society account to save for his own shop. He still enjoyed working with Bob and Andy but realised that he would get restless and need to move on. He still had a lot to learn about ordering the best meat and how to prepare it and decided to absorb as much knowledge as he could.

Chas took Lily out to the fields on good mornings and Ronnie would go on his bike after work to fetch her back to the stable. He still managed to play for the early closing team on a Thursday afternoon. He was becoming a fit, muscular, young man, finding it easy to lift the carcasses delivered to the shop. Sometimes he jogged to the field, going the long way round. He resisted his desire to buy a motorcycle, remembering Herbie's request and decided to have driving lessons and, eventually, to buy himself a van.

Chapter Fifteen

Grace and Valerie were going shopping. They made their usual visit to Thelma in the cake shop. She was busy, as she usually was on a Saturday. Across the road, the doors to the little Methodist Chapel were open. In between customers, Thelma and Stella craned their necks to see who was getting married.

Stella turned to Grace. "Lovely day for it."

Grace looked puzzled.

"For the wedding," said Stella.

"Oh. Oh, yes. Can I have my usual bread and two Chelsea buns, please."

Thelma leaned across the counter. "How are you, Valerie?" she asked.

"Alright, thanks, Aunty Thelma."

"See yer both." Thelma turned to the next customers.

As they left the shop, Valerie saw the bride and groom emerge from the chapel. She recognised Maureen Edwards, then all the laughing, chattering families spilled out onto the small, paved area. She spotted Ronnie and his parents and the bridesmaid, Patty. Then it was as if a knife had gone into her heart. Norman had come out. He bent his head towards Patty and was speaking slowly to her so that she could read his lips. Patty was concentrating on his mouth. There was an intimacy about them which tore at Valerie's senses. A searing feeling of jealousy almost made her reel.

Grace had spotted him. "Our Valerie, is that the chap you've bin gooin out with?"

Valerie managed to pull herself together to deal with her mother.

"I told you, Mother, he's just a friend."

Grace sniffed. "Well, he seems more than friendly with that one as 'e's talkin' to." And she turned to go into the fruit shop.

Valerie followed her. Usually they bought fruit and veg from the market stall but Grace had fallen out with them over a bad orange. Jenny was serving. She was surprised to see Valerie.

"'Allo, Val. 'Ow are things at the factory? Everybody still slaving away? I'm glad I'm out of it. Suits me 'ere, workin' with me dad, he ain't a slave driver." She turned and patted her father on his baldy head. Valerie just managed to nod and smile weakly.

The wedding party was dispersing. Valerie had to return Josie's wave, then looked away from them, hurrying along, causing Grace to quicken her step.

Inside the shop, Mr Dawes turned from the till and looked at Jenny.

"Is that the wench what had your job when you left, Jen?"

She nodded. "And she's welcome to it an' all."

He scratched his head thoughtfully. "An' did yer say as 'er used to do the post?"

"Yes, her an' Vernon between them while I was away."

Her father stood for a moment, then lifted his hands.

"Say no more," he said.

Jenny was shocked. "You don't think Valerie had anythin' ter do wi' me sick note goin' missing, do yer, Dad?"

"How can I say, Jen? But 'er got the job when you left."

She nodded. He polished an apple.

"Anyroad, Jen, just remember, in this life what guz round, comes round."

Valerie had spent a miserable weekend. Grace, mercifully, had not mentioned Norman again. Although Valerie had been unsure about her feelings for him in the past, she now realised how fond she had become of him and how nice it had been to think that she had a boyfriend, like other girls. She cried into her pillow at night and agonised on how she would cope with seeing him at work. She decided that, come what may, if he still wanted to, she would see him more often and risk upsetting her mother. Anything would be better than the anguish of losing him.

Grace was secretly glad that Norman had appeared to like the bridesmaid at the wedding. She resented anyone other than herself having Valerie's attention, even to the extent of feeling a stab of jealousy when she showed affection to young Mark or enjoyed an evening with Josie. She was not aware that Valerie visited Janice weekly. That was still a well-kept secret.

Norman was still friendly when he saw Valerie. He waved as they passed each other on their way in to the office block. However, he didn't ask her out again. She suffered agonies but never let anyone know how she felt, carrying on as normal at work and at home.

One day she confided in Janice, who said, "Tek no notice, gel. Plenty more fish in the sea. I was let down bad before I met yer Uncle Stan but now I'm glad. 'E turned out ter be a right drinker. Keeps 'is wife short o' money, by all accounts. 'E done me a favour finishin' wi' me. Our Stan'll skin an' 'eel 'im. Mind you, I was upset at the time."

Valerie always felt a little better for seeing Janice. She could never have confided in Flo, who was having problems of her own with Fred and Josie didn't seem the right person to confide in somehow. She threw herself even more into her work and her studies, determined, more than ever, to get on.

* * *

Wilf was having a nice, long soak in the bath. Ivy was round in her own house with Annie to keep her company. They had a TV set round there, which they enjoyed, with a shared bottle of stout. John was in the backyard, tinkering with his motorbike, Patty had gone over to the field with Ronnie to fetch Lily and to take Prince for a run. Nellie was in the front room taking advantage of the quiet to add up her housekeeping in her notebook. She heard John come into the kitchen to wash the oil from his hands.

She called, "Use the old towel, John. You never get all the black off."

He stood in the doorway, drying his hands. He stared down at the towel, looked up at his mother, then down again. He seemed to want to say something, then changed his mind and turned to go back into the kitchen.

Nellie called, "John." No answer. "John, come back in here a minute."

He appeared in the doorway. Nellie looked at him over her glasses.

"What's up, son? Come on, spit it out."

He raised his head and looked at her. "Can't hide anything from you, Mom."

"No, you can't," she agreed. "Come on, spit it out."

"I don't know how to spit it out, Mother. P'raps I'd be better talkin' to me dad."

Nellie took off her glasses and looked at him thoughtfully.

"John, you know you can allus come to me wi' yer troubles but, if this time, you want ter goo ter yer dad, that's okay."

"Yes, I know I can allus come to yer but this is really bad."

Nellie flinched. "'Ave yer got money troubles, son? Are yer bad or something?"

John hung his head. "It's Rose, Mom."

Nellie bridled. "'As 'er got somebody else? 'As 'er finished with yer?"

John stood up and turned away. He could not face his mother.

"No, nothin' like that." He took a deep breath. "'Er thinks 'er's pregnant."

Nellie was speechless. Nothing had ever happened in her family, or Wilf's, like that. She felt angry. She opened her mouth to berate her son, then she thought better of it. The chap was so upset and he needed her help.

"Well," she said, "I can't say as I'm 'appy about that, John."

He hung his head. "No, Mom. I dain't expect yer ter be."

She went on, "At your age I would 'ave thought you'd of 'ad a bit more about yer than ter goo an' get a gel inter trouble."

"I know, Mom, but it just happened."

They sat in silence for a minute, then Nellie asked, "Has Rose told her mom yet?"

"No. We thought we'd better do it together. Just need to pick the right time."

Nellie asked, "Do you want me to go an' see Nora for yer?"

John looked at her. She must be the best mother in the world. What would any of them have done without her? He put his head in his hands and broke down and cried. Wilf stood in the doorway, hair on end from his bath.

"What's up?" he asked, alarmed to see his grown son weeping.

Nellie got up and took her husband's arm. "Come on, Wilf, get yer coat on. We'll go an' meet our Patty." She whispered to him, "I'll tell yer on the way."

*　　　　*　　　　*

Josie put the finishing touches to Mrs Partridge's hair. She held a mirror so that the back could be seen.

"Very nice, thanks, Josie." She dug in her bag and gave the girl a shilling tip. Josie smiled at her through the mirror.

"Ta, Mrs P. See you next week."

"Ar, all being well," Mrs Partridge answered.

The shop was busy. Freda and Joe were away on a long-awaited holiday. The girls and Roger were working flat out. Brenda, the new junior, was a slow worker. She was a pretty girl who professed to be keen to learn the job but she wanted to run before she could walk and resented having to do the menial tasks.

Josie commented to Maureen, "Like gettin' blood out of a stone ter get a cuppa tea out of that one."

Maureen agreed. "Thinks she's too high an' mighty. We all had to do it when we started. Look at the state of these mirrers. I can't stand it. I'll have to give 'em a polish. Me mother's comin' in this afternoon an' she's sure ter notice the state thay'me in."

"Where's she gone now?" asked Josie.

"Probly havin' a sly smoke in the lav," Maureen answered. "I'll have a look."

She moved towards the staff room to fetch a cloth for the mirrors. As she opened the door, she heard a muffled giggle. She froze with shock. There was Roger with his arms round Brenda, kissing her passionately.

Nellie came on time for her appointment. She was quieter than usual but Maureen didn't notice. She was still upset about seeing Roger and Brenda in that clinch. She thought, "What if Josie had opened that door? What a shock it would've been for her."

Nellie thought, "How am I going to cope with facing Nora about Rose? I could do with talking it over with somebody, but who?" She spent her time waiting for her perm to take reading magazines and made a point of turning to the problem page in case she could come across any tips.

Maureen tried to keep a semblance of normality. She was agonising over whether to tell Josie or to confront Roger about his behaviour and make him tell her himself.

Both women carried on looking normal but deep in their own thoughts.

On return from Tresses, Nellie went round to Ivy's to let Annie know that she was back.

"Ooh, yer 'air does look nice, Nellie. Is it your Maureen what does it?"

"That's right, Annie. 'Er perms it at the shop an', as yer know, sets it at 'ome."

Annie scratched between her dinky curlers. "Ter be 'onest wi' you, I get fed up on windin' me 'air inter these things day after day. I might 'ave meself a perm. What do yer think?"

Nellie was pleased. She had been thinking of a gift for Annie from Ivy to thank her for all the time she spent with her and for all the help she was willing to give.

"Shall we 'ave a cuppa before yer go round 'ome, Nell?"

Nellie nodded. Would Annie be able to give a wise old ear to her predicament? She decided to confide in her old friend. After all, she had kept Ronnie's windfall a close secret.

The tea poured, she said, "Annie, if I ask you something, well, tell you really, can you keep it a secret?"

Annie laughed. "'Aven't I allus kept yer secrets, Nellie?"

Nellie agreed. "Well, yes, you have. I have a problem and I'm not sure how to handle it."

"Goo on," said Annie. So Nellie told her all about the unwanted pregnancy. Annie sipped her tea, thoughtfully.

"Well," she said, "this is how I see it. Your John thinks the werld o' that Rose. 'Er's a nice gel, not some Tatta who'd goo wi' anybody. Thay'me a genuine couple. They ain't the fust ter get copped and they won't be the last. Thay'me both old enough ter get married." She slid a sly look at Nellie. "I'm tellin' you this, Nellie, I was 'avin' our Jack when I got married. 'E was one o' them premature babbies wot weighed seven an' half pounds. If I'd gone full term wi' 'im, he'd a bin a whopper!"

Nellie had to smile. She thought no less of her old friend for disclosing this information.

"How did you tell yer mom and dad, Annie?"

"Well, it wore easy. We 'ad ter goo tergether an' face 'em. I couldn't a done it on me own."

Nellie frowned. "I thought I might go an' see Nora first."

Annie shook her head. "You can't keep carryin' 'em around all their lives, Nellie. Some things they 'ave ter do themselves. Goo wi' 'em, by all means, but let them do the talkin'."

Nellie realised that Annie was right. She resolved to have another talk with John when he came home from work.

Josie had cleared up her trolley and they had all helped Brenda to clear up the shop.

Maureen told the girl, "We are only helping you this once, Brenda. You'll have ter get yer finger out in future and clean up as you go along, otherwise I'll have to have a word with Freda when she gets back."

Brenda just shrugged. She was getting tired of the job anyway.

Roger poked his head round the door and called to Josie, "Jose, I'll have to clean up at home before me mom and dad get back so I shan't be comin' round tonight, okay?"

Josie was relieved to hear it. She was tired and they would be going out on Saturday anyway.

"Okay, Rog, see you tomorrow."

Maureen cringed. She wondered if he was seeing Brenda and wished that she could get to know somehow.

Ronnie had taken Lily to the farrier after early closing. He enjoyed his visits to the genial Ken Turner. The smithy smelled of burnt hoof and horse sweat, manna to Ronnie's soul. Lily stood patiently while Ken trimmed her hooves. He liked young Ronnie and they would reminisce about Herbie.

"'E done the right thing leaving Lily ter you," Ken said. "He knowed as you'd look after 'er. Gerrin ter be an old wench now, aye 'er?"

Ronnie nodded. "Ar, gerrin long in the teeth. The vet says as 'er aye too bad fer 'er age. I keep 'er warm in the winter wi' plenty o' good bran mash an' cool in the summer. When it's hot we don't tek 'er to the fields, 'er stops at 'ome."

Ken lifted Lily's big hoof. "'Er's better looked after than a good many. Mind you, there aye so many now, more lorries on the roads. I sid your Barry drivin' the coal lorry last wik. 'Ow's 'e gerrin on?"

"Oh, 'e's allus loved humpin' coal 'as our Barry. God knows why. Me mother gus on about the dirt but 'e seems to thrive on it."

Ken pared away at Lily's hoof. "'Ow's the butcherin' these days?"

"Great. We do lots o' things now. Bob's missis meks the best pork pies in the Midlands. 'Ave yer tried one?"

"Course I 'ave. The missis brings one every wik. I like me grub."

Ronnie could see that he did.

Ken went on, "That young Roger from the barber's is courtin', aye 'e?"

Ronnie's heart sank. "I think so," he said.

"I sid 'im wi' a little blonde wench. 'Er day look above sixteen. 'E must like 'em young, eh?" and he laughed.

Ronnie was puzzled. Josie had lovely, dark hair, unless she had done what a lot of young girls had done lately and bleached it. But she didn't look sixteen.

Nellie had prepared the evening meal. Ronnie came in, smelling of horse. She wrinkled her nose.

"Our Ronnie, you can get that smell off yer before you sit at the table."

"Okay, Mom, keep yer 'air on. Giz a chance ter get through the door. I've bin ter Ken's ter get Lily seen to."

"'Ow is 'e?"

Ronnie smiled. "Fine, you know Ken, never any different. Full o' gossip. Nothing gets past Ken." He went into the bathroom. "Chuck me a clean shirt an' trousers, Mom," he called.

Nellie sighed. She thought how suddenly her family had grown up and she still had the problem of John and Rose to face.

Ronnie emerged smelling sweeter. He had put on some Old Spice aftershave he had found in the bathroom cabinet.

Nellie asked, "Are yer goin' out tonight, son?"

He shook his head. "Why, Mom?"

"Well, if me and yer dad 'ave to pop out, can yer keep an eye on yer Gran? I doe want ter ask Annie ter do it, 'er's bin wi' 'er all mornin' while I got me 'air permed."

He said good-naturedly, "Course I will. I want ter watch telly tonight, anyroad. Goin' anywhere nice?"

That was a joke, Nellie thought. "No," she said. "We might pop to Nora and Jack's but we don't know yet."

Ronnie didn't query the reason for the visit. He was already ensconced in the sports pages of the evening paper.

Wilf and John came in together, having travelled home on the motorbike. They took turns to use the bathroom, thankful to be there before Barry, who always took ages. Nellie managed to have a word with John in the front room.

She told him, "I didn't go to see Nora. I thought I'd wait to see if you wanted me to."

John passed his hand over his eyes. "I think me and Rose should see them together first, Mom."

"Yes, that's what I thought, son. Me and yer dad can come down later, then we can get things sorted, if yer like."

John sighed. "Would yer, Mom? I'm dreadin' it. I never slept last night an' I doe know how I got through terday."

"Well, son, come and have yer tea. Our Patty's here now an' we can all sit down together for a change."

Nora Proudfoot was a tiny, bird-like woman. She attended the local Wesley Chapel. Her sons, Norman and Desmond, were no trouble to her. Rose was a nice enough girl but, at times, did tend to answer back. However, Nora thought her daughter hardworking and respectable, not like those flighty pieces that Nora was inclined to look down on.

Nora's house was spotless. She seemed to have a second religion – cleaning – fanatically doing her chores and cleaning whether it needed it or not. She had the sort of home which intimidated visitors, who sat on the edge of their seats and dreaded dropping a crumb. Not that she would have minded, she quite cheerfully would have cleaned it up after them. She was a good neighbour who would do anyone a favour. Her family accepted her for what she was, knowing that her strict, chapel upbringing was at the root of her personality.

Jack Proudfoot worked at the Town Hall. He was always clean and smartly turned out. He was pleased that Desmond and Norman had office jobs. He was a bit disappointed that his daughter-in-law, Mary, still worked at the factory but she was a quiet enough girl. The apple of his eye, Rose, worked at the Home and Colonial in the High Street. Although he loved his daughter deeply, he left her upbringing mainly to Nora. He was, like most men of his generation, out of his depth with the female of the species.

Nora had finished washing up and was putting the crockery away neatly in the cupboard. Jack was reading the paper, Rose was upstairs getting ready to go out. Norman had gone straight to college from work.

Nora turned to him. "Our Rose is quiet today. I wonder what's upset her? Hardly touched her meal."

Jack looked at her over the paper. "P'raps summat at work. She'll tell us all in good time. P'raps you've imagined it." The ways of women were anathema to Jack.

Nora folded the tablecloth. "I worry over our Norman."

Jack sighed and lowered the paper.

Nora continued, "I don't think he'll get anywhere with that Valerie Potts. Mrs Tranter at Chapel told me that her mother's so possessive with her that any man what takes her on will have to take her mother on an' all."

Jack folded the paper, resignedly. "Don't worry about summat as might never 'appen. Our Norman's no fool. I'll mention it, if yer like, but I don't want to push 'im towards her by interfering."

Nora put her hand on his arm. "Would you, Jack? Don't say as I've said anything, will you."

"No but I mightn't say anythin' meself yet. Is our Rose going out?"

"Yes, I think John's coming for her around half past seven. I think that's what her muttered when I asked 'er as 'er was going upstairs."

John called for Rose, as arranged, at seven-thirty. She was looking out for him from the front room window. Calling a quick "Tarra" to her parents, she ran out of the house to meet him.

Nora, sitting darning socks, said to Jack, "Our Rose seemed anxious to get out of the house, don't you think?"

Jack was half asleep. "Yes," he mumbled.

Within half an hour, Rose and John were back. They came in at the back door and were whispering in the kitchen.

Nora put down her darning and called, "Are you two going to stop in there or are you coming in here? While you're in there, Rose, pop the kettle on."

Rose appeared in the doorway. She had been crying and her face was streaked with tears. Nora jumped up and went to her.

Leading her into the room, she said, "Whatever's the matter? Are you bad? Have you had an accident on that bike?"

Rose sobbed. “No, Mom,” she said.

John followed them into the room. “Sit down, Mrs Proudfoot. We want to talk to you.”

Jack stirred and woke up.

“’Allo, you two,” he said, then, realising that his daughter was weeping, he woke up properly, with a start. “What’s up?” he asked, feeling helpless.

His wife shook her head at him. “She’ll tell us in a minute, Jack. Let her calm down a bit.”

John stood in front of the couple. “Mrs Proudfoot, I wish that I didn’t ’ave ter tell yer this but I’ve got to.”

“What? Tell us what, John?”

John looked at Rose. “Well, the fact is, and you’ll hate me for it. The fact is, Rose is pregnant.”

Nora sat with her mouth open. Jack put his hand to his face.

He said, “Are you standing there, in my house, tellin’ me that you’ve gone an’ got me daughter into trouble?” He went red in the face.

John took a step backwards. “I’m sorry, Mr Proudfoot, really I am.”

Nora sprang up from the sofa. “Sorry? Sorry? It’s too late ter be sorry. You’ve only been going out for a few months. Rose is only nineteen, you’re much older than she is. How could you, John?” She began to cry, her howls joining in with her daughter’s.

Jack stood, glaring at John, who wished the floor would open up and swallow him.

“We want to get married, Mr Proudfoot. Me mom and dad are coming at half past eight to talk to you about it.”

Jack grimaced. “So, they know, do they? They know what their son’s been up to? A fine carry on, I must say.”

John could have cried himself.

At eight-thirty, sharp, Nellie and Wilf arrived. They were very anxious about the situation and weren't sure what they were going to say.

Jack opened the front door to them. "Come on in," he said. "A tidy mess we've got on our hands, I must say." He gestured to them to take a seat.

Rose and Nora had stopped crying and were dabbing at their eyes. John sat, white-faced, wanting to escape but couldn't. Nellie's heart went out to him.

Rose said to her mother, "Shall me and John make a cup of tea, Mom?" Nora nodded.

Jack said, "I'll find the whisky out. I think we all need a drop."

Nora turned to Nellie. "I never thought a daughter of mine would end up in this mess."

Nellie answered, "It's not the end of the world. We can all rally round and help them."

Nora shook her head. "It's the disgrace of it all."

Nellie saw red but curbed her tongue. Slowly and deliberately she said, "I had my youngest daughter in hospital for ten weeks with meningitis. 'Er nearly died, it left 'er deaf. That, ter me, is a werse thing than being told that a new life is on the way."

Nora cringed. "It's what people will say that worries me."

Nellie retorted, "Bugger what people say! If they get married quick, it's nothing ter do wi' them, anyroad. There's nobody in this town's whiter than white. If you mix wi' folk what cant about other people's business then more fool you."

Nora was annoyed. "I'm no fool, Mrs Edwards. It's a big shock for my only daughter to have to get married. I wanted her to have a white wedding with all the trimmings and now it looks as if she'll have to go to the registry office."

Nellie accepted her cup of tea from John. Jack poured a drop of whisky into it.

"Here, Mrs Edwards, I think we all need a drop o' this."

His wife put her hand over her cup. "Come on, Nora, shift yer hand. A drop in a crisis won't hurt yer." So she allowed him to put some into her tea.

John sat with his arm round Rose. Nellie said, "I hope you don't mind, Mrs Proudfoot, but Wilf and me had a talk before we came. Did you know that we live next door to me mother? The girls, all except Patty, have lived there 'til they got married. Now Annie, her friend, and me take turns sleeping round there in case she wakes in the night, which up ter yet 'er never 'as. Anyroad, we thought that Rose and John could lodge there after they was married."

John could have kissed his mother. He had a dread that they would end up living with Nora and Jack.

Nora considered this, then said, "I never thought me daughter would end up as nursemaid to an old woman."

Wilf put his hand on Nellie's arm to restrain her. She breathed deeply.

"No way will anyone be a nursemaid to my mother, Mrs Proudfoot. I look after her myself and have done for many years. I felt it was the only Christian thing to do."

Nora flushed. The barb had gone home. "I was only thinking of my daughter. I meant no offence."

Nellie, gingerly, put down her cup and saucer on to the coffee table.

"Well, Wilf, I think it's time ter go. P'raps you'll keep us in the picture what's happenin', Rose? We'll be there to 'elp yer, yer only 'ave ter ask." She picked up her handbag. "Cheerio, Mrs Proudfoot, Mr Proudfoot." And, going to the front door, they took their leave.

Outside, she walked a few yards down the street and then she let loose.

"That bloody hypocrite of a woman! S'posed ter be a church-goin' Christian? The roof ought ter drop in on 'er next time 'er sets foot in theer."

Wilf held her arm. “Now, Nellie, that ain’t like you. Doe let ’er get to yer. It’s up ter John an’ Rose if they want ter lodge at Ivy’s. They’ll think on it an’ let us know.”

Nellie nodded her head. “Do you know, Wilf, for once I could do wi’ a drink.”

He laughed and they made their way to the Haymaker’s.

John came home from the Proudfoot’s at eleven o’clock. Nellie and Wilf heard him put his motorbike in the back yard. They waited for him to enter the kitchen. Taking off his crash helmet, he faced his parents.

“Hello, son,” said Nellie. “Do you need a bit o’ supper?”

“No, thanks, Mom. Rose and me went fer a walk and we had some chips. We’ve had a talk an’ we’ve decided what we’me gonna do.”

They waited for him to continue.

“We’ve decided we’ll lodge wi’ Gran ’til we can get a place of our own. We’ll go on the council list. Thay’me building some maisonettes an’ when we’ve got the little ’un, we should get some more points. Rose knows Gran’s no trouble an’ you look after her. ’Er mom’s got the wrong end o’ the stick.”

Wilf said, “You can say that again.”

Nellie smiled. “I know ’er ’ad. Anyroad, we’d better think about the weddin’.”

John said, “Yes. We’re gonna get a special licence an’ do it quick as we can. I’ve got some savings, thanks to you an’ our Ronnie, so we’ll be okay. We’re goin’ on Saturday to order a new bed an’ get some bedclothes. Rose’ll ’ave ter come an’ look round next door, if you don’t mind, Mom?”

“Not at all,” said Nellie. “’Er’ll find it clean but not spit an’ polish like ’ome.”

John laughed, dryly. “We don’t want it that clean, we want ter live in it, not look at it.”

Wilf yawned. "Come on, let's hit the sack. Ronnie ain't in yet so leave the catch off the door. Annie's next door wi' Ivy. We'll tell 'er about it in the mornin'. Let's 'ope we all gerra good night's sleep."

Ronnie let himself in the back door. He was dead tired after a hard day at work and then mucking out the stable. He had decided to pop into The Star for a couple of pints and a game of darts and had then stood chinwagging with his mates.

Nellie had left out bread and cheese, as usual concerned that her family were fed, so he did himself a sandwich and took it into the front room where the fire was still smouldering. Feeling cold, he moved the guard to feel the heat. He scanned the sports page while he munched his bread and cheese. His head began to nod. Before he could fight it off, he had fallen asleep in the chair.

Patty was in a deep sleep. She was tired and had gone to bed early. Prince was asleep on his blanket. He grunted and moved restlessly, then something assailed his nose. What was that smell? He got up and pawed at Patty. She turned over grumbling at him. He persisted.

"What's up, Prince? Do yer want ter go out? You went before we come to bed at half past nine, surely you don't want to go again?"

She pulled on her dressing gown, resignedly, and opened her door. She then smelled something odd.

Banging on her parents' door, she called, "Dad, come quick. Summat's on fire."

Wilf sprang out of bed. He was not very pleased.

"Bloody 'ell. I thought we was goin' ter 'ave a decent sleep fer once."

Nellie sat up, bleary-eyed. "What's up?"

"Doe know. I'm gooin down."

The smell was coming from the front room. As Wilf pushed open the door, he was greeted by the sight of Ronnie sprawled out on the chair, feet in the hearth and crepe-soled shoes smouldering nicely.

"Ronnie," Wilf shouted, "wake up, yer on fire."

Ronnie stirred. Wilf ran to the kitchen, grabbed the kettle, which had been filled ready for the morning, and poured it over Ronnie's feet.

Patty stood there, her hand to her mouth. When she saw that her brother wasn't hurt, she laughed until she cried.

Wilf couldn't see the joke for a minute, then he joined in her laughter. Nellie was just relieved that no harm was done. John slept through the whole drama.

Chapter Sixteen

It had been a hectic day at the butcher's shop. The next day, Christmas Eve, Tess and Bob had last-minute shopping to do. Bob planned to finish early, leaving Andy and Ronnie to clear up and serve the stragglers.

All the poultry and pork pies were labelled, ready to be collected. Ronnie had gone to see to Lily and Andy was in the flat, having his evening meal. They were coming back to the shop to tidy up and allow Bob to go home.

Alone in the shop, Bob put the catch on the front door. He went into the back to cut up some joints of beef. He telephoned Tess to tell her of his intentions. She wasn't too pleased.

"Can't you go a bit earlier tomorrow mornin' instead o' stoppin' tonight, Bob? Your tea's nearly ready, it's half past six now."

Bob commiserated with her. "I've still got to come early, love. You know what it's like. I want to close reasonable tomorrow so's we can fetch the bikes for the kiddies an' hide 'em while they're round at yer mother's. I can leave the lads ter clear up. They'll be back soon, anyway."

She sighed. "You'me right, o' course. I'll put yer meal on a low light. Try not to be too long."

Bob switched on the wireless. He was looking forward to Christmas with his children. They were so excited. He sharpened his knife, ready to cut into the beef. He knew some of his customers would want beef, rather than poultry, for Christmas dinner. He worked away, steadily. He was tired. He jabbed the knife into the meat, pulling it hard towards him. He felt a sharp pain. Looking down, he saw, with horror, that he had stabbed himself in the groin. Blood spurted from the wound. He grabbed some cloths and tried to stem the flow. Struggling to the phone, he dialled 999 and asked for an ambulance. He felt dizzy. He dialled his home number. Tess answered.

He tried to tell her, "I've stabbed. . ." Then he passed out.

Tess, on the other end of the line, was puzzled and alarmed. She could only think her husband was in trouble. She tried his number, it was engaged. Turning off the stove and running round next door, she asked Mrs Bladon to keep an eye on the children, who were watching TV. Then she got on her bicycle and rode round to the shop.

The ambulance men were trying the door. One of them went up to the flat.

"'Ave yer got a key ter the shop, mate? Somebody's hurt an' we can't get in."

Andy said, "No, you'll have ter force the door. It must be me gaffer. 'E was in the shop on his own."

He shouted, "Mandy, I'm goin' down ter the shop. I think Bob's hurt hisself."

Between them, they broke open the door. Bob was lying in a pool of his own blood. He looked ghastly and hardly seemed to breathe. The medics pressed on the cloths and added more pads to help to stem the flow. As Tess reached the shop, they were carrying her husband into the ambulance.

She dropped her bike onto the pavement. "Oh, my God, what's happened?" she cried.

"Are you is wife, love?"

She nodded, hand across her mouth. She was in shock.

"Get in, quick. We gotta go."

The bell rang all the way to the hospital. The ambulance men ministered to Bob. Tess could only sit there, frozen, in shock.

Bob was rushed straight to the operating theatre. Tess sat, waiting. Someone gave her a cup of tea, which she held, untouched, in her cold hands. Her mother arrived after being summoned by Mrs Bladon. Tess put her head onto her lap and sobbed.

A sister came to see them. "Your husband is on the ward now, Mrs Haynes. He is very ill, he had lost a lot of blood. You can sit with him, if you would like to."

Tess and her mother went behind the screens. Bob lay in the bed, his face as white as the sheets. Blood dripped into him from a transfusion. Tess kissed him and held his hand. At midnight, he quietly passed away.

Ronnie and Andy worked to clean up the shop. They were quiet and upset. Andy phoned Ben Jinks to replace the broken lock on the door. They had phoned the hospital to be told that Bob was in theatre.

Andy said to Ronnie, "All the times he's warned us about them knives an' told us we must never tek risks like that wi' em an' now 'e's done the very same thing isself. He musta bin tired or rushin' ter do the job. Anyroad, we shan't mek that mistek, poor sod. You might as well carry on 'ome now. We've got early start in the mornin'. I'll be 'ere, if there's any news, I'll let yer know."

Ronnie agreed to be there by five so that they could carry on where Bob had left off. They felt bereft, not knowing how badly he was hurt. Andy had a good idea it was extremely serious. He saw how much blood Bob had lost and how much time it had taken to clear it up. They had both baulked at the task but managed to cope.

The news of Bob's death hit them both very hard. His father-in-law had called at one in the morning to see Andy to break the news. Mandy had a hard task to comfort her husband. He felt disinclined to open the shop but she reasoned with him and he realised the day had to be got through somehow.

Ronnie, on reaching work next morning, had the bad news waiting for him. He functioned like a robot. The customers were all subdued. The Christmas spirit was gone.

Tess Haynes was devastated by the death of her husband. She vowed that she wouldn't set foot in the shop ever again and could not even pass it. Her father-in-law was keeping an eye on things. Andy and Ronnie were coping well between them. They needed a lad to help out. Andy mentioned it to a solemn Mr Haynes, who came daily to cash up and take the money to the bank.

"We'me managin' up ter now, Mr Haynes," he said. "We order the same as before from the wholesaler an' tek it in terns to do the cooked meats on a Monday. We could do wi' somebody ter do the pies and we need a lad."

Mr Haynes nodded. "Just put all the paperwork together each day. I'll tek it when I cash up. Tess can't face anythin' ter do wi' the shop. That's understandable, I find it 'ard meself."

Andy was concerned about the future of the business and said so to Ronnie.

"I'm wonderin' if Mrs Haynes will want ter keep the shop, Ron."

Ronnie answered, "I thought the same meself. Poor woman, I expect this place is the last of her worries."

Andy then dropped a bombshell. "We've bin thinkin' about emigratin' Ron, tekkin one o' them assisted passages. Me mate went last year."

Ronnie was taken aback. "Was yer, And? Where was yer thinkin' o' gooin?"

"Well," he answered, "we fancied Australia. Mandy's mom'll goo mad but we've got ter think of our future. We'me savin' 'ard. About a year, I'd think, or six months if we can."

Ronnie's world seemed to be crumbling around him. Bob, now Andy. He realised he may have to look for another job.

Chapter Seventeen

It took a while but Nellie persuaded Annie to have her hair permed. They sat with Ivy, having a cup of tea.

Nellie said, "Annie, go on, let our Maureen do yer a perm. You see 'ow nice 'er does mine an' Ivy's. It won't cost yer a bean. We only bought yer tea towels fer Christmas 'cos you'me allus sayin' as yer doe need nothing, so we'd like ter treat yer."

Annie was touched. "You doe 'ave ter do that, Nellie. I doe mind 'elpin' out. Think about it, I aye got much ter do all day. When I sleep 'ere Ivy never wakens till seven an' I'm allus up at six an' dressed by half past. I don't believe in stinkin' in me nightie, so it's no problem ter me at all."

Nellie persisted. "The hairdresser's quiet now Christmas an' New Year are over. They've got plenty o' time. I tell yer what, our Maureen'll book yer in."

Annie smiled. "Alright, gel, thank yer."

Tuesday was pensioners' day at Tresses. Maureen was looking forward to doing Annie's hair. She arrived at eleven and Brenda showed her to a chair by a washbasin.

Annie said, "Doe get me collar wet, will yer? I doe want a stiff neck."

Brenda grimaced behind her back. Maureen saw red. She was getting heartily sick of that little madam. She was still unsure what to do about telling Josie about the kissing incident.

Annie enjoyed every minute of the pampering. She met one of her old friends and their chatter brought smiles to everyone's faces. When she was all done and dusted, Maureen showed her the result.

"Ooh, it's just lovely, cocka. I'll 'ave to start wearin' me teeth again, even if they kill me. You never know, I might get meself a bloke now."

She left tips for all the girls and shuffled off, hairnet in hand, to show Nellie her new, glamorous image.

Nellie agreed with her old friend that the hairdo had been worthwhile.

"You woe 'ave ter keep puttin' yer dinkies in now, Annie, an' you'me just right fer our John's weddin' next wik. There's only a few on us goin'. As yer know, it's a register job."

Annie nodded. "Doe matter as long as thay'me 'appy and the babby's 'ealthy. I was sayin' ter me friend, worra shaerm about Bobby Haynes, aye it? All the years 'e's bin butcherin' an' fer that ter 'appen."

Nellie agreed. "I worry about our Ronnie. Wilf day want him in the steelwerks, thought as it was safer in the butcher's. Anyroad, it's med 'im extra careful wi' them knives. It's a shaerm fer 'is famly. Them three little 'uns'll miss their dad. Nice bloke an' all, 'e was."

"Is Tessy Haynes keeping the shop on?" asked Annie.

"We doe know. 'Er's still too shocked ter think straight. Bob's dad's runnin' it, as far as the bookkeepin' an' orders. Andy an' Ronnie seem ter be doin' alright. Anyroad, we can only wait an' see."

"Ar," said Annie. "Your Ronnie'll miss it if he 'as ter leave."

Mr Haynes came into the shop. "Andy, Ronnie, I'd like you to meet Paul, he's your new assistant."

They shook the lad by the hand.

Andy said, "We'll keep yer busy. 'Ave you done butcherin' before?"

"No," said Paul. "I started at the steelworks but I day like it, too dirty and noisy."

"Well," said Ronnie, "you won't be idle here. It's a busy shop. Do yer play any footie?"

Paul brightened. "Yeah, I love a game."

“Well, we’ll ’ave ter ’ave a butcher’s at yer, see if yer any good. Gerrit? Butcher’s at yer?” And they all laughed. “We could do wi’ some talent in the early closing team.”

Andy fixed Paul up with some whites and a striped apron.

“Now then, lad,” he said, “these knives are super sharp. You must treat ’em wi’ respect. Only wash one at a time, don’t risk one bein’ left in the bottom o’ the bowl. Yer ’eard what ’appened to our gaffer?”

“Yes,” said Paul. “I’ll be careful, don’t you worry.”

His first day went quickly. He discovered that he quite liked the work and realised that there was a lot to learn. Andy and Ronnie were hard workers and were good with the customers. Paul came in for a lot of good-natured teasing.

At the end of the day, as they were leaving the shop, Ronnie called to Paul as he was about to cycle off, “By the way, Paul, what’s yer surname.”

Paul cheerfully called out, “Potts, Paul Potts.”

It was the day of Rose and John’s wedding. Snow was on the ground, so everyone had to dress warmly.

Nora Proudfoot inspected her family and was satisfied that they would all pass muster. She had been concerned that Desmond’s shirt would fail the whiteness test, worried that Mary could not wash as clean as herself but, with Nellie’s training, her fears were unfounded.

She grumbled to Jack, “I just wish we could’ve had a white wedding. It’s what I’ve always dreamed of for our Rose.”

Jack gave his shoes a final rub. “Yes, so you’ve told me a dozen times, Nora. You’ll just ’ave ter forget it and make the best of today. It’s too late for that, anyway.”

Rose came downstairs. She had a smart, Chanel-style suit on, in blue, to match the colour of her eyes. It had a fur collar and a neat little hat to match. She was determined to enjoy her day.

Jack wiped a tear from his eye. "You look real pretty, love. It only seems yesterday, you was a little 'un an' now you'me gonna be a married woman."

She kissed him and said, "Oh, Dad, come on now, the taxis are here. Off we go."

She picked up her gloves and her envelope handbag and they set off for the registry office.

Nellie and Wilf weren't looking forward to facing the Proudfoots, neither was John, but they intended, like Rose, to make the best of the occasion.

The ceremony seemed very short. Nora felt that it was too brief to be binding but had to accept it. She sighed, resignedly.

The reception was at The Haymaker's and Jack Pearce brought Ivy and Annie along. Bert had a roaring fire going in the lounge and his missis had laid out a tempting array of food. There was a wedding cake ordered from Thelma at the cake shop.

Nora actually had a glass of sherry to toast the couple. Gradually, they all relaxed and began to enjoy themselves.

Desmond stood up to propose a toast to the bride and groom. He then made an announcement.

"Moms and dads, you are going to be grandparents. Me and Mary are expectin'."

They all applauded. Nora was shocked. How could he just stand up, in front of everyone, and just come out with it? She hadn't brought him up to broadcast a delicate subject like that to all and sundry. She had a further shock. Norman stood up next to his brother.

"Our Desmond ain't the only one to have an announcement. Me and Patty are gettin' engaged."

Nora gasped. Was there no escape from this family? Jack had a couple of pints and seemed as thrilled as the rest of them. Nellie and Wilf were overjoyed. Wilf shook Desmond's hand and patted him on the back.

"Drinks all round," he said. "I'm gonna be a grandad."

*   *   *

Mrs Shelley was impressed with Valerie's work and her reliability. She was having problems with Doreen Pritchard, a rather pretty girl who worked for Mr Harris, the Personnel Manager.

Doreen claimed that he was wanting more than a typewritten letter from her and was threatening to go to the managing director with her complaints about his conduct. A quick reshuffle was needed. Mrs Shelley summoned Valerie to her office.

"Sit down, Valerie," she said kindly. "I have a proposition to make to you."

Valerie was curious.

"Would you consider working for Mr Harris in personnel?"

Valerie knew there had been gossip in the office but had taken no heed. She had heard that old Harris couldn't keep his hands to himself but, as there was always some scandal going round, she disregarded it.

Valerie was flattered to be asked. She considered the post to be a good promotion and felt that some of the girls would be green with envy.

She answered the supervisor. "Oh yes, Mrs Shelley, I would like the position. I would learn a lot in that department."

Mrs Shelley sighed with relief. She felt that Valerie would not be a temptation to Harris.

"You will start at the beginning of next week and, of course, there will be a pay rise for you." She stood up. "I hope that you will be happy in your new post. Come to me if you have any problems."

Valerie nodded. "Thank you, Mrs Shelley, I will."

Some of her colleagues were envious. A few had been in the typing pool longer than Valerie Potts. Others didn't mind, they had heard things about old Harris. Some felt that she was just a creep.

Grace was pleased and proud of her daughter.

"You've worked hard for it, you deserve a good job."

She lost no time in telling Renee, Arthur and Flo.

Valerie called in at Janice's for her usual lunchtime visit.

"Come on in, cocka. You look perished. I'm gerrin proper nesh meself. Sittin' up the fire 'ole all the while. That's a nice blouse, is it new?"

Valerie nodded. "Yes, I thought I'd treat meself. I've been given a new job, working for Mr Harris in personnel."

Janice poured the tea. "Is that a promotion then?"

"Yes, I shall get a rise. It's more of a secretarial position. I'll learn a lot about hiring and firing and pensions. The firm's expanding and we're taking on more workers."

Janice gave her a plate for her sandwiches. "Am they tekkin over the factory next door? It's bin empty fer yonks."

"Yes, it's just the job. It's being rewired so the new machines can go in. I reckon we'll be in there in about three months."

Janice sat by the fire. "Our Paul's finished at the steelworks. Couldn't stand the racket. Stan warned 'im about it but he wanted to work with 'is mates. Anyroad, 'e's gorrimself a new job."

"Oh, where's that?"

"At Haynes, the butcher's."

Valerie's eyes widened. "Bobby Haynes's?"

"Yes, werkin' wi' Andy Bradley an' Ronnie Edwards, you know, Nellie Edwards's lad. Thay'me runnin' it for Tessy Haynes but 'er never goes there. Bob's dad 'as the dealin's with it."

Valerie sipped her tea. "Well," she said, "old Mr Haynes wants to keep his eye on the till with Ronnie Edwards around."

Janice was shocked. "Really? What's 'e done then?"

Valerie leaned forward. "Now then, Aunt, I don't want you to repeat this but . . ." and she told the story of Josie's necklace.

Janice sat quietly for a minute. "Well, I never woulda thought it. 'E seems such a nice lad an' 'e looks after that old 'oss o' Herbie Forester's. Yer know 'is sister rents Herbie's house? Ronnie rents the stable and looks after the 'oss."

"I had heard something about that," said Valerie. "It must cost a bit. Anyway, put Paul on his guard, we don't want him blamed for something he hasn't done." And she bit into a sandwich.

*   *   *

Flo was distraught. Fred was becoming unbearable. She hardly saw him and when she did, he was demanding a clean shirt or his trousers pressed. He showed little interest in Mark, leaving Flo to do the upbringing. Now she had received a letter from a person who claimed to be the new woman in his life.

One evening, Grace answered the door to a Flo who was upset and bordering on hysteria.

"'E's gonna leave me, I know 'e is. 'E ain't bin the same since I 'ad our Mark. Now the rotten sod's bin an' got another woman." She waved the letter under Grace's nose. "'Er says as it's bin gooin on fer two year. I can't tell me mother, 'er's never liked 'im. I don't know what I'm gonna do. 'Ow am I gonna manage if 'e leaves? Trust 'im ter goo an' get 'imself a freshun."

Grace led the way to the kitchen. "Sit down, Flo. I'll mek us a cuppa tea." She lit the stove. "'Ave yer ever thought as you'd be better off without 'im? You can't say 'e's bin that good ter yer, admit it."

Flo sank onto a chair. "'E wore too bad when we fust got married. 'E musta felt pushed out when I 'ad our Mark." She began to cry. "It's my fault, I've neglected 'im."

Grace snorted. "Rubbish! You done yer best. I tell you, 'e's selfish. Fred first and Fred last." She poured the tea. "You ain't tole mother and Arthur then?"

Flo shook her head. "No an' don't you tell 'em. 'E might not goo."

"Well, are you goin' ter show 'im the letter?"

Flo thought for a second, sipping her tea. "I don't know yet. P'raps if I ignore it, it'll come ter nothin'."

Grace certainly hoped so. Much as she disliked Freddie Burke, she didn't relish the idea of a divorce in the family.

*　　　　　*　　　　　*

Mrs Jinks wasn't well. The pain in her back was constant. It was worse after eating, so she was becoming reluctant to eat her meals. Ben was worried.

He told Grace, "Me mom's losin' weight. The doctor wants her to go for tests. 'E thinks as it might be 'er kidneys."

Grace commiserated with him and told Valerie when she came in from work.

"I'll pop round while the tea's cooking. Okay, Mom?"

Ben was pleased to see her. "Come on in. I ain't sin yer for a bit. Are you alright?"

"Fine, thanks but I hear your mom's poorly again."

He nodded. "Ar, 'er is." He ushered her to the stairs door. "'Er's 'aving a rest but you can go up and see 'er. 'Er'll be comin' down fer 'er tea later, not that 'er'll eat a lot."

Valerie looked round the bedroom door. Connie raised a hand.

"Come on in, Valerie. I ain't sin yer fer a bit. You look well, duck."

"Yes, I'm alright Mrs J, but what about you? What've you been doing to yourself?"

"I doe know what's up wi' me. The weight's droppin' off me." She pulled up the blanket. "Look at me spindly legs. I gerra pain when I eat. I've got ter go to th'ospital termorrer. Frank's 'avin' the day off work to go wi' me. Thay'me goin' ter do some X-rays."

Valerie patted her hand. "You'll be alright when they've sorted you out."

The old lady smiled. "I 'ope so, Valerie. I don't know what our Frank and Ben'd do without me. I want to get back to normal an' look after me 'ome. I don't like the chaps 'avin' ter do it."

Valerie kissed her on the cheek. "I'll pop tomorrow to see how you've got on. Try not to worry."

Grace was waiting to hear Valerie's verdict.

"How was Mrs J, Valerie?"

"Not too good, Mom. Lost a lot of weight. She's going for X-rays tomorrow."

Grace put the potatoes onto the plates. "S'pose the doctor's bin half-soaked again. I'll pop tomorrow after work. Poor soul."

*   *   *

Mr Haynes continued to call in each evening to collect the takings and leave the float for next day. Andy would take it up to the flat for the night. He was quite satisfied with the way that Andy and Ronnie were coping. Paul had proved willing to learn, however Ronnie had noticed that although the lad was friendly with Andy, he was rather reticent with himself.

"P'raps I've teased him too much," he thought. "Better lay off a bit."

He also noticed that, when Paul was in the shop, he hovered round him when he was at the till.

One day he turned to the lad. "Want something, Paul?" he asked.

Paul reddened slightly. "No, no," he said and carried the tray of chops he was holding to the window.

Ronnie scowled. Had Paul been watching him operate the till? He hoped the lad wasn't going to be light-fingered.

Ronnie was concerned about Lily. The vet had been to file her teeth. He had found a swelling in her mouth.

"I don't really know what it is but we will keep an eye on it. Let me know if there is any change. Is she eating?"

Ronnie said, "Ar, like an 'oss."

The vet laughed. "Perhaps we had better worm her again."

Ronnie told him, "'Er 'as all the best."

"I know. Herbie Forrester would be proud of the way that you care for her. She's very old now, isn't she?"

Ronnie patted the horse. "Yes but we'me not certain how old exactly. Annie, me nan's friend, thinks 'er's at least thirty."

"Well, you know she won't go on forever, don't you?" The vet packed his tools in his bag.

"Yes, I know but we'll keep 'er goin' as long as 'er's okay. I'd miss the old gel. I've knowed 'er since I was nine."

He cycled home, deep in thought. He had a driving lesson later and was hoping to buy a van. The GPO often sold their vans on and Chas was on the lookout for one. He thought about Andy hoping to emigrate and wondered who would run the shop. It was all very unsettling.

* * *

Freddie Burke was in hospital. He had taken a beating from his fancy woman's estranged husband. Flo had to leave Mark at Renee's while she visited him.

Grace and Valerie called in on the Friday evening.

"Glad you've come. Flo's at th'ospital. I doe know why 'er bothers. I wouldn't. 'E's a selfish pig."

Mark came in from the lavatory. Renee put her finger to her lips. Valerie dug into her bag for sweets for Mark.

"Ooh, thanks, Val. I love coconut mushrooms."

"Have you had your tea, before you scoff them?" asked Grace.

He nodded and settled to read his comic and stuff his face.

Renee grimaced. "Arthur spiles 'im rotten an' all. Still I s'pose it meks up fer you-know-who."

Mark looked up from his comic. "Who's you-know-who, Gran?" he asked.

"Never you mind." Renee put the kettle on. "'Ow's yer job goin', our Valerie?"

"Fine, thanks, Gran."

"Glad ter see you'me gerrin on an' doe ferget, 'ard werk never killed nobody. Yer grandad was a 'ard werker." Turning to Grace, she said, "Looks like our Flo's gorra gerra job. 'Er's thinkin' o' the twilight shift at the lock factry, so's 'er can fetch Mark from school. I'll 'ave ter go an' sit round theer. I s'pose I can watch telly round theer as well as at whum, that's if you-know-who aye theer."

Grace sipped her tea. "'E'll be there, Mother. Where else would 'e go? Our Flo's saft enough ter 'ave 'im back, more fool her."

Mark, absorbed in his comic, munched his sweets.

Chapter Eighteen

Vera Salt was worried. Roger now had a motorbike and Josie was frequently a pillion passenger. Steve tried to calm her down.

"'E's sensible enough, gel. You worry too much."

"I can't 'elp it. So many accidents. Them things am death traps."

Steve sighed. "There's nothing you can do about it, love, and I've med sure Josie's got a decent crash hat."

When the weather got warmer, Roger would collect Josie and they would go for a Sunday spin. Sandwiches and flask packed into the panniers, off they would go to the countryside or the coast.

Roger was ardent and desperately wanted to make love to Josie. She wasn't having any hanky panky, she was too scared of ending up like Rose and one or two other girls she knew, one of which had ended up in the mother and baby home and was facing the heartache of giving up her baby. She was finding it more and more difficult to fend him off. It caused arguments between them and they often returned home out of sorts with each other.

One Sunday evening, Roger had dropped Josie off when he spotted Brenda taking the family bull terrier for a walk. He stopped the bike.

"Aye up, Bren, that's some dog you've got there."

She laughed. "Ar, a dog an' 'alf's our Bruno."

He grinned back at her. "Do you fancy a spin?"

She nodded. "Yes, I'll take Bruno back an' then I'll be out in a jif."

Five minutes later, she came running across the street. "I've borrowed our kid's helmet. It's a bit wobbly but it'll do. I can't be out long, just a quick spin, okay?"

"Righto," said Roger.

She held him round the waist tightly. He drove around the streets, then made his way to the shop. It was dropping dark. He stopped and turned to her.

"Shall we pop in for a cuppa? I've got the keys."

"Okay," she said.

He unlocked the door and they went in. It all looked different in the gloom. They went through to the staff room and he closed the door before switching on the light. Brenda sat on the easy chair and switched on the electric fire. Roger switched off the light and they sat in the glow from the element. There were only the sounds of a dripping tap and the electric kettle, coming to the boil. He bent over her, she stood up. He put his arms round her and kissed her, hungrily.

Jack Pearce was patrolling the centre of the town, trying the shop doors to ensure that they were secure. He spotted Roger's motorbike outside Tresses and tried the door. It opened.

"Aye up," he thought. "Who's in there then?"

He walked, silently, through the barber's shop, then he heard muffled giggles coming from the staff room.

"I bet it's kids up ter no good," he thought.

He pushed the door open and switched on the light. There, on the floor, completely naked, was a young couple. They jumped up. The girl screamed and grabbed her coat to hold in front of herself. Jack immediately recognised Roger.

"What's goin' on then?" he asked.

Roger was as red as fire. "Nothin', Mr Pearce. We just come in fer a warm."

Jack had to laugh. "Well, I was only checkin'. You left the door off the catch. Be more careful in future."

Roger stammered, "I will. Thanks, Mr Pearce."

He pulled on his trousers and walked with Jack to the shop door.

"Mr Pearce, I would appreciate it if you didn't tell me mom an' dad."

Jack nodded. "O' course I won't. I was young meself once, yer know."

Brenda was crying and hurrying to get dressed.

"Don't worry, Bren, he won't say anythin'."

"I 'ope 'e don't or our kid'll half kill me an' you an' all."

Roger flinched. He knew Brenda's brother was a hard case. He made a cup of tea to calm her down and then they continued as they had left off. This time with the door locked.

Jack called in to see Annie. She had her hairnet on.

"God, Mother, you look like a kamikaze pilot in that thing."

"Well, I want ter keep me perm nice, Jack. It saves purrin me dinkies in all the while."

"I know but let the air get to it, Mother. That hairnet's a fortnight thick."

They sat, drinking tea and gossiping generally.

Jack said, "I see that young Roger's courtin' strong. You know, 'im from the barber's?"

"Yes, I know. Freda's son. 'E's goin' out wi' young Josie Salt."

"Oh," said Jack. "Only I saw him with young Brenda, the young 'un from the 'airdresser's. They was together on 'is motorbike."

Annie frowned. "I was sure as 'e was goin' strong wi' young Josie. They musta finished then."

Annie asked Maureen about Josie's romance when she was setting her hair round at Nellie's.

"There's no need to keep that hairnet on day and night, yer know, Annie."

"I know but I want me perm to last."

"Don't worry, I'll soon book you in for another one. It'll need cutting in a few weeks, anyway."

"Ar, our Jack says as I look like one o' them Kami knicker pilots."

They all dissolved into laughter.

"'E was tellin' me that young Roger's got a new girlfriend, seen 'em out on 'is motorbike. That young Brenda from the shop. I thought as 'e was goin' out wi' Josie Salt."

Maureen combed her hair. "Yes, he is," she said.

Maureen decided to talk her problem over with her mother. She stood, setting Nellie's hair in the kitchen. There was only Ivy present, sitting in the corner, oblivious to what was being said.

"Mom, what would you do if you knew somebody was being taken for a fool?"

"What do you mean, Maureen?"

"Well, Roger has been going out with Josie for about two years now."

"Yes, I know he has."

"Well, I saw him kissing Brenda in the staff room and now Annie says that Jack has seen them going out on his motorbike."

Nellie snorted. "The little double crosser. I don't know what ter say, our Maureen, burrif it was you, I would like yer ter know, so as you could gerron wi' yer life, away from 'im. Once a cheater, allus a cheater."

Maureen thought about it. "I don't want to go and tell her mother, Mom. Josie wouldn't thank me for it. Mind you, she won't thank me for tellin' her about it, full stop."

Nellie said, "I know but 'er could 'ave a decent chap, a nice gel like that. Young Roger's allus bin spiled, bein' the only one an' no shortage o' money."

"I think I'll tell Josie, Mom, but I don't know when I shall do it."

The opportunity arose next day. The shop was quiet, Brenda was clearing up and Josie and Maureen made the most of the lull to have a cup of tea in the staff room. Josie was looking at a magazine and showed Maureen a hairstyle she liked.

"That's smart, Jose, it'd suit you."

"Do you think so, Maureen? P'raps you could have a go at it for me one of the days when we're quiet?"

Maureen handed her a bag of biscuits. "Jose, I've been wantin' to have a word wi' you but couldn't find the time somehow."

Josie was curious. "Why's that, Maureen? Have I done summat to upset you?"

"No, nothing like that. It's Roger."

Josie frowned. "Roger? Why, what's he done?"

"Well, you'll probably hate me for tellin' you, Jose, but I've heard that he's seein' another girl."

Josie's eyes widened. "Who saw him? Who is it?"

"Well, I don't want to tell you who saw him or who the girl is but I can assure you that the person is reliable and not a tittle tattler."

Josie looked near to tears. "I'd best ask him about it. We're going out tonight."

Maureen smiled, sympathetically. "Yes, I think you should."

Josie could hardly wait to ask Roger about the allegations. They went to a film, which she sat through without really seeing, then walked back to Josie's.

"Are you coming in, Roger? Me mom and dad are in the shop, so we can have the living room to ourselves."

"Righto, Jose. Just fancy a few chips."

They went through the shop. Vera and Steve called hello. They were busy.

Josie put the kettle on and then she said, "Roger, I want to have a talk with you."

He cringed. "Oh yes, why's that then?"

"Well, somebody told me that you've been seein' another girl. Is that true?"

She stood there, hoping that it wasn't but the look on his face told her that he was guilty. He reddened and sat on a chair.

"It wore nothin', Jose, just a fling. 'Er come on ter me."

"Who come on to you?"

He looked up at her. "Don't you know?"

"I'm not saying whether I do or don't, just tell me yourself."

"No point," he said. "You won't believe me, whatever I say. I think I'd best go."

He got up and walked to the back door.

He said, "Cheerio, Jose, it's been nice but if you want ter believe things about me, it's no use us carrying on."

She almost felt guilty about accusing him, then realised he was twisting things. He wasn't worth bothering about. Although she felt a knife pain in her heart, she let him go.

Next day, she saw Freda and gave in her notice. Freda was upset.

"What's brought this on, Josie? We've always got on well and you're a bostin little worker. The customers like you. I don't want to lose you."

"Well, Freda, they're advertising for hairdressers at Butlin's holiday camp and, as you know, we went there last year. I fancy giving it a season. I think I need a change."

Freda peered closely at her. "It's got nothing to do with our Roger, has it, Josie?"

Josie shook her head. "Not really. We were getting tired of each other, anyway. It wasn't going anywhere. I feel like a change of scenery."

"Well, we'll be sorry to lose you. If ever you get fed up at Butlin's, you can always come back here."

"Thanks, Freda." Josie gave her a kiss and a rueful smile.

*　　　　*　　　　*

Mr Haynes called in the shop, as usual, to cash up.

He said to Andy, "Tess wants you and Ronnie to pop and see her one of these evenings, after closing."

Andy thought for a moment. "Would it be okay tonight? Only we've got a match on Thursday afternoon."

"Yes, I think so. The sooner, the better. Can you come about eight o'clock? The kids'll be in bed then."

Andy told Ronnie and they arranged to meet there.

Tess looked very drawn and pale. She offered them a beer and they all sat down. Mr Haynes opened the conversation.

"Tess felt that you should know what her plans are. She didn't want anything to happen without your knowledge and didn't want to cause you any problems or concerns."

She nodded and said, "Thank you for keeping the shop going for me for so long. I haven't been able to think straight for months. Anyway, I have decided what to do. I think it best if I sell the shop and this house and make a new start for me and the kiddies."

Ronnie said, "I understand, Mrs Haynes. It's been a very hard time for you."

Andy agreed. "We have been thinkin' about you and we wondered what you would decide ter do. We aren't surprised really."

Tess went on, "The shop will be advertised in about a week or so, as a going concern. I hope it will carry on as a butcher's but, of course, that will depend on the new owner."

They stood to depart.

Ronnie said, "Thanks for telling us yerself. We can think things through now."

Andy told her, "Mandy and me was looking into emigrating, Mrs Haynes, so don't worry about us. If the flat goes, we can stop with Mandy's mom."

Tess smiled with relief. "I hope it all turns out well for you both."

As they walked down the street, Ronnie said, "Poor woman, it ain't bin easy for her. I felt in me bones that the business would 'ave ter go."

Nellie and Wilf were not surprised about Tess's decision. They were concerned about Ronnie, knowing that he enjoyed his job.

He sat discussing it all with them, then he said, "Do you think I'm too young ter 'ave me own business?"

Wilf said, "I don't think so, son. I was 'opin' you'd consider the shop, if it ever come on the market. You've got yer money from Herbie, he'd like ter think you'd put it to good use. You werk 'ard and Andy's a good chap."

"That's the problem, Dad. Andy's goin' ter emigrate. I doe really know who I can get ter werk for me. If 'e's experienced, 'e'll be older and want to run the show. It's a problem. I know about orderin' and how to do the books but I've got ter get somebody reliable. I can't do it all on me own."

Wilf nodded. "You'me right. We'll 'ave ter look round fer somebody but it woe be easy."

Nellie asked, "Are you goin' to mek an offer then, Ronnie?"

"When I know how much Mrs Haynes wants for it but I dain't ask. I wanted to talk to you an' me dad first."

Wilf said, "Folks'll wonder where you got the money from."

"I'll tell 'em I got a loan from the bank. Anyroad, it aye nobody's business. I might tell 'em that!"

Barry was the first to be told that Ronnie was hoping to buy the shop. He was pleased.

"I wish I'd got the means ter buy the coal yard when Gerry retires," he said. "I reckon 'e'll be goin' in a couple o' years. Moanin' about his screws, 'e is. Mainly stops in th'office. I'm glad I learnt to drive. I'll keep me ear ter the ground fer a good bloke fer yer, Ronnie. 'Ow's that young Paul comin' on?"

"'E seems okay, seems ter want ter learn. A bit quiet wi' me but I musta tormented 'im a bit much when 'e started."

Barry laughed. "That's you all over. 'Ave ter be a bit more serious when you'me runnin' the show."

Within two weeks the shop was advertised and Ronnie had made an offer, much to the surprise of Tess and her father-in-law. They were only too pleased for him to have it. Andy was shocked to think that Ronnie could afford to take the business on but accepted that he had a bank loan. It would be a few weeks before he emigrated and he was grateful that he could still rent the flat until they went. He also said he would listen out for a butcher who needed a job.

Renee always bought her meat from Brian Jenkins. It was a stone's throw from her house and she had always shopped there. She remembered his dad with fondness and, being a creature of habit, was glad when Brian took over the family business. Brian, however, was not known for his generosity with his staff. He was, in fact, downright mean. He had working for him a young chap, Terry Dawkins. He had been with him for three years and was getting restless. One day he arrived at work and gave in his notice.

Brian was shocked. "What've I done to yer, lad, as yer want ter leave?"

"Nothing. I've got a new job and when I marry Hazel we can rent the flat over the shop."

Brian sulked for a while. “Where are you goin’ then?” he asked, reluctantly.

“To Bob Haynes’s old shop.”

“Oh, and who’s got it now?”

“A young chap, Ronnie Edwards. ’E’s worked there for some time now.”

Brian frowned. “Got plenty o’ money over the bonk then, ’ave they?”

Terry shrugged. “I doe know. All I know is, it’s all sorted.”

Renee came into the shop. “’Ow am yer, Terry? Are yer alright?”

“Yes, ta, Mrs Shaw. What can I get yer?”

“I just fancy a few brains fer me tea an’ a lamb chop fer our Arthur.”

Brian turned round from the window display. “Mek the best on it,” he said. “Our Terry woe be servin’ yer for long.”

She looked at Terry. “Why? Where you gooin then?”

“Bobby Haynes’s old shop. I’m gooin ter werk fer Ronnie Edwards, ’e’s buying it.”

Renee looked puzzled. “Ronnie Edwards? I doe know if I know ’im.”

That evening, Grace and Valerie called to see her. She was smacking her lips over the tasty meal she had enjoyed.

“Them was lovely brains on toast I ’ad fer me tea. I really enjoyed ’em.”

Valerie flinched. “Oh, Gran, I don’t know how you can eat them. Are you sure they’re fresh?”

“Course I am, you can tell by just lookin’ at ’em. Brian’s gonna be short staffed, ’e’s losing young Terry. I never thought as ’e’d leave. I thought as ’e’d be theer for life.”

Grace asked, “What’s caused him to leave then?”

“I doe know. All I know is ’e’s gonna werk ferra chap called Ronnie Edwards. ’E’s bought Bobby Haynes’s old shop.”

Valerie was gobsmacked. She felt a surge of hatred. Ronnie Edwards, with his own shop and at his age? It was too much to bear.

Valerie was 'spitting blacking'. She scarcely spoke on the way home. Grace, with her own thoughts, didn't seem to notice. When they reached home it was nine o'clock.

"I wonder if we should knock and see how Mrs J is?" Grace said.

"They might be ready for bed," said Valerie.

However, Ben was in the backyard, getting a raker out of the coal bunker to settle the fire for the night. He was pleased to see them.

"How's your mom got on at the hospital, Ben? They hadn't come back when we went out."

He pursed his lips. "Ar, it were a day's job with one thing an' another. 'Er was dead tired when 'er got 'ome. We got 'er to bed and 'er's asleep now. We woe know anythin' 'til next wik. The doctor'll let us know by Wednesday, they say."

Valerie said, "I'll pop round tomorrow. Put the washing ready and a list of anything you want from the shops."

"Thanks, Valerie, I'll be okay for the shoppin', werkin' in the town meself."

He went inside. Frank was making the cocoa.

"Who was yer talking to, Ben?"

"Oh, Valerie an' Grace. Thay'me collectin' the washin' termorrer, so put it ready an' they wanted ter know if we needed anything from the shops but I'll get that."

Frank poured the milk into the cups. "That's good on 'em. Young Valerie's terned out ter be a nice young woman. Pity 'er mother's so smotherin' on 'er."

Ben hadn't really noticed but, on reflection, had to agree.

*　　　　*　　　　*

Vera and Steve Salt were upset. Josie dropped her bombshell over Sunday lunch.

"Mom, Dad, you know I went out for the day a week last Thursday?"

"To Brum, yer mean?" asked Vera.

"Yes. Well, I went for an interview at the Grand Hotel."

Steve paused, fork halfway to his mouth. "What? Yer mean you'me goin' ter work in 'otel?"

Josie shook her head. "No, Dad. They were interviewing for jobs at Butlin's."

Vera gasped. "Come on, our Josie, spit it out."

"Well, I got a job in the hairdressing salon there."

It was Steve's turn to gasp. "Butlin's? Where we went last year?"

"Yes, Dad."

Vera felt close to tears. "What for? You've got a job here. You've only been away from 'ome with us, on holiday. How do yer think you'me gonna get on, away from 'ome?"

It was Josie's turn to feel tearful. "Oh, Mom, lots of young folk'll be there, working."

Steve snorted. "That's why we're worried."

Josie flushed angrily. "What do you think I am, Dad? I know what I'm about." She started to cry. "I just need a change."

Vera put her arm round her daughter. "We'll miss yer. Won't that Roger mind yer goin'?"

Josie shook her head. "No, he's got another girl, anyway. 'Er works at the shop, so I've got to leave. I can't work there with the two of them."

Vera looked at Steve over Josie's head and raised her eyebrows. He didn't get the hint. He put down his knife and fork.

"'As 'e upset yer? I'll 'ave a werd wi' that young man."

Josie protested. "No, Dad, don't. It's all finished. I'll work away for a bit, then when I get back after the season I can pick up the pieces."

He sighed. "Well, we'll be able ter come an' see you, stop for a couple o' short breaks, if not at the camp, we can stop in a boardin' 'ouse."

Josie kissed him. "Thanks, Dad. After dinner, I'll go for a walk round to Valerie's. Might as well tell her before somebody else does."

The room was silent apart from the ticking of the clocks, ash falling through the bars of the grate and occasional, gentle snores from Grace. The cat stretched out to his full length and yawned widely, showing his pink, rough tongue, his extended claws catching in the pegged mat.

Valerie looked up from her book. Grace sat in the armchair, the Sunday paper open on her lap, her head to one side. She looked so relaxed and peaceful. The room was getting dark and it was becoming difficult for Valerie to read. Grace always left it to the last minute to switch on the light to save electricity. Valerie did not want to disturb her mother.

They sat in companionable silence. Valerie gazed into the fire and dreamt of the day when she would be rich. Sunday afternoon was the only time that Grace had a rest and Valerie always looked forward to Sunday tea. Sometimes they would have salmon sandwiches. The tin stretched between Sunday tea and sandwiches to take to work on Monday. The bits of skin and bone, together with any juice and a little hot water, would be used to soak bread as a treat for the cat. Other times it would be sardines on toast or pikelets, toasted at the fire. Occasionally it would be butter on them, other times margarine would suffice. The pikelet man had not been round this week. He did miss sometimes. Whatever it was, they would enjoy it, unhurriedly, Grace appreciating the fact that she was not dog tired for a change. The cat decided that he wanted to go out, and urgently. He meowed loudly and sat looking at the door, waiting for one of his slaves to open it. Valerie obliged and the draught woke Grace.

"Nice sleep, Mom?"

"Yes, thanks, ready for a nice cuppa tea now."

Grace was contented and felt that her life could go on like this forever, just her and Valerie.

They were surprised to hear a knock on the front door. They never had visitors on a Sunday afternoon. Valerie was even more surprised to see Josie standing there.

"Oh, Josie. I wondered who it could be. Come in."

Josie asked, "Am I disturbing you and your mom, Val?"

"No, don't worry. I was just making a cup of tea."

Grace was also surprised to see Josie. She was slightly disgruntled to have her Sunday afternoon disturbed but tried not to show it.

"Hello, Josie. Your mom all right, and your nan and grandad?"

"Yes, thanks, Mrs Potts. Grandad's rheumatics are playing him up. S'pose it's the damp weather."

Grace stood, laboriously, and went to make the tea. "Yes, I know how he feels," she said.

Valerie and Josie sat down. "You don't look too happy, Jose. What's up?"

"Well, Roger and me are finished. It was two weeks ago."

Valerie gasped. "I thought it was serious."

Josie shook her head. "No. Anyway, I've decided to leave Tresses. I've got a job at Butlin's. The season starts in April, so I'll be off soon."

Valerie was lost for words for a moment. She felt near to tears. Her only friend was going away.

"You never said about you and Roger, Jose. You could've talked to me about it."

"I didn't feel like talking to anybody, Val, to be honest and I certainly don't want to go on seeing him day after day at the salon."

Grace brought the tea in and noticed the long faces. "What's up?" she asked.

Valerie stared at the floor. "Josie's going away to work next month, Mom. She's got a job at Butlin's."

Grace was elated but couldn't show it. "How's your mom feel about that, Josie?"

"She's a bit upset but she realises that I need a change. It's probably only for the summer season. It'll do me good."

Grace poured the tea.

Valerie said, "P'raps we could go for a holiday, Mom?"

Grace nodded but very much doubted it.

The next day Valerie sat on the bus, contemplating her life. Years stretched ahead of her. Working at the shoe factory, seeing Janice secretly once a week, Friday evenings at Granny Shaw's, weekend shopping and cinema with her mother, the occasional visit to Flo. It all looked very bleak. And to top it all Ronnie Edwards had his own shop. She had to do something, but what? She went into the house and put the kettle on. Clearing the ashes from the grate, she relaid the fire. There was a knock on the back door. Ben stood there with a pair of Grace's shoes.

"'Allo, Valerie, just poppin' these in fer Grace."

Valerie thanked him and turned to reach her purse.

"No need fer that. You do our washing. Exchange is no robbery."

She said, "I'll pop round later to see your mom."

"Okay," said Ben. "She'll like that."

Grace arrived with the fish and chips. She hung her coat on the door.

"Vera Salt's not happy about Josie gooin ter Butlin's. I could tell when I asked her but she seems ter be makin' the best on it. Anyroad, I told her 'er'll soon be back when 'er gets fed up wi' no mom ter wait on 'er."

Valerie unwrapped the chips. "Ben's brought your shoes back. He doesn't want paying, says it's in return for the washing. Are you coming round later to see Mrs J, Mom?"

"Might as well but I saw the doctor goin' in as I came past."

Valerie frowned. "Ben never said he was calling. Never mind, we'll soon know."

It wasn't good news for Connie. The doctor had called to tell her that there was a bed for her on the surgical ward and she was to be there for nine o'clock next morning. Ben and Frank were worried. Connie was philosophical about it.

"I s'pose they've had a butcher's at me innards an' found out what's what. Me cousin 'ad the same sort o' trouble. Gallstones, it was. They tried ter swayne 'em away but couldn't. Anyroad, as soon as they got 'em out 'er was a new woman."

Frank smiled at her. "I could do wi' a new woman."

Valerie said, "Have you some nighties ironed, Mrs J? Do you need anything?"

"I'm okay, love. Ben's packed me case already. You've kept the washing down for us. Thanks, you're a good gel."

Ben cut in, "You'll soon be eatin' them scratchins again, Mom."

Connie pulled a face. "Can't imagine it, son."

Doctor Johnson slid the X-rays on to the screen. He studied them closely then, frowning, turned to Staff Nurse Christine Edwards.

"Have you Mrs Jinks's notes there, Staff?"

She handed them to him.

"She'll be for theatre on Thursday. It doesn't look good, I'm afraid. I'll write up her pain control and pre-med while I'm at it."

Christine was sorry. Connie Jinks was a lovely woman. Her husband and son obviously adored her. She could only pray that the surgery would be successful. She tidied the desk. On reflection, life could be a pig at times.

At visiting time, Connie was waiting to tell Ben and Frank.

"I don't want you to worry. The doctor's real nice. The surgeon's comin' ter see me in the mornin' an' the one what does the anaesthetic. They've took some more blood an' some more X-rays. Doe gi' yer a minute ter yerself. The nerses am lovely. I like Staff Edwards. It's a small werld. 'Er's Nellie Edwards' gel – you know, their Ronnie's just bought Bobby Haynes's shop."

Ben patted her arm. "P'raps you'me talkin' too much, Mom. You'll be done up."

Frank touched him on the arm. "Let 'er talk if 'er wants to, son."

Connie smiled at them. "Anyroad, I'm in good 'ands, so stop worryin'. Are yer copin' at 'ome alright?"

"Yes, Mom, we'me okay. Allus the fish an' chip shop. Valerie's good an' Grace says 'er can allus cook some extra so's we can 'ave some. Valerie's comin' ter see yer when you've 'ad chance ter pick up from yer op."

"That'll be nice. 'Er's a good gel."

Ben was working at his shop, his mind on his mother. The morning seemed to drag. At twelve o'clock his telephone rang.

"Hello, is that Mr Jinks?" said a female voice.

His heart plummeted into his shoes. "Yes, speaking."

"This is Staff Nurse Edwards. Mr Jinks, Doctor Johnson has asked me to telephone you. He thinks that you and your father had better come along to the ward."

"Yes, oh yes. We shall be along shortly."

He telephoned the steelworks and asked that his father be given a message and then ordered a taxi. They arrived at the ward to be met by Staff Nurse Edwards. She showed them into the office and asked them to be seated.

"I'm afraid Mrs Jinks is very poorly. She hasn't come round from the anaesthetic yet. You may sit with her. I'll ask Ida, the orderly, to bring you a cup of tea."

Frank and Ben could only nod their thanks.

Connie never came round from the anaesthetic. She died peacefully with her husband and son at her bedside. The surgeon came to see them in the ward office. He indicated for them to sit down and began.

"I'm so sorry about your wife, Mr Jinks. I'm afraid that she had a massive liver tumour. We removed a lot of it but, as in many similar cases, the bleeding was excessive. She was in a weakened state already and must have been feeling unwell for a long time."

Frank nodded. "'Er warn't the sort ter moan and 'er wouldn't 'ave wanted ter linger, Doctor. It was drivin' 'er mad not bein' able ter do things at 'ome. Thank you an' the other doctors for tryin' ter do summat for 'er."

Ben couldn't speak. He felt as if his world had ended.

Grace and Valerie were grief stricken at the loss of their good neighbour. They offered their help.

Frank thanked them and said, "Ben can't face openin' the shop. I daresay it'll stop shut 'til after the funeral."

Valerie thought, then she said, "What about the folk who can't wait that long for their shoes?"

Frank shook his head. "I doe know."

She said, "I can open the shop on Saturday for you, if you like, Ben."

He was touched. "Thanks. Do you think as you'll manage?"

"Yes, course I shall."

He gave her a key and she went to put a notice in the shop window to inform customers that they could collect their shoes on Saturday. Ben was grateful. He knew that the shoes could not be mixed up. He had a ticket system and the cost of each repair was written on the ticket, attached to each pair of shoes.

Valerie quite enjoyed her day in the shop. Grace called in to leave some shopping for her to carry home.

"How are you gettin' on then?" she asked.

"Alright, Mom. I like serving, makes a change. There are some sympathy cards for Ben and his dad. I think most of the shopkeepers have pushed one through the door."

Grace picked them up. "What time are you closin' then?"

"About four o'clock, I think. Most of the shops are clearing up by then. It's been steady."

Grace picked up her bag. "I'll get the tea when you come in, no use lettin' it spoil."

She went over to the cake shop. "Nearly done, Thelma?"

"Yes, thank heavens. 'Ow's Valerie doin'?"

"Okay, seems ter 'ave enjoyed it really, except she's so sad about Connie."

Thelma nodded. "Poor Frank an' Ben. 'E really loved 'is mom. Such a nice bloke."

Grace agreed. "Such good neighbours an' all," she said.

Chapter Nineteen

In one week, Ronnie had good news and bad. First, he passed his driving test, secondly Lily was ailing. She had lost weight, although her stomach was swollen, and he decided to call in the vet. It was a young man, who had joined the local practice. He examined Lily thoroughly.

"She's very old, isn't she?" he said.

Ronnie nodded, a sinking feeling in his stomach.

The vet continued, "I can see from our records, and the conditions she is kept in, that she has been very well cared for."

"We do our best for her," Ronnie said.

"I'll leave some medication for her. She's been wormed lately?"

"Yes," said Ronnie.

"Then I'll see her in a few days. Perhaps get Mr Robinson to give her the once over. Sometimes they have an off time and then they rally but we'll have to wait and see."

Maureen and Chas were waiting to hear the verdict. Ronnie told them.

Maureen said, "Don't worry, Ron, thay'me good vets. We can only do what they say."

Ronnie sighed. "Ar, you'me right. I know we can't keep 'er forever. I shan't let her suffer, Mau. I couldn't bear that."

Chas put his hand on his shoulder. "Come on, mate, let's pop in The Haymekker's for half an hour. 'Elp you ter sleep."

They stood at the bar, chatting. "I think I've found a van for yer, Ron. I've gid it the once over and it seems a good buy. What do yer think?"

"Well, I could do with one for the business an' now I've got me licence, no reason to wait. When can I come an' 'ave a look at it?"

"I can bring it to the yard on Saturday afternoon, if yer like."

"Okay, that'll be fine. Summat ter look forward to."

The following Friday was Connie Jinks's funeral. Valerie and Grace had managed to get half days off. Ben and Frank were distraught. It was a cold day for the time of year and rain threatened, making it even more sombre.

Connie had been a Chapel-goer and the little building was full of fellow worshippers, including Nora Proudfoot. The singing of the beautiful, old hymns caused the tears to flow afresh and Frank sobbed on his son's shoulder.

They all went back to the house for a cup of tea. Thelma's cake shop had provided sausage rolls and sandwiches, which no one could find any appetite for. All in all, it was a very sad day.

Grace and Valerie took their leave.

"Anythin' we can help you with, just say," said Grace.

"You have enough to do wi' werkin'," said Frank, "but thanks, anyway."

Valerie gave them both a kiss on the cheek. "We'll still manage the washing, don't you fret but we'll talk to you about things another time."

Closing the door behind their visitors, Frank and Ben went into the empty house.

Mr Robinson came that evening to see Lily. She was no better, in fact, she had gone off her food completely. He examined her and, turning to Ronnie, said, "I think the old lady has finally had enough, Mr Edwards. If we leave her she will get weaker. It will be cruel to let her carry on. I could try medicine and an injection to boost her up but it will not last and it will mean a decision pretty soon, I think."

Ronnie turned away. He was very upset but he knew that there was only himself to make the decision. He couldn't run to his parents with this problem. He turned to face the vet.

"I think we will have to let her go, Mr Robinson. I can't imagine what it will be like without her but I always said I wouldn't let her suffer. Herbie has trusted me to do the best for her and he left me the means to do it. I'll have ter leave it to you ter see to her. I 'ave ter ask you, though, can it be done here? I don't want her upset. I don't think 'er's ever bin in a 'orse box."

Mr Robinson nodded. "Yes, of course. It'll cost a bit extra but I'm sure you won't mind about that."

"O' course not. Can it be done tomorrow? I want ter spend a bit o' time with her."

The vet arranged to come next day. Ronnie would leave the key at The Haymaker's. He then went home to collect a sleeping bag to spend the night in the stable.

Nellie and Wilf were woken by a hammering on the front door. It was two o'clock in the morning. Wilf leaned out of the window. It was Desmond, hair on end, eyes popping.

"It's Mary, 'er's started. I've phoned fer a taxi ter collect Nellie. Is 'er in?"

"Course 'er's in," said Wilf. "I'll open the door for yer."

"No, I'm gooin straight back." He picked up his bike from the pavement and pedalled like mad up the street.

Nellie was dressing quickly. Fortunately Annie was next door at Ivy's. Almost as soon as she was dressed a taxi pulled up outside.

"You stop 'ere, Wilf. Our Patty woe know where we've got to if you come."

"Okay, love. Let me know as soon as you can."

Waving her off he resolved to go on the waiting list for a telephone. It seemed they were in need of one more each day.

Mary was calmly sitting on the sofa waiting for her mother and the taxi. Nellie bustled in.

"'Ow often are yer pains, love?"

"About every twenty minutes, Mom. I told Desmond not ter panic but I'm glad you're here. Me case is ready, has been for a month." She laughed then a pain shot into her back.

Nellie escorted her into the taxi whilst a trembling Desmond locked the door, dropping the keys onto the pavement in his haste, then they were off.

An efficient night sister greeted them.

"Come along, Mrs Proudfoot. We'll settle you into your bed. Baby won't be here for a while yet."

Nellie and Desmond sat in the corridor. Sister reappeared.

"Right, Mr Proudfoot, pop in to say goodnight. You may telephone in the morning around eight o'clock."

Nellie didn't want to leave her daughter. Desmond was worried to death.

"You'd better come home wi' me, son. Can't wait all on yer own in an empty 'ouse."

Wilf was still up, couldn't settle. He made the cocoa. He realised what Nellie was going through. One of her chickens was suffering. They sat, dozing, in front of the front room fire. Patty was surprised to find them there when she came downstairs at seven o'clock.

"What's up?" she asked. "Has our Mary had the bab?"

Nellie shook her head. "Not yet, love. Desmond has to ring at eight o'clock."

Wilf and Patty set off for work. At last eight o'clock came and Desmond went across the road to the phone box. On his return, though jubilant, he could hardly speak. Nellie stood, hand over her mouth, wide-eyed. At last he managed to put her out of her misery.

"It's a girl, thay'me both alright." Then they both cried.

Nellie said, "Wait 'til I tell Wilf 'e's got a granddaughter."

Ronnie said his final goodbye to Lily. He kissed her nose and hugged her. She snuffled and nudged at him. Maureen had prepared some breakfast but he could only drink half a cup of tea. He rode to the shop, hardly seeing the road through his tears. As he approached the shop, he saw Desmond waiting for him, jubilantly waving his arms to bring him to a stop.

"Aye up, our Des. What's up?"

"I'm a dad. Little gel."

Ronnie shook him by the hand. "That's great, mate, just great."

Desmond got on his bike. "Must push off ter get ter me mom's. I ain't told 'em yet." And, with a cheery wave, he rode off down the High Street.

Nora was pleased at the news. She was thrilled to have a granddaughter but a little peeved that Nellie had known before her.

"You've missed yer dad but I can ring him at work. Have you had anything to eat?"

Desmond realised that he was hungry. "No, Mom, never thought about it."

"I'll get you some toast. What time can you visit?"

"Two o'clock."

Nora slid a sideways look. "On yer own?"

"No, Mary can have two visitors, no changing over."

"Oh, who's going with you at two then?"

Desmond was in a cleft stick. He swallowed his tea and tried to fathom a way out of the dilemma.

"Well, Mom, I can visit again at six. Would you like to come with me then?"

She sniffed. "S'pose I'll have to be satisfied with that," she said.

*   *   *

Valerie sat in the canteen, eating her packed lunch. Pat Sharpe came over to her table.

"Mind if I join you?"

"Not at all," said Valerie.

They chatted generally. Pat worked in the accounts office. She typed invoices which she found 'dead boring'. She chewed her food, contemplatively.

"You know," she said, "when you look at what we charge for shoes an' what the shops sell 'em for, there's a blooming good profit margin."

She offered Valerie a crisp.

"Ta," she said. "I never thought buying wholesale and reselling was such a good deal."

Pat answered, "Oh yes. Why don't you pop in our office an' I'll show you an invoice. You'll see how much we charge an' when you're in town, look at how much you've got to pay out."

Valerie was glad that Norman Proudfoot had left long ago. Had he been there she would never have set foot in the accounts department.

"When can I come?" she asked Pat.

"Now's as good a time as any, nobody in. Anyway, we're not doing any harm, are we?"

It was true. Valerie had never thought before that there was money to be made from selling shoes. She was intrigued.

* * *

Ronnie discovered that being the boss wasn't easy. He had the books to do as well as working in the shop. Terry proved to be a good worker and young Paul pulled his weight. Ronnie realised the young lad had stopped hovering around when he was at the till. He had a nasty thought – perhaps he had suspected him of dipping his hand into the takings. He mentally shook himself – never. He spotted Ben Jinks coming across the street. He entered the shop. Ronnie was unsure what to say to him these days.

"'Allo, Ben. How're you doin'?"

"Not so bad, Ron. I've only come fer some pig's pudding an' bacon. Quick tea fer us. 'Ow's yer famly these days?"

"Well, our Mary's had a little gel. Me mom knitted enough cloes ferra football team."

Ben laughed. "Your Christine was on me mom's ward. 'Er's a nice wench an' a good nerse."

Ronnie agreed proudly. "Ar, 'er is, teks after me mother."

He watched Ben cross the street back to his shop. He was a nice bloke. Pity he hadn't found a decent woman to marry. Come to that he hadn't found one himself, had he? Ronnie was in the back room sorting through some invoices. Terry popped his head round the door

"Can I have a werd, boss?" he asked

The shop was quiet and he had chosen his moment.

"What's up, mate?"

"Well, me and Hazel, we've had a fall out an' it looks as if the engagement's off."

"Sorry ter 'ear it, mate. Do you think you'll mek it up?"

Terry shook his head. "I doe think so. Fact is, 'er's met somebody else at werk, bin going on fer a bit, by all accounts. As bad as that Roger at the barber's."

Ronnie was interested. "What do yer mean?"

"Well, 'e's done the dirty on that young Josie. Bin knockin' the young un off, what's 'er name? Brenda. Anyroad, me sister 'ad 'er 'air done the other day an' 'er tells me as Josie's gonna werk at Butlin's."

Ronnie's heart sank. Just as he, fleetingly, thought he had a chance, she was going.

"I'm sorry, Ron, but we shan't be rentin' the flat after all. I feel I'm messin' yer about but I might as well stop at me mom's."

Ronnie put a hand on Terry's shoulder. "No worry, mate, somebody'll rent it."

Maureen had called in on her way home from work. She was showing Nellie the gift that she had purchased for Josie. Everyone at the shop had put together, including Roger, to Maureen's contempt. She had purchased Josie's favourite Blue Grass perfume, in a set, with talc and body lotion.

Nellie said, "That's nice, Maureen. She'll like it."

Ronnie came through the door. "Who'll like what?" he asked.

"Oh, hello, Ron. It's a leaving present for Josie."

He flushed slightly. "Oh, yes, I heard she was leavin'. Goin' ter Butlin's, ain't she? Which one?"

"Minehead, I believe. Went there on holiday last year wi' her mom an' dad. Went for an interview at Brum, starts next month."

Nellie said, "I bet Vera's upset, and Steve. They think the werld o' that gel."

Maureen nodded. "We'll miss her an' all. Good worker, always was, an' pleasant, even as a junior. Odds ter that young Brenda, no more use nor ornament, that one. Young Roger's gone sweet on her. I don't think as Freda's very pleased but what can you do?"

"Nothin'," said Nellie. So far she was satisfied with her children's choices. She hoped that Barry and Ronnie would soon find themselves decent girls.

* * *

The train journey to Minehead seemed never-ending. Josie arrived tired and apprehensive. She missed her mother already but was determined to stick it out. She realised that if she didn't break away from home now she would never do it. Anyway, she wasn't the only one. There were lots of girls in the same boat.

A coach was waiting to take staff to the camp. It all looked different, somehow. Perhaps because it was waiting for the holidaymakers. It seemed unwelcoming and artificial.

On the coach, she met a girl called Noreen. She was hoping to be a redcoat. She was able to sing and dance and she professed to love children. She was the same age as Josie and they became friends immediately.

"I wonder if we can share a chalet together?" Noreen said.

"I hope so," Josie replied. "Where are you from?"

"Birmingham."

"Oh, not far from me, that's nice. At least we have a similar accent. I get sick of folks taking a rise out of my accent. When I came here last year with mom and dad some cheeky sod called me Marlene."

Noreen laughed. "Oh yes, that's happened to me an' all. Have you any brothers and sisters?"

Josie shook her head. "No, have you?"

"One brother. He's a pain. Me mom and dad smother me. I felt I had to get away before I went mad. Do you know, me mom met me from school 'til I was thirteen? It was dead embarrassing. What was your job, Josie?"

"I'm a qualified hairdresser."

"Ooh, that's good. I've only worked in Lewis's. Got sick o' them toffee-nosed assistants. Thought they owned the shop. Me mom thought I was a cut above everybody working there. Anyway, I'm here for the season. I'll decide what to do when that's finished. Shall you?"

Josie thought. "Yes. I want me own shop one day but it might be a while before I can afford to start on me own."

Noreen was impressed. "Your own business? Wow!"

It was a good job that Josie had met Noreen. When they were allocated a chalet, they had a shock. It was basic and bare. They soon put their stamp on it with bits and bobs to make it more homely.

Meals were in the staff canteen. They soon became acquainted with the routine and met more of the recruits. The salon was passable. It had been redecorated so it was better than the chalet. Josie met her fellow stylists. They seemed a nice enough bunch. Two had worked there before. She thought it couldn't be bad if they had returned for another season. The food was much as she remembered it and the company at mealtimes was often hilarious. Gradually she settled into a routine.

Thelma popped into the fish shop.

"Two cod and chips, Vera, please," she said. "How are you these days now your Josie's left 'ome?"

Vera scowled. "'Er ain't left 'ome, only werkin' away for a season. Rang home last night, says 'er's okay. Med friends wi' a gel from Brum, sharing with 'er. Anyway, we'me goin' down in three wiks' time. Me mom an' dad are gooin ter see ter the shop fer a few days."

Thelma put salt and vinegar on her chips. "I bet young Valerie's gonna miss Josie. They've bin pals fer yonks."

"Ar," said Vera, "I know. I bet 'er'd like ter go fer an' 'oliday an' all."

Vera discussed with Steve the prospect of taking Valerie with them when they went to see Josie.

"You know, Steve, apart from day trips, I don't think that wench's even bin ter the sea."

Steve picked his teeth with a matchstick. "Do you think as 'er mother'd mind 'er gooin?"

"Well, let's face it, thay'me over twenty-one now an' if they can't 'ave a bit o' life, it's a poor show."

He agreed. "Well, you can only ask. As far as I'm concerned 'er's welcome ter come. They don't 'ave the main wiks at the shoe factry, do they?"

"I don't think they do in the offices."

"Well, goo on then, ask 'er next time yer see 'er."

Valerie called in the following Tuesday. She was getting fish and chips for Ben and Frank as well as herself. Vera looked up from the range.

"Oh, just the one I wanted to see. 'Ang on a minute." She finished serving the customer in front of Valerie and said, "Come on inter the back fer a minute. Steve, carry on fer me, will yer?"

"Okay," he said.

Valerie was curious to know what Vera wanted her for.

"Now then, Valerie, we're goin' ter see our Josie in three weeks' time for a few days. Steve's changed the van for a car, so there's room fer you ter come. That's if you want to."

Valerie was thrilled. "Oh, yes, please, Mrs Salt. I've never been away properly."

"Well, we shan't stop too long because of the shop. I would say about three days. Let me know if yer want to come, will yer, love?"

Valerie smiled. "Thanks, I will."

Her first port of call was the Jinkses. Ben had lit the oven to put the parcels of fish and chips in.

"Thanks, Valerie. Dad won't be long. You look mithered. What's up?"

Valerie told him about the invite to see Josie.

"Take yer chips round 'ome ter keep warm, then we'll 'ave a chat about it."

She did so, knowing that she had only a few minutes until Grace was home.

"This is 'ow I look at it, Valerie. You've bin a good gel ter yer mother and to us. I think as you should go an' see yer friend fer a few days. We can keep an eye out fer Grace. An' we'me on the phone now so you can allus give us a ring, can't yer?" He smiled his good-natured smile.

"Thanks, Ben. I'll talk to mom about it when she comes in." She dreaded it.

*   *   *

Rose's baby was born three weeks after Mary's baby. It was a boy. The whole family were jubilant, especially Wilf. Nellie was totally surprised at his reaction.

She told Annie, "I'm gobsmacked at our Wilf. 'E loved 'is kids, I know, but 'e left it all ter me. Now 'e does anything fer the grandkids. Even changed Patricia's nappy the other day when our Mary was out shoppin'. I said ter 'im you'me gerrin a proper stop at whum in yer old age. Reg doe see 'im at the loft so much now either."

Annie laughed. "'E's comfortable in 'is own 'ome, that's what. Gorra telly an' all 'e needs wi'out gooin out all the while."

Nellie nodded. "Anyroad, Annie, I don't want ter put on yer ter sleep round me mother's now there's gonna be a babby skrikin' fer feeds in the night. Me mom never wakes up, anyroad, so we'll let 'em get on wi' it. I'm round there early ter get 'er dressed an' bring 'er round 'ere. When our Patty's married, me mom'll come round 'ere permanent."

Annie raised an eyebrow. "When's the weddin' then, Nell?"

"I don't know, when they've got somewhere ter live. Trouble is our Patty woe go anywhere wi'out Prince. They could 'ave the flat over Ronnie's shop but there's nowhere for the dog, only a titchy back yard."

Annie thought for a moment, sipping her tea. "They could lodge wi' me. Do yer think they'd like to, Nellie?"

Nellie was touched. "I'll ask them, Annie, but you won't be upset if they say no, will yer?"

Annie shook her head. "No, course not. It's their lives. Thay'me a lovely couple an' I'm lonely at times. They could 'ave me front room. I wouldn't bother 'em."

"I know you won't. I'll ask 'em first opportunity I get."

Valerie didn't speak of the proposed holiday until she was at Renee's on the Friday evening. They all sat round the table, drinking tea. Flo was telling them that Fred was a reformed character since his good hiding. He had realised which side his bread was buttered.

"To hear her talk you would think as 'e was the best catch in the Midlands," Grace had said.

On this particular evening she was regaling them with how thrifty he had become and how he was saving up to take her and Mark to Rhyl for a week.

"I ain't bin away since we was married apart from the club trips."

Grace sniffed. "Me, neither. Chance is a fine thing."

Valerie started collecting the cups. "I've got the chance of going away for a few days," she said.

Grace spun round on her chair, "You have?" she exclaimed. "Where to, may I ask, and who with?"

Flo sat up, ears cocked. Renee sat, biscuit suspended midway to her mouth. It was soggy from dunking and broke off into her tea.

"Mrs Salt's asked me if I'd like to go with them to see Josie for a couple of days."

Grace flushed. "First I've heard about it."

"Well, I haven't had a chance to talk to you about it yet, Mom."

The room went quiet. Valerie started to wash up. She could have cut the atmosphere with a knife. She dreaded the journey home.

On the bus, Grace didn't speak. They sat in silence. Valerie dreaded the weekend if this was going to continue. They entered the house. Grace switched the light on.

Hanging up her coat, she said, "What other secrets 'ave you kept from me?"

Valerie gasped. "What do you mean, Mother?"

"I said, what other secrets 'ave you bin keepin' from me?"

"None. I was going to talk to you about seeing Josie. It won't cost me anything in fares and a couple of nights in a boarding house won't break the bank."

"I'm not talkin' about that. 'Ow do I know you're goin' with Vera and Steve? You could 'ave a bloke 'angin' about somewhere an' be goin' with 'im."

Valerie laughed derisively. "Don't be so silly. Mother. You can go down to the shop and ask Mrs Salt. I've got nothing to hide."

"What about me 'ere all on me own? An' I've not bin well lately. Don't know 'ow I've kept on goin' ter work."

"Ben says he'll keep an eye out for you, Mother. You won't be alone."

"So, Ben knows about it, does 'e? Well, I will be on me own, won't I? You won't be 'ere."

Valerie felt like crying. "I'm going to bed, Mother. Goodnight, see you in the morning."

She went to her room, feeling trapped. How could she convince Grace that she should go to Minehead without her having hysterics or giving out the silent treatment for days?

Next morning, Valerie and Grace cleaned the house in silence. Valerie got ready to do the shopping.

"Don't ask me if I want ter come," said Grace. "What I want counts fer nothing round here."

"Oh, Mother," said Valerie, "just put your coat on and shape yourself."

"Go on your own, if that's what yer want. Me knees are killin' me anyway."

Valerie knew that if she did her life would be even more unbearable for days on end.

"Come on, Mother. You haven't seen Thelma for ages. You'll enjoy a walk round the town."

Grace shrugged into her coat. Picking up her bag, she walked out of the door, leaving Valerie to lock up.

Later that afternoon Valerie called round at the Jinkses to see if there was any washing. Frank was cleaning the stove.

"Come on in, love," he said. "How are you and your mom?"

"We're fine, Mr J. How are you?"

He grimaced. "Missin' 'er, Valerie. I'm comin' up ter retirin'. We 'ad a lot of things we wanted ter do tergether. We planned ter 'ave a little caravan down Bridgnorth or Stourport but I don't want ter do that on me own. What'll I do all day wi'out 'er?"

Valerie put a hand on his shoulder. "You'll find something. The house and the garden. You can start going to The Haymaker's again with Ben."

He shook his head. "Ain't got the heart. I sometimes feel like giving it neck."

She continued, "Can't you help Ben in the shop? I quite liked that Saturday I did for him, meeting folks."

He pondered. "S'pose I could but I doe know if 'e wants me round 'im. 'E's used ter werkin' on his own. Aye up, 'ere 'e is. Closed at four, I expect, it bein' Satday."

Ben came in, loaded with shopping. "Hiya, Valerie. Okay, love?"

She nodded. Frank went outside to empty the bowl of dirty water down the drain. Ben looked closely at her.

"Somethin' up, love?"

She hesitated, then said, "Well, me mom's upset about me wantin' to go for a fer days to Minehead to see Josie."

He frowned. "You should put yer foot down and go. You've bin a good gel fer yer mother, a few days away'll do yer good."

She sighed. "I know but is it worth it?"

Ben started to put the shopping away. "Leave me to bring the washing round. I'll be round later."

True to his word, an hour later, he knocked on the back door.

"Hello, Grace," he said. "This is the last bit o' washin' I'll bother yer with, love. We've got a cleaner comin' in. 'Er's gonna do three half days a wik. Anyroad, we'll see how we get on."

"We don't mind doing a bit of washing, Ben," said Valerie.

"I know you don't but you and yer mom are werkin', you 'ave enough ter do. Anyway, me an' me dad 'ave decided that we'd like ter treat yer fer bein' so good to us."

Valerie and Grace both spoke at once. "No, no. We don't expect anything."

Grace said, "Your mother was good to me when I 'ad Herbert bad an' 'er kept an eye on our Valerie when 'er used ter come 'ome from school an' I was at work."

Ben raised his hand to stop her. "Well, whatever you say, we've med up our minds. The waiting lists have practically gone now, you can get a phone put in within a wik."

Valerie gasped. "A phone!"

Grace was not so sure about it. "We've done without one all this time."

Ben said, "I know you 'ave but I've been tellin' Valerie 'er should go an' see her friend an' if you've got the phone 'er can ring every day. That's beside us bein' there if you need anythin'."

Put like that, how could Grace object? She was dumbfounded.

Valerie went across to Ben and kissed him on the cheek. She had tears in her eyes. What a lovely man Ben Jinks was.

Chapter Twenty

The stable badly needed clearing out but Ronnie was unable to face it. He missed Lily badly. He could still smell her. Every time he opened the stable door there was her tack, hanging on the wall in front of him.

One Saturday afternoon, Chas took pity on him and made a start. He was under pressure from Maureen. There were mice nesting in the tea chests, stored at the back of the building, and Maureen was terrified. She was reluctant to peg out her washing on the line after seeing one run across the yard.

"We'll have rats next," she said, so Chas decided to bite the bullet and get on with the job.

For a joke he tied string round the bottom of his trouser legs. Maureen watched from the kitchen window, the door tightly closed. He picked one of the tea chests up.

"Blimey, this is 'eavy," he thought. "Must be full o' bricks." As he lifted it, the bottom split and the contents fell out. It looked like a heap of pewter mugs, candlesticks, gravy boats, salvers and dishes of all descriptions. The newspaper they were wrapped in had been chewed into tiny bits by the mice.

"Maureen," he shouted. She gingerly opened the back door. "Come 'ere, love. There ain't any mice."

She opened the top of the stable door to let in more light. Chas passed her one of the candlesticks.

She gasped. "I think it's silver, Chas."

"More like pewter, it's filthy derty."

"No, really. I think it's solid silver."

"Good grief," he said. "There's a pile in 'ere an' all."

Forgetting her fear, Maureen went into the building.

"I wonder what's in the rest on 'em? We'd better be careful in case the bottoms drop out o' the others."

Chas dragged the boxes outside, one by one, into the yard and proceeded to investigate the contents. There was more silver and lots of china and ornaments and figurines. One contained a load of old saucepans which had been repaired with washers and one nothing but mouldy old shoes, but mainly it was a newspaper-wrapped treasure trove. They carefully carried the items into the kitchen. Maureen washed all the china carefully. One by one they were cleansed and the true glory of the colours and workmanship came to light. Chas was despatched to Turdy's for a tin of Silvo and he set to work to clean the silver.

At six o'clock Ronnie called in with their meat order and to see how Chas was getting on. As he entered the kitchen he was confronted by their handiwork. Every surface in the two downstairs rooms was covered with the treasures. He gasped.

"All yours, brov," said Maureen. "All this was in the stable in them tea chests."

Ronnie sank down on to a kitchen chair. "I need a drink," he said.

Nellie and Wilf were astounded when they saw the find.

"Our Ronnie, this lot's just askin' ter be pinched," said Wilf. "If I was you, I'd pack it all up an' tek it ter the auction rooms."

Ronnie agreed but, being the businessman nowadays, said, "Yes, I know Dad, but will they give me a good deal on it?"

Nellie cut in. "Why don't you ask that solicitor chap? 'E should be able ter advise yer."

"Good thinkin', Mom. I'll ring 'im Monday mornin'."

Nellie was picking up the figurines and looking at the marks underneath.

"I think thay'me good pieces. Your dad's right. Get 'em sold afore they gets broke or pinched."

Ronnie nodded. "Would you like anythin', Mom? Or you, our Maureen?"

They shook their heads.

"Too much responsibility," said Maureen.

Nellie agreed. "I don't think so, son. It's all lovely but if I 'ad one I'd be frit ter death ter dust it."

Maureen said, "And I'd be worried ter death in case the bab broke it."

They all stared her, then Nellie cried, "Your bab?"

Maureen nodded, smiling smugly. They all laughed. Ronnie gently danced his sister round the kitchen, then shook Chas by the hand. Wilf clapped his son-in-law on the back.

"I think this calls fer a visit ter The Haymekker's ternight," he said.

Ronnie frowned. "We needn't tell anybody about this lot, though."

They all agreed. It was to be a well-kept family secret.

* * *

The following Monday Valerie went to see Mrs Shelley about taking a week's holiday.

"I'm sorry it's a bit short notice but I've been invited to go with the parents of my friend. They want to go before the season gets busy. We can get digs easier at this time of year."

She held up her hand. "Don't apologise, Valerie. You are a good worker. Apart from the odd half day for funerals, you don't ask for much time off. Of course you can take the week. I will get someone from the typing pool to do Mr Harris's work. Just you go and have a good time."

"Thank you, Mrs Shelley. I will."

On leaving the office, it dawned on Valerie that her supervisor had not looked at all well. Of course, like Grace, she was getting older but there was a look about her which disturbed Valerie. She had always found Mrs Shelley to be fair and kind. She wouldn't care to work for anyone else.

Ben fetched the small case belonging to Connie out of the cupboard. He spotted Valerie in the back yard and called to her.

"Valerie, I'm sure me mom would like you to 'ave this."

He put the case on top of the wall. "It's just the right size for a few days away."

Valerie was touched. "Thanks, Ben. By the way, did your cleaning lady come?"

"Oh, yes. 'Er's named Iris. A nice gel, widder wi' two schoolkiddies. Comes in the shop. Not a canter, quiet really."

"Glad you've got somebody decent, Ben."

"Ar, it'll tek the pressure off." He waved and went inside.

Grace saw the case as soon as she entered the kitchen.

"Gettin' packed already then?" she said.

Valerie answered, "Not yet, Mom. Ben's given it to me. It was Mrs Jinks's."

"Oh, I thought as you'd bought it."

Valerie put the eggs in to poach and made the toast.

"I've got the week off to go. When I get back I can spring-clean and wash the curtains and covers."

Grace sniffed. "If you like," she said.

Two days later the phone was installed. Grace was wary of it. Valerie wrote down her office number and Ben's number in a little book and showed her mother how to dial.

"Don't s'pose as I'll ever use it," Grace muttered.

"It's there for emergencies, Mom, and I'll be able to ring you, won't I?"

Grace grimaced. "I s'pose so," she said reluctantly.

* * *

Mr Foster had recommended a reputable firm of auctioneers in Birmingham for Ronnie to consult about his antiques. He telephoned them and they arranged for him to take some on a Thursday afternoon for valuation. Nellie rarely went to the city and Ronnie decided that she should accompany him and he would take her for a meal while they were there.

The expert, Mr Rhodes, was impressed by the silver. He gave an estimate of what to expect, which left them open-mouthed with astonishment. Nellie had made a note of some of the marks on the porcelain.

Mr Rhodes said, "You think that the silver is valuable? Well, the porcelain may be even more so, especially the figures. Have you decided what you want to do?"

Without hesitation, Ronnie agreed to let them auction the silver. He was given a detailed receipt and arranged to bring the porcelain the following Thursday. When they left the building, he drove into the city.

"Wheer are we goin'?" asked Nellie.

"Fer a nice bit o' grub."

"Wheer?"

"Well, there's one or two nice 'otels we can eat at."

Nellie was perturbed. "Am I dressed good enough, son?"

He laughed. "Good enough for me, Mom. Tek no notice, my money's as good as anybody else's."

He then confided in his mother that he had almost paid off the bank loan for the shop.

Over the meal, which Nellie felt she could have cooked for a tenth of the price, he asked her advice.

"Mom, if you was me, would yer invest in another shop?"

She thought for a while, then asked, "Wheer was yer thinkin' of, Ron?"

"Well, Frankie Pearce, the delivery man, says that Brian Jenkins's missis is bad. 'E's thinkin' o' movin' to the seaside. 'Er needs the fresh air. 'E's fifty-five now an' Frankie reckons 'e's got enough ter tek early retirement."

Nellie chewed her food reflectively. It was taking time to sink in that her son could have two shops at the age of twenty-two.

"It's a lot of werk, son, doin' the books an' that. Who'd werk there fer yer?"

"Well, there's a chap there, took Terry's place. I would ask him to werk in me High Street shop an' ask Terry ter manage Brian's. 'E's werked there before an' knows the ropes."

Nellie was concerned. "You ain't had an 'oliday since yer bought Haynes's. Don't let werk rule yer life, Ron."

"No, I shan't, Mom, but I want to get on. I want ter mek good use of Herbie's money, show 'im as I was the right one ter leave it to. Anyroad, I was thinkin' o' me an' Barry 'avin' 'oliday before I did get the shop over the bonk. They reckon Brian aye sellin' just yet and, o' course, he might change his mind."

Nellie agreed. "You an' our Barry'd enjoy that. 'E werks 'ard an' all. In a way I 'ope as 'e doe tek that coal yard on."

Ronnie patted her hand. "What other work would he do, Mom? He's bin at it since he was thirteen. Leave 'im be, 'e'll mek 'is own mind up."

Nellie was affronted. "As if I'd interfere, son. You're all good kids. I've no need to."

* * *

The three days at Butlin's which Valerie spent with Josie were the best of her life, so far. Josie had worked for three Saturdays and so was entitled to three days off. Vera, Steve and Valerie stayed at a homely bed and breakfast in the village. They bought day passes to go into the camp and because Josie was staff, she could show them round. Valerie was impressed. They swam in the pool and spent time on the beach. It was windy but dry and sunny. The meals were good and they were allowed, with Josie's pass, to see a couple of shows. Josie's piano skills were utilised, which she enjoyed. Her mother was very proud.

"I'm glad she 'ad them lessons, Steve," she said. "She can always fall back on her pianner playing."

Valerie telephoned Grace.

"Are you enjoyin' yourself?" she asked.

"It's okay, Mom, not as good as I expected," she lied.

"Bet you'll be glad ter get 'ome then?"

"Reckon so, Mom."

"The sooner, the better. I'm fed up on me own."

Valerie gritted her teeth. "See you soon, Mom," she said.

The three days were soon over. Valerie resolved to have another holiday as soon as she could. She needed the respite from Grace. Vera and Steve were a refreshing change. They never moaned. She envied Josie and wondered how she could bear to be away from such wonderful parents.

Ronnie asked Terry if he could cope for a week while he went on holiday. True to form, Terry reassured him.

"Course we can manage. You manage when I'm away, don't yer? So, it's no different. Get yerself off an' enjoy yerself. Where are yer goin'?"

"Butlin's."

"Which one?"

"Minehead."

Terry gave him an old-fashioned look. "Oh, yeah! That's where that Josie Salt's gone, ain't it?"

Ronnie flushed. "Has she?"

Terry laughed. "As if yer day know."

Barry was looking forward to his break. He actually went into town and purchased some new clothes. Nellie was delighted.

She said, "All 'e does is save, save, save. 'Bout time as 'e spent a bit."

Wilf said, "You should be glad as 'e saves. 'E coulda bin a waster."

She had to agree. "I know. The lad's set on 'avin' 'is own business. Gerry's sons doe want ter know. Thay'me at the university, they doe want ter run the business. Our Barry wants ter 'ave first refusal. I just wish as 'im an' our Ronnie could meet a coupla nice gels."

Wilf sighed. "You'me allus sayin' that. Anyroad, 'as our Patty decided when the weddin's gonna be?"

"No. Can't find anywhere to live. Thay'me still thinkin' over whether to lodge at Annie's while they save ter buy 'ouse."

Wilf grimaced. "As long as they doe end up at 'is mother's."

Nellie laughed. "Oh, yes, 'er'd love ter 'ave our Prince sleepin' up 'er stairs."

*   *   *

Valerie came back to earth with a bump. Grace had missed her and let her know it. To compensate, Valerie began the spring-cleaning on the Thursday, as she had promised. Being at home meant that she would meet Iris, Ben and Frank's cleaner. Valerie spoke to her as she was pegging out the curtains.

"Morning. Nice day."

Iris smiled. She was an attractive woman of around thirty years of age.

"Just the job," she said.

"How are you getting on working at the Jinks's?"

"Okay, fine. They're no trouble and so kind. I've got two other cleaning jobs, fit in with the kiddies. I like to be home when they get in from school."

Valerie asked, "Are they boys or girls?"

"One of each," Iris answered. "Nine and ten."

"I lost my dad when I was eight and a half," Valerie said. "I still miss him a lot."

"Yes, I know how you feel. I miss my husband all the time and the kiddies do too, although they don't say."

Valerie finished pegging out the curtains. She almost asked Iris to come round for a cup of tea but thought better of it. Grace would not have approved.

That evening, she mentioned to Ben that she had met his cleaning lady.

His face lit up and he said, "Yes, Iris is a lovely girl. She comes into the shop, brings shoes for them what can't get. Her kiddies are smashin', a credit to her."

To her surprise, and shock, Valerie felt a stab of jealousy. It quite shook her and she made a quick exit. She had to be alone to sort out her feelings. How could she feel like that about Ben? He was so much older than she was. She had known him all her life. She had never thought romantically about anyone since Norman. What was wrong with her? Ben was almost a father figure, wasn't he?

Chapter Twenty-One

The antiques from Herbie's realised a surprising amount. Ronnie realised that he could easily afford Brian's shop if it came up for sale. He decided to wait until it came on the market and not pre-empt things by putting in an offer. In the meantime, he would keep his ear to the ground for a replacement for Terry, in case Brian's bloke was unsuitable.

Barry became quite excited about the holiday. He was determined to get his hands clean and wore gloves at work for the deliveries. He had his leg pulled by workmates and family alike.

Wilf said, "'E'll be gerrin one o' them manicures next, proper pansy like."

Nellie was pleased. "'Bout time he got hisself organised. The Zam-Buk's done 'is cracked knuckles a power o' good. Still gorra bit o' black o' the coal where it's healed but not as bad as they was."

While the lads were away, Christine was coming to stay for the week to spend some time with her parents and her nephew and niece. Nellie was proud of her daughter and so excited to hear that she was being promoted to ward sister. Annie and Nellie told everyone they met about it.

Grace heard Nellie telling Thelma about it in the shop.

After she'd gone, Grace said, "You wouldn't think as Nellie Edwards had ever 'ad ter scrape fer nits, would yer?"

Thelma was shocked at her friend's cattiness. "Now Grace, we've all 'ad ter do that at some time, ain't we?"

Grace sniffed. "Ar," she said, "some more'a others."

* * *

On their arrival at Butlin's, Barry and Ronnie were allocated a chalet on the singles section of the complex, over the opposite side from the family section. The accommodation was basic. There were two single beds, a wardrobe and a washbasin. Across the green area was a toilet and shower block. They were quite happy with the set-up and soon unpacked. Barry decided to have a shower and Ronnie had a walk round the camp to investigate.

"See yer later, Ron, doe get lost."

"I shan't." He wondered if he would come across Josie on his travels.

Ronnie strolled round. He found the swimming pool and the dining hall, located the bars and the coffee bar. The door to the ballroom was unlocked and he could hear someone playing the piano. He went inside. Walking over to the stage, he had the shock of his life when he saw that it was Josie playing. He had only been there an hour and he had found her.

Approaching her from behind, he said, "Play it again, Sam."

She jumped and turned round. Their eyes met. She was astounded.

They just stared at each other, then she said, "What're you doing here?"

He laughed. "Deliverin' meat, what do you think?"

She smiled. "Get off, don't be daft."

He continued, "And pork pies, pig's pudding, chitterlins and brains, liver, faggotts and a nice rabbit."

"Stop, stop, you're putting me off me meal."

"I'm on holiday, yer saft thing. What do yer think as I'm doin' 'ere?"

"Oh, right. You on your own?"

"No, me brother's 'ere with me. Our Barry. I finally got him away from the coal yard."

She looked away from him. "Well, it's a small world. I hope you enjoy your holiday." Then, reluctant to let him go, she said, "How are all your family these days?"

He sat down on the edge of the stage. "Well, Mary's got a daughter, our John's got a son and, you'll never guess what."

"What?" she said.

"Our Maureen's expectin'."

She put a hand to her mouth. "Oh, I am pleased for her. I used to like working with Maureen."

They lapsed into silence, then, "Are you goin' into tea, Josie?"

"Yes, in a minute."

"Are you allowed to sit with us at the table?"

"If there's room. Will Barry be there?"

"Yes, I 'spect so, if 'e's not fallen ter sleep in the chair."

"I'll tell them you're my cousins," said Josie, "then there'll be no trouble about me sitting with you."

Over the meal, they all chatted animatedly. Ronnie was interested in the work that Josie was doing and, particularly, in her time off.

"I have most evenings off. I do have to socialise and sometimes I play the piano but mostly I finish around five-thirty."

Ronnie was pleased to hear it. They were enjoying their apple pie and custard when Noreen came over.

"Aye up, Jose, who're these then?" she asked.

Josie introduced them and she sat down and joined in the conversation. Ronnie noticed that Barry had gone shy until Noreen, determined to draw him out, asked him about his work. That was one subject that Barry could talk about. Then it turned out that Noreen's brother supported the same football team as he did. The ice was broken.

That evening, over a drink, Ronnie asked Josie, "Do yer miss yer mom an' dad?"

"Yes, course I do. They were here last month, came for three days for a visit."

"Nice," said Ronnie. "When's the season finish?"

"For me, September. It'll soon go."

He nodded. "Shall you come back again next year?"

"No, I don't think so. I want to open me own shop, always have."

Ronnie said, "I know the feeling. It's hard work, though, Josie, a big responsibility."

"You've managed to do it, though."

"Yes, yes, I have," he said.

She then said, "Valerie came with me mom and dad."

He looked at her. "Valerie?"

"Yes, Valerie Potts."

"Oh," he said, "Poison Pottsy."

"Now that's my friend you're calling names, Ronnie Edwards."

He held up his hands. "Sorry but she's no friend o' mine."

"No, I know," said Josie. "Anyway, let's go to the ballroom and see what Barry and Noreen are up to."

By the end of the week Nellie's wish had come true. Barry and Noreen were smitten with each other and Ronnie and Josie were head over heels. It would be a long five months until the end of the season but the lads arranged to come as often as they could for Sunday visits and, of course, they could phone and write. Ronnie knew that Josie had been worth waiting for.

*　　　*　　　*

Valerie was finding it awkward to keep an eye on Iris. The only way she could discover the extent of Ben's feelings was to bring her into the conversation when she popped round to visit him and Frank. One evening she called in with an apple pie that she had baked. Frank's eyes lit up when he saw it.

"I'm partial ter a bit o' home med apple pie. Only trouble is I doe know 'ow ter mek the custard."

Valerie offered to make some. Ben came into the kitchen.

"Summat smells nice. Oh great, apple pie. I was upstairs an' I thought as I could smell summat nice." He put the kettle on. "Cuppa tea, Valerie?"

"Yes, please, Ben. Me mom's dropped off in front o' the telly, so I won't be missed for half an hour."

They sat enjoying their pie.

"How's business these days, Ben?"

"Oh, nice and steady, as usual. I'm lucky, I'm the only cobbler fer miles."

Valerie said, "Mom was grumbling last week about having to go all the way into town to buy a decent pair of shoes."

"Ar," said Frank. "The thing as we could do with round 'ere's a shoe shop."

The cogs started working in Valerie's head. "How are you getting on with Iris?"

Frank said, "Okay, never see her though. Ben just leaves her money. It's just as if the fairies have bin."

Ben agreed. "That's right. I ain't sin 'er fer ages but we allus knows 'er's bin. Apparently 'er's getting married again, according to Thelma at the cake shop. I 'ope as it doe mean as 'er's gonna gi' up our cleanin'. We mayn't get anybody as good."

"No," agreed Valerie, inwardly rejoicing.

September came. Mrs Shelley was not at all well and word spread round the offices that she was planning to retire. Valerie was hoping that she could take her place, although she realised, deep down, that she was a bit young for the post.

The position was advertised and the letters of application began to arrive. Valerie always opened the post arriving in the personnel office. She read all the letters and the ones which looked most qualified to get the supervisor's job she discarded. Mr Harris, together with Mrs Shelley, conducted the interviews. They were finding it difficult to find anyone suitable.

Mr Harris had got along well with Paula, who worked for him while Valerie was on holiday, so when Mrs Shelley suggested that Valerie could do the supervisor's job on a temporary basis, he was in agreement. The week before her twenty-third birthday Valerie was given the post.

* * *

Vera and Steve Salt were glad to have Josie back at home. Steve had redecorated her bedroom and the piano had been tuned. On her first evening back, she sat down for a meal with her parents and grandparents. It was a happy gathering and the meal was delicious.

"I've missed mom's cooking and me nan's baking," Josie said. "It's nice to be back and I'll be able to see my boyfriend more often now."

Vera sat up, ears pricked. Steve stopped eating. They all waited.

"I've been seeing a chap while I've been away."

"Oh, yeah?" said Steve. "Where's he from then?"

Josie smiled at him. "Round here," she said. Steve was relieved.

"Was he working at the camp?" asked Gran.

"No, he came for a holiday with his brother. We didn't tell anybody because we didn't know how it would go."

"Who is it then?" asked Gran.

Josie smiled round at them. "Ronnie Edwards," she said. They all gasped.

"Ronnie the butcher?" asked Vera.

"Young Ronnie what went ter school with you?" said Gran.

"That's him," answered Josie.

Steve frowned. “I can remember the little matter of a necklace.”

Vera nodded, then Gran piped up, “’E’s alright is that lad. I allus liked ’is mom. ’Er’s a good gel is Nellie Edwards, brought her kids up right. Thay’me all doin’ alright, ’ard werkers, all on ’em.”

Josie smiled gratefully at her. She had given Ronnie and his family a good reference.

“He’s coming later to meet you all properly and then he’s taking me to meet his mom and dad.”

Vera started to clear the table. “Better get the place tidied up then.”

Barry borrowed Ronnie’s van to go to Birmingham to collect Noreen. She introduced him to her parents and her brother. Barry and Don got on famously, as fellow football supporters would, and her parents took to him straight away.

At 34 Ingram Terrace Josie was being made welcome. Nellie was overjoyed. Wilf had to smile, he was as pleased for her as for his son.

He said, “One thing about it, we woe starve, what wi’ our Ronnie’s butcher’s an’ your mom an’ dad’s fish an’ chip shop.”

Barry and Noreen arrived. They took the girl to their hearts. Again, Nellie was scarcely able to contain her glee. At last Barry had a girl and it looked as if it could be serious.

It was agreed that Barry was in need of a vehicle, so again Chas was coerced into finding him a reliable van.

To enable Chas to work on the vehicles belonging to family and friends, Lily’s stable was being used as a workshop.

Ronnie told them all, “I’m glad ter see it being used. I still miss her.” But with tools and cars around the yard, the stable became less bleak and he could bear to visit once again.

*   *   *

It was Valerie's birthday and it was Friday. She accompanied Grace to Renee's. Arthur had left an envelope for her. She put it into her bag to open later. Flo had bought her a pair of leather gloves.

Mark was now eight and doing well at school. Valerie liked to sit to hear his reading and to help him with his arithmetic. Flo, Grace and Renee sat doing their favourite thing, grumbling.

"'Ow's you-know-who, Flo?"

"Same as usual. Gone to the dogs with Arthur."

"Do yer get yer 'ousekeepin' afore 'e guz?"

"Course I do, Mother. Anyroad, did yer go to the doc's terday like I told yer to?"

Renee grimaced. "I did, much good it done me. They doe bother about we."

Flo sighed. "What did 'e say?"

"It's arthuritis in me joints. Nothin' as they can do 'cept rubbin' an' asprin. Mrs Peters told me ter get some o' that dog oil. Says it's done her knees the werld o' good."

Mark raised his head from his book. "Dog oil, Nan? Is it med from dogs?"

They all ignored him. Flo said, "I'll get yer some termorrer, Mother. Did yer get ter the shops terday?"

Renee nodded. "Ar, I just popped ter Brian's fer me meat. 'E's sellin' up. 'Is missis aye well. 'E's gorra place in Wales an' thay'me movin' theer."

Grace asked, "What's 'appenin' ter the shop? Will yer still 'ave a butcher's? If not, it'll be a buz ride fer yer meat."

Renee answered, "Oh, it'll still be a butcher's, somebody from over the bonk's bought it. He's already got one shop, they say."

Valerie's head shot up. She sat as though turned to stone.

Her mother said, "What's his name? Do you know, Mother?"

"Ar, I think it's Richards, or was it Edwards?"

The next day Josie called round at Valerie's with a card and present. Valerie was pleased to see her. They sat companionably, having a cup of tea and chatting.

Grace asked, "Are yer glad ter be 'ome now, Josie? I bet you missed yer mom and her you. I'd miss our Valerie if she ever went away like that."

Josie sipped her tea. "I'm back now anyway and I'm stopping. I'm looking for a job. I don't mind travelling into the town, the buses run regularly."

"Not goin' back ter Tresses then?"

"No, I need a fresh start."

"Our Valerie's acting supervisor now Mrs Shelley's left."

Josie smiled. "Good on yer, Val. You've done well."

Grace went out of the room and Josie plucked up the courage to tell Valerie about her relationship with Ronnie.

"I've been seeing a feller while I've been at Butlin's."

"Oh yes," Valerie said. "Does he live far away?"

"No, he lives round here."

Valerie was surprised. "Does he work at the camp?"

"No, he came for a holiday. You know him."

Valerie racked her brains. "Not Roger again?"

"No, not likely. It's Ronnie Edwards."

Valerie was speechless. She couldn't look at Josie, who said, "I know you've never liked him, Val, but he's alright really and we get on really well."

Valerie pulled herself together. "I don't like or dislike him but I'm surprised at you Josie, especially since the necklace incident."

"Oh, that's gone now. He's sworn to me he didn't take it and I believe him. It must have been one of his mates, playing a trick."

Valerie said, "How's he getting the money for his shops? That's what I'd like to know."

Josie answered, "I don't know but I'll tell you Valerie, he's got it honestly."

Valerie collected the cups. "Well, to me it's a mystery," she said.

*   *   *

Norman had put down the deposit on a house. It was two doors up from Mary and Desmond and three doors from Betty and Reg. He had a good job at an accountants in the town and was keen to get married. They had decided on a December wedding. Maureen would have had her baby by then, so they arranged it for the beginning of the month, as Ronnie would be run off his feet for the festive season.

Nora wasn't looking forward to her last chick leaving the nest. She was secretly disappointed that her son had fallen for a girl who was deaf but she daren't say it to anyone but her husband.

"How's she going to hear a baby cry?" she asked him. "It's worrying me to death."

He sighed. "Don't worry, love, mothers have an instinct."

"Humph. I just hope she does or I can see meself there all the while."

He patted her arm. "Mary's close by and Betty. She'll have plenty to turn to."

"They don't know much about babies themselves. I dread to think what could happen."

"Well, you're crossing bridges before you come to 'em. They may not 'ave any babies."

She polished the table vigorously. "I s'pose we don't know what that illness done to 'er. You might be right."

*   *   *

Valerie was coping with the supervisor's job. She had never become familiar with the rest of the girls in the offices. She took dictation from the managing director and sat in Mrs Shelley's office on her own, allocating work to the rest of the girls. She wouldn't admit it, even to herself, but at times she felt very lonely. She expected high standards and behind her back the girls called her Pansy Potter. In a way she was relieved to get out of the personnel department. It had become monotonous. She had needed a change. Even so, each day was much the same and life for her was generally dull. She found that she looked forward to seeing Ben and Frank for a chat, popping round a couple of times a week.

One evening Frank announced that he was taking his redundancy. His section of the factory was relocating. He was coming up to retiring age anyway, and he had money in his pension fund. Ben was surprised but not displeased.

"You can do the decorating now, Dad," he said.

Valerie suggested, "You can give Ben a hand in the shop."

Ben laughed. "The customers would be gettin' two left shoes, that's fer sure but the shop could do wi' a lick o' paint."

Frank said, "I'll be better off stoppin' at werk, you'll kill me off."

Ben then announced, "The shop next door's gonna come empty. Mr Brittle's finishin'. Shame that is. 'Is famly 'ad that shop fer years, allus bin a sweet an' tobacconist as long as I can remember.

Valerie was interested. She still had her heart set on opening a shoe shop. Frank went to the bathroom.

"Ben," she said, "how do you feel about a shoe shop in the High Street?"

"Ar, you mentioned that afore, Valerie. I 'adn't really thought about it."

She leaned towards him. "How about I find out what the profit margin is? Would you be interested?"

"Well, I don't really know. It's an altogether new trade ter me, gel."

"Would you think about it?"

"Course I will but I ain't promising anything. What gid yer that idea anyroad?"

"Well, working at the factory and seeing the invoices and how much we sell the shoes to the trade."

"You'd need capital, Valerie."

"I've got some savings but I'd need a business partner to invest."

Ben patted her hand. "I'll sleep on it. We'll talk about it another time. No rush. Mr Brittle's not sellin' just yet."

Valerie just hoped that he wasn't too set in his ways to help her out.

* * *

It was all hands to the pump when Patty and Norman got the keys to their house. All spare time was spent scraping walls, removing and refitting fireplaces. A builder was employed to do the bathroom. As with Herbie's old house, it gradually took shape. Again, Aunty Betty and Patty were busy sewing curtains and dresses. As Christine was her only unmarried sister, she was to be bridesmaid. Her dress was to be blue, to set off her blue eyes and lovely blonde hair.

Jack Proudfoot helped. He hung new doors and repaired window frames. Nora kept an eye on the progress. She was asked to accompany Patty and Norman to select a table and chairs, which they had already decided upon, which pleased her and helped to keep her sweet.

Nellie's fears of her house becoming empty were unfounded. There was always someone popping in or a baby to be minded. Ivy was very old now and getting frailer. When Patty had gone to her own house, she would be moving in to her room. Negotiations to get Rose and John's name on the rent book were underway. If there was any problem, John had decided that he would purchase the house. Indeed, Nellie was going to enquire about the possibility next time she saw the rent man.

* * *

Vera and Steve Salt were having a family discussion with George and Eva, Josie's grandparents. They also had heard that Mr Brittle was thinking of selling his shop. They felt that it was in an ideal position for a hairdressing business.

Vera said, "Our Josie always wanted her own shop. I know Tresses is popular but there's always room for competition."

Steve nodded. "What'll we do then? We can always give 'er the money ter get started. The shop'll need fittin' out, if we get the say so. That'll cost a pretty penny."

Eva said, "Well, Steve, we can put towards it. 'Er may as well benefit now as after we'me jed an' gone."

George nodded. "You'me right, Eva. 'Er's allus bin a good wench an' 'er could do wi' a bit on a boost after the disappointment 'er's 'ad."

Vera said, "Don't ferget that's over an' done with now, Dad. 'Er's gorra good chap in that young Ronnie."

"You'me right," he said. "Be nice ter see 'er settled. Yo'de better look inter that shop, Steve."

"I will, George, but I shan't tell 'er unless it looks a likely proposition."

Ben had thought over the prospect of buying the shop next door. He would miss Mr Brittle. They would, on occasion, have a cup of tea together. He decided to have a chat with him.

"Hello, Ben. How's your dad?" Mr Brittle was pleased to see Ben.

"He's picking up now, Mr Brittle. Don't know how he'll be when he retires, though. I've popped in to see you about a bit o' business, actually."

Mr Brittle put the kettle on the little stove in the back room. "Sit down, lad. As you know, I only close for half an hour." He opened his sandwiches and offered them to Ben. "What can I do for you, lad?"

"Well, I hope as you don't mind, I only wondered how much you was thinkin' the shop would fetch?"

Mr Brittle looked quizzically at him. "Were you interested for yourself or for somebody else?"

"Well, I'll tell yer because I know as you won't go an' tell all an' sundry. I was thinkin' o' gooin inter partnership wi' young Valerie. 'Er's lived next door ter me all her life and 'er's got the idea of openin' a shoe shop."

Mr Brittle thought for a while. "Well, I think that's a good idea. Folk round here have to go into the big town for shoes. She's got her eye to business by all accounts."

Ben was pleased to hear Valerie praised.

"Yes, 'er's a good, 'ardwerkin' gel. 'Er's got 'er 'ead screwed on. Done all the bookkeepin' at college an' that."

"Well, all I can say, Ben, is that you will get first refusal. I've always respected you and you've been a good working neighbour. Let me know what you decide."

"I will, Mr Brittle, thanks."

Ben decided to have another talk with Valerie. He needed to discover exactly what she had in mind and how much money she had. The opportunity arose when he saw her coming home from work that evening.

"'Allo, Valerie. Alright?"

"Yes thanks, Ben."

"I'm glad as I've bumped inter yer. I wanted to 'ave a chat about that business idea you 'ad."

"Okay, when would you like me to pop round?"

"Well, dad's goin' out at last. 'E's got a domino match, so can yer pop round about eight o'clock?"

She nodded. "Sure, see you then."

Grace came home, tired out. She complained about her feet and knees aching, although she sat down all day.

Valerie told her, "Go and sit in a nice warm bath Mother. I'll cook the tea."

She was paving her way for her visit next door. Grace agreed and Valerie cooked belly pork, potatoes and peas, which her mother enjoyed, then switched the TV on to a favourite programme.

Valerie washed up, then called to Grace, "Just popping next door, Mom."

"What for now?" asked Grace.

"Just a quick word with Frank, nothing important."

"Can't you phone 'im?" asked Grace.

"No, I'll interrupt your viewing. Won't be long." And she made a quick exit.

Ben had a cup of tea ready and a pen and paper to work things out as far as they could.

"Sit you down, Valerie. Make yerself at 'ome."

He felt comfortable with her, not threatened or shy.

"Now then, I don't know about this shop venture. It'll need fittin' out wi' shelvin' an' footstools and chairs. Then there's the stock. The counter's there an' the till. It'll need a coat o' paint an' a sign. What worries me is the stock. 'Ow do we know what's gonna sell in our High Street? An' who's gonna man the shop? You've gorra good job, you won't want ter give it up after all you've put into it."

Valerie started to cry.

"Well, whatever's the matter?" Ben asked. He felt uncomfortable and unable to cope with a crying Valerie.

"'Ere, 'ave a drink o' this tea an' tell me."

She managed to stop crying. "Well, Ben, I've been acting supervisor for some weeks now. Anyway, they've found a replacement for Mrs Shelley. I didn't even know they were still looking. Now they want me to be the managing director's permanent secretary. I can't stand the man and I feel they've done a dirty trick on me. I feel used."

Ben was concerned. "After all you've done for them lot! Never mind, gel."

She went on, "I've thought about the shop, Ben, and I realise it's too much to ask you to take a gamble like that. I've got some money but it's not a fortune, just some me Gran left me and some savings. I think I know what stock would sell. I enjoyed the day I spent in your shop, meeting people." She paused. "I s'pose I've got a right cheek asking you to come in with me, Ben. Sorry."

He moved round to sit beside her and put his arm round her.

Patting her shoulder, he said, "I can't think of anybody I'd rather be in partnership with, Valerie. I've allus thought a lot of yer and me mom thought the werld o' yer. I aye short and I can't see how the shop could lose money, really."

She blew her nose and turned to face him. Giving him a watery smile, she kissed him on the cheek. They just sat there, looking at each other.

The next step, after the new shop had been secured by a deposit, was to prepare Grace for the news. Valerie knew that it would be a shock for her mother and she dreaded her reaction. She left it for two days before touching on the subject. It was a Sunday afternoon and all was peaceful. Valerie had washed up the dinner things and Grace was reading the Sunday paper.

"Mom, did you know Mr Brittle was selling his shop and retiring?"

"Yes. Thelma had said something about it. It won't be the same without that shop, unless whoever buys it carries on the same trade."

"I think we could do with a shoe shop in the High Street, meself."

"Yes, I s'pose we could. It's a ride inter town we could do wi'out but there's little 'ope o' anybody openin' one o' them."

Valerie took the bull by the horns. "I wouldn't mind a shoe shop meself."

Grace's mouth dropped open. "You? How could you get one?"

"Well, I could get a business partner. He could finance me until I could pay him back, or a bank loan. And I could run it."

Grace snorted. "Pie in the sky, that. Who's gonna do that? Anyroad, doe yer like yer job? You've got a good job you have, werked hard for it an' all. Better than a good many round here."

"Well, I'm sick of me job. I never told you but they're taking the supervisor's job off me. I'm just going to be Mr Lucas' secretary. I can't stand him all day. I need a change, Mother, and I'm seriously thinking of getting one."

Grace was speechless, then she found second wind. "You must be mad, our Valerie. Where can you get money from, anyway?"

"The bank gives business loans, Mother, and I see the profit margin on the shoes from working at the factory. The shop's in a good position. I'm sick to death of that office."

"You'd rather be a shop assistant then?"

"Don't be silly, Mother. It would be my shop."

"Folks wouldn't know that. They'd think as you was only the assistant."

"Don't be a snob, Mother. Most folk round the High Street would know me, anyway."

Grace was not convinced.

"I'll just have to make sure they do then," said Valerie.

Josie was disappointed about the shop being sold. It had gone even before she had a chance to make an offer.

Ronnie said, "Don't worry, another one'll come up. We'll keep an ear to the ground and look in the adverts. You've got a job in the meantime, it ain't the end of the world."

Nellie sympathised. "If you was meant to 'ave it, you would've done. There's summat else fer you, wait an' see."

Wilf agreed. "Don't worry, Jose, you've got the money behind yer, so the right opportunity'll crop up. Anyroad, who 'as got Brittles? Do yer know?"

She shook her head. "No, and we don't know what sort of shop it's going to be either. Not a hairdresser's, I hope."

Ronnie said, "Watch this space." And they all laughed.

Eight weeks later the workmen moved in to refit the shop. Ronnie was curious. He couldn't discover what was happening. Ben feigned ignorance, even the workmen were cagey. Although Valerie still saw Janice, she had not told her about the venture, preferring to keep it to herself, especially as Paul still worked at the butcher's. Grace had been sworn to secrecy, even from Flo and Renee.

Four weeks later the shop was ready and the new sign arrived. Everyone crowded to the windows of the butcher's and the cake shop to see it.

There it was, in all its glory:

VALERIE POTTS – QUALITY SHOES

Ronnie was speechless. He had to sit and have a cup of tea before he could phone Josie to tell her. She, in turn, was astounded.

"Ronnie, you're joking. It's another one of your pranks."

"No, honest, Jose. On me mother's death bed. Come and see for yerself."

"I shall and if you're having me on, I'll kill you."

When she had finished work, Josie arrived at the butcher's and saw that Ronnie was telling the truth. She didn't know how she felt, really, that her friend had kept such an important thing all to herself. Also, pipping her to the shop rankled quite a bit.

Ronnie put his arm round her. "I've got an idea. Why don't we alter the flat upstairs into a shop for you?"

Josie gasped. "Really? What a good idea, Ron. Can I go and have a look at it?"

He gave her the key. There was a bedroom, a living room, kitchen and bathroom. It could be fitted out, if they got permission. The stairs weren't too steep for customers to climb. She was excited and could hardly wait to get home to tell her parents.

Chapter Twenty-Two

Valerie and Ben were getting on well. They were astonished to discover they cared for each other. They decided to keep it a secret, especially from Grace and Frank.

After the first excitement of opening the shop, life settled into a pattern for them. They would close for lunch and sit in the back room of the shoe shop. It was comfortable in there. They had two chairs and a table and a small tabletop cooker and a sink.

Valerie did not frequent the butcher's. If they needed anything Ben would fetch it or she would go to the Home and Colonial. They were quite happy to let their relationship develop gradually, in private, away from the critical eye of parent or acquaintance.

When, one Saturday, the wedding of Norman Proudfoot and Patty Edwards took place at the little Methodist Church in the town, Valerie felt no resentment. She was secure with the relationship which was blossoming with Ben. Her friendship with Josie had, for the moment, floundered.

She still called in at the chip shop and Vera greeted her cordially enough. There were times when Valerie wished she could pop into the back room to chat to her friend but time went on and it looked as if there would be no turning back.

Ronnie and Josie could not get permission to convert the flat into a salon. Ronnie silently cursed Valerie Potts for snatching Brittle's from under their noses. And she seemed to be doing very well with it.

His new shop, 'over the bonk', was thriving under Terry's management. One day he phoned Ronnie.

"Hey, Ron, you'me lookin' for a shop for Josie, ain't yer?"

"Ar, I am. Why?"

"Well, there's a shop comin' empty next door but one to here. What do yer think?"

"I'll tell her. Thanks a bunch, Terry."

Josie was excited. Steve went with her to have a look. It was just the job, needed fitting out but they could manage that. It was in a good position. Josie was over the moon.

Steve said, "Our Josie, why don't you have some drivin' lessons? Then you can 'ave a little motor. I think we can run ter that."

She hugged him. "You're so good to me, Dad."

"Well, you're a good gel and, as Gran says, you might as well 'ave it now."

Barry and Noreen became engaged. Her mother was upset at the thought of her daughter moving away from the family but had to come to terms with it.

Her husband said, "'Er could've met somebody from th'other end o' the country at that 'oliday camp. You should be grateful 'e's only ten mile away."

She had to agree.

Ronnie's van had seen good service in the courtship and, at last, Chas came up trumps with an A35 van for Barry.

One day Annie and Nellie, fearing rain, were unpegging their washing.

Annie said, "'Alright, Nellie? It's black over Bill's mother's, aye it? A right bilin' piece. I see your Barry's gorra motor then? The street's fillin' up wi' 'em now."

Nellie agreed. "Sign o' the times, Annie. We'me alright for a lift, anyhow."

Annie laughed. "You'me right theer, cock, spiled fer choice, I'd say."

"How's Jack, Annie? Is 'is foot better?"

"Ar, a lot better now. Fancy, our Barry's engaged now, Nell. 'Er seems a nice wench, even though 'er's a Brummie."

Nellie smiled. “Yes, ’er is. Only a few months agoo I was ’opin’ as ’im and our Ronnie’d find nice gels, now they ’ave.”

Annie screwed up her face. “Odds ter our Jack. ’Er’s a stuck up madam. I ’ardly siz ’er, as you know. I doe know what I’d do wi’out you lot. You’me more like famly than me own.”

“I know,” Nellie had to agree. “I’m glad ter ’ave you an’ all, Annie. You’me like a mom ter me. Come on, we’ll ’ave a nice cuppa tea.”

Annie noticed how peaky Ivy looked. Nellie was worried about her.

“Me mom’s losin’ weight, Annie, but ’er seems ter be eatin’ the same.”

Annie agreed. “P’raps the doc had better tek a look at her. That new doctor, Blair, aye it? Seems ter ’ave a bit o’ oil in ’is lamp. They reckon as ’e’ll skin an ’eel the old un. Good riddance, I say. ’E’ll look at her proper, the new un.”

Nellie said, “I’ll get our Ronnie ter tek us. ’E’s usually quiet on a Monday.”

She thought about what the vet had said to Ronnie about Lily, when he saw her mother.

“Your mother’s a very old lady, Mrs Edwards. You can see that she’s been well cared for.”

“Yes, Doctor. What’s wrong with her do you think?”

“Well, I’m not sure but we’ll get some tests done. How long has she been unable to care for herself?”

Nellie thought and was rather shocked herself when she said, “About twenty years. It don’t seem five minutes, time flies.”

The doctor stared at her. “You’ve looked after your mother for twenty years? Remarkable.”

Nellie said. “What’s remarkable about it, Doctor? We look after our own round here.”

He smiled. “I know you do but it isn’t the same everywhere, you know.”

He wrote out the form for a blood test. “Take her to the outpatients between ten and three tomorrow. If she gets worse, send for me, otherwise I will see you next week with the results.”

Nellie feared the worst but, before they got the results, Ivy caught the flu. All the family had coughs and colds but Ivy fared worse than any of them. The doctor was sent for.

“I’m afraid it’s pneumonia, Mrs Edwards. You mother would be better in hospital.”

Nellie had to agree, though reluctantly. Ivy was admitted and put into an oxygen tent. Three days later she passed away.

The shop was doing well. Valerie stocked a good variety of footwear for men, women and children. She also sold handbags and shopping bags. Women coming in for shoes for a special occasion could choose a matching bag. She stocked Wellington boots, working boots and plimsolls. Her quiet practicality ensured that all her customers felt comfortable in her shop. She catered for older ladies with wider feet and Ben did a good trade in shoe stretching if anyone had a problem.

Grace was getting more pain in her joints and complained all the time. Valerie accompanied her to the doctor who, again, told Grace that she arthritis. Valerie realised that her mother would have to give up her job. She was becoming more morose by the day.

Thursday half-closing was used by Valerie to clean the house. Each day she brought home shopping from the High Street and called at Vera’s once a week for fish and chips. Often, on a Friday, Valerie would have to visit Renee’s alone. She was considering taking driving lessons. Life would be easier if they had a car. Grace, as usual, disagreed.

"We can manage without a car, we live close to everything. It'll cost a fortune an' you'll 'ave ter leave it out in the street."

Valerie said, "Oh, Mother, other people leave them on the street. We can do with something now you're getting worse. You can hardly get to see Gran or Aunty Flo."

Grace sniffed. "They doe come over 'ere a lot, do they?"

Valerie had to agree. "No, they don't but Gran's old now, we should go to see her."

After giving up her job, Grace wanted Valerie at home every spare minute that she had. If only they had a car, she could be dropped off at Renee's or Thelma's or even Flo's and Valerie could have a couple of hours' respite from her. If she didn't have Ben to talk to, she felt she would go mad.

One day, when she and Ben were having their lunch, she talked to him about her ambition to learn to drive and eventually have a vehicle.

He chewed thoughtfully on his sandwich and then said, "If you get a car, your mom will expect you to go home every lunchtime, Valerie."

She gasped. "Of course, I never thought of that. Good job you did. She's against the idea anyway."

"Well, I think you should have lessons if you want. P'raps one lunch hour a week? She wouldn't know but don't be in too much hurry to get a car. You can hire a taxi to tek 'er to your Gran's or wherever."

Valerie was ecstatic. "Good idea, Ben. We only have our lunch hours, we don't want to lose them." She smiled and kissed him. "You're so good to me, the best friend I ever had."

He held her hand. "Do you think we'd ever be able ter get married, Val?"

She paused to think, then said, "I don't know, Ben. I've got me mother, you've got your dad, we'd better wait and see what pans out. Go on as we are for the time being. What me mother doesn't know, she won't grieve about."

"I know, love. Sometimes I feel like just sellin' up and runnin' away. I never bothered wi' gels, as you know. Folk'll think as I'm too old fer you, Valerie. It'd be 'ard round 'ere with all the gossip."

She had to agree. "P'raps we will one day but, as it is, we're doing okay. I'll soon be able to pay you back if business goes on like it has been, then I can really start saving."

He squeezed her hand. "You know you don't have ter pay me back. You pay me rent on this place."

She nodded. "I know but I will."

He smiled at her. "Anyroad, if anything happens ter me, I'm mekkin sure you're okay."

Her eyes widened. "What about your dad, Ben? You should think about him first."

"Oh, he's okay. Don't worry, I won't leave 'im short. Anyway, he's allus looked after his money and the house is in 'is name."

Valerie feigned surprise. "You own the house, Ben? I thought that you paid rent."

"No, me mom paid the rent man for yer mom when 'er was at werk an' I popped it in after 'er died. We day want all an' sundry ter know our business. Now yer mom's at home, o' course, 'er pays it herself. I doe 'spect as 'er's noticed old Russell don't call at ours."

Valerie sat, taking it all in. With any luck, she would be set up for life.

Grace was waiting for Valerie to return from work. She was in a perverse mood. Valerie had told her that she would be out that evening, going for a meal with some of her old colleagues from the shoe factory. As soon as she entered the house, she felt the atmosphere. Grace was at the stove, poaching an egg.

"Hello, Mom, had a good day?"

"Not really, it's a long day on yer own."

Valerie carried on. "Is that all you're having for your tea?"

Grace buttered the toast. "No point in cookin' just fer meself is there?"

Valerie said, "I could have got you some fish and chips."

"S'pose you could. Anyroad, I'm 'avin' this now. Not that I've any appetite."

Valerie poured the tea. "Mom, I've been thinking."

Grace looked at her. "Oh, ar?"

"I think you're right."

"What about?"

"Getting a car."

Grace sniffed. "I thought it was a daft idea."

"Yes, and thinking about it, you're right."

Grace paused, fork halfway to her mouth. "How do you mean, I'm right?"

"Well, it's a lot of expense. I can walk to the shop and we have stuff delivered there. I can choose the stock from catalogues, so I wouldn't use it for the business. It'd only be standing around."

Grace smiled smugly. "Told you that."

Valerie continued, "If we want to go anywhere we can use a taxi."

"That'll cost."

"Not as much as running a car, though. I'll write the number down and if you want to go anywhere you can phone. Why don't you use one tonight and pop to Flo's or Thelma's? And you haven't seen Peggy for ages."

Grace shook her head. "No, not tonight."

Valerie gritted her teeth. "Well, I'll get ready. The girls are meeting at half past seven."

"Well, don't be late back. I can't sleep while you're out."

Later, in the restaurant, Valerie and Ben sat enjoying their meal. It was a refreshing change to be away from the shop and their parents. They had taken a bus into town and gone to a place where no one would see them.

"I must be home by ten, you know, Ben."

"How are yer goin' to do that? You won't digest yer meal. We'll get a taxi, don't worry."

"It's just that if I'm late, mother will be unbearable to live with."

Ben put his knife and fork forcefully onto the table. "Valerie, you'll just have to stand up to her. 'Er's run yer life for too long now."

"I know, Ben, but she's got nobody else."

"Neither has me dad but 'e don't rule me like Grace rules you."

"Listen, Ben, don't let her spoil our evening. We'll get a taxi and I will be dropped off round the corner."

"Okay an' I'll be dropped off at the end o' the street in case 'er's in the winder but we'll 'ave ter sort summat out better than this."

She held his hand and he smiled all over his good-natured face. She could not wish for a better chap than Ben.

The engagement of Ronnie Edwards and Josie Salt was announced in the family column of the local paper. Grace, with time to read every last word, spotted it. She could hardly wait for Valerie to get through the door after work before waving it under her nose.

"Thay'me engaged then," she said. "Josie an' that Ronnie Edwards. I should think as 'er wants summat ter do gettin' mixed up with that lot."

Valerie read it. "It's her choice, Mother."

"Well, I'm glad you never did."

"No chance, can't stand him anyway."

Grace reread it. "Wonder what Vera Salt thinks? Set her up in her own shop, they have. Wonder if that's got anythin' ter do with it?"

Valerie's eyes widened. "You mean marryin' inter money?"

Grace pursed her lips and nodded. "Could be, could be."

Valerie said, "It's a complete mystery how he's got two shops. It took me all this time to get one and I'm still paying for it."

Grace looked at her closely. "How much do yer owe now?" she asked.

"Not much, just a couple of hundred, soon be done with."

Grace shook her head. "Don't like debts, never 'ave. You warn't in debt when you was in that office. It was a good job you 'ad."

Valerie seethed. "It'll be okay. Soon be in clear street, the shop's doing well. You don't go short of anything, Mother."

Grace reddened. "Nor you dain't when you was a kiddie. I sacrificed a lot fer you, our Valerie."

Valerie was getting tired of this conversation. "Oh, Mother, don't start. I've had a busy day and I'm tired."

"That's goin' out of a night and gerrin in late."

"Late? Late? I don't call half past ten late. For God's sake, Mother, I'm twenty-four years old nearly. If I want to go out I will."

Grace sniffed. "Ar, don't we know it."

She shuffled off to switch on the TV. Turning at the door, she said, "And don't tek the Lord's name in vain. You'me getting proper common."

Next day, Valerie confided in Ben about her mother's outburst.

"I don't know how much longer I can stand it, Ben."

He put his arm round her. "Tek no notice. 'Er's on 'er own too much, that's 'er trouble. Too much time ter think. Me dad's a bit lonely an' all. Does 'er knit or sew?"

"She used to crochet but she hasn't done any since her hands got so stiff."

Ben made a cup of coffee and put bacon under the small grill.

"Open the window, Ben, we don't want the smell in the shop."

He did so, then he said, "Valerie, we could get married. Needn't live too far away. We could pop and see 'em most days. I could ask Iris to go to your mom's a couple of mornin's a week."

Valerie shook her head. "Mom doesn't like her."

"Why? She don't know her."

"I know. I think it's because she's remarried. She says if she had loved her first husband, she'd never have married again. She might say it to her face."

Ben shrugged in despair. "I don't know what ter say, love. We can't keep goin' on like this, it ain't right."

She agreed. "My nerves won't stand much more. I dread going home every day."

He patted her hand, feeling helpless.

That afternoon, after closing, he went across to Ronnie's to collect his meat order. As he walked along, he noticed a sign in the pet shop window: "KITTENS FOR SALE". On an impulse he went in. There, all alone in a cage, was a ginger kitten. Berny Priest came over to him.

"How much?" Ben asked.

"Five bob ter you, Ben."

"Okay, wrap him up."

"Who's this for then?" asked Berny.

"Me next door neighbour. 'Er lost 'er cat over a year agoo."

"Will 'er look after 'im, Ben?"

"Oh, ar, 'er will. Got nothin' else ter do, as 'er?"

Grace was sceptical. "Well, Ben, I'd say thanks but I never really wanted another cat. He's homeless, did yer say?"

"Yes, Grace. Nobody wanted 'im. I thought, I know somebody who'll look after him, 'til somebody else can tek 'im, that is."

She grimaced. "Ar, 'e'll be looked after all right. Don't know what our Valerie'll say when 'er gets 'ome but thanks anyroad."

Ben went round home, grinning.

Frank said, "You look like the cat what got the cream."

Ben laughed and laughed.

"What's so funny, lad?"

Ben told his father about the kitten.

"Ar, about time Grace 'ad summat ter occupy 'er. I know what it's like ter be on yer own all day and I find things ter do with meself."

Ben realised that Frank spent a lot of time in front of the television set or listening to the radio. He was getting a proper pot belly. He decided that it was about time he got him a dog. He would have a word with Berny next day.

The result was a little Jack Russell. Frank christened him Sparky. He certainly livened the place up and kept Frank busy, taking him walks, feeding and grooming him and, between dog naps, playing with his ball. It all took the pressure off him and Valerie. Frank and Grace would chat over the yard wall about their pets, finding great pleasure in relating their exploits. Ben only regretted that he hadn't thought of the idea months before.

Janice was in the habit of calling in to see Valerie when she was in the High Street. If the shop was quiet they would go into the back room for a cup of tea. One day she complained to Valerie how bored she was becoming at home all day, on her own. Stan had changed from shifts to days, so, when Paul left for work in a morning, she had all day to herself.

"I've polished everythin' ter death. Sometimes I think ter meself, is this all me life's about? Stan comes in dead beat and, after his tea, he's asleep in his chair. Our Paul's off out with his mates. I feel like an 'ousekeeper sometimes. I go once a week to the Bingo with me friend but I can't afford to go more than that. I've watched the telly till I've gone square-eyed."

A customer came into the shop. Valerie left her to finish her tea.

On her return, she asked. "What was your job before you had Paul, Aunty Janice?"

"I worked in Peacock's. I thought as you knew that. I liked it an' all, meeting folks."

"Oh, I bet you did miss it."

"I certainly did, still do, sometimes."

At lunchtime, Valerie told Ben about her talk with Janice.

"Do you think I should ask her to do a couple of half days, Ben? It would give me time for myself. My mother needn't know an' if she finds out, it's my business anyway."

He agreed. "Get yourself into town to shop, have a driving lesson, get the books done instead of 'avin' ter do 'em at 'ome."

The next time Janice called in, Valerie offered her some part-time work for a trial period. The only snag was if she cottoned on to Valerie and Ben's relationship, but Valerie knew she could trust her aunt to keep her mouth shut about that.

Maureen had offered to work two-and-a-half days a week for Josie, who was thrilled to have her. She found another young mother, Janet, to work on Monday, Tuesday and Wednesday.

Nellie was chief baby minder, which she enjoyed. She needed to fill the void left by Ivy's death. Maureen and Chas needed the money if Chas was to have his own garage one day. One of the first customers at the shop was Flo Burke.

"'Allo, Josie," she said. "Long time since I sin you. You was only a little un. I racked me brains where I knowed you from, 'til I realised you was our Valerie's pal."

Josie didn't put her wise to the rift between her and Valerie.

"How's Mark, Mrs Burke?"

"Growin' up and cheeky with it. 'E's football mad. Never see 'im 'ardly, allus over the park wi' 'is mates. Comes whum when 'e's 'ungry."

Josie laughed. "Proper lad then."

"You can say that again."

Josie asked. "Do you see much of Valerie these days?"

"Not so much, 'er's busy wi' the shop an', of course, her mother. 'Er ain't easy, our Grace. 'Er's a good wench ter 'er mother. You can cut a bit more off if you like, love. If our Valerie got married, it'd kill our Grace. Not that there's much chance o' that. Keeps 'er on a tight leash, 'er does."

Josie realised then that, although Valerie had a successful business, she was in a trap and unable to get out of it easily. She no longer envied her getting Brittle's shop.

The following Friday evening Valerie rang for a taxi and took Grace to Renee's. Flo was already there.

She grumbled, "Our house is dead. Mark's footballin', Fred's at the dogs with Arthur, as usual, nothing any good on the telly. Did you bring some shoes for yer Gran to try on, Valerie?"

Valerie produced a bag containing three pairs of wide-fit shoes.

"Here you are, Gran, try these."

Renee moaned. "Me bunions are givin' me some gip, I can tell yer." She pushed her foot into a shoe.

"Pull your stocking up properly, Gran."

Valerie knelt to help her. As she did she got a whiff of a decaying, musty smell when she was close to Renee. She had a sense of foreboding.

Flo chattered on. "Like me 'air, Grace?"

"Yes, very nice."

"Why don't you get yours permed?"

Grace bridled. "Mine's alright as it is. As God made it."

Flo continued. "I 'ad it done at the new stylist's."

"Which one?" asked Valerie.

"Your pal Josie's, 'er new shop. Does a good job. I'll goo theer again. Don't overcharge neither."

Valerie signalled to Flo with her eyes that they should go into the front room.

"What's up, gel?" Flo whispered.

"It's Gran, Aunty Flo. There's a funny smell from her."

"I aye noticed it." Flo looked shocked.

Valerie said, "Does she bath herself?"

"Yes, why?"

"I think you should bath her and p'raps have a look."

Flo wasn't hopeful. "I'll try but her mayn't let me."

Grace called out, "Flo, Valerie, nice cuppa tea."

Flo grimaced. "'Er doe like us talking on our own."

On the way home, in the taxi, Grace could contain her curiosity no longer.

"What was you an' Flo plottin' in the front?"

"Nothing, Mother. I was asking her about Gran. I don't think she's well."

Grace sniffed. "'Er's not the only one."

Valerie gritted her teeth.

Flo had decided to go back to work on the twilight shift. That meant that Fred had to stay in with Mark, except on Fridays, when he took him along with him to the dog track. However, he managed to put a bet on the horses most days.

He won some and he lost some. Mark was keen to learn the betting game. He soon got the hang of it and couldn't wait to grow up so that he could gamble himself.

Renee said, "It's in the blood. Our Flo's got 'er 'ands full with that pair. You should 'ear young Mark talkin' ter Arthur. Knows as much as 'im, studies form an' all."

Grace said, "Good job our Flo's got 'er money ter fall back on but 'er shouldn't 'ave ter go back ter work at 'er age."

Renee disagreed. "Do 'er good. 'Er went fer a bit when 'er 'ad that trouble wi' Fred, got 'erself some mates an' was a different wench. I cor see ter young Mark now, too cheeky by half."

Valerie checked with Flo if she had managed to find out how Renee's health was.

"No, I ain't had the chance, Valerie. Every time I ask 'er she says 'er's 'ad a bath. I know 'er keeps washin' rags out, there's half a dozen on the line. I doe think thay'me dusters, 'er aye that 'ouseproud."

The next Thursday, half-day closing, Valerie decided to go to see Renee herself. She was very surprised to see her.

"Come on in, gel. Is yer mom alright? Did 'er know as you was comin'?"

"No, Gran, I wanted to talk to you."

"Come on then, 'ave yer gorra problem? Is it our Grace? Time as you stood up to 'er. You'me a woman now, shouldn't let 'er dictate to yer. Anyroad, what's up?"

Valerie sat down. "Gran, if there was anything the matter, would you tell us?"

Renee looked shifty. "Depends on what it was. I've got arthuritis but so's most on we old uns. I'm eighty now. Gorra 'ave summat up wi me, aye I?"

Looking out of the kitchen window, Valerie asked, "What're all those rags on the line, Gran?"

"Dusters, o' course."

Valerie looked round at the dusty room and then at Renee, who said, "I'm tellin' lies, ain't I?"

Valerie nodded. "I think maybe you are, Gran. Do you want to tell me now?"

Renee began to cry. Valerie poured a cup of tea, then reached the whisky bottle from the cupboard. She put a good measure in Renee's cup. When she had calmed down, Renee told her what was wrong.

"It's me bust, yer see. It's nearly gone on the one side. I 'as ter put rags on. It's nasty an' would come through me frock."

Valerie patted her hand. "Did you show the doctor, Gran?"

"Not likely. I doe like 'ospitals. Anyroad, I've 'ad it a long time."

"Can I take you to the doctor, Gran?"

"No! No, you can't. I ain't gooin. I tek Aspro fer the pain. I can see to it meself."

Valerie felt helpless. "Gran, please let me ask the doctor to see you. He won't send you to the hospital if you don't want to go. He can get the nurse in to dress it for you and give you some better painkillers."

Renee waved her hand at her granddaughter. "Let me think about it. I've never bin bad in me life 'til I got the arthuritis. I've bin lucky. I dain't understand how bad yer dad was an' I'm sorry about that now."

Valerie silently forgave her for doubting the seriousness of Herbert's illness.

She said, "Gran, I'm going to see Aunty Flo. She'll take you to the doctor. Please promise me you'll go."

Reluctantly, Renee agreed. "But I ain't goin' ter no 'ospital," she said.

Next day, Flo telephoned Valerie at the shop. It was bad news. Renee had advanced breast cancer. It was a matter of weeks.

"'E wanted 'er to go to th'ospital. 'E said because of 'er age it'd bin growing slow. It's just a matter of mekkin 'er comfortable. O' course me mother woe goo to th'ospital, 'er went mad when 'e suggested it. Anyroad, 'e's gerrin the nerse in ter see to it."

Valerie was upset. She knew the brunt of the care would fall on Flo.

"I'll do what I can, Aunty, but you know how Mom is."

Flo said, "I s'pose I'll 'ave ter give up the twilight shift now. Still, it's me mother an' you only get one, doe yer?"

Next morning the police contacted them. Renee had been found at six am, floating in the canal.

Ben and Valerie had been plucking up courage and looking for the right opportunity to tell Grace that they intended to get married. Ben felt that Frank would not be a problem, then the tragedy happened and they had to put it off yet again.

Valerie was glad that she had, in a way, made her peace with Renee and realised that her gran was truly sorry to have misjudged Herbert all those years ago. She confided in Ben, yet again, how all this time she had disliked her gran.

Grace reacted to the news of her mother's demise with hysterics.

"The disgrace of it! Suicide! What a disgrace on the famly!"

"Mother, how do we know it was suicide? You can't say that, Gran was confused."

Grace went on, "Everybody'll point a finger at us. 'Them's the Shaw gels, their mom committed suicide'. I'll never be able ter 'old me 'ead up again."

Valerie was getting cross. "Don't be silly, Mother. Where's the proof? Anyway, if Gran did commit suicide we should feel even more sorry. You are only thinking of yourself, not of how afraid she must have been."

Grace glared at her. “How dare you speak to me like that? Me own daughter and me just lost me mother. I’ll never forget what you just said, not to me dyin’ day.”

“Oh, Mother, don’t be so dramatic.” Valerie was fast losing patience with her.

Grace retorted, “It’s all right fer you, you’ve got all yer life in front on yer. I’m ’ere hour after hour on me own, and now me mother’s gone.”

Valerie sighed. “You were never that close to your mom.”

Grace bridled. “What do you know about it? ’Er was me mother an’ now ’er’s gone an’ we’ve got a suicide in the famly.”

Valerie knew she was on a hiding to nothing. Her mother was immovable.

Chapter Twenty-Three

Ben came into the back room of the shoe shop. He looked happy about something, rubbing his hands and smiling.

Valerie commented on it, saying, "You're happy today, love. What's happened?"

He kissed her. "I've got something for you, got it Satday afternoon."

He reached behind the door and produced a cake box.

"Oh, yes, what's that then?" He pushed the box across the table. "Cream cakes? They'll be stale by now if you got them on Saturday."

She laughed as she opened the box. In it was a small, iced fruit cake and, nestling on the top, was a small parcel.

"Open it," Ben urged.

She did so and inside was a ring box. As she flipped the lid open she gasped. Inside was a beautiful, solitaire, diamond ring. Ben eagerly watched her face for her reaction.

"Like it?" he asked.

"Oh, it's lovely, Ben."

"It's an engagement ring, love. 'Bout time as we med it official."

She tried it on. "It's a bit loose."

"Don't worry, it can be altered for you."

She had tears in her eyes. "Thank you. It's so lovely. I never in all my life dreamt that I would own such a lovely ring."

He was thrilled. Beaming all over his face, he said, "The cake's our engagement cake. Go on, cut it."

She did so and popped a piece into his mouth. Then she had a nasty thought.

"What will mother say?"

He shrugged. "I don't care anymore. We'll tell her tonight, after tea. I'll come round at eight o'clock. It's time 'er learnt you ain't her sole property. You'me nearly twenty-five and deserve a life of yer own."

Valerie admired her ring.

He said, "I'll tek it across Henderson's ter be altered. They'll have it ready fer closing time or, better still, you tek it. I'll watch the shop. They can measure yer finger proper. Goo on, yer won't be a minute."

Valerie said, "Janice'll be in at two o'clock. Shall I tell her?"

"Doe see why not, 'er's one o' the famly. We need all the allies we can get."

That afternoon Valerie sat doing the books and orders, while Janice served in the shop. She was doing well and Valerie was pleased with her. Ben locked his door at four o'clock and popped over to Henderson's to collect the ring. He then went into the shoe shop.

"'Allo, Janice. Valerie in the back?"

"Yes, Ben, shall I call her?"

"No, thanks, I'll go through."

After a couple of minutes they both came back into the shop. Ben had his arm round Valerie. Janice's jaw dropped.

"Surprised, Janice?" asked Ben. "Show her, Val."

Valerie held up her left hand. The light caught the diamond on her ring finger. Janice was speechless.

"Aren't you going to congratulate us, Aunty Janice?"

"Yes. Yes, of course." She kissed her niece. "What a lovely surprise. I knew you was friends but this is a turn up for the books."

Ben put his finger on his lips. "Keep mum," he said. "Grace doe know yet."

"Oh, blimey," said Janice. "Don't envy you, facin' 'er with your news, not by a long chalk."

"Anyway," said Valerie, "have a bit of our cake."

Janice laughed. "Don't mind if I do," she said.

After closing they walked home together, not caring anymore if anyone saw them, not going their separate ways round the corner, as they usually did.

However, facing Grace with the news that she and Ben were courting, and intending to get married, was the hardest thing that Valerie had ever had to do. When Valerie opened the back door, she felt physically sick. Grace was frying sausages and onions, potatoes were bubbling in the saucepan, Whisky lay stretched out on the mat. All looked peaceful. A peace which Valerie knew was not to last long. Ben was coming round at eight o'clock and bringing Frank with him. Grace looked round from the stove.

"Had a good day?" Valerie asked.

"Quiet, as usual," Grace replied. "Sausage an' mash fer tea. That tap's drippin', drivin' me mad. Needs a new washer on it."

Valerie fiddled with the offending tap. "Yes, it does. I'll ask Frank or Ben to pop round later to see to it."

Grace poured the tea. "Th'ouse is dropping ter bits. I told the rent man about the roof last Friday. Good job as it's summer or we'd be in a right state."

Valerie drained the potatoes and mashed them. She looked at the clock. Six-thirty. Time was slowly ticking towards take-off. Grace placed the plate of sausage and mash in front of her. Her stomach churned. She picked at her meal. Grace, of course, noticed.

"What's up? You always like sausage an' mash. Are yer sickenin' for somethin'?"

"No, Mom, just not very hungry."

Grace sniffed. "S'pose you've bin scoffin' at the shop."

Valerie wouldn't bite. "Not today. I've been busy trying to do the books between customers. I could do with some help in the shop."

Grace looked at her. "Does it run to it? You'd need somebody reliable, not light-fingered."

"Yes," said Valerie. "I've got somebody in mind."

Grace's ears pricked up. "Who?" she asked.

"I'll tell you later. I'll just ring Frank and ask him to pop in to see to the washer on the tap."

Ben answered the phone. For her mother's benefit Valerie just asked for help with the tap.

Putting the phone down, she said, "Frank'll be round at eight o'clock. Ben'll come an' all."

"Good on 'em," said Grace.

Valerie washed up. She turned the radio on. Grace went into the front room to watch her TV programme. To occupy herself, Valerie ironed a blouse for the next day. At last it was eight o'clock and the men came round.

Valerie said, loudly so that her mother could hear, "Thank goodness you two have come. This tap's been driving me mom batty all day."

Frank tested it. "Don't worry, gel. I've got a washer round whum. I'll soon fix that for yer."

Valerie signalled to Ben with her eyes that Grace was in the front room.

He said, "No need to do it yet, Dad, we've got summat ter tell yer and Grace."

Valerie went to the middle door. "Mom, Ben and Frank are here."

Grace was interested in her programme. "Oh, yes," she said, absently. "Mek a cuppa tea. I'll settle wi' them for the tap later."

Valerie said, "They haven't just come for the tap, Mother. We want to talk to you."

Grace dragged her attention from the TV set. "What's up?" She paused, then, "You in trouble wi' that shop?"

Valerie ushered Frank into the room. Grace looked puzzled.

"Sit down, Frank, and you, Ben," said Valerie.

Ben sat next to Grace on the settee. She looked nonplussed. Valerie sat opposite to her mother. She nodded to Ben and he turned to Grace.

"Grace," he turned to his father, "and Dad, Valerie and me have got summat ter tell yer."

Grace looked alarmed. Frank sat, patiently waiting.

Ben continued, "Me and Valerie, well, we think a lot o' one another and we want you ter know that we'me courting."

Grace was speechless for a moment, then she spat out, "Courtin'? You and 'er?" She nodded in Valerie's direction. "You'me old enough ter be 'er father." She turned to Frank. "Aye 'e? Old enough ter be 'er father?"

Frank sat, shaking his head. "Well, Ben," he said, "this is a right 'ow's yer father. 'Ow long 'as it bin gooin on?"

"There's nothing 'gooin on', Dad, but we've thought a lot o' one another fer some time now."

Grace was fuming. "A right fool you've med o' me. I s'pose everybody knows about it, laughing behind me back."

Valerie was angry. "Don't be silly, Mother, nobody knows. We're sure what we want, so we decided to tell you before anybody else."

Frank had sat quietly for a while, then he spoke up. "Life's too short ter be on yer own. My missis allus thought a lot o' you, Valerie. If yer can be 'appy yer should goo fer it. You woe allus 'ave me an' Grace an' you'll be on yer own. Age doe matter as long as yer look after each other. I 'ad an' 'appy married life and I 'ope our Ben does an' all."

Grace rounded on him. "My husband died an' left me ter bring 'er up on me own. Now 'er's gonna leave me and marry a man old enough ter be her father. After all I've done fer 'er."

Ben held his temper but said, "You left your mother when you got married, Grace, or have you forgot that?"

She retaliated by bursting into tears.

She said, "Don't you talk about my mother, she's dead an' gone, poor soul."

Frank stood up. "Well, I'll say this, it's a selfish parent what doe want their child ter be 'appy." Facing Ben, he said, "I'll see you round 'ome. I'll pop a washer on top o' the wall so's you can fix the tap, son, an' I'll wish good luck to the pair on yer."

Grace continued to snivel. Ben and Valerie went into the kitchen to make a drink. He put his arm round her shoulders.

"We've done it now. It's all one way fer us. Don't worry, as long as we stick together, we'll make it."

She dissolved into tears. The strain had caught up with her. Ben wiped her eyes on the teacloth. Taking the ring from his pocket, he slipped it onto her finger.

Grace watched from the doorway. Sniffing, she turned and went upstairs.

*   *   *

Josie was debating with her mother whether or not to invite Valerie to her wedding.

"I feel that I should, Mother. We were friends from infant school, good friends 'til I told her about Ronnie."

Vera frowned. "Can't imagine how anybody could bear that bad a grudge, right from infant school 'til now. What exactly did 'e do to 'er?"

"Well, he used to tease her. You know what a plague he can be. It wasn't only Valerie. His sisters tell me they had a right life with him when they were kids. He's as good as gold really but him and Valerie just never got on."

Vera asked, "What does he think about asking her?"

"He says I can please myself. Most of the High Street shopkeepers'll be coming to the evening do anyway. He doesn't have to bother with her."

Vera said, "They only buried her gran the other week. P'raps leave the invite for a week or two, sleep on it."

Josie saw the sense in that and agreed.

The decision was finally made. Valerie was to receive an invitation to the wedding. It was addressed to Valerie and 'friend'.

Josie said, "I think she'll feel better if she can bring someone with her, Mom. More likely to come and less likely to feel like a fish out of water."

Vera looked doubtful. "Don't be too disappointed if she don't come, Jose."

"Well, I'll take it round myself. Be better than posting it, break the ice."

Steve said, "You wenches, you're too complicated fer us chaps ter cope with. I'll be glad when it's all over an' we can settle down again."

Vera was indignant. "It's your only daughter's wedding you'me on about, not a surgical operation."

He grunted. "Cor be no werse, at least you ain't worried all the time about upsettin' somebody."

That evening Josie called at Valerie's. She answered the door and was nonplussed for a moment but, if the truth were known, she was glad to see her old friend. Grace was ensconced in front of the TV. She nodded at Josie. She was still aggrieved and giving out the silent treatment. The atmosphere in the house could be cut with a knife.

Valerie said, "Come on in, Josie. Long time, no see. We'll go through to the kitchen. I'm just having a sandwich." Grace had not prepared a meal. "You can keep me company while I eat it."

Josie looked at Grace. "Hello, Mrs Potts, how are you?" she asked.

Grace answered reluctantly, "Fair, how's your mom?"

"Oh, she's fine, thank you." She followed Valerie into the kitchen.

"Would you like a sandwich or a biscuit, Josie?"

"No thanks, I've had my tea. I just called to give you this." From her bag she produced the invitation.

Valerie flushed. "Oh. Oh, thanks. I didn't expect this, Josie. We haven't seen each other for ages."

"That doesn't mean that we aren't still friends, Valerie. Do you think you will be able to make it?"

Valerie was quite overcome. "Oh, Josie, I will do my best." She whispered, "I can ask Janice to cover for me at the shop." She kissed her friend. "Anyway, I've got something to show you."

She reached her handbag and took out the ring box. Slipping the ring onto her finger, she held out her hand to show it off.

"Ooh, that's beautiful, Valerie. Who's the lucky man?"

Valerie slid her a look. "Well, you'll be surprised when I tell you."

"Go on," urged Josie.

"It's Ben. Ben Jinks."

"Next door?"

"Yes."

Josie smiled. "He's a lovely man. We use his shop a lot. How long have you been courting then?"

"Oh, a long time. We kept it quiet."

Josie nodded at the front room. "Any problems?" she asked.

"A bit," whispered Valerie. "Not talking at the moment. She'll get over it, she'll have to."

Josie went to the middle door.

She said to Grace, "I bet you're pleased that Valerie's settled with a lovely man like Ben, Mrs Potts?"

Grace just grunted.

"I have brought her an invite to my wedding."

Grace nodded. "When is it?" she asked.

"Five weeks' time. Hope the weather holds out. Isn't Valerie's ring lovely?"

Grace inclined her head. She hadn't even seen it. Josie returned to the kitchen. She made a face at Valerie and rolled her eyes.

"Shall you bring Ben to the wedding, Val? If you can make it, that is."

Valerie nodded. "Yes, we'll try our best. It's a Saturday afternoon, so he should be okay. Anyway, I'll let you know."

Josie lowered her voice. "When do you think you'll tie the knot?"

Valerie shrugged. "We haven't planned yet. Lots to think over first." She inclined her head towards the front room. Josie nodded understandingly.

Quietly, she said, "Don't leave it too long, Valerie."

The silent treatment went on for three days. Valerie had been waiting for an opportunity to tell Grace that Janice had been helping out at the shop before anyone else could tell her. With a clear conscience, Valerie and Ben went out as a couple, to the cinema or a for a meal. On a Thursday afternoon they went into town, window shopping and had tea at the Kardoma. They were a happy couple. The only blight on them was Grace. On Friday evening, they called to see Arthur. He was pleased to see them and shyly shook Ben's hand.

"Well, our Valerie, I'm glad to see you settled. 'Ave yer sin Flo?"

"No, not yet, Uncle. It'll have to be on a Thursday afternoon, her being on the twilight shift."

"Ar, 'er comes and siz ter me washin' and does a bit o' werk for me. I doe see much on 'er. Young Mark allus comes fer 'is pocket money on a Satday. Sometimes 'is mom pops wi' 'im."

Valerie said, "I'm taking my driving test next week, Uncle. If I pass I'll be able to bring mom over more often."

"Don't mither yerself about me, I'm alright. I get me dinners in the canteen at werk. It's nice ter see yer anyhow."

They took their leave so that he could get ready to go to the dog track.

On their way home, Ben said, "I could have ended up like that if I hadn't got you, Valerie."

She squeezed his arm. "Don't think about it," she said, knowing full well that she could have ended up like that also.

"Whisky? Whisky, where are yer?"

Grace could hear him meowing upstairs but where was he? She hunted high and low.

"You silly cat," she muttered. "Allus gettin' inter scrapes. Probly stuck somewhere."

She looked in Valerie's room. She could hear him crying. She looked under the bed, in the wardrobe – no cat. Behind the chest of drawers and the dressing table. No Whisky. Then she realised he must be shut inside a drawer. She pulled out the top ones in the dressing table then, bending down creakily, she laboriously tugged at the bottom drawer. It came out askew and out jumped Whisky. He must have curled up in there and Valerie, not realising, must have shut him in.

Grace struggled to get the drawer back in straight. It was stuck, so she gave a pull and it came out completely. It was too heavy for her to manoeuvre, so she decided to leave it on the floor for Valerie to put back when she came home.

As she bent to pick up the indignant cat, she spotted something on the base of the chest. Picking it up, she discovered that it was a Post Office savings book. Curiously, she opened and began to read.

On her return from work Valerie was surprised to find that her mother was cooking a meal, the first one in a week. Grace actually answered when Valerie said, "Hello."

The meal smelled very appetising and Valerie inwardly gave a sigh of relief. Perhaps Grace was accepting the inevitable.

They sat eating the meal.

Valerie said, "Nice chops, Mom. Where did you get them?"

"Frank picked 'em up for me. He took Sparky for a walk to get 'is bones and asked me if I wanted anythin'."

"Kind of him," said Valerie. They ate companionably.

Grace asked, "Any luck gettin' help in the shop?"

It was the chance Valerie had been waiting for.

"Oh, yes. I've asked Aunty Janice to do a couple of half days. She'll relieve me any time if I need her. I need time to do the books and the ordering."

Grace looked at her. "Thelma popped in today."

"Oh, yes."

"'Er says as Janice's bin in the shop ferra couple o' wiks now. Why dain't you tell me?"

Valerie thought quickly. "She was on trial, to see if she'd cope. Seems okay."

Grace looked straight at her daughter. She spoke slowly and deliberately. "Why dain't you tell me?"

"In case it didn't work out, Mother. She's still on trial but, so far, she seems to be doing okay."

Grace stopped eating and, waving her fork, said, "Did 'er know about you an' 'im next door?"

Valerie began to get riled. "His name's Ben, Mother, not ''im next door'. And no, she didn't know, nobody did."

Grace didn't look convinced.

After a silent pause she said, "Whisky was lost this mornin'."

"Oh, yes? He's here alright now, though."

"Guess where I found 'im?"

"Where?"

"In the bottom drawer of your dressing table."

Valerie laughed. "He must have snuck in when I was getting dressed. Is he okay?"

"Yes but I can't get the drawer back in."

"Don't worry, I'll do it."

Grace put a dish of rice pudding on the table. In front of Valerie, she dropped the Post Office savings book.

"I found this. It was under the drawer."

Valerie froze. She managed to stutter, "Oh, thanks. I'd lost that. There isn't much in it now."

Grace leaned towards her. "No but there was, wasn't there?"

Valerie was angry. "You shouldn't look in my private things, Mother."

Grace glared at her. "Where did you get all that money to save? You was only an office junior."

Valerie thought quickly. "I won it."

Grace bridled. "You dain't tell me."

"I decided to save it."

"I could see that. I wouldn't 'ave 'ad it off yer. Anyroad, why did you save it in dribs an' drabs?"

"To stop folks talking."

"What folks?"

"Anybody who saw me in the Post Office."

"Like who?"

"People behind me in the queue."

Grace didn't look convinced. "Seems funny ter me. Did you tell anybody else about it?"

"No, why would I? You know I always wanted me own business. I decided to save up for it."

Grace pondered. "That wouldn't be enough. Where did you get the rest?"

It was Valerie's turn to speak slowly and deliberately. "From the bank. I got a bank loan."

Grace sniffed. "Ben, more like. Did 'e know about these savin's?"

Valerie was getting nervous. "Yes, he knew I had some savings, Mother."

Grace changed her tack. "I could've done wi' many a thing over the years. I 'ad ter get me washer on H.P. an' struggle ter pay fer it an' you 'ad that money all the while."

Valerie said, "I gave you as much as I could out of my pay, Mother. I never had a lot fer myself."

Grace picked up the plates. "No but 'ad that money, dain't yer? 'Ow many other things 'ave you kept from me, I'd like ter know?"

Valerie decided to prepare Ben in case her mother brought up the subject of the money.

"Me mother found me bank book this morning and she looked in it."

He tutted and she went on, "She wanted to know how I had saved it all up. I told her I had had a win through work. Anyway, me Gran Potts made me swear not to tell anybody about what she gave me. It would have caused trouble in the family. She left quite a bit to the others but as me dad had died she said I should have his share."

Ben nodded, understandingly.

Valerie went on, "She's mad because I didn't tell her about the money. If she knew that me Gran had given it to me she might let on to Janice and that would cause big trouble, so I'm only telling you. I know you can keep a secret."

He smiled. "Course I can. You doe 'ave much privacy in you 'ouse, do yer?"

"I don't know what I'd do without you, Ben. Now I want to talk to you about Josie's wedding. We're invited. Will you come with me?"

"Course I will. Be our chance ter go as a couple. I could do wi' a new suit. I think I'll treat meself. Now, when Janice comes in on Monday, why don't you go an' get yer 'air done an' buy somethin' nice to wear?"

She thought about it. “I’ll ring Josie and make an appointment.”

The following Monday saw a transformation in Valerie. Josie cut and permed her hair in a soft, face-framing style. She went to a good dress shop and steeled herself to pay for a quality suit and blouse. She had the perfect shoes and bag in her shop to go with it. Then she went to the optician and made an appointment to have her eyes tested. There were lots of stylish frames. She would ask Ben to accompany her to choose one. When Ben saw her hair, he was pleased.

“’Bout time you did what you wanted instead o’ bein’ frit o’ what Grace thinks. Now, why don’t you go every wik ter ’ave an ’airdo? Right?”

“Right!” she said.

Grace was scathing about the hairdo.

“What was you thinkin’? All them chemicals on yer ’ead? You ’ad lovely ’air, allus looked neat in that plait.”

Valerie gritted her teeth. “I needed a change, Mother. Anyway, Ben likes it.”

Grace snorted. “What does ’e know about it?”

Valerie decided to ignore this remark.

*   *   *

The wedding of Josie Salt and Ronnie Edwards was a great success. Nellie and Wilf were in new outfits. Josie’s parents and grandparents had splashed out in Lewis’s in Birmingham. The bride looked stunning in a designer dress. Maureen was matron of honour. Patty, who was expecting, looked radiant.

Valerie had been nervous about facing the Edwards clan. She needn’t have worried. The reception was a sit-down meal at a hotel. The atmosphere was one of informality and laughter. Valerie and Ben were seated next to Nora and Jack Proudfoot. They were soon to get their measure.

Nora said, "I'm Nora and this is Jack. Our kids are Norman, Desmond and Rose. That's our daughter-in-law, Patty."

Valerie thought, "As if I didn't know."

Nora lowered her voice and leaned towards Valerie. "She's expectin' in four weeks."

Valerie nodded and smiled, hiding her feelings. "That's nice."

Nora continued, "She's deaf, you know." Again Valerie nodded. Nora continued, "Had meningitis." She pursed her lips. "I'm worried about the bab."

Ben asked, "Why's that?"

"She mayn't hear it when it cries."

Jack said, "I keep tellin' you not to worry. 'Er'll be okay. Sensible gel."

Nora continued, "That's my son, Desmond. Married Mary, Patty's sister, and that's my daughter Rose, married to John, Patty's brother."

Ben laughed. "Happy families, eh?"

Nora smiled weakly. "Yes, if you like," she said.

Valerie could not help feeling relief that she had not married Norman Proudfoot. How would she have coped with Nora and Grace, both trying to control her life? Heaven only knew.

Speeches over, the dancing began. Ben went up to Ronnie to clap him on the back and get him a drink.

Ronnie said, "See you're with Valerie then, Ben. How's things?"

"Great, mate. We're wearin' her mother down bit by bit. We're 'opin' ter get married as soon as we can find somewhere ter live so's her mom and me dad can come an' all."

Ronnie's eyes widened. "Do you think that's a good thing to do, Ben? Wouldn't you be better on yer own? Me and Jose are only goin' ter be in the flat over the shop for a bit while we save up fer a house but at least we can have a few werds in private."

Ben nodded. "That's what I think, mate. We'll 'ave ter see. Anyroad, all the best to yer."

"And to you," said Ronnie.

Chapter Twenty-Four

It was domestic unrest in Pipers Row. Sparky had chased Whisky and Grace had had words with Frank.

She told Valerie, "That blasted dog's a menace. Our Whisky can't look for 'im. Frank says 'e don't mean any 'arm but 'e'd kill our Whisky if he got 'old on 'im."

Valerie tried to pour oil on troubled waters. "Mother, he's only a puppy yet. They do chase things. They'll have to learn to share the yards. Leave them alone and they'll rub along."

"Never," said Grace. "That kitten's all I've got. Some days all I talk to. I don't want him chewed up by that blasted dog."

Later, talking to Ben, Valerie was almost in tears. "How are we all going to live together when Sparky is after Whisky? Me mother's sure that Sparky'll kill him. It's no good, Ben, we can't all live together."

Ben was upset. He'd just located a bungalow and had wanted Valerie to take a look at it. Also she had passed her driving test and he was on the lookout for a reasonably priced car. If they didn't have the problem of their parents' disagreement their outlook could be rosy.

With the help of Chas, Ben had found a car for Valerie. It had to be big enough to seat four but not too big to park in the street.

Valerie told her mother, "I'll still walk to and from work. There's nowhere to park it near the shop anyway. I'll be able to take you more often to see Arthur and Aunty Flo."

Grace sniffed. "I doe know why, they doe come 'ere very often, do they?"

"No but it's a jaunt and Uncle Arthur's working and he's not so fit as he was and Aunty Flo's still on the twilight shift."

"You'll mek excuses for 'em. Anyroad, I s'pose it'll be a change."

Valerie was pleased with the Ford Escort car. She planned to take them all for a spin on Sunday to Barr Beacon or Sutton Park. Frank asked if they could take Sparky along.

"'E can sit on me lap, 'e'll be no trouble. I can tek 'im for a good run, get some of the devilment out on 'im."

Valerie agreed, much to Grace's disgust. She had turned well and truly against the dog. Valerie was still despairing of them ever living under one roof. Ben had told her about the bungalow.

"It's big, Valerie. It has four bedrooms and it's built so the living rooms are in the middle, so they won't have ter be under one another's feet. There's room to extend an' all."

Valerie was tempted to go and look at it but she was afraid of liking it too much and being disappointed if they couldn't have it. Ben had told her where it was and, on the Sunday outing, she drove past. It was ideal, not too far from the High Street to get to work but on the outskirts of the town and far enough away from the factories. It had a nice garden.

Grace piped up. "Look, that's for sale. Nice, that is. Wonder 'ow much they want fer that?"

Frank said, "Oh, ar, that used ter be a gaffer's 'ouse, that 'ad. I bet as it's a tidy price. Looks big."

Ben nodded. "We could do wi' a place like that for us lot."

Grace laughed. "Us lot? We'd be under each other's feet." She turned her face away from Sparky's panting breath. "I'm alright in me own house, I am. Me an' our Whisky. Can't see me ever wantin' ter leave. Bin there too long, I reckon."

Valerie gritted her teeth.

That night Valerie lay in her bed, thinking. If she got rid of Whisky, would her mother agree to moving into the bungalow with Ben and Frank? She could put the cat in the car, drive for miles and then let it out . . . couldn't she? Failing that she could find it a good home somewhere, but where? Ben's good deed, bringing the kitten, was backfiring on them. It would be a hard task to get her mother to move but with the cat it was impossible. Could she be so callous as to dump it? Could she take it to the vet to be put down? Would the pet shop find it a new home? No to all of these questions. Much as she was losing patience with Grace, she could not let the little cat bear the brunt of it.

"I must be getting soft," she thought.

She really liked the bungalow. She could visualise living there, ideally just her and Ben but that was out of the question. No way could she run the shop, go daily to visit her mother and run a home. She mulled it over in her mind until she was getting overtired and tearful. Perhaps she would find the solution in the morning.

* * *

Josie and Ronnie had enjoyed their honeymoon at Butlin's. They went there for sentimental reasons. Some of the old crowd were there and Josie was pleased to see them. One day Ronnie told his wife about Herbie's legacy.

"I waited 'til we was married, Jose, because it's always bin a famly secret an' now you're one o' the famly."

She was surprised to hear how the old chap had owned his own house and about all the antiques.

"He was a quiet old man, didn't seem to have two ha'pennies to rub together. Used to come in the shop. He enjoyed his fish and chips, I remember that and I remember the old horse."

Ronnie smiled. "My Lily. I miss her, you know. One day, when we're rich, I shall have a horse again but we'll need a house in the country. What do you think, Jose?"

She sighed. “Yes, I’d like that. I’ve never been on a horse but I’d like to.”

“I’ve never ridden a horse in my life either. Although I had Lily, ’er wasn’t a ridin’ horse, ’er was a dray horse. I can still smell ’er now, even though Chas uses the stable for his cars.”

Josie asked, “You don’t want any more shops, do you, Ron?”

He laughed. “Why not? I thought I’d have a string o’ shops like Marks and Spencer.”

“But you’re alright with the two you’ve got? You work hard enough.”

“We’ll see, Jose. We want to save for that ’ouse, don’t we? Shops can wait an’, as you say, I’m doing alright with the ones I’ve got. It’s gettin’ the staff what’s the trouble. Though young Paul’s quite experienced now and Terry’s runnin’ the one over the bonk a treat. You don’t want any more hairdressers, do you, love?”

She laughed. “Not likely. I’m glad I’ve got the one but I want a family and kids and work don’t always mix. Me mother’s gettin’ tired now. Me gran and Grandad are gettin’ too old to help with the shop. Me dad’s retiring soon. He likes the shop but without me gran and Grandad to take over, they can’t go on holiday like they used to.”

Ronnie thought for a minute. “Do you think they’d like to sell the shop eventually, Josie?”

“I don’t know, why?”

“’Cos if they do, I wouldn’t mind first refusal.”

She gaped at him. “You? You and fish and chips? You’d be even more tied than you are now.”

“No, I wouldn’t run it. I’d put a manager in.”

She looked doubtful. “I don’t know about that, it could be a load of worry.”

He had to agree. “Yes, you’re right.”

"And," she said, "what about our house in the country? That's what our money's for now."

He kissed her. "Don't worry, we'll get it some day. Trust me."

*　　　　*　　　　*

Ben realised that if he didn't make an offer soon for the bungalow it would be snatched from under his nose. He still had some money in the bank from his pools win and Valerie had almost repaid his loan to her for the shop. He decided to go for it. On the Thursday afternoon he arranged for a viewing. It was vacant, so the estate agent arranged to meet them there at two o'clock.

Valerie was unable to analyse her feelings. She half hoped that she would hate it. She dreaded the task in front of them if they had to persuade Grace to move. Frank was no problem. As long as he had his garden and his little dog, he was content.

At two o'clock sharp they arrived. Mr Perks, the estate agent, greeted them.

"Good afternoon, Mr and Mrs Jinks."

"Oh, we're not married yet," Ben said.

Mr Perks flushed. "Oh, I'm sorry. Anyway, I must tell you that this is a very desirable property. We have had a lot of interest."

"I'm sure you have," said Valerie.

When they entered, they both knew, straight away, that this was the house for them. It had a central hallway, a living room, dining room, study, large kitchen, two bedrooms at one end of the bungalow and two at the other. It needed some redecoration but that was easily dealt with. They looked at each other and Ben asked the price. He realised that he could afford it and a bit extra, if necessary. There and then he offered the asking price.

Mr Perks was surprised. "Will you have to wait for a mortgage, Mr Jinks?" he asked. "Because we have some others interested."

Ben said quietly, "No, it will be a cash sale."

The agent was rather taken aback. "Oh, well, there's no problem then, is there?"

"No," said Ben. "No problem at all."

Valerie wished that this were the case.

Next day, Janice came to the shop. Valerie was in the back room, working on Ben's books. She knew she had to talk to someone. Making a pot of tea as soon as it was quiet, she popped her head round the door and asked her aunt to come through for a cup.

"Aunty, I'm in a bit of a fix."

Janice looked at her. "Your mother?"

"How did you guess?"

"Well, everythin' else seems okay, so it's got ter be 'er."

Valerie told her about the bungalow. "Ben's set his heart on it. What am I to do?"

"Well, this is how I see it. Your mother's fifty-five now, she could live another thirty years. You will have had no life if you don't put your foot down now. It won't be easy, you'll just have to give it to her straight. No goin' round the 'ouses, just come out with it. If 'er don't move with you 'er stops where 'er is, on 'er own."

"Oh, Janice, I wish it was that easy. Frank's dog chases Whisky. Me mother can't stand him now and Frank thinks the world of him. I can't stand the thought of going home every night to a row. Ben needs a bit of peace and quiet after being at work all day."

"Valerie, watch me lips. Just go an' tell her. She and Frank and the animals have got to get on. The dog and cat have got to learn to live together. They've just got to, right?"

"Right. I might need a brandy before I tell her but I'll do it."

As they walked home that evening, Valerie told Ben that she was going to take Janice's advice.

"If you hear screams from our house tonight, Ben, don't worry. I'll try not to kill her or the blessed cat."

He laughed. "No, but I might come round and do it," he said.

Frank was pleased to hear that Ben had decided to buy the bungalow.

"We'll be okay there, son. I'll put this place on the market. I think your mother'd be glad for us. Be nice ter 'ave a bit more gardin. Sparky'll like it but what about Grace? Oh, ar, an' will you an' Valerie be gettin' married afore we all move?"

Ben replied, "Course we shall. I can't see Grace approvin' of us livin' under the same roof unless we am, can you, Dad?"

"No but 'er won't be 'appy about you gettin' married either."

Ben shrugged. "Too bad, Dad. It's time ter put it on the line. 'Er either comes or 'er stops, it's 'er decision but we'me definitely gooin."

The reaction from Grace was as expected when Valerie told her about the purchase of the property.

"Well, I told you, don't expect me ter goo. I'm not movin' from my house. I've lived 'ere a long while. It's got memories fer me, 'as this place. Anyroad, you ain't even married. What'll folk say? I shan't be able ter 'old me 'ead up round 'ere."

Valerie sighed. "We intend to get married in a few weeks' time, Mother, as soon as we can get something organised."

Grace humphed. "Registry Office, is it?"

"No, actually. Ben has seen Mr Lucas, the Methodist minister. He comes in the shop. He says to call in at the manse when we are ready and we can sort it out."

Grace sniffed. "White weddin', is it?"

Valerie flushed. "No, Mother, just a quiet ceremony, close friends and relatives, but we haven't decided how soon yet."

Grace turned to go into the kitchen. "Well," she said, "let me know, won't yer? If I'm too lonely I can always tek in a lodger."

Janice was pleased for her niece.

She said, "I wish I had bin there when you told our Grace. It ain't natural fer a mother to cling to her daughter like she does, Valerie. Everybody has to have freedom." She rubbed at a pair of shoes ready for the window display. "I dread the thought of our Paul leavin' home but I know he's going to go one day. Mind you, he's just a ship that passes in the night these days. Took a fancy to young Jenny, you know, her from the greengrocery. She's older than him but he needs somebody with a bit of oil in their lamp to steady him down. 'E's done well with young Ronnie Edwards, learnin' the butcherin'. I think 'e'd like ter manage a shop one day."

Valerie nodded. "He could do worse, I suppose," she said.

Josie also was pleased for her friend. Vera was surprised that the wedding would be so soon.

She said, "I thought as it'd be years yet afore she plucked up the courage to leave her mother."

Josie said, "Ben's the instigator. He's bought a bungalow big enough for the four of them but, of course, Mrs Potts is kicking up a fuss about going."

Vera laughed ironically. "I can't see her stopping on her own. Oh, 'er'll mek a stand but it'll only be for effect. 'Er'll goo eventually, you'll see."

Josie was annoyed on Valerie's behalf. "She's trying to spoil things. How spiteful can you get?" She kissed her mother on the cheek. "I'm glad you're not like that, Mother."

Valerie called in at the cake shop. Thelma was glad to see her.

"'Allo, Val. Everything goin' alright, love?"

"Yes, thanks, Thelma." She looked round. No one was in earshot. "Well, no, it isn't really. Mom's decided she isn't moving with us when we go."

Thelma tutted. "Well, 'er'll be lonely on 'er own. As well as missin' you, Frank's bin a good neighbour to her. 'Er'll miss 'im. Don't worry, 'er'll come round. Either that or 'er'll be a lonely woman."

Flo was disgusted with her sister's attitude.

She remarked to her, "Our Grace, many a one'd be glad ter get the chance ter live in a nice bungalow with their daughter. Not many gels ask their mother ter live with 'em. You don't know you're born, you don't."

Grace sniffed. "Well, I've bin a good mother, ain't I? I allus put her first."

Flo sighed in exasperation. "And 'er's allus put you first an' all. You can't grumble about our Valerie. And you should be glad 'er's got a decent chap who's gonna look after 'er, an' you an' all."

Grace pursed her lips. "I might a knowed you'd be on 'er side."

Two weeks later, on a Saturday afternoon, Josie accompanied Valerie to choose a wedding outfit. Valerie confided once more in her friend about Grace's obdurate attitude.

"She says she's staying put, Jose. How can I leave her on her own? I'd never sleep at night for worrying about her. She won't even have Frank to turn to."

Josie sympathised with her. "She'll come round, Val, she'll have to. You won't be able to keep going there every day. I see my mom a couple of times a week. I'm busy at the shop and looking after the flat. No way will you be able to cope. You'll have to get someone in to help her."

Valerie grimaced. "She won't have anybody in the house and if she did she'd find fault with them."

Josie patted her arm. "Poor you. Anyway, let's forget it now, we'll have us a nice afternoon."

Valerie settled on a shift dress with a matching jacket in a soft peach colour. It suited her perfectly. A cream hat was purchased and, of course, she had the perfect shoes and bag at the shop. She had decided on a clutch bag and she would pin flowers onto it to tone with her outfit. She felt a little happier.

She said, "I'll take mother into town next week for her rigout and I'll get the Spirella lady to call to fix her up with some new foundation garments."

They laughed. Josie said, "Have you tried the new Playtex Living Girdle? I used a tin of talc in a week on mine. When I take it off I'm covered in pimples from the holes and I'm boiling if I wear it in the shop. I think I'll go back to my old roll-on."

Valerie giggled. "What we do for beauty," she said.

Josie persuaded her to buy some cosmetics but Valerie was doubtful about applying them. Josie was insistent.

"You'll look lovely. The lipstick is the exact shade of peach. I'll show you how to put it on, if you like."

"Okay, Jose. I'll have to prepare me mother for me transformation." She dreaded it.

It took a whole afternoon to get a costume for Grace. She was reluctant to go at all, moaning about her feet and knees and she had no intention of being easily pleased. The last resort was C&A. They had plenty of choice.

Valerie said, "Come on, Mother, surely we can find something here?"

"Well, I want something I can wear after. Nothing too fancy, a nice beige or brown crimplene'll do."

Valerie sighed. "Yes, okay." She searched along a rack of suits. "Here, try this, it's your size."

Grace moaned, "Me feet are killin' me. I could do wi' a cup of tea."

"Try this first then we'll have tea at Lyon's. I'm getting tired as well as you, Mother."

Much to Valerie's relief, the suit was a perfect fit.

"Now a nice blouse," she said.

"White'll do," said Grace.

"No, Mother, not with beige. A nice duck egg blue, I think."

"Peach," said Grace.

"No, Mother, I'm wearing peach."

"Are yer?"

"You know very well I am. Stop being obtuse."

Grace screwed up her face. "Ohh, la di da, big words."

Valerie gritted her teeth.

Later, she told Ben about the ordeal.

"P'raps we should sneak off an' come back married," he said. "It seems too much for Grace even to take part in a quiet wedding."

Valerie agreed. "Shall we, Ben? Shall we?"

"P'raps not, she'd be even worse if we did. Any luck with her moving in with us?"

"No, she still intends to stop in Pipers Row."

"So be it," he said.

* * *

Flo had a bad cold. She called to see Grace, red-nosed and sniffling.

“Doe breathe all over me, Flo. I doe want yer germs. It’s only three wiks ter the weddin’.”

Flo blew her nose. “I know, that’s why I’ve popped in. Me and Arthur want ter know what ter get our Valerie fer a weddin’ present.”

Grace thought. “Well, they’ve got everything from next door. Frank’s got some good stuff. Connie allus bought good quality.”

“What about from ’ere?” asked Flo.

“Nothin’ from ’ere, I need it. I’m stoppin’.”

Flo gasped. “Still?”

“Yes, I am.”

“Well, our Grace, I’m surprised at yer. As I said before, you’me bein’ silly ter yerself. It’s a long day on yer own.”

Grace shrugged. “I’ll manage. Me an’ Whisky’ll be alright.”

Flo waved her hand in the air. “Well, it’s up ter you. Anyroad, I think as I’ll get our Valerie one o’ them candlewick bedspreads. A nice, deep pink. I sid one in the town. Nice an’ warm, they am.”

“Please yerself,” said Grace. “Anyhow, how’s your Mark these days?”

“Same as ever. Chip off the old block ’e is. I wish I ’ad a daughter, I can tell yer. ’E only comes in fer ’is meals and ’is bed. I’m thinkin’ o’ gerrin a day job. It’s a long day on me own. I miss me mother.”

“Ar, an’ me,” said Grace.

Three days later, Grace came down with a cold. It quickly settled onto her chest and developed into bronchitis. Valerie rang Janice and asked her to go into the shop. Then she rang Doctor Bladon. He called in after surgery.

“Well, Mrs Potts, you certainly have a bad chest there.” He looked round the bedroom and noticed the discoloured patch on the ceiling where the roof had leaked. “You could do with moving to a less damp room, you know, once you start getting bronchitis."

Valerie nodded her agreement. "My fiancé and I are trying to persuade mother to move with us to a nice, warm bungalow, Doctor, but she wants to stay here."

He handed her the prescription. "Well, the landlord needs to sort this roof out." He turned to Grace. "If you stay here you'll likely be bronchitic every winter but, of course, it's your choice."

Turning to leave, he winked at Valerie. "Best of luck," he said.

Grace stayed in bed for four days, during which Valerie again debated what to do about Whisky. While her mother was out of the way she could dispose of the cat. Somehow she couldn't bring herself to do it. One morning she put him into a cardboard box and placed it into the boot of the car, only to think better of it and release him into the back yard. As Grace never went to see Janice, she offered to give Whisky a home but, again, Valerie couldn't do it. Josie was behind the scheme.

"As long as he's got a good home, Val, I shouldn't worry. Your mom would soon get over it. Anyway, she might decide to stop in Pipers Row, even without the cat."

"I know, Jose, but it's more likely that she'll move if she hasn't got to keep Whisky and Sparky apart."

Josie reiterated. "They'd just have to get on with it if they were mine. Can't let animals rule yer life."

Valerie sighed. "I think it's just an excuse, Jose. She don't want me to get married or leave Pipers Row. She just makes heavy weather about every single thing."

Josie said, "Well, it's just up to you to call her bluff then, Val."

Ronnie was reluctant to go to Valerie's wedding.

"I can't see why I should have ter go, Jose, there's no love lost between me an' Val Potts. I'd feel like a hypocrite."

Josie hugged him. "For me, do it for me, Ron. After all, they came to ours and you know how much you like Ben. He's done nothing to deserve your indifference."

"No but she has. Okay, okay, I'll come but don't expect me to be all over her."

She kissed him. "Thanks, Ron. I know you two have never got on but we've been friends all our lives and Val has a right life with her mother."

Ron grunted. "Ar, you can see who 'er teks after."

Paul was bringing Jenny to the wedding. She read out the invite to her parents.

Her dad said, "I remember 'er when 'er 'ad your job at the shoe factry. I've knowed Ben Jinks fer years, a nicer bloke you couldn't wish ter meet. His dad's a nice bloke an' all. I doe envy 'em wi' that Grace Potts fer an in-law. Dead miserable, 'er is, allus got her gob screwed up like a cat's arse."

Jenny laughed. "Oh, Dad, you're so crude, you are. Tell 'im, Mom. Good job Paul's not here to listen to your opinion of his aunty."

He retaliated. "Well, I doe care. You doe see me gooin inter that shoe shop, do yer? I wouldn't gi' her me custom."

Jenny smiled at her mother. "He bears a grudge, don't he, Mom? Glad I tek after you. Anyroad, I'm glad I come into the shop. I could run it meself now."

Her dad laughed. "I aye jed yet," he said. "Yo could be on the pension afore you get ter run this place."

Chapter Twenty-Five

Frank often went to the market, accompanied by Sparky. He liked to browse round the stalls and meet people. He saw many a familiar face and would stop to have a chinwag. He specially liked to meet old workmates. They would compare notes on coping with retirement. Most of them were glad to be finished with the daily grind and had found new interests.

One Friday he was sorting through some tools on a stall run by a young, Indian chap, when a voice said in his ear, “You doe want ter find yerself werk now you’me retired, Frankie.”

Looking up, he met the kind, brown gaze of Ranjit Singh, an old workmate.

“Wharro, Ran. How’s tricks? Am yer enjoyin’ yer retirement?”

“I am. I’m helpin’ me lad on the stall, keeps me out of mischief. I see your Ben when I tek the shoes in. He looks well.”

“Ar, ’e’s gerrin married at long last.”

“That’s great. You could be a Grandad yet then.”

Frank just nodded. “We’re movin’ soon, got a nice, big bungalow. Needs a bit o’ decoratin’ but I’ll enjoy that, gi’ me summat ter do.”

“What about your ’ouse, Frank?”

“I’m sellin’. It’s a bit of a wrench but Connie’d want me ter move on. The new un’s got a lovely, big gardin. Me little dog’ll love it an’ it’s only a bus ride from ’ere.”

Ranjit nodded. “Me lad’s lookin’ for a house, Frank. What’s it like down yer street?”

“It’s okay. Most folks am gerrin on now, quiet really. You can come an’ ’ave a look if yer like.”

“Can we come when we’ve finished today?”

"Course you can. I'll be in, mek yer a cuppa. 'Ave yer got a bit o' paper? I'll write the address down."

Grace was much better. She was up and about most of the day. She should be completely recovered for the wedding. Pottering round, she found things to do, peeling potatoes for the evening meal, washing Whisky's dishes. Tidying out a drawer, she found some old photographs. There was Herbert smiling out at her.

"What am I to do, Herb?" she asked him. She went into the front room. Looking at herself in the mirror, over the fireplace, she saw a sour-faced woman, greying hair pulled back into a bun, lines of discontent either side of her mouth. Her old-fashioned glasses looked back at her from the mirror. She was looking at a younger edition of Renee. She sat on the settee and cried.

Wiping her eyes, she got up to go into the kitchen. She heard voices, men's voices. Peering through the net curtain, she saw two men, wearing turbans, looking at Frank's front door.

Maureen called out, "Josie, call for yer."

Josie excused herself from her client and went to answer it.

"Hello? Is that Josie?"

"Yes."

"This is Mrs Potts, Valerie's mother."

Josie had a sense of foreboding for a second.

"Oh, hello. Anything wrong?"

"No, no, nothing wrong. I just wondered if I could come over to you to get me hair done."

Josie was speechless for a moment. "Yes. Yes, of course. When would you like to come?"

"Any morning next week."

"Right, I can fit you in on Wednesday at ten o'clock. Is it a perm?"

"Yes, I think so."

"See you then, Mrs Potts. Bye."

Josie turned from the phone and said quietly to Maureen, "I don't believe it! Val's mom's booked herself in for a perm. Miracles do happen."

The voices were in the back yard now. Grace peered through the kitchen window. The two men were talking to Frank and looking at the garden. They looked happy, chatting away, the younger one laughing and showing his beautiful, white teeth. Knowing that Ben would tell Valerie about Frank's visitors, Grace decided to keep it to herself.

Frank was cooking the evening meal when Ben came in from work at six o'clock.

"What's that smell, Dad?"

"Oh, I fancied a bit o' tripe an' onions. I've done you stew. I'll have some o' that termorrer fer me dinner." They sat down to eat. "Guess who I saw terday?"

"Who?"

"Ranjit, you know, from werk."

"Oh, how is he? He says he's enjoyin' his retirement when he comes in the shop."

"Ar, 'e 'elps 'is lad on 'is stall an' 'is other lad in the shop. Got three grandchildren an' all. 'Is missis minds 'em while the gels 'elp in the shop. Seems 'appy enough. Nice bloke, 'e is." They ate companionably. "They come 'ere ter look at th'ouse. You ain't long missed 'em."

"Oh, ar, and what'd he think?"

"Well, it's for Vik. They seem ter like it. Should suit 'em, this street, mostly old uns so nobody ter bother 'em. He's got one little gel, 'er's three an' thay'me expectin' another soon. They live with Ranjit but need to be on their own."

"Ar, I can imagine," said Ben.

Next day, Ben told Valerie about Ranjit and Vik's visit.

She gasped. “Me mom’ll go spare if they move in. I can just imagine the moans and groans, specially about the cooking smells. I reckon that’ll make up her mind about moving to the bungalow.”

“Thay’me a nice family, Val. Me dad werked with Ranjit fer years. Anyway, we’ll see. Can’t mek her come. P’raps after a time on her own she’ll change her mind. Anyroad, Iris says she’ll do for her if we like. She won’t have me dad’s ter clean. See what ’er says.”

“I don’t hold up any hopes.”

They decided to get one bedroom, the kitchen and the bathroom done first and then a living room. The other rooms could be done at leisure. Frank would stay in Pipers Row until his house was sold. Grace would stay while she decided, finally, what to do.

Valerie liked the new G-Plan furniture and decided that the main rooms would be furnished with it. Frank would bring what he required and the rest could be left if the new occupants could use it. It was an exciting, though stressful, time.

Grace phoned for a taxi to take her to the hairdresser’s. She was nervous and almost changed her mind.

Josie greeted her. “Nice to see you, Mrs Potts. Sit over by the washbasin. Claire will wash your hair for you. Have you decided on a style?”

“I thought that bubble cut. What do you think?”

“Yes, it’s popular and easy to keep. P’raps a set every other week? If you bring your wedding hat the week before the wedding, I can style it to suit. I’ll only do a very soft perm to start with. It won’t last so long but it’ll give you a chance to get used to it.”

It was nice to be pampered. Claire thoroughly washed her hair, then Josie approached to cut it. The locks fell to the floor.

Annie Pearce, who was sitting at the next basin said, "You'll feel better wi'out that lot, wench. I 'ad mine permed an' I've never looked back. Come every wik now. Lovely gels, these am. Allus come ter young Maureen, I do, knowed 'er from a babby."

Grace and Annie decided to share the taxi home.

"I 'ad a lift from me son but I doe like ter keep askin' 'im. Where do you live then?"

"Pipers Row."

"I think I sid you in the town. 'Ave yer gorra daughter?"

"Yes, she owns the shoe shop," Grace was proud to say.

"Is 'er married?"

"No, she's getting married in a couple of weeks."

"You'll miss 'er."

"Yes, s'pose I will."

"You'll 'ave ter come down the Bingo. Good night out, it is. I usually goo on a Friday night wi' Nellie from next door, that's young Maureen's mom. Lovely famly, like me own, they am."

"I might just do that. I'll ask me friend, Thelma. Why don't you come in for a cuppa?"

So the unlikely friendship of Grace and Annie began.

What a shock and surprise lay in wait for Valerie when she got home from the shop. Grace sat in all her glory, casually reading a magazine.

"Ooh, Mom, how nice you look. What a transformation! Where did you get it done?"

"Josie done it. 'Er cut a lot off. I must say it's cooler now. 'Er's goin' ter do it ter suit me 'at for the weddin' an' I've decided to 'ave new glasses."

Valerie still couldn't take it in. Grace, who had looked sixty-five, if a day, now looked her fifty-five years. Also the expression on her face had relaxed, helping her to look younger.

Frank called round with some paint charts for Valerie and stood, transfixed.

"Well, Grace, you look ever so nice, not the saerm wench. Bet you feel better an' all."

She nodded and poured him a cup of tea. "Are your friends coming again, Frank?"

"Friends?"

"Them Indians what was here the other day."

"Oh, you mean Ranjit and Vik? Yes, thay'me comin' termorrer, bringing Vik's missis to see th'ouse. Nice famly, them am. Got a little un, three, an' another on the way."

"Be nice to have a couple of kiddies round the place."

Frank and Valerie were gobsmacked.

Nellie was concerned, in fact, she was worried to death. Patty was having a difficult pregnancy. She was enormous and the heat was getting her down. Norman, with the help of Betty and Nellie, had managed to get her to rest but when she was eight months gone she had to go into hospital.

One evening, Wilf was reading his gardening magazine. Nellie was doing the ironing.

"I'm worried sick about our Patty. None of us 'as ever 'ad any trouble 'avin' babbies. I wonder if it's got anythin' ter do with 'er illness, Wilf? I wonder if 'er's gonna be alright? Poor gel allus seems ter draw the short straw."

He was just about to say 'don't worry' when a short rap came on the back door and Norman came in. He was wild-eyed and sweating. They looked at him aghast.

Wilf was the first to speak. "What? What's 'appened?"

"I just 'ad a phone call." He sank onto a chair. "We've got twins, a lad and a girl."

Nellie gave a little squeal, then burst into tears.

Wilf asked, "Am they alright?"

"I think so. I'm goin' now. Will you come with me, Nell?"

She switched the iron off. “Sure, I will. Try an’ stop me.”

Grace saw Vik and his pretty wife arrive on the Friday afternoon to look at Frank’s house. With a little shock, she realised that she knew the girl. She had worked on the assembly line at the factory. Grace remembered her as a quiet, shy, little thing. She had liked her, so she was pleased to see her next door. Holding her hand was a pretty little girl, chattering animatedly to her parents. She skipped excitedly from the van to Frank’s front door, her piping child’s voice echoing in the quiet street. Grace happened to be in the yard when they emerged to look at the garden. Gurpreet recognised her immediately.

“Hello, Grace. How are you? I didn’t realise that you lived here. I haven’t seen you since you retired.”

“Hello. I’m fine, thanks. Is that your little gel?”

“Yes, this is Sunita. Say hello to Grace, love.”

“Hello, Gace,” said the child, giving her an engaging smile.

Grace was lost.

The day of the wedding dawned. Valerie drew back the curtains. The sky was overcast. She shuddered. “Please don’t rain,” she thought. Her stomach churned with nerves. Grace was up and about.

“Don’t look very promising, our Valerie. Better find the brollies out.”

“Yes, I will. Anyway, it might blow over. Still a few hours to go yet.”

They sat, drinking their tea. “I ’ope the weather stops dry fer your weekend.”

“And me but there’s plenty to do in Blackpool if it rains. Shall you be okay while I’m gone?”

"Yes, course. The cupboards and the fridge are full, I've got the phone, Frank's next door. Anyroad, you'll soon be back."

Valerie couldn't believe the change of tune!

"Frank says he'll have the kitchen paintwork done by the time we get back. We're pleased with the decorating. That Bobby Turner's a good chap. You'll have to come and see next week, Mom."

"Yes, I might ask him to do some here for me."

Valerie kept her tongue between her teeth.

The day brightened. All was ready. Valerie carefully applied her make-up as Josie had shown her. She entered the front room in trepidation, dreading her mother's comments, but none came. Grace looked smart in her crimplene suit. Josie had done her hair in a becoming style and her new glasses were a success.

The car arrived to drop off Arthur, who was to give Valerie away, and to take Ben, Frank and Grace to the chapel. Arthur was so nervous. He hated being in the limelight. Valerie poured him a drop of whisky to calm him down as they waited for the car to return for them.

"You look real nice, our Valerie," he said. "I wish as yer Gran could be 'ere ter see yer."

"I know, Uncle. When we're settled, you'll have to come over to us for a nice Sunday dinner."

"Ar, I'd like that," he said.

On arrival at the chapel she felt as if she was on another planet. Her legs trembled slightly as she walked into the building. There was Ben, beaming as usual and waiting for her. She felt safe and wanted. The ceremony was touching and she felt a lump in her throat. Grace wiped a surreptitious tear from her eye.

So Valerie emerged from the chapel a married lady. The gold ring glinted on her finger. It was a strange feeling, one of achievement and pride. Ben was obviously over the moon.

Off they all went to the hotel for the reception. Flo, Fred and Mark, Janice, Stan, Paul and Jenny, Thelma and her husband, Peggy, Josie and a quiet Ronnie, together with Vera and Steve Salt.

Grace behaved impeccably, as if it was she had always wished to see her daughter married. Flo couldn't get over it, Grace laughing and chatting. She had been dreading her sister's sulks. Perhaps that was all to come later.

Frank made a speech, congratulating the couple. He wiped away a tear when he mentioned how pleased Connie would have been to see them settled. Ben thanked everyone for coming and for the presents. It was all over by six o'clock and they went home to load the luggage into the car and set off for Blackpool.

Later, Grace sat watching TV. She looked at the clock. They would be in Blackpool by now, she calculated. It was strange to think that Valerie had left home. She stroked the cat on her lap and shed a tear.

The phone rang. "Alright, Mom?"

"Yes, 'ave ter be, won't I?"

"Yes, well, I'll ring tomorrow. We'll be back by tea time on Monday."

"Okay, have a good time."

"Goodnight."

"Goodnight."

Whisky cried to go out. She opened the back door. Frank was in the yard with Sparky.

"Alright, Grace?"

"Yes, you?"

"Ar, bin a nice day, all in all."

"Yes, s'pose it has."

"Goodnight then, Grace."

"Goodnight."

The doors closed on two silent, empty houses.

Nora sat in Norman and Patty's front room. She looked all around. It certainly appeared to be clean enough. It was a bit untidy with clean baby clothes and nappies folded and piled on a chair and bits of baby paraphernalia all around. Norman carried in a tray of tea. Patty sat in an armchair feeding Ruth. David slumbered in his carrycot. Nora checked her cup before she drank.

"How are you managing, son? You must be run off your feet."

"Not really. Betty and Nellie are good as gold and we really appreciate your doing the washing for us. They've only been home for two days and we can't remember what it was like before we had them."

"How do you manage at night? You must have to get up when they cry?"

"No, Patty does it. We have the bottles all ready in the fridge, she only has to warm them up, then she has a lie in and a nap in the afternoon when Nellie's here."

Nora was nonplussed. "How does she know when they're crying then?"

"Prince tells her."

"That dog's upstairs with them babies? Do you think that's hygienic, son?"

"Why not? He's always slept upstairs. You know me, I never hear a thing. He's uncanny. Every time one on 'em cries he paws at Patty 'til she wakes. We reckon it must get on his nerves and he wants peace and quiet."

"Well, don't go round tellin' all and sundry that dog sleeps up there. Folks'll think as you ain't clean."

Frank kept himself busy. It was strange at the bungalow at first and he missed Pipers Row. The weeks that he had spent there alone had increased his resolve to move. The garden kept him occupied, together with taking Sparky out and painting his living room, ready for his furniture. He took the bus into town twice a week and the time passed quickly.

The removal van arrived to take the rest of Frank's bits and pieces. Grace watched the men loading it. She thought to herself, "I'll see how he gets on before I commit meself." She had missed him being around but wouldn't admit it to anyone, not even herself.

The next day Vik and Gurpreet arrived to open up ready for their furniture to arrive. Grace took them a cup of tea and wished them well in their new home. Gurpreet looked tired.

"Come and take the weight off your feet, let the men do the graftin', then you can go round and tell them where to put everythin'." Gurpreet accepted gratefully.

"Where's the little un?" asked Grace.

"With Vik's mom. She'll be here later. I hope she settles okay, Grace, it's a big thing for a three-year-old to move into a new bedroom."

Grace patted her hand. "She'll be alright, don't worry."

The following Thursday afternoon Valerie called in. She was amazed to find her mother sitting on the settee, reading nursery rhymes to Sunita. They certainly looked cosy, sitting there.

"Hello, Valerie. This is Sunita. She's come to live next door. Say hello to Valerie, love."

"Lo, Valerie. Gace is readin' me a story."

"So I see," said Valerie. "Shall I put the kettle on, Mother?"

"Yes. How's the bungalow coming on? Has Frank sorted himself out?"

"Yes, he's fine. Bobby's started to decorate the other bedroom. Things are taking shape. You'll come to dinner on Sunday, won't you? Then you can see for yourself."

Grace nodded. "Ben alright?"

"Yes, he's gone home to help finish some painting. Never seen so many doors in a place." She poured the tea. "I wondered if you'd like a lift to Josie's next Thursday to have your hair done. We could go together."

"Oh, thanks but I've arranged to share a taxi with Annie next Tuesday. It's pensioners' day and termorrer night me and Thelma are goin' to the Bingo. Annie reckons as it's a good night out."

Valerie was speechless.

The arrival of the new baby next door saw Grace more in demand to help. She looked after Sunita regularly while Gurpreet got on with her chores. She came to love the little girl dearly and Sunita looked on her as a second grandmother. Valerie did not mention Grace moving again. She decided to wait and see what transpired. Grace was loathe to move into an area where she knew no one. She could not catch the bus into town as Frank could and she knew that she would miss Gurpreet and the children.

Vik had taken on her garden as well as his own, carrying on Frank's good work and, occasionally, he would take her to the doctor or to have her feet done at the chiropodist. He was becoming a good friend. She knew that she would miss this little family if she moved. And, of course, there was still the question of Whisky.

So the time went on.

Chapter Twenty-Six

1998

Nellie sat gazing into the fire. She was reflecting on her many memories and the way that her family had developed and grown up around her. Wilf had died four years ago and she missed him badly. Since his retirement they had been happy together and been on many lovely holidays, both together and with members of the family. Annie was long gone. Sometimes when she looked out of the kitchen window when washing up at the kitchen sink or pegging out her washing in the garden, she thought that, out of the corner of her eye, she had caught a glimpse of her old friend. She often chatted to Wilf and Annie as if they were still there and told them all the latest news about the family.

Yesterday had been her seventy-ninth birthday. She looked at her cards, displayed around the room. So many of them. The family had all assembled at a restaurant to celebrate. She had sat beaming with pride at them all. Christine had sent a video of her family from New Zealand. She had watched it twice already and marvelled at the way the children had grown up since the last time she had seen them, when Wilf and herself had gone for a long visit. She thanked God for them all and counted her blessings every day.

Ronnie and Josie had the house that they had always dreamed of. It was in the countryside. It had five bedrooms and an adjoining cottage, also stables and a paddock for their beloved horses, including a white pony called Lily-two. They had three children. Ellie was twenty-two and a staff nurse at the local hospital, Annie was twenty and at university, Billy had just had his eighteenth birthday and was the proud owner of a little red car. He was also going to university and would need it to get home at weekends to his family and his horse.

Ronnie had asked Nellie to move in with them. There was room and she had spent a few weekends there but she was reluctant to leave the house which held all her memories and she would miss the town, although the people she knew were getting fewer by the week.

Vera and Steve had retired. They lived in the bungalow adjoining Ronnie and Josie's house. Steve was getting more confused by the day. Josie was concerned that her mother was becoming worn out with caring for him but she stoically carried on and would not consider any help or hear of Steve going into residential care.

John had been made redundant from the steelworks and had bought the fish and chip shop. He now had three in the area and was doing well. Rose was happy to work alongside him. They had two sons, both happy to work in the shops for their father.

Maureen had bought the hairdresser's shop from Josie and Chas had his own garage, modest but profitable. They had one daughter, Patricia, who was married. This resulted in Nellie becoming a great grandma to a little girl, which delighted her.

Barry and Noreen were still running the coal yard. They had two sons, Peter, who was studying accountancy, and Craig, who was happy to help his father.

Patty and Norman were as happy as ever. The twins, Ruth and David, were quite grown up now. Ruth was engaged and David was in the navy, which was quite a shock to Nellie as no one in the family had ever been to sea, to her knowledge.

Ronnie had expanded. He now had five butcher's shops which he managed quite well. Paul Potts still managed the one in the High Street for him. Sometimes Ronnie worried in case Paul decided to leave and work with his wife, Jenny, in her fruit and veg shop across the road but he reassured him that he had no liking for weighing 'taters' and would prefer to carry on as he was.

Holding the card from Bethany, her great grandchild, Nellie smiled and spoke to Wilf.

"You'd love her, Wilf. The image of our Christine, she was at 'er age an' so pleasant. I could eat 'er, I could. I just wish as you an' Annie was 'ere ter see 'er. An' last night were a lovely party. You'd be proud of all on 'em. Well, you was proud, warn't yer? Our Billy's the spit of 'is dad at 'is age. I can see you in 'im an' all. I love 'im ter death. Cheeky with it, you know. I doe know what ter do really. Our Ron wants me to move over theer. I'd miss this 'ouse. Would yer know where to find me? And Annie? I'd miss the town an' all, though there aye many as we know nowadays. P'raps I'll wait a bit longer, eh?"

She went through to the kitchen to make a cup of Horlicks. She felt tired and, although it was still quite early, only half past eight, she decided to go to bed and perhaps have a little read.

She jumped as the doorbell rang. She had been wary about answering the door since one of her friends at the Over 60s had been robbed. Ronnie had put in a spy hole for her. She looked out, nervously. There standing on the pavement was Annie, Ronnie's youngest daughter. Opening the door she gave an exclamation of surprise.

"Come on in, love. What a surprise ter see yer." She hugged her granddaughter. "Come on, in, sit yer down. I'm just mekking a drink."

"Not for me, thanks, Gran."

Annie sat on the settee. Nellie sat in the armchair, facing her.

"Are you alright, love?"

"No, not really. Can I talk to you, Gran?"

"Course you can, love."

Annie took a deep breath. "Well, I've got a problem, Gran."

Nellie smiled encouragingly. "Oh, ar?"

"Well, as you know from the teasing I got yesterday, I've been seeing a lad." Nellie nodded. "Well, I'm pregnant."

Nellie sat, speechless for a moment, then she asked, "What about your studies?"

"I don't know. My dad is so keen for me to do well. If I leave uni now I'll be letting him down, and badly. I don't know what to do."

Nellie thought for a moment. "I can't advise yer, love. It's a big thing, rearing a babby on yer own."

"Oh but I wouldn't be on my own. We want to get married."

"So, what's the problem, apart from tellin' your dad? I know he'll blow his top but he'll come round. Has he met your chap?"

"No, Gran. I was going to bring him home next weekend. He graduates soon but I've got a year still to do."

"How far on are yer, Annie?"

"Fourteen weeks."

"Shall you 'ave it?"

"I think so. I couldn't get rid of it, Gran."

"Well, we 'ave a task ter tell yer mom an' yer dad. Do you want me ter be there, love?"

"Will you, Gran?"

"Course I will, love."

"Only we have another problem."

"What's that?"

"It's Martin. He's black."

Nellie was taken aback. "Oh, well, he must be a nice chap if you love him, gel. Don't worry, we'll see it through together. Your dad'll be okay. He's a decent bloke, never judges a book by its cover. What's he want ter do when he passes then?"

"He's going to be a doctor so there'll not be much money for some time. Gran, can I stop here tonight, please?"

"Course you can. The bed's allus ready. Ring yer mom and tell 'er."

Nellie went into the kitchen to make a hot drink, leaving the girl to use the phone. As soon as Annie put down the phone, it rang again. It was Maureen.

She called, "Gran, Aunty Maureen wants to speak to you."

Nellie brought the tray through and put it on the coffee table. She picked up the phone.

"'Allo, Maureen. Are you alright?"

"Yes, Mom, thanks. I was just phoning to see if you wanted to go to the supermarket tomorrow."

"What time, love?"

"Half past three okay?"

"Yes, thanks, love. You'me a good gel."

"And you're a good mom. See you tomorrow then. Goodnight."

"Goodnight, love."

Maureen put the phone down. She was so glad that Nellie had remained fit for her age. She knew that Nellie worried in case she 'lost her marbles', remembering Ivy, but her mind was as alert as ever. She understood why her mother wanted to stay in her own home but with them all scattered into better areas now, she worried about her and was in touch constantly.

Next morning, Annie managed to eat some dry toast and drink a cup of weak tea. Nellie finished her breakfast and suggested that they ring Josie to come and collect her, then Annie could break the news to her mother on neutral ground.

"Okay, Gran, that's a good idea. Dad's busy today, so mom can come without any problem."

Nellie picked up the phone and dialled Ronnie's number.

He answered. "Oh, hello, Mom. Are you okay? Is our Annie okay? They still like to stop at yours, don't they, even now thay'me grown up?" He laughed. "I 'spect you've spoiled her, as usual."

"Is Josie around, Ron? Only Annie could do with a lift home."

"I'll get her, just off out meself. I'll have to dash. See yer, Mom. Cheerio."

Josie agreed to collect Annie in about an hour. Annie couldn't settle. She paced around the front room and kept looking out of the window to see if her mother had arrived. At last she came. She was a little concerned and puzzled and had a feeling of foreboding. Annie darted into the bathroom. Nellie answered the door and took her jacket.

"Sit down, love," she said. "Annie, your mom's here, love."

Annie came through and sat, twisting a tissue nervously in her fingers.

"Okay, Annie, what's wrong?" asked a discerning Josie.

Annie began to cry. Of course, Josie cottoned on immediately.

"Oh, Annie," she said and took her daughter into her arms.

Nellie came back with a tray of tea. Josie looked at her, over her daughter's head, raising her eyebrows.

Nellie nodded, then she said, "Come on, Annie. We 'ave ter face up ter things. Tell yer mom, that's a good gel."

So Annie confided in her mother. Josie was upset. What would Ronnie say? He was a successful businessman who wanted the best for his family. He had put his daughters on a pedestal. He wouldn't want Annie to drop out of university. How would he react to the fact that she was pregnant and he was to have a black son-in-law? What a predicament.

Martin was trembling in his shoes when Annie took him home to meet her family. Ellie was on duty at the hospital and Billy was at the stables, so they had peace to discuss the situation.

Nellie had paved the way well. She had spoken to Josie and Ronnie and prepared them for the emotions that she knew they would experience.

"I coulda gone mad when our John come 'ome to tell us that Rose was expectin' an' look at 'em now, 'appy as pigs in muck, they am. Lovely kids they've got an' they think the werld o' one another. There's werse things than 'avin' ter get married an' it doe matter what colour the chap is, as long as 'e's good to 'er."

They had to agree but Ronnie, who had put his daughters on pedestals, had taken it hard.

"I just wanted her to get her degree, Mom, and she's so young."

"Young? I 'ad our John when I was her age. I never regretted it. I married Wilf 'cos he thought the werld o' me an' I needed ter get away from yer nan. No, I never regretted it. Anyroad, they can allus come ter me if they need a roof over their heads."

Ronnie shook his head. "There's no need fer that, Mother, but I still think she's too young."

When they met Martin they were pleasantly surprised. He was a fine, well-mannered young man and Josie could see why Annie had fallen for him and he obviously adored her. There were a few tears from Annie and Josie but all was resolved. It was decided that they would marry soon and they would all assemble to discuss the wedding at Martin's parents' home the following evening.

Josie and Valerie met for lunch. Josie didn't mention to Ronnie that she was seeing her friend. He still disliked Valerie, so it was a quieter life if he didn't know about their monthly meetings.

After ordering their meal, Josie asked, "How's your mother now, Val? Has she settled in?"

"Just about. She's getting forgetful, watches the clock all the time. Expects me to come home at lunchtime because I did it a couple of times when she first moved in. That was a mistake, I can tell you. I had forgotten how tiresome she could be. Are your parents any better?"

"Dad's getting worse. Mom gets a bit cross with him but he can't help being so vague. The doctor says it's Alzheimer's, so he won't get any better. Good job Mom's fit for her age but I'm still worried that she's going to wear herself out. How's Ben?"

"Not too good lately. He's sixty-four now. I think he should retire."

"What does he think?"

"I don't know really. I expect he'd miss the shop and the customers but his fingers often feel numb. He doesn't need to work now. We've got the other shops and we could do with taking more holidays."

"What about your mom?"

"I could ask Janice to stop. I don't think she'd mind."

"What about Flo?"

"I don't know if she'd put up with me mother's moaning. I s'pose I could ask her, though."

"What'll you do with Ben's shop if he does decide to retire?"

"Sell it, I reckon. The chemist wants to extend so I don't think we'd have much trouble getting rid of it."

Valerie realised that her life would be easier if Ben was at home to be company for Grace. She would have to work on him to get him to retire soon. She sipped her mineral water.

"Anyway, Jose, how are your lot these days?"

"Well," Josie paused, then decided that it might as well come out. "Our Annie's getting married."

"Oh? What about her university course then?"

"Well, it'll have to go on hold."

"Why's that?"

"Well, she's pregnant, Val."

"Oh, I see. How's Ronnie taking it?"

"He's come to terms with it now. He's disappointed about the university but Nellie sorted him out for us. Only there's more."

"What do you mean, more?"

"Martin's black. His father's a doctor in Brum."

"Oh, I see. Well, do they love each other?"

"Oh, yes, they do and he's a lovely chap. He'll be finishing this year but he's got a lot to do. He's going to be a doctor. We'll help them and so will his parents."

"Well, that's alright then, Josie. I just wish I had some children to help."

Josie smiled sympathetically. "I know, Val. Anyway, they should be getting married in the next month or so, just family coming. They'll live with us for a while 'til they get settled. Martin says they'll get a flat when he knows which teaching hospital he's at. We've got space, so they may as well use it."

Valerie looked at her. "Are you looking forward to being a gran, Jose?"

"I hadn't really thought about it but, yes, I s'pose I am really. Ellie and Billy are away most of the time. Nellie's thrilled to bits, knitting like mad already. Mom's chuffed, given her something to look forward to."

They chatted away amiably until Valerie had to leave to go to the town shop and they arranged to meet the following month as usual.

Grace sat in the conservatory, watching the squirrels. She was bored. She felt neglected. With Valerie and Ben at work all day, time seemed to drag. She missed Thelma and Vik and Gurpreet and Sunita. Flo came occasionally and, once a week, she took a taxi to see her sister in her council flat but time seemed to drag. Last time she had seen her sister she had said that she was finding it hard to make ends meet. Grace was puzzled. Fred had died before he could retire. He had been in the work's pension scheme and was well insured, so why Flo was struggling she couldn't fathom. Grace didn't know that Flo had confided in Valerie and asked her to put the money from Fred's legacy in safekeeping. This was to prevent Mark wheedling it out of her if he got into trouble; he was still gambling, and so that she could claim benefits to supplement her income. She had told Valerie that she wanted her money to go to her two granddaughters when she died. Mark was separated from his wife and she and the children were in Rhyl, near to her mother.

Mark lived in a flat over the betting shop that he managed. He had a lady friend. Flo had yet to meet her. She often voiced her disapproval to Grace.

"Livin' over the brush! I just 'ope nobody round 'ere ever gets wind on it. I won't be able ter 'old me 'ead up."

Chapter Twenty-Seven

Steve Maynard sat in his bedsit eating, without relish, a takeaway meal and watching TV. The accommodation was basic and had no real home comforts. The smells of cooking drifted up the staircase and across the landing of the Victorian terraced house and a medley of noises accompanied them. He stood up to turn up his TV set and heard a noise outside. Putting his plate down, he went to the window to check that his car was unscathed. Three lads were kicking a can along the pavement.

His day at the superstore had been tedious. The general manager was away and he had had to deal with the niggling problems associated with the employment of a largely female workforce. The sound of his mobile phone playing its tune broke into the drone of the TV. Turning down the volume, he answered it.

"Dad, is that you?" asked a young voice.

"Yes, poppet. How are you today?"

"Okay. Usual day at school. Melanie was so nasty, Dad. I wish you were here. She needs you to sort her out. Mom's too soft with her."

"I'll be there to pick you up a week on Sunday. We'll go out for a burger or something. Tell your mother I'm at work this weekend. The manager's on holiday."

"Ooh, Dad," she said in a whiny voice, "a whole week before you can come? It'll seem just ages."

"Sorry, love, can't be helped. See you then, okay?"

"Okay, s'pose so. See you, Dad."

He switched off the phone and turned up the sound on the TV.

Valerie was doing the weekend shopping. The superstore was very busy. She browsed along the aisles. Such a vast variety to choose from. She needed food for Grace which could be easily chewed. Ben had developed a sensitive digestion, so bland foods for him. She could eat anything herself. She was settling on an Indian takeaway meal when she felt an agonising pain in her ankle. Someone had pushed a loaded trolley into her. The pain was so severe that she almost fainted. She leaned against the fridge to stop herself sinking to the floor. Steve Maynard put down his clipboard and went to her aid.

"Are you alright, madam?"

Valerie found herself looking into a pair of striking, blue eyes. "Oh, I felt quite sick for a moment. It's my ankle, it really hurts."

He picked up her bag, pushed her trolley to the side of the aisle and escorted her to the cafeteria. Seating her at a table, he went to get two cups of tea.

"Oh," she said, "thank you. What a fuss I'm making. You're so kind."

He studied her covertly, noting her expensive clothes and haircut, her good bag and shoes. She wore understated but obviously valuable jewellery. He calculated that she must be in her mid forties. She looked what she was, a successful businesswoman. Gradually, as she sipped her tea, the colour returned to her cheeks.

"Thank you," she said. "I must be keeping you from your work."

He shrugged. "I was due to have a break. Do you have to get back to work yourself?"

"Oh, no. I try to keep Friday afternoons for my shopping."

He stirred his tea. "And what work do you do?"

She flushed slightly. "I have three shops, shoes, but I have good staff in all of them, so I can have some time for myself. I work quite flexibly these days."

He smiled at her, showing his perfect, white teeth. "May I have your details? I need to enter them in the accident book.

And your phone number, if you don't mind. I shall need to ring you to check that your leg is no worse."

Valerie dug into her bag and produced a business card. "Use my mobile number, it will save any confusion."

"I will," he said. "Are you alright? Feeling better?"

"Yes, thank you. I shall be able to finish my shopping. I only have a few things to get now."

"I'll ring you next week," he said.

Ben was concerned about the bruise on his wife's ankle.

"I bet that came sharp, love. Did you complain?"

"No, the woman went before I could say anything. Anyway, the manager put it in the accident book and got me a cup of tea. I soon felt better."

Grace was putting the shopping away. "Where's me tinned rice, Valerie? 'Ave yer forgot me tinned rice?"

"No, Mother, it's in the car. Ben'll get it."

She had bought plenty of fish for the freezer. Ben had digestive problems and needed a light diet. Some days Valerie felt as if she was running a home for the elderly. She was getting bored. She could do with a little excitement in her life.

On the Monday morning, Valerie's phone rang just as she was entering the High Street shop. Fortunately Ben had gone into his own shop, so she was able to answer it in peace. She went into the back room for privacy.

"Hello."

"Hello, Mrs Potts, Steve Maynard here. Just ringing to see how you are."

"Oh, yes, much better now and my name is Jinks. Potts was my maiden name."

"Sorry. Potts is on your card."

"Yes, I know. Anyway, thank you for phoning."

"Well, I did want to ask if you would like to have lunch some time?"

"Oh," she stammered, "I don't really know, er, yes, I suppose that would be alright."

"Could you make it tomorrow? It's my day off. I've to go flat hunting and I'll need a good lunch to keep me going."

"Oh, yes, tomorrow will be fine. I have to go into town tomorrow anyway."

"See you then. Station Hotel okay?"

"Yes, twelve-thirty, right?"

"Right, bye."

She switched off her phone and just stood there, not believing what had happened. She wouldn't go, of course. It wouldn't do, would it?

After lying awake until midnight, Valerie finally fell into a restless sleep. Ben snored gently in a trouble-free slumber. Next morning, she awoke early. Looking at her husband, sleeping like a cherub, her heart sank. She lay wrestling with her conscience. Surely it could do no harm to have lunch with someone? She would treat it as she would a meeting with Josie. Just friends, that was it, just friends.

She arose and showered, taking extra care about her appearance, taking time to do her hair and make-up. Of course, Grace noticed.

"Where are you goin' today then, Valerie? You'me looking smart, ain't yer?"

"Not particularly, Mother, just into town to the shop, seeing some reps and organising the sale."

"Not comin' 'ome lunchtime then?"

"No, not today, busy day. I'll try to finish early. Teresa will be coming in to do the bedrooms, so you won't be entirely on your own."

Grace sniffed. "Lick an' a promise, I expect. I shan't keep mekkin her tea."

Valerie gritted her teeth. Ben came through to the kitchen to have some toast. As usual, he was affable and sweet tempered.

"You look nice, love," he said.

She was quiet in the car. "You okay, love?" he asked.

"Oh, yes, just thinking about the sale at the town shop. Take it easy today, Ben, you look a bit tired."

"S'pose I am a bit. P'raps we'll talk again about me retiring. Anyroad, I think we both need a holiday. See if you can get somebody to stop with Grace, will yer?"

"Yes, I'll see."

He kissed her and waved as she drove off. By the time she had reached work, she had got over her doubts and was looking forward to her lunch date.

The morning passed quite quickly. Valerie left the shop to walk to the hotel, deliberately making sure that she was five minutes late. Steve sat at a table, sipping a glass of red wine. He stood up as she came over and they shook hands.

"How's that ankle?" he asked as he signalled to the waitress.

"Fine, thanks. The bruise has come out well. Just a mineral water for me, please."

They studied the menu. Valerie decided to have fresh salmon with salad and new potatoes and Steve settled on steak with fries and vegetables.

"How is the flat hunting coming along?"

"I've only seen one, a bit grotty actually. I need one with parking space. I'm in temporary accommodation at the moment."

"Where did you live before?"

"Nottingham. My wife kept pestering me at work, so they transferred me. I'm afraid she's a bit of a nut case. I can't live with her and I can't live near to her. She's taking me for everything. I could end up with nothing after years of hard work."

Valerie commiserated. "Poor you. Any children?"

"Yes, two girls. I see them for the occasional Saturday or Sunday. I've got a fight on my hands to do even that. She's so vindictive, you can't imagine." He looked at her out of sorrowful, blue eyes. "Anyway, enough about me, tell me about yourself and call me Steve. What's your first name?"

"Oh, Valerie. Well, I've been married for twenty-two years nearly. My husband's a lot older than me. As I told you, I have three shops. We've both worked hard, no children and my mother is living with us now."

They chatted throughout the meal, then Valerie said, "I may know of a flat. I can ask my friend and perhaps give you a ring about it."

"Fine." He wrote his number on a slip of paper. "And, Valerie, I'd very much like to see you again. I admire a woman like you, with brains and business acumen. Most women are boring but you certainly aren't."

She flushed. "Thank you, kind sir. Please, let me pay my way."

"Certainly not. I wouldn't hear of it."

They left the hotel and he took her hand. "Bye, hope to hear from you soon. Don't leave it too long."

He kissed her on the cheek. It sent shivers down her spine. Starry-eyed, she walked back to the shop.

"And 'er 'ad ter bring young Kyle wi' 'er. 'E's 'ad the earache. Tekkin 'im to the doctor's tonight. 'E's a nice enough lad but I wish as 'e wouldn't chobble 'is sweets, fair puts me teeth on edge. Valerie? Valerie! I don't think as you've just 'eard a word I've said."

"Oh, sorry, Mom. I was miles away."

Grace grumbled, "I sometimes wonder if you're on this earth or Fuller's sometimes. I miss our Whisky, at least 'e used to listen to me."

"Sorry. Anyway, did Ben phone?"

"Yes, he says 'e won't finish late. 'E got the meat. You can pick him up at the usual time. I've med an appointment to get me 'air done early termorrer, so you can drop me on the way to work."

"Right, do you want me to pick you up after?"

"No, I'll get a taxi to Flo's. 'Er ain't too good. That Mark don't do nothin' for 'er. I'd wash me 'ands on 'im. Good job there's not much money there or 'e'd be after it. That wench as 'e's shacked up with's bin round the track a few times an' all."

"Oh, Mother, you don't know, she could be alright."

Grace sniffed. "Don't think so. If 'er is 'er must be bad off ter peck fer 'im."

Steve rolled over and reached for his cigarettes. He grinned at the girl snuggled under his duvet.

"Light me one," she said and giggled. He passed the cigarette to her and squeezed her hand.

"I'll have to be goin' soon. Carl'll be home before me if I'm not careful."

"Make something up. Say you had to work your half day."

"He'll notice me pay slip, goes over it with a fine-tooth comb. I'll have to say I went to me mate's, she'll cover for me. I've done it for her often enough."

They compared their work rotas so that they could meet the following week and then she dressed hurriedly and made her exit. He waved to her from the window. Their relationship was purely a self-indulgently sexual one. They had both done it many times before and, no doubt, would again, with different partners.

Ronnie couldn't see his daughter living over the shop in the High Street. He called into his local estate agent's to see what was on offer near to him and Josie. He found a semi-detached house just two miles away. It needed renovations but he was prepared to get them done.

"Do you think that's the right thing?" asked Josie. "Don't you think they may want to fend for themselves?"

"How can they? He's still at university, she can't work in her condition."

"Well, let them pay rent. They may feel better. Before you buy it, test the water."

He had to agree.

The following Wednesday Josie and Valerie met for lunch. Josie noticed that her friend looked different somehow, she had a softer, happier look about her.

They chatted generally, as usual, then Josie said, "Ron's thinking of buying a house so that Annie and Martin can live near to us. We're going to talk to them about it tonight. I can't see them coping in the shop flat with a baby somehow."

"Oh, is the flat empty then?"

She had guessed it was. There had been no curtains at the windows for months.

"Yes. Ron likes to have someone there, more security."

"I may know someone who would rent it. He's new to the area, moved with his job."

"Oh? How did you meet him then?"

"Through work. Anyway, can I tell him about the flat?"

"I s'pose so. Better tell him to pop into the shop. Paul will give him Ron's number. Be better that way." She looked closely at Valerie. "Is that all he is, Val? An acquaintance?"

Valerie flushed. "Yes, of course. A nice chap, had some bad luck and needs a bit of help, that's all."

Josie thought to herself, "Unlike Valerie to concern herself with some lame duck. I wonder . . .?"

Ben woke with a start. The pain in his side was excruciating. He groaned and Valerie stirred. He got out of bed and staggered into the bathroom. Bent over in pain, he turned on the tap to get a drink of water. The pain intensified and he sank to the floor. Valerie came in. She was shocked at his appearance. He was grey and sweating. She wiped his face with a towel. He vomited into it.

"I'll get an ambulance, Ben. You do look bad." Hands shaking, she dialled 999. "Please come quickly, my husband's very ill. He's in terrible pain." Giving the address, she returned to Ben. He was rolling about the floor in agony.

Valerie woke Grace. "Mom, Mom, Ben's bad. I've sent for the ambulance. I'm going with him."

Grace looked at her blearily. "Oh, do you want me to get up?"

"No, stay where you are. I'll ring you to let you know how he is."

She returned to Ben. He was no better.

"Sorry, love," he gasped.

"What for?" she asked. "It's not your fault. Anyway, the ambulance is here, soon be seen to."

The paramedics were very good. They assessed the situation and administered pain control to Ben. By the time they got him into the ambulance, the pain was slightly easier.

Valerie put her coat on over her pyjamas and followed in her car. Ben was admitted. He had kidney stones and was to be kept in for investigations.

Next morning, she felt like a wrung-out rag. She phoned round the shops to tell them that she would not be in. Grace was very concerned about her son-in-law. Despite herself, she had become very fond of him.

Valerie sat in her car to phone Steve. He was a bit put out that she could not meet him for lunch but, by the time the conversation had ended, he was already plotting to meet up with one of his lady friends. He also decided to go into the High Street butcher's to find out about the flat.

Ben had his operation and was discharged a week later. He was very weak and it took some time for him to recuperate. Valerie had her work cut out to sort his customers out with their repaired shoes. She decided to leave a key at her High Street shop for people to call and ask her assistants for them. When all the shoes had gone, she negotiated the sale of the shop to the chemist next door.

Steve had contacted Ronnie and arranged to view the flat. They met there on a Friday afternoon and it was decided that Steve would take on the tenancy for six months to see how it worked out. It had been redecorated and there was an enclosed area at the rear for his car. He felt that it would do nicely, better than the crummy bedsit which he now occupied.

He told Ronnie very little about himself but was able to supply a reference from his store manager and, at this stage, Ronnie had no idea that he was a friend of Valerie's.

Annie announced to her parents that she and Martin would be waiting until he qualified before getting married. She felt that it would be a strain on them to cope with a new baby and the hours that he would have to put in at the hospital. Ronnie was quite shocked.

"I never thought one o' mine would be an unmarried mother an' live in sin an' all."

Josie secretly agreed with him but said, "Now, Ron, you know how times have changed. They love each other now but let them go through the hardships first and see how they feel in a couple of years' time. Be better than a divorce. I think they'll stick it out. Let's face it, they've both had privileged lives. Martin's dad is a doctor and he had a private education and, you must admit, our Annie's never gone short. So let them see how things go. They're both so young."

Nellie was taken aback. "Well, our Annie, I'd never be able to 'old me 'ead up if I was you."

"Oh, Gran, loads of couples have their family before settling down."

"Well, it's an arse-about-face way of doing things ter my mind but I s'pose you know what you're doin'. I just can't get me 'ead round what goes on these days. Good job yer Grandad ain't 'ere, 'e'd goo mad."

Valerie and Steve managed to meet more often. Ben was getting stronger and was content to potter in the house and the garden. He caught up with lots of little jobs which needed doing. He found an interest in the garden and spent many hours in Frank's greenhouse. Grace would join him, bringing cups of tea and biscuits and chatting to him. They developed a companionship which was comfortable and Valerie could go about her life with a clear conscience.

Care had to be taken when she went to see Steve at the flat. She always telephoned first and approached from the back so that he could unlock the gate for her to slip through quickly. He had two full weekends off a month. One he spent with his daughters and the other he and Valerie managed to slip away with the excuse that she was going to a fashion show or trade fair and needed to stop overnight.

She was besotted with him and would buy him expensive presents. A watch, cufflinks, wide screen TV, stereo equipment and clothes. She always paid if they stayed at an expensive hotel.

He once told her, "I wish that I could pay for us but my wife is bleeding me dry. She still won't divorce me. I feel as though I've got a millstone around my neck. I don't know what I'd do without you, Val."

She sympathised with him. "Don't worry. I've more than enough for both of us. I know you'd do it for me, if you could."

"I really love you, Valerie, you know that, don't you?"

"Yes." She stroked his hair. "Yes, I know you do, Steve. Don't worry, I'm married too. My husband is so good to me, more like a father really. He's happy in his own way. What he doesn't know isn't going to hurt him."

He looked into her eyes. "He's a lucky bloke. You're a real treasure."

He stroked her arm and she gave a shudder of pleasure. She felt that she could die for him, he was so delectable. She had never felt like this in her life before.

When they managed the weekend away, she felt so privileged to be seen with him. She was spending more on clothes and hairdressers and having her nails manicured. She watched her diet closely and, of course, Grace noticed.

"You'me losing weight, our Valerie. You don't eat proper. What're you worrying about? Is it Ben? He's okay now. Is it the shops?"

"Oh, Mother, don't go on. I eat enough. Anyway, I've no worries, everything's okay. I was thinking, would you be alright if Flo came to stay for a few days? I reckon Ben could do with a little holiday."

Grace nodded. "Yes, you both could. I'll be okay. Ask Flo if you like."

Valerie was gobsmacked. That evening she talked to Ben about taking a break in the Lake District. He was delighted and, next day, Valerie obtained brochures from the travel shop. They decided to go with a coach firm so that Valerie could enjoy herself without the chore of driving. The break coincided with Steve's daughters' weekend visit, so she felt that the time away from him wasn't wasted.

Valerie and Ben walked, enjoying the scenery. They ate well, although Valerie still counted her calories. Ben was so contented.

"Best break we've ever had, Val. We'll have to do it more often."

She agreed. If Flo and Grace got on well, it could be a regular thing and would be salve on her conscience.

On their return on the Wednesday she opened the front door in trepidation. She had phoned her mother daily and all had seemed well but she was dreading Grace's grumbles about Flo. As it happened Flo was still there and quite cheerful. Grace seemed quite amenable and Valerie gave a sigh of relief. They appreciated the gifts of Kendal Mint Cake and fleecy slippers Valerie had chosen for them. So, a precedent was set. Weekends away with Ben, trips away with Steve, visits to the flat, outings to the theatre and concerts, which she said she was attending with Josie.

Grace was washing up the breakfast dishes. Teresa was cleaning the lounge. She liked to have the wireless on while she was dusting and was humming to herself. Grace rolled her eyes to the ceiling. She felt that it was an imposition for Teresa to play the radio in her employer's house but, these days, it seemed anything went.

She decided to take Ben tea and biscuits out to the potting shed. At least there they could have peace and quiet. She shuffled down the path to the shed. Putting the tray on a bench, she pushed the door. It wouldn't budge. Again she pushed. It appeared to be stuck.

"Ben?" she called. "Ben, are you in there?"

No answer. She went to the greenhouse. No sign of him. She peered through the shed window but could not see him. Going back into the bungalow, she checked the toilets and bathroom. No Ben. She began to get alarmed. Going into the lounge, she switched the radio off. Teresa, startled, looked up from polishing the coffee table.

"What's up, Mrs P?"

"I can't find Mr Jinks. I thought he was in the shed but I can't open the door. There's something stopping it. He might be on the floor. What shall we do?"

"Ring Valerie. She'll know what to do."

Valerie was in the High Street shop, interviewing a prospective assistant. When her phone played its tune, she was alarmed by her mother's panicky voice.

"I'll ring the police, Mother, and ask their advice and I'll be right home."

She turned to the girl. “I’m sorry, I’ll have to go. An emergency. I’ll telephone you at home. Will you leave your number with Glenda in the shop, please?”

She rang the police, who agreed to send someone round, and made her way home. They took the hinges off the door of the shed to get to Ben, who was on the floor. He had been dead for some time. Valerie was numb. She knew that she had lost her best friend.

Chapter Twenty-Eight

Steve was unsure about his feelings when the news of Ben's death was broken to him. He had been quite contented with the set-up which had allowed him freedom to see his daughters and his lady friends. Now, he knew that Valerie would require more of his time.

Six months after Ben's death, Valerie decided to tell her mother that she had met someone.

"Where's he from then?"

"Nottingham."

"And what's he do?"

"Manager at the superstore."

"And how old's he then?"

"A bit younger than me."

"Toy boy?"

"No, Mother. Anyway, we're just friends really."

"Oh, ar. Where's he live?"

"In a flat in the High Street but he's looking for somewhere better."

Grace sniffed. "Seems funny ter me. Man of his age should have better than a flat over a shop. Has he got a wife?"

"No, he's divorced," Valerie fibbed.

"Oh. Any kids?"

"Two, he sees them at weekends. Anyway, I told you, we're just good friends. He's coming to meet you tomorrow, so be polite to him."

Grace humphed. "I'm allus polite. Anyway, it don't matter if you'me just friends, does it?"

It was decided to take Grace out for a meal so that she could meet Steve on neutral territory. He set out to charm her and appeared to have succeeded.

When they arrived home, Grace went into the kitchen to make the Horlicks. Valerie put the car into the garage. As she entered the kitchen, Grace turned from the stove.

"He's a nice enough chap, our Valerie."

Valerie smiled in gratification. "Yes, he is."

"Pity," Grace said.

Valerie frowned at her. "Pity what?"

"Pity he's after your money."

Valerie was shocked and annoyed. "No, Mother, he's not."

Grace gave her an old-fashioned look. "Oh but he is. Remember me words. Do as you please but he's after all he can get. At his age – no home, no pension to speak of. He's got to feather his nest somehow."

"No, Mother, it's not his fault. It's his wife. Avaricious bitch, she is. He thinks the world of me and I trust him."

Grace sniffed. "Do yer?" she said, as she shuffled to the door. "Well, just be careful."

It seemed that they had reached stalemate. Valerie couldn't ask Steve to live at the bungalow and Grace was resentful if she was left on her own too much. Occasionally he would come for a meal, perhaps Sunday lunch. Grace was barely civil to him. He certainly had his work cut out there. He tried his very best to charm her.

They managed a week in America while Flo stayed with Grace but Grace was upset.

"Anythin' could 'appen to me while our Valerie's all that way off. 'Er'd goo ter the moon if 'e wanted to. Besotted, 'er is an' I bet as 'er's payin'. 'E's got nothing, by all accounts."

Flo tried to pacify her. "You'me better off than me with our Mark, Grace. At least you'me bein' looked after an livin' in comfort. You doe want fer anythin'."

"Ar, if that un doe 'ave it all off 'er."

At last Valerie could confide in Josie about Steve.

"How long have you known him then, Val?"

"Oh, some time, just friends, but now it's more serious."

"Is he the chap who rents the flat?"

"Yes, he wants to move but he can't yet."

"Does your mom like him?"

"Not really but you know her, Josie, she's back to wanting me all to herself again. I'm so sick of the carping. Anyway, Steve wants to go away again soon and I must consider him, so she'll have to lump it. Flo's good. She stays, they grumble together. How's the choral society going?"

"Oh, lovely. Such nice people. You must come to our concert. Do you think your mother would like to come?"

"I'll ask her and Flo. Be a night out for them."

That would mean a free evening for herself and Steve.

That evening, Josie mentioned to Ronnie that she had come across Valerie and she had a new man in her life.

"Who's than then?" he asked, not really interested.

She explained that it was his tenant.

He gasped, then he laughed. "Steve? Over the shop? Paul reckons he's a right finger, more women than hot dinners."

It was Josie's turn to gasp. "What do you mean?"

"Well, he has one or two popping to visit him. He don't go short, I can tell you."

"Well, well, what a turn up. Anyway, he's obviously on to a good thing. She thinks he's the best thing since sliced bread."

Josie resolved than she would not tell her friend about her lover's infidelities. She knew that she would get no thanks and would lose the friendship which had lasted many years.

It was an icy day. Valerie had to drive carefully. She was on her way to the town shop. One of the assistants had flu. She wasn't seeing Steve for a couple of days, which made her feel quite low-spirited. The bad weather kept the customers away. She managed to do quite a bit of bookkeeping. At twelve-thirty she decided to go home for lunch. As she opened the front door, she heard a weak cry. She looked in all the rooms. No Grace. Then, going through to the kitchen, she heard it again. Grace was in the cold utility room on the floor. She was blue with cold. As Valerie approached, she fainted. Her leg was twisted underneath her at a peculiar angle.

"Mom, oh, Mom, whatever have you done?"

Grace groaned and opened her eyes. Valerie ran for a throw from the settee in the lounge to cover her, then she telephoned for an ambulance.

Grace had fractured her hip. She was too shocked to have an operation and was suffering from hypothermia. Within three hours she had developed pneumonia. Next morning, at seven o'clock, the phone rang. It was the hospital, asking Valerie to come. By the time she arrived at the ward, her mother had died.

Staff Nurse Edwards was sympathetic. "Your mother told us what a devoted, wonderful daughter you were, Mrs Jinks. She told us how you always cared for her." She smiled at Valerie with Josie's eyes. Valerie realised that, apart from Flo and Janice, she was all alone in the world. And, of course, she had Steve.

The funeral was a quiet affair, just Valerie and Steve, Flo and Mark, Janice, Stan, Paul and Jenny and Josie. They assembled at the bungalow for refreshments and Steve went to work to charm everyone. Josie chatted to him, tongue in cheek, knowing what a philanderer he was. Seeing for herself how besotted Valerie was, she knew she had to keep it to herself.

Flo had been staying to keep Valerie company. After the funeral she was going back to her flat. Mark was taking her. He gave Steve a quizzical look. He felt that he had seen him somewhere before but couldn't think where. He asked his mother what she knew about him.

"Well, he's from Nottingham, according to our Grace. Split up with 'is missis. 'Er's a bit of a nut case, by all accounts. Plagued him when he was at werk, so he had ter ask fer a transfer, that's why 'e's 'ere. Took 'im fer everythin' 'cause 'er's got the kiddies. 'E sis 'em 'op an' a ketch, says as 'er can be okkard about 'em comin' over 'ere."

He puffed thoughtfully on his cigarette. Suddenly it dawned on him where he had seen Steve before. He had relieved the Nottingham betting shop manager a couple of years before, where Steve had been a regular customer.

He said, "I hope our Valerie keeps control of her money, Mother. I remember 'im. 'E was a heavy gambler, owed quite a bit, by all accounts. Paid 'is debts off but 'eaven knows where 'e got the money from."

Flo gasped. "Do yer think as we ought ter warn our Valerie, Mark?"

"No point. 'Er's shrewd enough and it looks as if 'er's well an' truly smitten, so 'er wouldn't listen anyway. Keep it to yerself, Mother. Just watch an' listen."

Valerie couldn't settle on her own in the bungalow. It didn't seem right to ask Steve to move in there. She decided to sell it and buy a new house. The area in which Josie and Ronnie lived appealed to her, so she asked the estate agents to send details of properties in that area to her. Steve was pleased that he would get a good roof over his head and dismayed that he would lose some of his freedom to entertain his lady friends. However, he planned to overcome this difficulty somehow. Three months later they moved into a brand new, detached house, two and a half miles from Ronnie and Josie and three miles from the golf club. Of course, Steve persuaded Valerie that he must join and their social life took a new turn.

Ronnie complained to Josie, "That bloke Val Potts is shacked up with, the one that used ter rent the flat, is a member at the club now. I hope that don't mean we have ter mix with 'em at the clubhouse, Jose."

"Not if you don't want to, Ron. Anyway, I don't come very often, only for the awards dinners and the odd Christmas bash."

"Well, I shan't bother with 'em, he seems right fly bugger ter me."

Josie had to agree. She wondered what Valerie had got herself into.

One morning Valerie was getting ready for work when she had a pain in her chest. She sat on the bed and waited for it to subside. She had eaten a good breakfast for a change and decided that indigestion was the problem. She rooted in her handbag for a peppermint and, gradually, the pain subsided.

"I must get some Rennies and Alka-Seltzer," she thought.

She was feeling very tired these days. Steve liked a full social life and she felt that she should keep up with him.

The last time she had called in to see Flo she had said, "You look a bit peaky, our Valerie. Am you doin' too much? Wrong side o' fifty now to overdo things, my wench. And you'me losin' weight. Our Grace used ter worry about yer dietin' all the time."

"I'm okay, Aunty. We're going away in two weeks' time for a holiday, so I'll get a rest then."

"See that yer do."

Janice called in to the High Street shop to see her.

"How are you, Valerie? You can come and see us, you know. Just 'cos Stan's at home, don't think as you ain't welcome."

"I know, Aunty Janice. Anyway, I wanted to ask if you and Uncle Stan would stay at my house while we're on holiday? I'd like you to stay there, if you wouldn't mind, only the house next door was burgled last week."

"I'll ask him. It'd be a change for us. Paul'll drop us over. Is the man comin' in for the garden?"

"Yes and Mrs Banks comes on a Monday and Friday to clean."

So it was arranged that they would house-sit for the week. When Paul took them over to the house, he was astounded at the luxury of it.

"Blimey, Mother, I should think our Valerie's Fun a Puss, as they say. Ben musta left her well off."

Janice was overawed but Stan was sceptical. "Money aye everythin'. 'Er's got no kids ter leave it to."

Janice said, "No, she only has that Steve bloke. Let's hope as 'er lives to a good ode age."

The holiday was tiring. They stayed in New York and went on the town, seeing all the shows and shopping at all the best stores. Valerie had her indigestion problem a couple of times. She kept it to herself but resolved to see her doctor when she got home in case she was developing a stomach ulcer.

Laden with clothes and presents they returned to find that Janice and Stan had enjoyed their stay and were willing to do it again. Valerie felt that, at last, she was living. It was what she had waited for as long as she could remember, to be well off and to do as she pleased.

Chapter Twenty-Nine

At last Annie and Martin decided to get married. They had a little lad, William, who was adored by all the family. They had settled into the house bought by Ronnie and he had purchased the one next door to them for Ellie, who had become engaged to a male nurse.

Martin's parents were very supportive to the couple and Nellie was pleased to hear that they were settling down properly at last. Billy was working hard at university. Ronnie and Josie were debating what to get him for his twenty-first birthday.

"I think he should have another car, Jose. His has done a lot of miles, you know."

"I think you're right. Will you take him along to buy it or will it be a surprise?"

"Well, I know he keeps looking at a convertible. I think I might order one for a surprise."

"As long as it's red, he'll be happy."

So a new, red convertible was decided upon for Billy.

*   *   *

The lift door clanged shut. Pauline Maynard held her breath against the stench of urine and vomit which permeated the small space, even though it had been cleaned that day. She would not lower her shopping onto the floor, where there was a pool of what looked like motorcycle oil, preferring to hold onto it. Her feet ached after a day serving in the local newsagent's shop. Mentally she totted up her expenditure for the week. She had lost her home and income when Steve had settled his debts and gone. She had had a hard time since then but was now hoping to move into a house. How she was going to furnish it, heaven knew. He came to Nottingham, occasionally, to see the girls. Now that they were older, he would meet them in town for lunch and take them to see his parents. His mother was still besotted with him and secretly thought that it must have been Pauline who had got them into arrears by not paying the mortgage on their detached house. His father, however, had always known that his son had feet of clay and was glad that they also had a daughter, Molly, who was honest and dependable. They tried to help by buying the girls cheap items of clothing but, as they were on a pension, were limited to how much they could afford.

One Saturday, when Steve's car was at the garage for repairs, Valerie gave him a lift into Nottingham. She declined to meet them, deciding to do so if his divorce came through, and he secretly felt it best that they never saw how comfortably he was living in her new house. She dropped him off and Suzanne caught a glimpse of her as she drove off.

Later she told her mother, "You've got no need to worry, Mom, she's older than him. I reckon he picked her up at a Grab a Granny night. She's lots older than you."

Pauline asked, "What sort of car was she driving?"

"A BMW, I think."

"There you are then, duck, that's the attraction – money."

The doctor agreed with Valerie that the chest pains were caused by indigestion.

"I thought that was what it was, Doctor," she concurred.

"You must slow down and eat regular meals. Take your time, we don't want you to get an ulcer, do we? You've gone through a lot lately, Mrs Jinks, losing your mother and husband. You're bound to get some reaction."

He gave her a prescription and bade her good day.

She went for a facial and a manicure. Perhaps she would take a few days and stay at a health farm, have a rest and some pampering. It was worth considering.

Josie and Ronnie were having a family get together, a pool party. There was plenty of noise and music. The smell of barbecued food drifted on the air. All the family was there, including a thrilled Billy, admiring his new car. He had a girlfriend now. She did not live far away, indeed, he had met her at school and was pleasantly surprised when he met her again and found that she had turned into a beautiful young lady. She was coming this evening to meet everyone.

Ronnie smiled benevolently at everyone. His life was a happy one, especially now that he was a Grandad. Everyone was tucking in and drinking, except Billy, who declined any alcohol. He wanted to take Lucy home in his new car.

The golf club was crowded. Steve had ordered the meal. He sat looking like the cat who had the cream. Valerie had a slight feeling of dread. She didn't know why. She pleated her skirt nervously between her fingers. She was trying not to dwell on the phone call she had taken at the shop that day from a woman trying to tell her things about him. Lies, all of it, she was sure. She knew better than to ask him why he was looking so smug. He would tell her all in good time. She always found the food at the club a trifle rich. She tolerated it rather than complain, hoping that her indigestion wouldn't flare up later. The waiter arrived with a bottle of white wine. Steve tasted it and nodded.

"Fine, thanks, and we'll have a bottle of red with the main course, please."

Valerie protested. "Don't forget you're driving, Steve. The lanes around here are dark and winding."

"Don't be a killjoy, Val. You know, as well as I do, that I'm a better driver when I've had a few."

"Well, I'll drive. I don't need a drink, water'll do for me."

"Oh, suit yourself. I'll soon polish it off."

The evening was warm. The restaurant hummed with conversation and loud laughter reached them from the bar. Those hearty types weren't Valerie's cup of tea but she tolerated them. Either that or stay at home alone. She somehow didn't quite trust Steve out of her sight too often. Putting down his cutlery, he leaned towards her across the table.

"I've had news today. I thought I'd save it 'til we were here. Guess what?"

"I can't, you tell me."

"Pauline has finally decided to give me a divorce."

Valerie gasped. "Really?"

"Yes, really. We'll be able to get married."

She sat there, pondering. Was this what she really wanted after all? Oh, she loved him alright but she was never really sure that she could keep him.

Giving herself a mental shake, she smiled and raised her glass. "To us," she said.

He poured a glass of wine for her. "A proper toast – to us," he said.

At last she was to be his wife instead of living a lie. All his faults faded into insignificance as she looked into those blue eyes and basked in his lovely smile. She was lost and he knew it. They went into the bar and were swallowed up by the jovial crowd. She always felt out of place but managed to stand and smile and chat a little about inconsequential things, such as holidays, with the other women. She was always glad to make her escape at the end of the evening. At last it was time to go. Steve had consumed two brandies, as well as the wine, and was in good spirits. He had a game of golf arranged for next day. Calling out their 'goodnights' everyone waved and smiled indulgently at him.

"Good old Steve, not a mean bone in his body. Always good for a drink. Good old Steve."

The cool air hit them as they walked to the car. Valerie was tired, she felt a headache coming on. The smell of the leather in the car made her feel nauseous and she felt the start of an indigestion attack. She would be glad to get to her bed.

Steve fumbled with his seat belt, grunting and grumbling.

"Sod the thing." He let it slide back and promptly fell asleep. Valerie left him to it and concentrated on reversing the car out of the tightly-packed car park. She hated driving in the dark. The lanes around the club were unlit and she had to strain her eyes and concentrate hard to negotiate the bends. The tightness in her chest was getting worse. Then a light shone in her eyes. Some idiot had not dipped his headlights. The pain went across her chest up into her jaw and down her arm. She swerved. There was a bang, then nothing.

Josie sighed and reached for her book. She hoped that Billy would soon get back from taking Lucy home, then Ron would settle down for a good night's rest. He got so uptight about the kids, especially now that Ellie was Casualty Sister and regaled them with gruesome stories. He came through from the bathroom, grumbling and started to pull on his jeans.

"Where are you going, love?"

"I don't know. It's two o'clock. I can't settle while he's out in that car. I've tried his mobile, it's switched off."

"Probably smooching somewhere."

"Well, I'm worried. I don't like it, Jose."

"He's a really good driver, Ron. Don't worry so much."

He looked at her. "Hark who's talking!"

"I know. Anyway, let's put the kettle on. I can't settle myself now."

"Kettle, be blowed, I need a stiff whisky."

The shrill of the door bell made them jump. The dogs began to bark frantically.

"He can't have forgotten his key. I'm sure he put it with the car key," muttered Ron, as he went to answer it.

Josie pulled on her dressing gown and followed him. There, on the step, in the glow from the porch light, were two police officers.

Ron staggered back and Josie gave a little scream. "Oh God, oh God!"

"Mr Edwards? Mrs Edwards? May we come in, please?"

Ron stood back, his face ashen. Josie grasped his arm. Ellie came downstairs. Josie clung to her. The police officers followed them into the sitting room. To Josie the rest was a blur. She came to, on the settee. Ellie was sponging her face and sobbing. Ron sat in the armchair, a tragic, broken man. His only son was dead, killed only a mile away in a car crash in the lane.

Ellie was on the phone. "Uncle John, can you come? Something terrible has happened. Can you get Uncle Barry, please. There's been an accident." She broke down again and sobbed bitterly.

As the police officers prepared to leave, Ron asked, "Was there another car involved?"

"Yes, unfortunately there was. It appears the driver had a heart attack."

"Any idea who it was?"

"Well, I shouldn't tell you really. Her passenger was killed as well. He wasn't wearing his seat belt. It seems it was a lady who lived not far from here. Her name was Mrs Jinks, Valerie Jinks."

Ron sat, as if turned to stone. Josie fainted clean away.

Pauline Maynard opened the envelope. Inside was a letter from an insurance company and a cheque for a sum which made her gasp. Steve had been insured at work for three times his yearly salary. The money was to come to her as his next of kin, together with pension money which had accrued. It would seem that her money worries were over.

The solicitor sat facing Janice, Stan and Paul, together with Flo and Mark.

“As Mrs Jinks died intestate her property is to be sold and, together with any money, it will be divided between you all as her next of kin, after the funeral expenses, of course. Rest assured you will all receive a substantial sum.”

They sat in stunned silence for a while, then he shook their hands. They thanked him and went on their way.

Married with one daughter, Norma was born in Walsall in the West Midlands. She trained as a nurse at Walsall Sister Dora Hospital. She worked as an industrial nursing sister and as a sister in a sanatorium before training at Aston University to qualify as a Health Visitor, working in the Black Country.

The Flawed Inheritance is her first novel, written after her retirement.